The Death Of Tommy Quick And Other Lies

DJ Wiseman

Published 2016
Askance Publishing

ISBN 978-1-909009-27-1

British Library Cataloguing in Publication Data.
A catalogue record for this book is available from the British Library.

Set in 11pt Aldine401BT by Askance Publishing
Printed in the United Kingdom

DJ Wiseman was born and educated in Essex. Having lived on the South Coast and in Bristol, he settled in Oxfordshire in 1973. He's divided his time between Nova Scotia and the UK since 2011.
Lifelong interests include travel, maps, reading and photography. For more than twenty years he's had a passionate interest in genealogy, discovering branches of his family scattered round the globe.

Other titles
A Habit of Dying *2010*
The Subtle Thief of Youth *2012*

The Death Of Tommy Quick And Other Lies

1

And so it ends.

It should have been a comforting thought, a satisfying conclusion to another successful project, but it felt lifeless, hollow. Finding a home for the Brenton medals had been too easy. A wasted detour with Ada Brenton had been quickly compensated by a fast response to Lydia's message-board posting: *Seeking Francis Bellinger b. 8th May 1930, Hampshire, England. Or any connected family. Son of Alfred Bellinger and Lillian Brenton, grandson of James Brenton.* It was the kind of request that can go unanswered for years, but in only a few weeks it had brought her to Bedford on a drizzly Saturday in July. James Brenton's medals sat beside her on the passenger seat of the rattling Nissan, neatly wrapped in brown paper. Freshly cleaned and snug in their new velvet-lined case, they were heading to their rightful owner.

The apparent ease of finding a descendant who might treasure the medals was not the only unsatisfactory aspect of Lydia's latest quest. She'd never met or even communicated with Francis, only with Monica, his helpful neighbour. It had been Monica Sanders who'd responded to her message, it was Monica's information which confirmed that Freddie Bell at number twenty-seven was more properly Francis Bellinger. Now in his eighties, he'd become a resident of a nursing-home where he was waiting for the last few weeks of his life to drain away. According to Monica he could be bloody-minded and rude. So far as Lydia knew, Francis had no children, no nieces or nephews, nobody close who might give the medals a long-term home. She consoled herself that in passing them on she would at least have done her part and in doing so she might also bring a small pleasure to a dying man.

'Ah, yes, I'm so sorry, but Mrs Sanders left a message for you. She sent her apologies, but she's unable to meet you this morning.' The moon-faced girl with puppy-dog eyes who greeted Lydia in the entrance hall of Willoughby House imparted this news with more compassion than the message warranted.

'Oh, er, well, thank you.' Lydia was slightly nonplussed.

Wide-eyed, the girl brightened instantly with, 'But I know Freddie's really looking forward to seeing you, he's talked of nothing else this morning.' Instant, on-demand enthusiasm had replaced the graveyard sympathy. 'You haven't been here before have you? Shall I come along with you?'

'Er, no, er, thank you,' she glanced down at the badge, 'Sharon, yes please, that would be good.' Lydia clutched her bag and the precious brown-paper parcel, suddenly unsure of herself. The prospect of making unaided small talk about the dying man's grandfather was not appealing.

They walked along a carpeted corridor, past the rooms of the terminally ill, past hints of music, past bland paintings and cut flowers overflowing their vases, drooping in the heat, dropped petals crowding round the bases. At the last room they paused and the girl found her serious face and a confidential voice. 'There's just one thing, before we see Freddie, one thing you should probably know, be ready for.' The girl's voice dropped to a whisper. 'Freddie can be a bit, um, rude, if you know what I mean, a bit explicit sometimes.' As her voice grew smaller so her eyes grew larger. 'And now and again his hands can, well, you know, wander a little. It's partly the medication, they lose their, you know, inhibitions. He'll probably be fine.'

'Oh,' was all Lydia could manage by way of response.

'And I know you'll be quite prepared for this too, but what with the drugs and the pain relief you might find the conversation can wander too. He's been good this morning, conversation and hands all staying where they should be, if you know what I mean.' She gave a little conspiratorial grin and dipped her head by way of indicating that the seriousness had finished.

Without knocking she swung open the door and announced in her bigger, smiley voice, 'Hello Freddie, here's the visitor you've been waiting for.'

The room was as bland as the corridor, plain to the point of minimalist but without the style. Seated in one of two uneasy chairs cramped together by the window was the last of a man. It was this impression that Lydia would always have of him, a once great big man, broad, tall and strong, now reduced to a hulk washed up on this empty beach, all the guts and life worn away and the fussing seagull nurses wheeling around him. Beside his chair two bags of clear liquid hung from an IV drip-stand while behind him drizzle streaked the window until another gust splattered a heavier dose across it.

Francis Bellinger shuffled his feet and gripped the arms of the chair as if to rise and greet his visitor, his head thrust forward with the effort.

'I'm so pleased to meet you Mr Bellinger. Please don't get up,' Lydia said as she advanced to meet him. He sank back with a grunt.

'Just call if you need anything,' said smiley-face, adding in the same happy-campers voice, 'and none of your tricks today, Freddie,' as she closed the door behind her.

'Silly cow,' retorted Freddie, his voice as big and slow and empty as the man himself. It came from way down inside, echoing through distant tubes before it left his body.

Lydia was about to add some word of defence for the girl but thought better of it, she had not come to talk of his care or take sides in a petty difference. She would attend to the business of her visit, give and take such pleasure from it as she could, and continue on her way to lunch in Grantchester.

'I hope Monica Sanders has explained what I've come about, Mr Bellinger.'

'Maybe she has. Why don't you tell me, eh?' He indicated the other seat with the slightest movement of head and eyes.

'Oh right, yes.' Lydia looked at the chair, closer than she might have wished to her host.

'You gonna stand all prissy like that or sit down?' He gave extra emphasis to the last two words, making the question an order. 'What did she say, I might bite yer, eh? Yeah, well, I might, mightn't I?' He opened and closed his mouth to show his yellowed teeth in a weak snarl.

Lydia eased herself into the chair, adjusting her position so that their knees did not touch. Then, with her own slightly self-conscious smiley-face, she told Francis Bellinger the story of his grandfather's medals awarded for service in the Great War. Nothing exceptional, no conspicuous gallantry, no mention in despatches, just the deadly grinding horrors of killing in the trenches of Flanders. She explained how she'd bought the medals at an auction, how she enjoyed finding the living descendants of the people who'd once possessed such treasures and re-uniting them with those who might keep the memories and breathe new life into them. Without going into all the detail of the records, the censuses, the web sites, the vast bank of information so readily available to her, Lydia told how she'd traced the deaths of Freddie's grandfather, his parents and sister and finally, a little fortuitously, found Freddie himself with the help of Monica Sanders. Through it all the old man appeared to listen attentively, nodding slightly as names and dates were mentioned. Once or twice he raised a shaky hand to wipe away imagined dribble from the corner of his mouth.

When she came to the end of the story and the moment was right to pass over her little parcel, Lydia hesitated. Of course she did, she always hesitated at this moment, whether it was a photo album or a Bible, medals or love letters, it was the end of a story. Sometimes it had been a story that had engrossed her, consumed her for months or years, but not now. Now she was almost as detached as the day she'd first bought them, and if anything, she felt more connection to the man who'd earned the medals than to his grandson.

'So, these medals, what d'yer want for 'em?'

'Oh, no, I don't want anything for them, they're your grandfather's, they're yours.'

'What's it to you then, eh?'

'I just enjoy it, it's my hobby if you like.'

'I dunno as I do like, poking yer nose in where nobody asked yer. Like that other old cow what got yer 'ere in the first place. Never asked me, she didn't.'

Lydia felt her smile slip away along with the lingering sympathy she'd felt for Francis since she'd first heard of his situation. She could easily leave, be out of the room and out of Willoughby House in less than two minutes, taking the medals with her. They remained as saleable as when she'd bought them, perhaps more so. So much for giving and getting small pleasures.

'Perhaps I'd better go, Mr Bellinger.'

'Only just got here ain't yer? Christ, what's up with yer?'

Lydia set her jaw and summoned up a little more civility. 'Would you like to see them?'

'See 'em?' Freddie's face creased into a smirk. 'Don't get an offer like that too often round here, leastways, not without they wanna dip their little fingers in me wallet.' Before Lydia could fully comprehend what he was saying, he added, 'Freddie, call me Freddie. What yer clutching then, girl? Better see what yer got, eh?'

For a fleeting moment Lydia had a sense of a former Freddie, one whose rheumy eyes once held laughter and sparkle, whose hollow voice once boomed above bar-room chatter, a great big affable bear of a man engrossed in life and all it held. Nearly all of him had gone and what remained sat slumped in dull acceptance, being slowly desiccated by the heat that was intended to bring comfort. The passage through life from squealing birth to opiate-lulled exit never seemed so short as it did in this brief glimpse.

She groped mechanically for the leather case within the brown paper, withdrew it and fumbled to unfasten the little brass clip. The three medals, the three standard nothing-special medals, issued to millions after the Great War, looked at their best. Lydia had carefully cleaned them and tenderly pressed out their ribbons from their previous crumpled state. The black velvet-lined case had been her own indulgence, but she felt the medals deserved it after their decades squashed in a brown envelope. She passed the open case to him.

'There, there they are.'

He considered them for a moment. 'Pretty, ain't they? Whose d'yer say they were?'

'Your grandfather's. Your mother's father.' Lydia reached over and lifted the Victory medal from its place. 'Can you see? Here's his name on the edge, James Edward Brenton.'

'James Edward Brenton,' he repeated the name, weighing the medal gently. Lydia thought it might weigh as much as the skeletal hand that held it. 'Fancy that, dear old grampy.'

'He probably never saw them, but your grandmother must have had them.'

'How's that?'

'Well, although they were for service in the war, they weren't actually issued until some time after. Your grampy...' Lydia hesitated, distracted by using the word Freddie had used. She tried it again, 'Your grampy's were only issued a day before he died.' It sounded no better the second time.

'Yeah? Bugger me, how d'yer work that out?'

'It wasn't difficult. His death certificate has the day he died and the medal record gives the date of issue.'

The medal remained in his hand, the case rested on his knees while his eyes focused somewhere in the past. After a few moments he looked at Lydia and said, 'Yeah, I don't remember all that stuff.'

'No, you wouldn't.' Lydia could have added 'because you weren't born', but it seemed uncharitable to press him. 'Do you mind if I ask why you're called Freddie? I mean, it's not a common nickname for Francis is it?'

'Always been Freddie. Like mum was always Tess.'

'Tess? That's unusual too. A pet name I expect, something your dad called her maybe. What was she like, Freddie?'

'Who? What d'yer wanna know all this stuff for then, eh?'

'Sorry, I don't mean to pry, it's none of my business, I'm just curious. It must have been a terrible time to lose her like that. And your sister.'

'Yeah, terrible it was.'

'Freddie,' Lydia said gently. She had no wish to upset the old man, it really was none of her business, but curiosity had the better of her. 'Freddie, your grandfather's medals are yours, but I wonder if I could ask a favour?'

'You can ask, but I ain't got no money.'

'No, money isn't the thing.' She smiled in what she hoped was her most disarming and sincere way and felt a little sick at her own deceit. 'Do you have your birth certificate here, in your papers and things? Monica Sanders sent me a copy of it, it's why I'm here, but I just want to be sure of something.'

Freddie Bell weighed the medal again, gently up and down.

'A favour, eh? One good turn, eh? In the cupboard over there, my little case, in there. Bring it 'ere.'

Lydia fetched it, an old faux-leather brief-case circa 1965 covered in faded and torn stickers from all corners of the globe. She slipped the latches and turned it to Freddie.

'You get it,' he said. 'In the envelope on top.'

It was exactly as she'd seen before, it was the birth certificate Monica had scanned and sent to her, it was Francis Bellinger's birth certificate, or rather, a copy issued in 1956.

'Seen enough, have yer?'

'Yes, thank you. And I suppose being Freddie Bell was just a convenience, shorter than being Bellinger.'

'One favour, not two. My turn now. Hold me hand will yer?'

Lydia stiffened at the suggestion, not just because of the warning she'd been given by smiley-face, but because his hands seemed so uninviting, so cold, so transparent and the request so blatant. He saw her hesitation but couldn't taste how dry her mouth was as she said stiffly, 'Just a hand then Freddie.'

'That fat little cow been telling tales has she? You dunno the half of it. Always leanin' over pushin' herself in yer face then says she needs payin' for favours. Thievin' little tart she is. Forget it, yer nosy bitch. Get out and leave me in peace and take yer fuckin' medals wiv yer.'

Lydia flinched and shifted awkwardly, shocked by the accusation and the force of his abuse which bore witness to his sincerity. Steeling herself for what might follow, she leaned forward holding out her hand palm up. Freddie need only move his an inch or so to grasp it. 'Just a hand then, Freddie,' she repeated, then added, 'If you like,' hoping he would not use the one with the stained tape holding down a cannula.

'Good girl,' he said and laid his hand in hers. The feel belied the appearance, he was warm and soft with the lightest of touches despite covering her little hand twice over with his bear's paw. She felt the smallest of pressures as he closed his eyes. 'Good girl. I need to tell yer something, maybe ask a real favour.'

7

Before he could continue the door opened and smiley-face leaned into the room. 'I just thought I'd see if...Freddie Bell!' she exclaimed as if talking to a six-year-old. Lydia snatched away her hand as if she'd been caught stealing sweets from a jar.

'Can't a bloke hold hands wiv 'is daughter now?'

Smiley-face lost her smile and looked from Freddie to Lydia and back again. 'Oh, I'm so sorry, I didn't know. Freddie, how wonderful.' Her lips struggled to recover their smile.

'Well,' Lydia began, 'I'm not really...' but she thought better of it and let the lie linger a while longer by grasping the bear's paw.

'Now piss off.'

'All right Freddie, no need for that. I'm off now till Monday, I'll see you then.' The condescending kindergarten voice returned along with the smile. 'None of your nonsense while I'm gone.'

The door closed behind her.

'Oh dear,' said Lydia awkwardly, at a loss for anything more meaningful. His fragile grip tightened a fraction. He wasn't looking at her, his eyes were closed, his mouth a little twisted. 'Are you all right?'

Freddie groaned, struggling to find a word to describe the intense pain in his back, even dulled as it was by morphine. 'All right?' he managed after a few moments, 'Course I'm not all right, fuckin' dyin' ain't I?'

Lydia could find no answer to his blunt assessment, no bridge from her living world with its future promise and potential to his bleak future-less one. She would be on her way soon enough, never to return to this warehouse of the dying, while he would probably never leave it. Touching hands and knees, sharing his grandfather's war medals, she wished for a moment that she might really be his daughter and bring him some relief from dying among strangers.

'Tell me about Tess, tell me about your mum, Freddie.'

'She was a great old girl she was, tough as old boots though. Bleedin' had to be in them days.' His eyes remained closed but his mouth slowly untwisted. 'It was all bloody tough, right through. We still had a laugh though, plenty of that about, even if we was

8

short of everything else.' He drifted to another place, nodding slightly to himself at the memory.

'You must have missed her so much, and your sister. And then your dad when...' The words were spoken before Lydia caught herself and she grimaced at her own crassness. The last subject she meant to return to was death, and certainly not such painful recollections as both parents and a sister.

'Missed 'em all, but that was it. No choice, eh?'

'What happened to you afterwards?'

'Not a lot, wandered about, all over. Seen some fun, all over.'

'I meant, were you adopted or...' To use the word orphanage seemed insensitive yet Lydia could find no alternative.

'Adopted? Adopted?' Freddie opened his eyes, scanned the room as if unsure of his whereabouts. 'What's this about?'

'Nothing Freddie. I'm sorry to have brought back bad memories. I'd best be leaving soon. Shall I put the medals away for you or would you like to keep them right there?'

He looked down at the case as if for the first time, let go her hand and traced a finger down the red-white-and-blue ribbon of the Mons Star. He collected himself back to the present, 'Mine, you say?'

'Yes, awarded to your grampy.' The word came no easier than previously.

'You worked it all out, then?'

'Yes. It wasn't very difficult.'

'Could you find anybody?'

'No, sometimes it's impossible, sometimes it just falls in your lap.' Lydia's smile was genuine as she added, 'You rather fell in my lap.'

Freddie Bell sank deeper into his dressing gown, giving Lydia the impression he was visibly shrinking. His eyes closed as the twist returned to his face. A little stiffening jerk of his legs caused the black case and its contents to fall to the floor.

'I'll get them, Freddie,' she said softly.

'Good girl, eh. You get 'em,' came a hoarse whisper. 'You come far?'

'I'm on my way to Cambridge, almost passing the door, so it was no trouble.'

'No trouble, eh.' He looked at her, then beyond her to somewhere far distant and shook his head slightly. 'I ain't got long,' he said, almost casually. 'You comin' back?'

Lydia hesitated. She could easily come back, she could come back every day for a week, she was on holiday with only herself to please. Time with Stephen was, as usual, flexible and uncommitted. She had a few ideas of an outing here, a visit there, so yes, she could come back if she wished. But she didn't really wish to, she didn't wish to be drawn deeper into this dying man's life, even though she'd barged into it. There was also an uncomfortable hint of emotional blackmail, yet he'd already enlisted her sympathy, already made her an accomplice in his convenient lie. And out of compassion for a lonely death she'd held his hand.

'Monica...might she call in...drop in to see...' It was a feeble attempt to deny what her heart had already decided.

'Nosey cow, thinks I dunno what she's up to. Wants it all, she does, there'll be a surprise for 'er all right.'

Lydia suddenly saw the medals in their new leather case with the black velvet lining becoming Monica's, by default or perhaps worse. She would have no claim to them but they could still become hers to do with as she wished.

'Yes, Freddie, I'll come back. We can talk about your mum, your dad, your sister, we can talk about anything you like.'

'Come tomorrow. Linda, I wanna talk about my Linda.'

∞

The Old Rectory had become familiar. Lydia had felt comfortable in Stephen's house right from the start, but over the months - and her frequent visits - it had begun to have the feel of a second home, although when she thought more deeply about it, it felt more holiday-home than real home. She rarely needed to exert herself beyond making coffee or pouring a glass of wine, any other task was a distant thing delegated to the unseen housekeeper, Mrs Webb. She and Stephen ate meals prepared by her or by any number of chefs in the many Cambridge restaurants where they generally dawdled away Saturday nights. Lydia slept in a bed made by Mrs Webb, between sheets washed by Mrs Webb. She walked on lawns mown by the gardener and picked vegetables he'd planted and tended. For all the welcome, for all that Lydia had the run of the house to do as she pleased, she was at pains to take nothing for granted. It remained Stephen's house, the house he'd raised a daughter in, the house he'd lived a married life in. And it was still a house where both living daughter and deceased wife kept a presence in their different ways.

Since the horribly uncertain start to their friendship, which Lydia would privately concede was due to her own insecurities, they'd greatly enjoyed each other's company and shared both the little successes of life as well as the disappointments. However, they had not shared a bed, although more than once the opportunity had seemed imminent, more than once the suggestion had been only a breath away. Their embraces were those of good friends, their kisses usually chaste. Stephen was far from cold, on the contrary he was warm and open and frequently affectionate, but just as he was not cold neither was he passionate. Lydia's own desires were muted and confused. Much as she enjoyed his company, she wasn't at all sure she would want it every day and surely the sex thing would complicate matters, all that intimacy and angst. Worse, the sex thing might change everything. Having met on holiday, their relationship had become fixed in that mode: for all that they stayed together in Stephen's house, it might just as well have been a country hotel. It might all be an illusion, a holiday romance that never quite blossomed, change one part of it and it might disappear altogether.

When Lydia stood at the door, suitcase in hand, it was without any great anticipation of change. He opened it almost as soon as she touched the bell. His familiar, ready smile welcomed her.

'I heard the car, you don't have to ring, you can just come in.'

'Yes, I know. Hello Stephen.'

They hugged as they always hugged, he stooping a little to be cheek to cheek, she on tip-toes to meet him half way, lips touching briefly to confirm affection. To Lydia their physical contact always underlined his height and slimness, emphasised her own podginess.

'I was beginning to wonder where you'd got to. You do know you always arrive at exactly the time you say you will?'

'It took longer than I expected.'

'All safely delivered? Another satisfied customer?'

'Not exactly.'

Their customary summer lunch of salmon, salad fresh from the garden, warm bread and chilled wine was spread out waiting for her, not on the terrace under the sunshade as they might have hoped, but the next best thing, the luxuriant conservatory filled with all manner of exotic plants and scents. Lydia was reminded of just how easy this life was, how little effort it took beyond the drive from Oxford and the always-more-difficult return. The warmth and humidity of the conservatory, the vivid splashes of colour against the tropical greenery all reinforced the sense of visiting a stately home or the botanic gardens. There was a time when she might've cringed at the contrast to her house in Osney with its cramped little garden and the pots she sporadically tended between bouts of total neglect.

'I've still got the medals. He wants me to go and see him again,' she blurted out before they'd sat down.

'Ah.'

'I said I would, he hasn't got long.'

'Oh.'

'I'm, er, going back tomorrow.'

'Right.'

'I didn't think you'd mind.'

'I don't.'

'I mean, we don't usually do anything. And I was going to stay over till Monday or Tuesday anyway.'

Stephen saw the unease, the awkwardness in her, and wondered what might have caused it. He'd become accustomed to a Lydia who'd shed her burden of self-doubt, at least while she was in his company, and now here she was tentative and apologetic again. And Monday or Tuesday, hadn't it been Tuesday for sure? He opened the wine, her favourite he thought, but now he wondered where he got that idea, whether it was simply that he always bought it and she always drank it. He poured the bubbles and they chinked their glasses.

'He didn't want them?'

'He wanted me to hang on to them.'

'But even so, that was the point of it wasn't it?'

'Yes. No. The thing is, he has no one to leave them to.'

Stephen just nodded. He saw what she meant, yet surely there would be more to it than this. He'd seen it before, this involvement she felt for the objects and the people she found in her quests. He'd seen the reluctance in the final parting.

'I know it's hard to say goodbye after all the work you put in.'

'It's not that,' she said and smiled when she added, 'not this time. I don't know what will happen to them when he's gone. I don't think he knows either, but the way he spoke just made me think they might disappear into someone's pocket. I mean, who would know? Who would know he ever had them? Nobody would miss them, there're no grandchildren who've been promised them or anything like that.'

He still thought this was no more than an excuse to keep the medals. Once she'd parted with them it would be none of her business what happened to them, although he could see that if the old man only had them for a few days or a month, then Lydia might feel aggrieved if some stranger collected a windfall by selling them. But for some reason he had yet to understand, she was a little tetchy and he let the subject of Freddie Bellinger and the medals drop.

'Is there anything you'd like to do? There's a table at Mimi's tonight, but we can cancel and eat here or go to the pub. Whatever you like.'

A forkful of smoked salmon paused on the way to her mouth. Yes, whatever she liked. Yet it was all so unsatisfactory, there was nothing she liked enough to put it before anything else. Indecision reigned supreme. The wine, the comfort, the ease of it all had let another, older, unwelcome feeling creep up on her: she was unworthy of such choices, unworthy of his friendship, of his affection, his generosity. She was not even any good at the one thing she supposedly excelled at, weren't the wretched medals still in her room instead of being where they belonged? Now, almost too late, she recognised the expanding cloud of depression threatening to condemn her past, present and future to utter failure. Once she might have run, through any door, by any means, but there was no escape without drama or worse, explanation. With far greater effort than her face betrayed she concentrated on the fork and brought it carefully to her lips, tasting the texture and smokey sweetness of the fish, willing it to consume her senses.

Stephen, dimly seeing some silent struggle taking place, waited until Lydia swallowed and took a sip of her wine. 'It doesn't matter, you know. We'll just stay in and read, maybe watch a bad film.'

'Yes, thank you,' she said, pushing the cloud back a little further. He was, she thought, such a good man, almost innocent in his kindness and consideration. Perhaps it came with a different age, a different world. Her unworthiness briefly threatened to return.

The afternoon grew wetter and colder, pushing them in from the conservatory to the comfort of the sitting room armchairs. Lydia would have walked to change her mood, even in the rain, had she been in Oxford where a hundred variations of route were available from her doorstep, but in Grantchester the choices were few and crossing the fields through the squalls to the Cam was uninviting. At length she sank into *Brighton Rock*, plucked almost at random from Stephen's bookshelves and far removed from all her troubles. In the evening they heated frozen pizza - emergency rations, Stephen called it - followed by ice-cream with strawberry jam as a topping. The kitchen cupboards groaned with food that needed time and careful preparation, the garden offered fresh everything, but they chose the convenience of the freezer, along with more wine. Skipping Mimi's also saved her from trying to tame her unruly hair or fit her body into clothes it was never designed for.

On the point of heading to her bed, Lydia turned back and asked, 'When you were younger, what did you call your grandfathers, either of them?'

'I never knew my father's father, and my mother's father I hardly saw. He died when I was about eight or nine I think. I don't remember calling him anything.'

'Do you remember what other people called him, how your mother might have said 'your grandfather' or 'your grandpa' when she spoke of him?'

'Granddad, I think, yes she would have said granddad. I think I called him granddad too.'

'And what about your father's father? The same?'

'No, my father rarely spoke of him. He would have said 'my father' I think. And he was my grandfather but he was never a grandfather in his lifetime, he never knew his grandchildren. Why?'

'Something Freddie Bell said. He called his grandfather, the medals man, he called him 'grampy' and I couldn't work out why it felt wrong.'

2

'He's picked up an infection from somewhere, so he's not so good this morning. I'm afraid you'll see a difference from yesterday.' Smiley-face's place had been taken by a woman whose eyes were so sad she appeared to be carrying the cares of the whole world on her shoulders.

'Poor Freddie.'

They followed the same route as previously, passed the same wilting blooms, through the same stuffy heat, the wisps of music as stale as the air. At Freddie's door there was a pause to sanitize their hands and a token knock, but no cautionary word about the patient's behaviour.

Lydia was not prepared for the change. Freddie had not left his bed. He was propped up on a bank of pillows, attached to the drip, eyes closed. Each breath announced the struggle for life, the air rasping in his throat as it was defiantly drawn in. Lydia swallowed nervously, wishing beyond anything that her compassionate hand-holding had not been the source of infection. Involuntarily she wiped the palm of her hand down the side of her jeans.

'Freddie, Linda's here to see you again,' said the carer gently.

He stirred slightly as his breathing paused and he made a sound which might have been an acknowledgement.

'It's Lydia, Lydia Silverstream,' Lydia whispered to the carer.

'Oh, oh right,' she said, puzzled. 'I'll leave you two. I'll come back in a while, it's a busy morning. Use the buzzer,' she indicated the red button on a cord on Freddie's bed, 'if you need to.'

Unsure of whether to disturb him or let him wake himself, Lydia stood by the window and watched the wind driving the rain across the garden at the back of Willoughby House. It was no more than a large rectangle of lawn with a single wooden bench seat along each side. Below her, to her right, a black van was backed into the basement entrance. She was just considering what might be delivered on a Sunday when with a start she realised it was an undertaker's van, not delivering but collecting. The instinct was to look away, yet she was transfixed by the process she was witnessing through the gap between the van roof and the doorway. From within the building unseen hands were manoeuvring a wheeled stretcher carrying a grey body-bag into the rear of the van. After a pause, a second trolley followed the first. When was it exactly that death and all its paraphernalia became secret, unseen and unspoken of? When was death so euphemised that it stopped being part of everyday life?

'What d'yer want?' Freddie's feeble but unmistakeable voice brought her back to the living.

'Hello Freddie, I said I'd come today. I hear you're not so well.'

'Is it really you? Is it Linda, you've come to see me?' Each word was a struggle and he groped towards her as a blind man might do.

'Lydia, it's Lydia.'

Freddie appeared to give this some thought, although he may simply have been gathering his strength to continue. 'Lydia, eh,' he paused again, 'Sure it were Linda, she told me Linda. We said Linda.' Mind and body sagged in unison, never was a man more disappointed with a name.

'Tell me about her, Freddie, tell me about Linda.'

'Nah, not doin' that.' He shifted his head round slightly, looking intently at her. 'Never say nothin'. Safest bleedin' way. They said you was her.'

His eyes closed again and the tentative conversation faltered. Lydia couldn't find the right words to set Freddie off, set him going on memories, happy memories that might bring her closer to exploring the great blank of his life. Between his father being killed in 1943 and the present day she knew nothing, had not needed to know anything. Monica Sanders had conveniently bridged that gap for her.

'Have you travelled much Freddie, seen much of the world?' It was the hairdresser's gambit, but all she could manage.

'Will do when I get out, eh? Have some fun then.'

'Where will you go? Somewhere warm and sunny?'

'Back to Oz, that's where. Warm and bleedin' sunny there, eh.'

'When did you go, Freddie? I'd love to hear about it,' she said, and she meant it. He'd noticeably brightened, found a little reserve of energy from somewhere.

'Go? I dunno, twenty, fifty years back. Went all over, did it all. Sweat buckets out there you could, like a bloody oven then freeze yer arse off. God, we drank that shit beer like it was water. Cold piss it was, but piss or not we had to 'ave it, eh? I won't do no more of that, not now, gettin' past all that shovelin', shiftin' all that dirt. Someone else can do all that, I'll sit and watch 'em, eh?' He made a deep guttural sound, an unhappy substitute for a laugh.

'Sounds easier, Freddie, was it gold you were after?'

'Gold? Yeah, that's good. Gold, silver, anything you like. Kings of the bloody castle we were.' He nodded to himself at some new thought that crossed his mind but didn't share it with Lydia. Having found a way into his memories, she was keen to keep them on this happier track, but itched to guide him round to his family. She risked mentioning girls, surely a happy topic for an old miner.

'I bet the girls were all over you with gold in your pockets.'

'Girls? Yeah, most likely.' He spoke as if he wasn't really sure what she meant and couldn't be bothered to ask. Lydia tried another tack.

'Did you ever get married, Freddie?'

'Married?' He considered the question, nodding, rolling the idea around as a hypothetical problem. 'Nah. You ever killed a man?' Before Lydia could fashion an answer he continued, 'Nah, not you, eh?' then some new thought wrinkled his face into half a smile. 'I coulda killed a few I can tell yer. Killed a few more'n what I did anyway.' Again the humourless laugh gurgled in his throat.

Struggling to hang on to some thread, Lydia gratefully thought of the services and dismissed mobsters and hit-men from her mind. 'Was that in the army, Freddie? Korea or Malaya?' Her history failed her, the exact sequence of wars that dotted the last half of the century was beyond her recall. When Freddie didn't answer she tried tentatively, 'Kenya?'

'Yeah,' he said at length, although he seemed to have moved on from killing to some fresh vista.

A sudden thought, a memory of her own from not that long ago came to Lydia. Her much-loved grandmother, an intelligent and feisty woman right up to her death, had spent the last years of her life in a retirement home. Pain killers and antibiotics were dished out freely and in some combinations could have an unwelcome side effect. Too often it was written off as senility, only for the real coherent person to emerge once the course of drugs was completed. Freddie had been sharp enough yesterday.

'What's yer name again?'

'Lydia.'

'Lydia, eh?' he looked away, far beyond the room and all of Bedford. 'I knew her once, clever little madam she were. Didn't do her no good. Washed up on the beach one day. Not a mark on her. Dark hair she had, all straggled across her face. Little bits of seaweed in it and sand in her nose. White lips she had, lyin' there, white as the rest of 'er, white as snow.' He turned to her, his eyes intense, fearful, 'And blue. White and blue as snow on a sunny day.' Whoever she'd been, he saw her now with stark clarity.

More death, not the subject of choice, but the one which Freddie was drawn back to. Little wonder perhaps, when his own was close enough to see, close enough to reach out and touch. Lydia tried to imagine how it might be when her time came, to know for sure she wouldn't see next Christmas, the next birthday, another spring.

'When was all that, Freddie?' she asked with little expectation of an answer.

'I dunno when, long time. Lovely sunset. Red sky at night, eh?'

She could just get up and leave him, slip out of the room quietly and he'd probably not notice or even remember she'd been there. She could leave him to his drugged wanderings through scenes of his life or his imagination, probably a cocktail of both. Instead she looked at her lap and wrestled with her conscience, questioning her motives for being there in the first place. What if the roles were reversed, how would she feel about being used by a stranger for their own strange satisfaction? Her hands lay in her lap, with the feel of unnatural cleanliness that comes from a sanitizer. And the feel of it brought her back again to Freddie's infection.

'Red sky at night, shepherd's delight. That's what we said Freddie, was it the same for you?'

'Shepherds?' he was almost indignant. 'Sailors more like. See what they'd think about bloody shepherds down the docks. Shepherds? Might as well say bloody…say bloody…say bloody anything,' he ended lamely, the strength of feeling already exhausted.

'Down the docks? Were you in the docks?'

'Docks? We was all in the docks, till we was bombed out. They was some red skies they were. You wouldn't believe the stuff we used to get up to in them days.'

'What kind of stuff Freddie?' With mention of bombing Lydia had the connection to the history she knew: the deaths of his mother and sister, his father a couple of years later.

'Used to pick up bombs, them fire bombs and stick 'em in buckets of water before they got goin', can't see kids today doin' that, eh? Fat chance.' His smile and laugh were cut short by a cry of pain and a tensing of his body. The animation left his face as he fell back on the pillows. Lydia half reached for the red buzzer and wondered what constituted an emergency on a busy morning.

She watched him intently until after a minute or so he stirred again. 'What you 'ere for then? Come to say prayers have yer? 'Cos yer wastin' yer time, prayers ain't gonna do me no good now.'

'No prayers, Freddie. I came to see you yesterday, about your grandfather's medals. My name is Lydia.'

'Yeah, yeah, medals. Did you find Linda?'

Lydia hesitated before saying, 'Not yet, I'm looking though. Did she have another name? Was she Linda Bell?'

'Bell?' He seemed confused again, struggling to connect the word to anything.

'Or Bellinger, Linda Bellinger? Did Linda have your name Freddie?'

He stared at his hands limp across the sheet in front of him, at the tube dripping fluids into his body. The question held either deep meaning or no meaning but Lydia had no way of guessing which.

'Dunno, maybe. Who knows, eh?'

'I'll see what I can find,' Lydia persisted. 'I'll look for Linda Bellinger and Bell. When did you know her Freddie?'

'Never knew 'er. Thought I saw 'er once, walking down Oxford Street, just like that. Lovely she were, just like her mother.' His slow and broken voice couldn't hide the emptiness of love lost.

'You knew her mother, then Freddie?'

'Yeah.' A shiver ran across him and trembled the IV bags hanging beside him. 'All gone. It's all gone now, nothing left.'

A faint sound at the door announced the return of the sad-eyed carer.

'Hello, how are you getting on?' She smiled weakly and put a hand on Freddie's wrist. He made no move or sound.

'He's been a bit rambling, you know, makes sense one minute and not the next. I think he's had some pain.' Lydia whispered, at the same time wondering why she felt the need to provide a bulletin.

The carer looked down at her and kept the contempt from her voice as she said, 'Yes, he will have had some pain.' There was a great deal more she might have said had she been less experienced, had she never previously encountered a Last Minute Loved One. They usually arrived about now, a little while before a death, full of regrets for not coming earlier, regrets for not visiting their grandparent for twenty years, full of hope that it was not too late to be remembered in the will. Sometimes they arrived a few days after death, outraged that nobody had told them, demanding a complaint form, cursing their cousins.

'Yes. Obvious. Sorry.'

The carer nodded. 'It's OK,' she said flatly. 'He needs to sleep.'

Freddie appeared to have already fallen asleep, or fallen into whatever state passes for sleep on the threshold of death in the land of morphine.

∞

Lydia had never returned from an outing on her own to The Old Rectory. Arriving straight from her job in payroll admin on a Friday night, it was right and proper to ring the bell and wait for Stephen to open the door. It was somehow quite different to swish

21

back up the gravel only a couple of hours after sharing breakfast with him. She'd let herself out of the house without assistance, so maybe she could let herself in. The front door was still too formal an entrance, so she ducked through the drizzle to the conservatory at the rear, calling out as she went in. He returned her hello from his study.

'We'll see, Laurence,' he was saying as she came into the room. 'Yes, at twelve, I'll let you know if not.'

Lydia grimaced. From this single fragment of a conversation she knew exactly what was spoken of. She had promised to meet a colleague of Stephen's, Laurence Durham, to see what help she could give his genealogy research. So full of Freddie and medals, she'd quite forgotten the arrangement. She nodded frantically, mouthing yes, yes, as he said goodbye.

'Ooh, I had forgotten, sorry, but yes, yes, of course we must see him,' she implored.

'It's fine, it's all set. What about Freddie, how is he?'

'He has an infection. I think he may die. I mean today, tomorrow, die soon anyway.'

'Not good.' Asking anything more was suddenly irrelevant.

'I'm going to do a little work on him, you know, checking to see about…well, you know.'

'Yes, I do. But I think you mean checking on yourself.' As happened so often, Stephen spoke straight to the point. 'But there can't be any mistake can there?'

'Not unless there were two Francis Bellingers born to parents of the same name on the same date in the same place.'

'Not likely.'

'No, not likely,' and she smiled and wondered if ever a man was more sympathetic than Stephen Kellaway. There were times, such as this, when he felt almost a part of her, so well did he read her moods, so effortlessly did he slip into step beside her. Yet the inner man remained a little elusive, hidden beneath his even-tempered surface. It was he who fell into her step, rarely she into his.

Through the chill of the afternoon they each worked on their interests, he preparing an article for a journal he contributed to, she searching and extracting information about Francis Bells and

Bellingers. Experience had taught her the tricks to use, the variations of name, the widening of date ranges, the inclusion of the most unlikely sources. In this instance she was simply repeating the process she'd completed weeks previously. After an hour or so her carefully recorded notes had little more to offer than she already knew. She confirmed Freddie's parentage and that of his mother Lily, according to the record Francis 'Freddie' Bellinger was James Brenton's only surviving grandchild. She did however, have a few other strands that might yet be relevant. There were several F Bells and a Bellinger who'd travelled to Australia in the 50s and 60s, two in the autumn of 1956, a few weeks after Freddie's new birth certificate had been issued. She'd also found a reference to Mrs Bellinger in a diary of the attacks on Bristol in World War II, where Freddie's mother and sister Maud had died. The link to the original text was broken and there was no ISBN, but it was a lead, possibly to her Bellingers, and it might cast more light on the events. At the other extreme she had more references in voter lists and telephone directories than she could make use of.

The Old Rectory was a comfortable home in all respects, but it performed least well on a cold drizzly summer day. With log fires and central heating both in their seasonal 'off' positions, Lydia's fingers grew cold tapping keys. As the dampness seeped into her she became restless, pacing the room, trapped by the weather, her mind full of unresolved questions. The little lie and promise she'd given Freddie about looking for Linda had felt deceitful at the time, now they added to her discomfort. She had no dates, no place and only her own suggestions of a surname. She couldn't look for Linda without something more to go on. And why would she look for her anyway? If Linda were Freddie's daughter or just possibly a niece, finding her would certainly give the medals a better home than Monica Sanders. That might be motive enough to search. Hadn't he spoken fondly of Linda in his vision of a girl in Oxford Street? The more she thought about it the more Lydia felt it was the fondness of a father, heightened by separation. And the comparison to her mother, that said something too, although he might have spoken of a niece in a similar way. She wondered if men ever saw their sisters as beautiful. Even when she tried she couldn't see her own brother in anything approaching those terms.

Just as the new quest was taking shape, just as she was planning to see Freddie again tomorrow, ask him directly about Linda, her date with Laurence Durham popped back into her head. The arrangement was a duty more than a desire. Of course she'd agreed when Stephen had asked her, it was impossible to say no even if she'd wanted to, but she had little appetite for tracing a stranger's ancestors. It seemed to her that it was nowhere near as challenging as it once was, unless it involved a family beyond the reach of search engines. Care still needed to be taken, it was still easy enough to make the wrong connections, to rush to join the dots on paper where they were never joined in life. But however much care was taken, however diligent she might be, the end result was always incomplete, it could never be otherwise. Since she'd already done as much work as was reasonable on her own family, her preferred new research was always to move forward in time through the generations rather than backward, the opposite of what was recommended. Her way, there was a satisfactory conclusion or, at worst, a puzzle waiting to be solved another day.

Stephen looked up from his papers as she came in. 'Done checking?' he asked.

'For now, yes, there's very little to go on. Nothing new. I might never have found him if his neighbour hadn't found him for me. What about your friend Laurence, do you know exactly what he wants?'

'No. I was talking about you, I mean what you do,' for a second he was flustered, 'er, your research and finding people, like the medals, and...' a little colour came to his cheeks as he sought the correct phrase. Lydia couldn't help but smile, it was a rare moment for Stephen to be lost for words. But she enjoyed it enough to let him struggle unaided. 'Well, anyway, he became very interested, asked how you went about things, and was very keen to know if you were, well, trustworthy I suppose.'

'What did you tell him?' she asked with as straight a face as she could.

'Well, naturally I told...yes, well, you know what I told him.'

He accepted the little joke at his expense with a smile. For all their easy friendship such moments were not common between them. For a few seconds neither spoke as they considered each other, he liking how much she stood so relaxed and teased him in his own study, she liking the look of him half turned from his work, looking up at her with such warmth in his eyes. It was a moment that might lead to other moments, might take them down new paths. But no sooner had they both recognised it for what it was, it had passed.

'But he didn't say what he wanted, didn't say specifically?'

'No, he was interested, very interested, and asked if he could meet you next time you were here. I think his words were something like you might be exactly the person to help him sort something out.'

'Is he coming here?'

'No, I thought we'd see him in college, have lunch together, plus the optional sherry beforehand. I thought you might enjoy the occasion even if Laurence turns out to be a waste of time.'

'What does he do, what's his subject? Is that the right question?'

'Good enough, but his subject is administration or more precisely, money. He's the college bursar. He's a bit of an odd bird in some ways, but you can make your own mind up, you don't have to do anything if you don't want to. I promised him nothing.'

Lydia nodded, reminded again of her own promise. 'Stephen, if you were to tell me about a time you saw your niece, Phoebe, or perhaps someone who looked like her, would you say how lovely she was, perhaps like her mother? Is it something you'd say?'

'I don't know, I might.'

Lydia was about to ask if he might say it of his daughter, Jacqueline, but stopped herself, knowing the answer without asking. But Stephen had already asked it of himself.

'I would say it about Jacqueline,' he said, adding as an afterthought, 'Any father would. I'm sure that there isn't a daughter in the world who isn't lovely in a father's eye.'

'Yes, I expect you're right.'

'This is connected to Freddie,' he said, no question, just an observation.

'Yes, it is. I wonder if he had a daughter. It might all be just ramblings, like the dead girl on the beach and killing people in the army. It could be just stories or some film he saw once.'

'Go and see him again tomorrow, Laurence will understand. You might not have long to talk to Freddie.'

'No, we'll see Laurence tomorrow, then I'll see Freddie on my way home on Tuesday. He'll last till then.'

∞

The Armoury is a very private dining room perched in a corner overlooking Second Court. It was serving its customary exclusive lunch for those few elite members of the college and their guests who were about in the middle of July. A single table was laid with white linen for eight diners. Upon it gleamed silver cutlery without a hint of stain or tarnish despite two centuries of use.

From the walls of the ancient room portraits of a dozen or so of the college's earliest Masters, resplendent in their heraldic insignia, stared sombrely down as Professor Sir Stephen Kellaway ushered Lydia into this holy-of-holies. Laurence Durham was waiting for them, standing awkwardly clutching a glass of sherry by a side-table on which seven other glasses and a decanter waited. As a mere employee, no more than an administrator, Laurence was in the Armoury as Stephen's guest, he had no rights to the inner sanctum himself despite controlling the purse that funded it. This was a room used exclusively by the privileged few, never let out for parties or meetings. By tradition only lunch was served here, and by the same tradition only eight places were laid, never more and never less, regardless of the number of would-be diners. In an anteroom were eight hooks for eight coats or gowns and any latecomer who saw all eight in use could quietly slip away to find a lesser meal elsewhere without disturbing those already seated.

'Ah, Stephen,' exclaimed the bursar, 'and Miss Silverstream, I presume. What a pleasure, thank you. Stephen has spoken so well of you.' He offered her a clammy hand.

'It's Lydia,' she said, surprised to be feeling less ill-at-ease than he appeared to be. There's nothing like another's obvious discomfort to calm the nerves within.

Laurence was a round man, round of face and of waist. His podgy hands showed only dimples where his knuckles should be. Protruding from his knife-sharp trouser legs were highly polished, round, black toecaps. His piggy eyes met Lydia's smile through circular frames perched on a round nose, even his perfectly placed bow-tie had rounded corners and a pattern of coloured balloons. Lydia understood immediately why Stephen had described him as an odd bird.

Small talk and sweet cloying sherry, not at all to Lydia's taste, took them through to lunch. There were no other diners. The meal was served silently, almost invisibly, by a dark-haired and beautifully lean young man who came and went through a door disguised as part of the panelling. He doubtless had some way of observing them, for no sooner had a decent interval passed after the last mouthful of a course than he appeared to remove the dishes.

They spoke of college things, of traditions, of present problems and past scandals, of Cambridge spies and government treachery. But they did not speak of anything remotely connected to family history or touch on how Lydia, trustworthy or otherwise, might be of assistance. The table had been cleared before she realised that so far it had all been an interview, she was being assessed for suitability. Stephen's recommendation had brought her only so far.

When coffee had been served and the handsome young man had been finally dismissed, Laurence Durham turned his round face to Lydia. 'Are you working on anything at the moment? Stephen said you might have just finished with something.'

'My lost-and-found work, you mean? I should've finished, I thought I'd finished, but something came up and, well, I'm still involved.' It gave her the perfect get-out should his puzzle seem uninteresting.

'I see.' The bursar considered this for a moment. 'Do you think you would have time for something new?'

'I don't know, it depends what it is.'

He looked from Lydia to Stephen and back again, still unsure of whether to share his mystery.

'Laurence, I can leave you two alone if it would help,' Stephen offered, ever the diplomat. 'But I hope you know whatever it is, it will remain confidential.' He spoke for himself, but his assurance covered Lydia too.

'Right. Yes. It's an odd thing asking a stranger about your own family.' He shifted nervously in his seat, re-arranging his body into a different set of spheres. 'All right, it is this. I would like to know who my father is. Or perhaps who he was, he may be long gone for all I know.'

So, thought Lydia, no long trail back through the centuries, no looking for a lost title, no claiming the throne of Ireland. Any of which might be easier than finding a lost father. Hadn't she said more than once that the dead were easier to find than the living?

'Can you help?' he said, then seeing her hesitation, 'I would pay whatever it costs of course, I should have said that.'

'Oh, no thank you, I don't charge, there's no fee, I'm not professional, but there are plenty who would help you.' She paused, uncertain of her ground. 'I wonder if it might be something for a private detective, an enquiry agent or whatever they're called these days. I've never tried to find anyone's father before.' She ended rather lamely, with a look beseeching Stephen to intervene.

He did, but not as she might have wished. Instead he sought to draw Laurence out, ignoring the difficulties until a better picture of the problem emerged. 'I wonder if you have much to go on, Laurence? A name, dates, places, anything that might be a starting point? I can't speak for Lydia, she's the expert in all this, but I'm sure she'd want to have an idea of what's involved.' It was his turn to look to her for support.

'Oh, yes, I should've said, yes,' she said with an enthusiasm she didn't feel.

'That's just it, I do have lot's to go on, too much to go on.' He hung his head and stared at his coffee cup. 'Too much.'

It was moments like this when the theory, the record searching, the building of family trees became something quite different, something intimate, something vitally important to the person involved. Lydia had seen it before and it always brought her up short, reminded her that all those names and dates, all those births and deaths were joy or tragedy for someone.

'Laurence,' she said, a little warmer than her previous tone, 'would you like to tell us anyway? My first question is always whether or not you've asked relatives about your family. They're often the best source, I wonder about your mother, did she say...?'

'My mother? Yes, she says a lot, most of it nonsense, and all intended to deceive.' He spoke with that unique resentment and contempt that a child can have for a parent.

'Your mother won't say who your father is? I suppose it's silly to ask if he's on your birth certificate?'

'My mother has told me many stories about my father and each time it's a different story, often at odds with the last version, and yes, there is a name on my birth certificate. My mother says it was just a joke.'

'Do you see your mother often? I mean, is it something you often talk about? Is she,' Lydia hesitated over her choice of words, Freddie Bell's ramblings fresh in her mind, 'is she aware of what she's saying?'

'Is she senile, is that what you mean? No, she's as sharp as a razor. My mother is coming up for her eighty-second birthday. She walks two or three miles a day and I see her every day, we live in the same house. She wouldn't have it any other way.'

Lydia wasn't quite sure if there was a sarcastic undertone or it was simply the way he drew out the last word he spoke. Now and again one heard of men who'd lived with their mothers their whole lives, who appeared to function quite normally, as Laurence did, and yet who'd had no experience of life beyond their mother's orbit.

'Is there nobody else in the family?'

'So far as I know only my grandmother. She's in her late nineties, also as fit as a flea. She and my mother are two of a kind.'

'You've spoken to her about your father?'

'Once or twice.' His voice took on a nasal tone and a higher pitch as he mimicked his grandmother, 'How should I know who your father was, she says, ask your mother, she says. Then she'll add

29

some…' he paused, looked up and saw her questioning expression. 'My grandmother often speaks quite graphically. Obscenely.'

'Is she…?' Lydia paused, regretting that she had started the question.

'Senile? No, not a bit of it. No excuses, she's just bloody minded, likes to shock. You get used to walking in the street and hearing everybody effing this and effing that, but there's still something quite unpleasant hearing a five year-old use foul language. Well, it's the same with a ninety-eight year old granny too, the more so when it's done for effect, believe me.'

'Your grandfather, perhaps, did he…?'

'Hah! One thing at a time. Probably another joke.' He paused, stifling the anger or tears or both, before continuing, 'Sorry, I haven't talked about this with anyone before.'

From a few questions about his family history the conversation had moved rapidly to revealing unsavoury intimacies. Lydia had the impression Laurence was relieved to be sharing them, unburdening himself of anxieties as he might to a therapist. These were a lifetime of secret resentments, a lifetime of longings for a father denied to him for reasons as yet unclear. He seemed to be struggling with other demons too, pulling at his mouth, twitching the muscles of his cheeks. Lydia felt sure tears would follow soon.

'Do you have any brothers or sisters, Laurence?' she asked as gently as a priest might ask of a recent widower, but with a view to finding safer ground.

'Not that I've ever seen or heard of. Which is an odd way of saying it, isn't it? Anybody else would be able to say either yes or no.'

'And your father's name on your birth certificate, even though your mother says it was a joke, have you looked for that person yourself? You'll have wondered if perhaps it was not a joke?'

'I haven't looked like you might look, it's just a name. Maybe the joke's on me, maybe it's real.'

'Do you have it with you?'

He reached into his inside pocket and drew out an envelope. Lydia had seen so many certificates over the years that the fold and size of it was instantly recognisable. He passed it across to her.

'What do you think?' he asked. The swell of emotion had drained away leaving no hope or expectation that she would find anything to interest her.

It showed the entry for Laurence Harvey Tweddle, born 29th September 1954 to Florence Ada Tweddle at an address in Dover. The father's name was also given as Laurence Harvey. The father's occupation was shown as 'own means', otherwise there was nothing remarkable about it at all. The name Tweddle was not one Lydia had previously come across and for a son to have a father's full name as his given names might be a little out of the ordinary, otherwise it was of no special interest. Neither was his mother's joke apparent, unless it was the complete absence of the name Durham from the document.

Lydia looked up at the bursar whose face held no expression. 'Tweddle? Harvey?' she said.

'Tweddle,' he said flatly.. 'Tweddle, or Harvey.'

'May I see?' Stephen frowned at the two of them and took the paper as Lydia passed it to him.

'My mother changed her name to Durham and changed mine along with hers. I don't know when, I've never been anything but Durham.'

Lydia said distractedly, 'I've not seen the name Tweddle before.' Her gaze shifted from Laurence to the square of lawn visible through the Armoury's medieval window. Stephen recognised her interest immediately. She was already hunting for Tweddles, sifting the Florences from the Floras, listing the Harveys and Harvies, seeing where the pairings might fit.

'When did you find out you weren't Durham?' Stephen asked, partly to fill the gap she'd left.

Laurence stared for a moment as if waking from a dream, almost surprised to find Stephen sitting beside him. 'Some time in my twenties, when I needed a passport,' he said, recovering his composure. 'I stayed Durham because it was easier, everything I had was Durham, school, college, everything.'

'Laurence,' Lydia said with something like urgency, 'you said something about having too much information, having different stories from your mother. Is there anything of substance in them, names of people or places, dates perhaps? And memories, I would need to know anything you can recall from childhood, places you've lived, holiday places, photographs, anything.'

Laurence smiled ruefully. 'I've listed them for you, but it's a short list. A few children's books, Peter Rabbit and so on, an *I-Spy In The Street*, a train-spotters book of engine numbers from 1962, an old autograph book that I think was my grandmother's, I've no idea how they escaped the purge. I have a box of oddments, like old conkers and an Eagle badge. And I have my stamp album,' he said. 'Oh and a couple of pictures of my mother and me and my grandmother and me. There may be others but my mother doesn't hoard such things. She burns them. She burns today's post if she thinks anyone may see it.'

Stephen said, 'You have memories, though.'

'Yes, some. But what do we remember from our childhood? Scenes, that's all. We know we did certain things because we have evidence or we're told we did things and we imagine we remember them. But we don't. We don't know the names of the people our mothers talked to, wrote to or entertained after we'd been packed off to bed. At least, I don't.'

'Those scenes, those fragments might be important, Laurence.'

'Yes, they probably all are, but they are still only fragments. Here's one that sticks with me. Once, perhaps more often, I'm not sure, my mother and I went to an office of some kind. I remember the shiny blue lino and pale wooden desks with drawers down one side. Looking back now I think they were what they called 'austerity furniture' from the war, but that may be wrong. Before we went my mother coached me on speaking properly. I remember I had to practice saying "Thank you, father", but funnily enough I can't remember actually saying it on the day.' The slight tremble returned to Laurence's lips and he clenched his jaw to control it.

'That's so sad, so, I don't know, so bleak,' Lydia managed, blinking back a hint of tears in her own eye. 'Your stamp album, did you mention it for a particular reason?'

'Yes, it's a link to something, it may be nothing but I've always had the idea it was important in some way. I've always believed that my father gave it to me. And it may contain some connection, I'm not sure. I may be wrong but I think it's the one place that my mother has never bothered about. I don't think she's ever looked in it. When I was a child, if I had a secret to keep that's where I'd keep it.'

Having come so far, having given Laurence the opportunity to share his innermost pain, an opportunity he had grasped with both hands, Lydia saw no reason to hold back. She could see the precious volume, crammed with coloured squares from every corner of the Empire, even before she asked, 'What secrets were they? What kind of things went into your stamp album?'

'Sometimes I would get cards on my birthday or Christmas, from people I didn't know or with no name on them. Mother would collect them all up after a day or so and burn them. Sometimes I would hide one in my stamp album. Once, I took an envelope from the ashes of a bonfire in the garden because I wanted the stamp.' He hung his head, still ashamed of having deceived his mother more than fifty years previously. 'Then I asked her for some of the other envelopes of the letters she burned, and she'd laugh when she gave me one, saying "here, take a letter, Laurence" in a gruff voice. Once, by mistake I think, she gave me an envelope with a letter still in it. It was so secret I dared not look at it for years. I thought it might be from my father, and if I didn't look then I could always think that it was.'

Lydia hardly dared ask how this tragic detail of his young life had concluded. Her own childhood had been a sunny haven of joy compared to the cruelty Laurence was hinting at. Briefly she wondered if it was all in his mind, exaggerated by a child's-eye view of the world, distorted by repressed emotions. His mother, far from being as irrational as he painted her, might be entirely reasonable, motivated purely by protecting her only son. From what? From himself? He appeared quite genuine, quite rational, had the full range of social capacities, yet who knew what disturbances he'd shown as a child, what medications he might still be using.

Stephen couldn't resist the simple question. 'When you looked, what was it, what did you find?'

'Nothing really. A letter to my mother from, um, Broadstairs, I think. It was signed Paul and asked if Harry had recovered from some illness. I have no idea who Paul or Harry might be.'

'Do you still have it?' Lydia asked.

'Oh yes. And copied. In the last few years I've taken a copy of everything I had and everything I get.'

'Do you have a safety deposit box or somewhere like that?'

'No, that would mean a letter from the bank, and that would mean questions needing answers. It's easier to avoid questions, the lies get found out. Long ago I grew weary of trying to remember the lies. No, I have a copy of all my papers here in the safe in my office.' Eyebrows raised, he dipped his head at Stephen as if seeking approval for his actions.

'Yes, good idea, I'm sure,' he said, although he was far from sure about anything.

'Where did you grow up? Here in Cambridge?'

'We came to Cambridge when I was about twelve or thirteen. We were in the city at first. Before that there were many places. I would do a term at one school then a term at another, sometimes I went back to the same school again, sometimes to the same house. Places in Kent and Essex mainly. Norfolk for a year I think, maybe longer.'

'Do you know why you kept moving?' Stephen asked, fascinated by the contrast between this and his own stable childhood.

'No, it seemed quite normal. Only looking back does it seem strange.' Laurence saw the next question before Lydia could ask it. 'Yes, I did ask her once.'

∞

They took the bus back to the car park, looking out at the greenery of Cambridge from the top deck. They said little beyond noting the houses along the Trumpington Road. From their vantage point they could see above some of the high fences to the private villas beyond. In one of them, Florence Durham prepared for her son's return at the end of his day's work. Tonight, she would have his tea ready for six-thirty. If by chance he should not be at the table by six-thirty-one she would sweep the food straight

34

from the plate into the compost bin. He'd given Lydia and Stephen this insight to his domestic life quite casually in speaking about the excellence of the lunch they shared.

In his office Lydia had accepted from him the envelope of papers, almost reverentially as if it were a sacred object. In its way it was just that, the visible traces of Laurence's sixty years. She'd said yes, she would see what she could find, see what a quick run through the records might throw up, but she'd also been at pains to say that on the face of it there would be little she could do. His mother, and only his mother, held the certain knowledge of his parentage. From what he'd said, that certainty might remain denied to him, regardless of what Lydia might find.

In the late afternoon, as the clouds were blown away, Grantchester and all the land around it was bathed in that special light reserved for an English summer when recent rain has made glistening jewels on every blade of greenery. With the conservatory doors thrown open, she and Stephen shared a pot of tea while considering the day.

'So, two projects. I expect you'll still see Freddie on the way back to Oxford.'

'Yes, but how could I say no to Laurence?' Lydia pleaded.

'It was difficult, I know.'

'That poor man, I was nearly in tears when he said about his birthday cards being burned on a bonfire.'

'I thought he would break down at one point. I don't think I'll ever look at him the same way again.'

'How often have I told myself never to go by appearances, never judge anyone by appearances, yet I still do it. We can never even guess what goes on behind closed doors, we have no idea how other people really live.'

'True,' he said, 'we never know.'

He spoke in the abstract, but his thoughts quickly turned to his own closed doors and what happened behind them, which was probably not as other people imagined. It troubled him from time to time, and tonight might be one of those times. Their friendship grew richer with each visit Lydia made to Cambridge, yet with no sign that she wished for more. On the contrary it seemed to

Stephen that she wished for nothing beyond conversation, good food and white wine. And her laptop. If he was honest with himself it was a very comfortable arrangement for him too, but there was a subtle pressure for definition if not progress in such relationships, not least from his daughter Jacqueline. She had more than once enquired if Lydia was 'here for the long term'.

'Would you think of coming back tomorrow night?' he asked suddenly, before he had time to reconsider.

3

Smiley-face was distinctly less smiley than when Lydia had previously encountered her. She avoided eye contact and looked enquiringly at Lydia's signature when she registered at Willoughby House.

'Are you, um…?' she began.

Lydia guessed there had been some conversation about her, some discussion with Freddie about his new visitor, his daughter or so he'd claimed. Lydia was not inclined to help the enquiry, after all, she had been complicit in his little lie.

'It's Silverstream,' she said, 'my writing doesn't get any better.'

'Hmm, oh yes,' said smiley-face.

They walked in silence to Freddie's room. At the doorway the carer said, 'He's a bit brighter today,' and showed her in. 'Here you are Freddie, your daughter's here to see you,' she said mischievously, almost taunting him with his own lie.

'Lovely,' he replied from his chair by the window. 'Now piss off.'

Unsmiley-face scowled and closed the door behind her.

'Freddie, I'm so glad you're feeling better.' Lydia crossed the room to sit close to him as she had done so unwillingly on her first visit.

'What d'yer want now, then?'

Lydia's heart sank. One more try, just one, she promised herself.

'My name's Lydia, I brought you some medals, your…' she hesitated, his word still unsettled her, 'your grampy's medals. I found you by tracing your mother and your birth and then a neighbour of yours, Monica Sanders put me in touch with you.'

'Nosy cow, she is. Medals, yeah, yer said, is that it, is that all?'

'No, you told me some stories, about bombs and a girl on a beach. And you asked me to find someone called Linda.' She struggled to keep a condescending tone from her voice.

'Linda, eh? Did yer find 'er?'

37

'No, Freddie. I can't find her without more details.' Before he could answer she quickly added, 'Even then there's no guarantee. All I'm saying is I'll try, if you still want me to.'

'Yeah.' He seemed to consider this idea, closing his eyes and turning his face to the window.

After a minute or two, with Freddie still lost in thought or sleep, Lydia fidgeted in her chair, uncertain whether to interrupt him. At length she said softly, 'If you like, Freddie, we could talk about something else, your adventures in Australia, anything you like.'

He turned to her and said, 'Wanna go out? Wanna go for a walk?'

'Can we? I mean, can you? I'm not sure.'

'Walk, and push, you'll 'ave to bleedin' push, won't yer? I'll ride.' His laugh may have been cracked and broken but the humour which drove it remained.

'Oh, yes, if you like.'

After a few raised eyebrows a wheelchair was provided, along with some warm blankets. Once again Lydia was reminded of her grandmother's last few weeks, how she'd hung on to life regardless of the ever-nearer ending. How light she'd been to push around those leafy avenues, talking of everything and nothing, until the leaves began to turn and the conversation faltered to its final close. Freddie weighed nothing at all, she could easily push him with one hand. After a short distance they turned into Shaftsbury Avenue and from there into a little park where they were tempted to stop, but a glimpse of the river lured them to its banks.

Oxford and her beloved Thames it was not, but it suited their purpose well. A few visitors strolled, but for the most part it was a quiet place, and they found a seat by the Butterfly Bridge to sit and enjoy the sun. Could she make sure he was back in an hour, they'd said, but that would hardly have given them time to turn round before heading back. He was so improved she could scarcely believe she'd feared his death was imminent. Sunshine and laughter are still such natural tonics at any stage of life, thought Lydia. Freddie listened while she spoke of her parents, of childhood and her brother, of her hobby and the places it took her. Freddie prompted her for a little detail here, a date there. Each time she tried to bring the conversation round to his life he turned it back or fell silent with closed eyes.

After a few minutes, she realised he was checking on her, seeing if she was who she said she was, listening for the truth, alert for a lie. It was her second interview in two days and she told him so.

'Well, do I get the job or not? Will you tell me about Linda?'

'Yeah, it don't matter much now.' He lowered his voice almost to a whisper. 'See what yer got on Linda Meadows, or maybe Bright. Her mum was Sylvie Bright. Bright as a button, that's what we said, and she was too. See what yer got on 'em. Fifties it was.' He paused, staring out across the sluggish green river, debating another question with himself. 'Yeah, mid-fifties. Meadows or Bright, yeah, maybe somethin' else. Shouldn't be, but who knows. Now get me back, I got somethin' for yer. In me case. Before I change me mind.'

'Where was she born, here in England, Australia or somewhere else?'

'Australia?' He was indignant, how could she think such a thing? 'Here of course, not bleedin'…'

'All right then, it's a start. Anything else, or is that all I get?'

He grimaced and tightened his skeletal fingers on the blanket, holding it close to his chin while his mouth hung slack and open.

'Are you cold?' she asked, stupidly.

Freddie gave a low croaking moan.

'Oh God!' she cried, jumping up, 'Oh God no! Freddie, hold on Freddie, let me get you back.'

She could think of nothing but getting him to the comfort of his bed, the relief of morphine. Her assurance that she'd have him back within the hour rang hollow in her head. He made no sound other than a grating intake of breath. In seconds she was pushing him as fast as she dared along the river bank, almost running, avoiding the questioning looks of those she encountered. Every stone on the path, every crack in the concrete threatened to derail their progress. She dared not stop to comfort him or check his condition. They bumped over the little bridge by the boating lake and for a moment she lost her bearings. Crossing the river had been a mistake, returning on the opposite bank compounded the

39

error. She was hot, sticky, close to panic while her patient grew paler by the moment. At least he still breathed.

'Soon be there Freddie,' she gasped, 'soon be there,' as she crossed the road and turned into a half familiar avenue. She heard him groan again, saw the blanket fall from his grasp. Stopping, she dropped to one knee to see him better, tuck the blanket tighter round him.

From the depths of his chest came his disembodied voice, slow and deliberate, 'Easy girl, I ain't done yet.'

∞

She was turning off the Botley Road, across Town Bridge onto the island when she remembered Freddie had promised her something from his case. She'd been so anxious to see him safely back to Willoughby House, back in the care of professionals, even the less-than-smiley-face, she'd completely forgotten his offer. So had he. He'd been well enough to pretend he was better than he was, simply to protect Lydia from criticism, but she knew he'd suffered more than he should. Once back in his room, she'd wished him a hurried goodbye and fled to the car where she'd sat for five minutes recovering her breath and composure before heading for home. Recalling the forgotten item only made her regret the whole excursion again.

Not that she didn't have enough to be getting on with before her promised next visit on Thursday, en route once again to Grantchester. To start with there was his list of Lindas who had a Sylvie for a mother, they would take long enough. In addition she had photocopies of envelopes, pages from the old stamp album, and a handful of photos from Laurence. To do his sad quest any kind of justice she'd need to pore over the papers for many hours, absorbing any nuance of meaning they might contain. Busy she could certainly be, but the chances of any worthwhile results were slim. And none of it required her to be at home in Osney. Every search could have been made as effectively at The Old Rectory.

She'd almost accepted Stephen's invitation to stay the week, nothing would have been easier, but her reflex always tended to the negative, the positive required more consideration and he'd given her no warning. He'd been disappointed, more perhaps than she'd expected, with her response. She had nothing fixed, only ideas of things she might do, and yet she'd put up those ideas as commitments that required her presence at home in Oxford. Stephen hadn't pressed her, he would never do that, but there was a hint of coolness in their goodbye. Back on Thursday for a couple of days? Yes, of course she'd be welcome, it would be a chance to finally meet his daughter Jacqueline, lovely for them both. All the words were there, and all in the right places, but the enthusiasm was muted. His suggestion to stay longer had been so much more than that and she'd declined too quickly, made excuses when they weren't needed. No amount of backtracking could take back what had been said in haste.

She squeezed the car into a space a few yards from her house, then stood on the narrow footpath by her door fumbling for keys with her arms full of envelopes and bags. Once inside, the house pressed in on her. It always did after a stay in Grantchester and it became more noticeable with every visit. A year ago her home in West Street had been her favourite place, cosy in winter and ideal for a single woman. It was perfect for walking the paths and riverbanks of Oxford and a safe and solitary refuge when one was needed. But it had become less welcoming and more confined on every return from Stephen's spacious luxury. Much as she enjoyed every moment of her time at The Old Rectory, she had a nagging resentment that it had sewn the seeds of dissatisfaction with her own space.

The pleasure she found in his company also came at a higher price than once it had. For years she'd been more than happy on her own, unconcerned about how her solitary life appeared to others, although she knew well enough what they thought. In recent times she'd begun to see the weeks between her visits to Grantchester as interludes to be negotiated as quickly as possible instead of taking any pleasure in them. Once, she'd been delighted to leave the competition for men and sex and glamour to those who enjoyed the race, notably her work colleagues and in particular her friend Gloria. It had never occurred to Lydia that she might one day find shades of those desires rekindled in herself, yet it seemed that a slow fuse had been lit. This too was unsettling, this too left her slightly dissatisfied with the course of her life.

And then there was Jacqueline. In all the visits to Grantchester, Lydia had yet to meet her. They had come close, once by a matter of minutes, but their avoidance of each other was a carefully orchestrated arrangement between father and daughter. Her presence was permanent, her influence often apparent, but physically she was never there. Lydia had seen more of the housekeeper and gardener than she had of Jacqueline. This had seemed so considerate at first, that a loving and understanding daughter would avoid cramping her father's style. But as Lydia's visits to Grantchester had increased, this avoidance had begun to feel less benign, more disapproving. Now the weekend ahead might bring them together at the very moment that Stephen and Lydia might benefit most from a diplomatic absence.

In an hour or so, these cares and conflicts fell away and she eased back into her world. She threw open doors and windows and let the summer airs blow through. The house was a little damp at the best of times, sucking up moisture from the river whatever the season. The summer had been wetter than most and the Thames ran high. In a corner of her garden she found some sunshine through the leaves of the neighbouring trees and pulled a chair across to enjoy the afternoon. She opened a bottle of wine despite being sure it was too early in the day, and sat with Laurence's envelope of papers along with her own collection of post from the doormat. Even though she knew Freddie's puzzle was the more urgent of the two, she was in no mood to sit and trawl through births looking for Sylvie and her baby. It was an afternoon for sitting outside, for leafing through Laurence's memorabilia and catching up with her mail.

Sifting through the letters, mainly a mixture of junk and the predictable, one white envelope caught her attention. She recognised the name of the firm of solicitors from a few months previously. They'd written to her when her former mother-in-law, Cicely Fordham, had died and left her some jewellery along with some money, although the amount had not been specified at the time. Lydia expected this letter would be reporting progress in settling the old lady's estate. They hadn't been particularly close while she'd been married to Cicely's son Michael and the jewellery had been a surprise, the more so since Michael had a much newer wife who might have received it. She slit open the envelope carefully and was pleased to see a cheque stapled to the letter. She was even more pleased when she saw it was for £2,517. Hardly a fortune, but more than enough to pay a few bills and treat herself to a luxury or two. Thank you ex-mother-in-law Cicely, she thought as she raised her glass.

The accompanying letter brought more good news, although less specific. It seemed that the bulk of the estate was in property and investments which had been her ex-father-in-law's when he'd died a few year's previously. Now, with the death of Cicely, under the terms of his will some portion of that would also pass to Lydia. Where relations with Michael's mother had been little more than friendly, his father, John, had always been more effusive and had often spoken of her as the daughter he'd never had. When he'd passed away there'd been no mention of Lydia being an ultimate beneficiary. Perhaps it had slipped Michael's mind. Lydia raised her glass again, this time speaking aloud as she thanked both of her ex-husband's parents.

The biggest envelope was Laurence's, but the day slipped on and it remained unopened. Afternoon drinking was another habit she'd begun to acquire from her visits to Stephen, and another that she was not pleased with. It was always so easy to sit in comfort with him, inside or out, and enjoy whatever he'd chosen for that day. Now, here in West Street she'd started to drink the same wines, albeit in less comfort and from cheaper sources. A bottle a week had become two and then three quite easily. Her clothes had noticed the change too, as a little less of her fitted comfortably into them. Laurence and his missing father would have to wait for another day.

∞

Pleasure, anticipation and regret are an odd mixture of emotions, but all three vied for Lydia's attention when she woke. The regret was not limited to her headache, nor the amount of alcohol she

43

had consumed the previous day. She regretted lazing away an afternoon, regretted the foolishness of leaving Grantchester, regretted Laurence's envelope remaining untouched. Most of all she regretted losing a day of research for Freddie's Linda, a day she might easily make up, but a day Freddie could probably ill-afford.

Pleasure had a smaller part to play and was confined to what she might do with £2,517 and the possibility of a second, similar windfall. For once, she managed to repress her natural instinct of unworthiness, that Michael's parents had been wrong to remember her. She accepted it with a good grace, comforted by the thought that if she didn't receive the legacy then it would go to someone even less deserving.

Almost to her surprise she was looking forward to every aspect of the last few days of holiday: research for Freddie, seeing him again, returning to Stephen's house, even meeting Jacqueline. It was time to meet her, of that she was suddenly convinced. And she'd find a way to set the record straight about running for home instead of staying with him the whole week. Where all this new-found confidence had come from she had no idea, but it invigorated her, gave her the energy she needed for new discoveries.

The first run through the birth index did not offer much encouragement. There were plenty of Linda Brights and Meadows along with all their predictable variations. Adding in Bellingers and Bells, just in case, turned the plenty into more than a thousand for the 1950s. Linda was a popular name with all those post-war families, along with Lynda and, surely mistakenly she thought, a single Linder. Narrowing the search to the middle of the decade still produced hundreds registered all over the country. As far as the record was concerned, there wasn't a single Bright who'd born a Linda and registered the child with any of the four surnames. Unless it was a second name, in which case there were hundreds more possibilities, all represented by the initial L.

If not Linda, then why not Lydia, hadn't people confused the two all through her own life? Weren't Freddie and the staff at Willoughby House still doing so? It took only a few more minutes to recast the searches and come up with nothing more tangible. Freddie's Linda might well be among the lists in front of her, but without a way of narrowing the field she would remain one of the hundreds. There were simply too many to think of investigating them all.

Remembering what Freddie had told her, there hadn't been any doubt when he'd spoken of Sylvie being 'as bright as a button', something he recalled quite clearly and with little scope for error. Even though it had been overshadowed by his sudden attack there was no mistaking the name Bright, whereas Linda's surname was far less certain than her mother's. Neither was the name Linda certain either, hadn't he said something about being told it was Linda? She hadn't paid much attention, the medals had been all that mattered. She'd taken the treasures to him and to her shame was listening for gratitude and wonder, little else. The more she thought about that first day with Freddie, the more some other aspect of it picked at a corner of her mind, like a piece of a jig-saw that seems to fit until a few more pieces are put in place when it stands out like a sore thumb.

So if Sylvie Bright was a lot more solid than her child, a few searches for her as a mother might prove more useful. Whether they were right or wrong, the results were certainly more manageable. In the mid-fifties the record showed only eighteen Lindas born to a mother named Bright. From Linda Carruthers to Lynda Wyman they were spread from Aberdeen to Devonport. It was hardly a conclusive result, many people chose to lie to the authorities when reporting life's events, and over time many of those lies became accepted as truths. But eighteen entries was a good result. Even including those with an initial L only increased the count to thirty-four, still manageable.

By the time lunch was calling, Lydia had tabulated all the information from the records she'd found. It was her way to note every detail available, whether it was from a straightforward index or the complexities of an old photograph. After a snatched sandwich and successfully resisting the idea of a glass of *pinot*, she added information about all the births of Sylvia Brights between 1925 and 1939. She chose these dates as being most likely for a Sylvia who grew up to have a baby called Linda in the fifties. To fill out the picture she tentatively identified those who had married and linked those marriages to her original list of Lindas. Almost as an afterthought she added a few deaths to her spreadsheet, and noted possible links to births.

At five the call of the grape became irresistible, justified completely by her satisfaction with the day's work. She had enough information to present Freddie with a list of Lindas, eight of whom Lydia thought might have real possibilities. Showing him what she had might also jog his memory enough to reveal some critical detail. And if none of it fitted, none of it came to anything, she consoled herself that she'd now kept her promise. Taking her glass to the garden chair she found the post from yesterday, exactly where she'd left it, half of it unopened and her inheritance flapping in the breeze, unpaid into her account. At some point she'd planned to go to the bank. At some point soon afterwards she'd completely forgotten the plan.

A vision of her shortcomings, real and invented, rose up in a black tidal wave of depression ready to break over her. Never was anyone so full of good intentions and so feeble at fulfilling them. Never was anyone so adept at failing to grasp opportunity when it presented itself. Nobody was less deserving of good fortune than Lydia, whether it be the presence of Stephen in her life or the kindness of former in-laws. How self-important she was with her bountiful quests to find a worthy home for a hero's medals or the fanciful notion she could find a wretched man's father. How people must roll their eyes and snigger behind her back. Hadn't Michael told her all those years ago how boring she was, how he was being bored to death by her emptiness. What possible future could Stephen imagine with her of all people? She, whose prized possession was a cramped little cottage with walls so thin you could hear the neighbour's kettle boil.

Paralysed by the suddenness of the attack, the crippling descent from high spirits, Lydia fell back in the chair as if punched, spilling her drink as she did so. She watched uselessly as the wet patch spread in a darkening circle across the knee of her jeans. Her hand trembled and the vibration sent bouncing ripples across the surface of her wine, catching the light as they did so. For a moment she focused on the ripples, unable to control the tremor, unsure as to

46

whose hand held the glass. She hung on the pattern, the way the light fluttered across her fingers until the all-consuming blackness retreated a little as the panic began to subside.

There was nothing new in her feelings, but their intensity and abruptness were alarming. A lack of confidence had blighted life from her first school report to the prospect of any significant advancement in work. She'd never had a single girlfriend who wasn't slimmer and more beautiful, whose smile wasn't wider and whiter, whose voice wasn't more melodic than hers. She'd never had a man who hadn't dumped her, sooner more often than later. Michael was almost the exception but, as she'd told herself and others had agreed, he was hardly a great catch in the first place.

As the black tide slowly ebbed away it left Lydia exhausted, utterly depleted. The fear and the blackness had passed, but nothing of her former humour remained. The image of a naked woman, laid bleached and lifeless upon a black shoreline entered her head. A smooth white and blue shape, the last forgotten snowdrift of spring, with gritty black sand congealed in her nose. For confusing seconds, perhaps minutes, she wondered if this other Lydia was her own death. Later she would remember how casual this question seemed, a quite matter-of-fact enquiry with no personal implications.

The rest of the day passed in mindless attention to the details of domesticity. By nine she had emptied the bottle without enjoying anything beyond the first mouthful and took herself to bed, pushing down the persistent nag that she should postpone her trip back to Cambridge. Fitful sleep followed until the first strands of light showed in the summer sky, when she woke with a single thought: Belinda, what about Belinda? Freddie's girl might have been named Belinda.

∞

'He was asleep. They said he'd had a bad night. He'd needed extra pain relief. I sat for half-an-hour but he didn't wake. He stirred a couple of times, might even have opened his eyes I think, but that was all. They said he was all right, you know, as all right as he can be.'

47

'You'll try again tomorrow.'

'Yes, I think I owe him that.'

Stephen continued with the coffee making, then, after a sideways glance, said, 'Did you look in his briefcase, see what it was he was going to give you?'

'No! Certainly not. How could you think such a thing?' Lydia was truly shocked at the suggestion, how could Stephen have thought it, even if the idea had crossed her own mind as she'd sat by the sleeping Freddie.

'Oh, I didn't think such a thing,' he said, keeping his deadpan face, 'I was teasing you.'

'Ah,' she smiled with cast-down eyes. 'Am I forgiven?'

'For what? For taking a break and going home?'

'No, for the way I did it.'

'It was nothing. I was a bit sniffy too, quite put out to be turned down, I suppose.'

'You were right to be.'

Here was another moment when a conversation might lead somewhere or nowhere. Another opportunity to speak of their friendship and how it might become more, or to say nothing and accept it for what it was and might always be.

'The thing is…' she began with no idea of how she would continue.

'Yes?' he said, expectantly.

'The thing is, I'm pretty confused at the moment, about everything. I'm not at all sure what I want. I don't mean just about us.'

There, she'd said it, in just two words, *about us*. From *you and I* they had become *us*. Before long they could be *we* and *we* could do things. Stephen nodded his understanding, his sharing of confusion, albeit not quite so all-embracing.

'It's lovely here, everything is lovely but,' she hesitated again, already on a track that she'd given no thought to taking. Stephen offered her no help beyond his undivided attention. 'But it's always here, always your house, always Grantchester or Cambridge. Always your home ground.' No sooner had she spoken than one simple answer occurred to her, namely that she had never asked him to Osney, never felt able to offer him a night, certainly not a long weekend, crammed into her damp little box. What would they do in West Street that didn't involve bumping into each other at every turn? The same answer also occurred to Stephen, but it didn't need to be said, this wasn't point and counter-point, this might be far more important.

'Yes, I've thought about that too,' he said. 'I wondered about getting away.'

'Do you mean The Lakes? Are you going this year?'

He smiled at the memory of their first meeting, how her enthusiasm had so attracted him despite her diffidence. 'Well, no. I was thinking of going abroad, guaranteed sun plus some point of interest other than food and drink.' He paused to see if this met with approval but she said nothing. 'I was thinking we might go together. It would be somewhere we could plan together. Neutral ground, you might say.'

'Oh.' The suggestion had been signalled clearly enough, but still it caught her unprepared. *We* had started doing things already. The reflex refusal formed in her throat. 'No, I...' but at the critical moment words failed her.

He held up a hand to stop her, 'And I know you always like to pay your way, and it might be more expensive than...'

'No, it's not that,' she interrupted him. 'Anyway, I had some luck with a little inheritance, so no, it's not that.'

'I see,' he said, although he didn't.

She pushed away the dreadful cliché of it being about her, not about him, and yet it stuck with her, it really was about her and not about him. He was completely relaxed, at ease with every aspect of his life, if appearances could be relied on. But wasn't it only a few days ago, listening to Laurence Durham's remarkable story, she'd reminded herself how deceptive appearances could be? Under that relaxed easy manner what did Stephen want? Lydia had little idea of what she was trying to say, beyond a vague dissatisfaction with the state of their friendship and the comfort of staying at The Old Rectory. Now he'd confused her further by talking of a holiday together. She could think of no words.

'Lydia, maybe I've taken too much for granted, you must tell me if I have. We seem to get along very well, I certainly enjoy your company, enjoy having you here. I enjoy being with you. I thought you enjoyed those things too. I love your projects, they fascinate me, I love what you bring to them.'

As she looked and listened to this most agreeable of men, and realised how close they had become in so many ways, she marvelled at her good fortune and her own stupidity and indecision. If he were to hold her a little longer in a welcoming hug, linger a little more with a goodnight kiss, her uncertainty might so easily be dissolved. She felt her heart thumping and was sure he'd be able to hear it, see her chest beating out its rhythm. She smiled weakly, inviting him to continue.

'But perhaps we're slipping into a comfortable, convenient groove. And as much as I like it, perhaps we've simply seen too much of each other in the last few months.'

Seen too much of each other. Each word pricked her like a little dart. Her lips took on an awkward shape she could barely control. When she felt she could trust the muscles she said, 'I don't really know what all that means. I don't know what you want, maybe you only want that comfortable convenient groove,' but what she wanted to ask was whether this was how it was when he was married, whether he was back in the same effortless stride.

'Would you like more than this, more than the way we are together?'

'That's just it, I don't know what I want.' A moment previously she'd thought she did know, but with the little barbs of *seen too much of each other* still scratching her eyes, the simple answer escaped her. She could have stamped her foot in frustration with both Stephen and herself. 'But I might like to find out,' she said, a little louder than she'd meant.

Stephen answered carefully. 'And you'd be happy to risk what we have by finding out.'

'Would you?'

'I'm a little too old to be acting on instinct and hormones,' he said a little regretfully.

'I'm a little too old to be doing much else.'

He stepped to her, and stooping a little, bent to kiss her as she stretched up to meet him. They'd shared kisses many times before in the way that friends, close friends, do. But this was neither hello nor goodbye, good morning nor goodnight. It wasn't even Happy Birthday. Unfamiliar with this new territory, each mirrored the other in their tentative embrace and broke off awkwardly, unsure of what had changed. Their confusion remained, perhaps deepened by long-neglected desire resurfacing.

∞

Freddie Bell was a little stronger when Lydia saw him the next day. He was still in his bed, still attached to his drip, and a machine monitored his vital signs, but he was awake most of the time. When he drifted off, it was for minutes rather than hours and in the long pauses Lydia found the rhythmic pattern of his heartbeat mesmerising. She couldn't help but imagine the point at which the trace would cease its regular peaks and troughs. It might be any moment, the next peak or the next might be the last. She stared at the machine, waiting for the final blip, the infinite plateau.

'Am I still here?' Freddie startled her.

'Oh, yes, yes, still here. A way to go yet.'

'Third time unlucky I reckon.'

'Third time? You've had a…' Lydia hesitated, what should she call a previous brush with death when speaking to a dying man? 'You've had a close call before?'

Freddie coughed and produced a gurgling from deep in his chest. 'Close call? Funny girl eh? Yeah, had a few. Dead and buried twice.' The low growl of a laugh emerged again, his mouth stretched wide in a bloodless smile.

'How was that?'

'Never you mind, funny girl. Tell me about Linda, tell me what yer got.'

'Well, nothing definite, but I have a fairly short list of possibles. I found nothing at all for Linda Bright or Meadows, not for the fifties, not with a mother whose name was Sylvie Bright. Or anything Bright for that matter.'

He grunted his disapproval.

'And just so you know, I've looked for Linda Bell and Bellinger after you'd mentioned her the first time.'

'What yer got on this list then?'

'Well, there are a dozen to start with, the best guesses really. Oh and they include Belindas, what do you think about Belinda?'

'Dunno,' he said, but was clearly weighing the possibility. What process he used, what memories were relevant he didn't say, but at length he repeated his first thought. 'Dunno.'

'I'll go through each one, read out the names and dates and so on, anything else I've found, you tell me what you think. No hurry, how's that?'

He nodded and closed his eyes. It was impossible not to glance at the heart monitor, although it would hardly tell her if he were awake or asleep. One by one she read the details from her list, the name and recorded surname, the date and the registration district. For those entries with an additional note, she made reference to it without going into all the details. After half a dozen, he'd said nothing and she paused. Peak, trough, peak, trough. His heart still pumped.

'Freddie?'

'Yeah?' he said after a moment.

'Just wondered if you were awake. Anything interesting?'

'Nah. Don't mean nothin.'

She continued for three more then at Belinda Andrews, Freddie interrupted her.

'Say that again, Andrews was it?'

Lydia read it back to him, a girl registered in Stepney, London, in the last quarter of 1956, mother's maiden name Bright.

Freddie considered the facts while shaking his head slowly. 'Andrews. And her mother was a Bright, yer say. No name just Bright.'

'Yes, to find out the name I'd have to get a copy of the certificate. It can be done.'

'Don't make any sense, not Andrews.'

'Did you know an Andrews back then?'

'Yeah, you might say I did. Little Caesar, he was Andrews. I dunno, all a long time ago.'

'What do you think, could this be Linda?' She ached to ask him if the Linda they were looking for was his daughter.

'Nah. Bleedin' sick joke if it were.'

Lydia scribbled a note to herself before continuing with her recitation. The Lindas of Richardson and Rutter, Seaton and Steward followed in steady succession, none of which elicited any reaction from Freddie. At the sound of Linda Thompson's name, his eyes opened.

'Thompson?' he said, 'When?'

'She was registered between the end of September and the end of December 1956 in London. In Stepney, like Belinda Andrews.'

'And her mum was a Bright, eh?'

'Yes.'

He stared out the window, oblivious to her presence. She sat silent to let him relive the memories this Linda Thompson brought back. Beside him the peaks and troughs followed each other across the screen a little quicker and a warning light blinked yellow. He closed his eyes and his face relaxed, revealing a hint of once-youthful good looks. It was as if all the cares of a lifetime had fallen away. Seconds became a minute then more. The peaks and troughs resumed their former pace and the yellow tell-tale blinked off.

At length she thought to disturb him. Putting her hand on his, she said gently, 'Freddie, would you like to hear the other names, the other possibilities? Or is this the one, shall I stop here?' This time she couldn't resist the added question. 'Is this your Linda, is she your daughter?'

He turned his head to look her square on. 'Daughter? Yeah, maybe. There's some who'd like to know that, even now. How long do you reckon, to find her, eh?'

'I've got no idea. A week, a month, a year, maybe never.'

'Huh. A month, a year, how long d'yer think I got? Funny girl ain't yer?' His hand closed round her wrist, tighter than she would have thought he could manage. A hardness entered his eyes as he told her, 'See what yer get, just you and me. No talkin' to that other nosey cow, knows it all and knows nothin', she does.'

4

She was half way back to Grantchester, her mind busy with all that Freddie had said and all that he hadn't, before she remembered that today she would meet Jacqueline. The once-worrying prospect had been so long in coming it would be a relief to have it done with. Only a few days ago, meeting her brimmed full of significance, now it seemed almost peripheral to greater concerns. Seeing Freddie, seeing what mattered to a man who knew his time was almost done, put a clearer perspective on so many things. Having no children of her own didn't mean that Lydia was without insight to parental feelings. As she had once reminded her sister-in-law Joan, Lydia had parents herself, and many years ago she'd even been a child. But more than that she'd observed others and their relationships with a keen eye. Many parents imagine that the childless have no understanding of children, whereas the childless sometimes have clearer vision, unclouded by parental prejudice.

Stephen often spoke of his daughter, her visits to Grantchester, vaguely of her social life, a trip she might take, but said little of substance. He'd mentioned occasional university teaching but apart from that and her work in TV, Lydia's picture of Jacqueline was confined to childhood anecdotes and snaps of teenage awkwardness. The only portrait on display hung on the upstairs landing close to his bedroom. It was a beautifully executed painting of her, radiant in a blue ball-gown, golden hair cascading across her shoulders. From this and the pony club photos, Lydia had detected a likeness to her mother, whose image in a black and white studio portrait from forty years previously, sat on Stephen's desk. If the daughter's looks were her mother's, her willowy figure came from her father.

No sooner had Lydia returned to The Old Rectory and gone to her bedroom than she heard Jacqueline arrive. Thinking to give her and Stephen some privacy to say hello, she waited briefly before going down to the sitting room. They were still hugging each other affectionately, Jacqueline's blonde head buried in his neck. At the sound of her step, the daughter turned a fraction to look, and having seen, turned back into her father's neck. In the brief glimpse of fringe and eyes she saw a beautiful woman. Before they stepped apart Jacqueline kissed her father on his cheek, holding his face to her mouth a fraction longer than necessary. Seeing Lydia hesitating in the doorway they moved to stand side by side, he with an arm round his daughter's waist, she with two round her father. Stephen wore his usual smile, a little broader perhaps, his pleasure quite apparent. Jacqueline grinned, eyes wide. Lydia thought they looked a handsome couple, all the more so since Jacqueline wore exactly the same page-boy hairstyle, exactly the same make-up as her mother had done for the photograph on the desk. The wide-eyed grin seemed as much challenging as welcoming.

'Lydia, this is Jacqueline,' Stephen said, motioning her nearer.

Lydia smiled and held out a hand, which Jacqueline ignored. 'Hello Lydia,' she said, 'I suppose you know Daddy's told me all about you, how passionate you are,' she let the slightest pause creep into the sentence, 'about your investigations.'

She spoke with a honeyed sweetness that fell just short of condescension. To her father it was melodic and welcoming, to Lydia it spoke of shared confidences between father and daughter, an alliance from which she was excluded. What had Stephen ever shared with her about Jacqueline, beyond the trivial and everyday? What passions did his daughter have? Lydia had not been given such insights.

'Jacqueline, at last, how lovely to meet you,' she said, stepping forward with the idea of an embrace to soften the moment. Still the daughter made no move from her father's side, no hand was extended, no embrace was forthcoming.

Stephen appeared oblivious to the subtleties of the exchange and put an arm round Lydia's shoulder and offered her a peck on her cheek. 'So good to have you here this weekend,' he said to neither of them in particular. Lydia felt wooden and resistant in comparison to their previous night's kiss and cuddle, awkward as that had been. How long, she wondered, before Stephen would tell Jacqueline of their idea for a holiday together, of their tentative steps towards a deeper relationship.

For the rest of the afternoon, right through preparations for the evening meal, Jacqueline was the perfect daughter and the stand-in wife. She took charge in the kitchen, putting the housekeeper's suggestion to one side and starting a new meal from scratch while delegating a few of the menial chores to Lydia. Where previously Lydia had been given equal rights around the house, even though she did not exercise them, now she played second fiddle. She was included in everything but given the minor role: conversation, chopping vegetables, pouring a drink for Stephen, deciding where they might go on Saturday evening, Jacqueline made sure Lydia had no doubt whose home it was she stayed in. Nor who it was who had first call on Stephen's touch or kiss, be it received or given.

Lydia consoled herself by rationalising her discomfort. She was after all, an expert at finding the fault in herself rather than others. Jacqueline's assuredness was only to be expected. This was her home, had been her home for many years, she'd grown from child to woman at The Old Rectory, shared the laughs and loves and tragedies of family life here. Maybe over the years she'd accompanied Stephen to functions, standing in for her mother. A loving daughter familiar with the role was bound to have acquired the outlook to go with it. And yet it was a little more than that. Lydia's presence made no difference to her. The relief of finally meeting the golden child was washed away in a flood of uncertainty.

Sitting together as the evening drew on, the conversation was of Stephen and Jacqueline's worlds, of academia, of having met this chief executive or that bishop. They spoke with an ease and familiarity that would be the envy of many fathers and daughters, indeed, it would've been the envy of many husbands and wives. Nothing to exclude Lydia, and yet it seemed to her that nothing included her either. Where she and Stephen had sat in comfortable silence many times in the same room, each in a book or simply deep in thought, now it was filled with conversation. Stephen was engaged with everything she had to say, more alive than Lydia had ever seen him. It was a side to him that surprised her, she had never imagined him anything but quiet and self contained, not unlike herself. Perhaps he was both, perhaps he possessed that happy chameleon ability to adapt perfectly to his surroundings.

Sleep was long in coming to Lydia that night. She left father and daughter still in animated discussion at midnight, Stephan barely pausing to offer her the briefest of kisses to her cheek. Rarely had she felt more ill-at-ease than she did climbing into the bed, Jacqueline's bed, Lydia's normal and very comfortable bed when she stayed at The Old Rectory. Today its owner had graciously given it up. 'No, no, I'm more than happy for you to use it when you visit,' she'd said, adding, 'Best bed in the house, I wouldn't have you anywhere else.'

∞

On Saturday Lydia resisted the invitation to visit The Fitzwilliam. She would have gone happily enough had it been just she and Stephen, although it occurred to her that he'd never suggested such an outing. Jacqueline was keen to see *The Art of Love,* a new exhibition which included a piece by an artist she knew. It was not enough for her to go alone, she spoke for them both when she invited Lydia to join them and her father made no protest. Again the sense of role reversal hung in the air, Lydia, not Jacqueline would make the crowd when two would be company. Luckily, Lydia's excuse was ready-made and genuine. There was Freddie's Linda to find and Laurence's papers to sift through, more than enough to occupy her for the whole day.

When they'd left, arm in arm in their immaculate summer casuals, the house fell silent and Lydia wandered from room to room listening to the peace. Would it, could it, ever be more than a holiday home? If she and Stephen were to become closer it was a question she might need to consider, although that seemed a very long way off. The promise of something more, the notion of intimacy that a shared holiday suggests, all that was yesterday, apparently forgotten. Stephen was so taken up with his dazzling daughter he showed little more than mild affection for Lydia. As for the distant idea of being step-mother to Jacqueline, it was

57

almost laughable, so much so that it took her from her reverie and back to the practicalities of finding Linda.

The sketchy searches she'd made to provide Freddie's short list only took her so far. The chosen record had no extra notes attached to it. If this was the girl Freddie was seeking, then a birth certificate was essential, regardless of what else she might find. Having selected it and paid extra for express service, she added Belinda Andrews to the order, mindful of Freddie's reaction to the name. Next, she set about a methodical search for all things connected to Linda Thompson, born 1956, registered in Stepney.

What once might have taken months of research was at her fingertips in a matter of minutes. The all embracing powers of the search engine and the database gave her six life-events for Linda Thompsons born 1956: three marriages and three deaths, variously for assorted Lindas, Lyndas and Lynnes. The deaths would be individual, but the marriages could be for the same person, according to what name they felt like using for that particular wedding.

Beyond the shores of Britain more than thirty other lives were noted with nuptials and burials from Tasmania to Texas. In her own careful and precise way, Lydia began recording her researches with names, dates, events and connections, leaving space for a dozen more snippets in case they should be needed. Her spreadsheet tables with their ease of sorting and filtering were her favourite tool, one she'd adopted for years and one which had proved itself time and again. Long ago she had found virtue in letting probability be her guiding light. It never excluded the possible-but-unlikely, but it did help concentrate effort where it might find most reward.

In another hour Lydia had exhausted the searchable lines of strictly family history enquiry, carefully tabulating all the details thrown up by her researches. Taken over all, it did not amount to much and didn't hold any promise of special interest. Freddie's Linda might already be half-way to being found, happily married and leading an unexceptional life in the London suburbs. And if she was, what then? Nothing then, most likely. Freddie would be content with some discovery and when he was gone Lydia would be left with no use for that stub of knowledge. Apart from the medals! The thought suddenly recurred, finding a long-term home for the medals was the very reason she was doing this work at all. That, and a certain sympathy for Freddie, although it nagged at her that he might be undeserving of any.

It was unlikely to produce any results that Freddie would see, but she also posted a few messages on the 'looking-for' websites. She was not a great fan of these, but it was one such which had brought her to Freddie in the first place. The name was too common, too often subject to variation to think of searching the social networks, there would be a thousand Linda Thompsons posting their latest likes and dislikes. Until she had something more than a name to go on, tracing a living person would have to wait, but it didn't prevent a few general searches. Experience had shown time and again that unexpected opportunities for investigation could present themselves and lead along some fascinating byways and backwaters.

The name Linda Thompson gave a long list of results, many of them relating to a singer, a handful more to a minor actress. Both had interesting careers with the usual spice of showbiz thrown in, and neither were born with the names they worked under. Which set Lydia thinking about how, for the great majority of people, names are fixed at birth, sometimes again at marriage, but otherwise don't change much. For a small minority they are quite disposable, and a pen name or a screen name can easily become far more significant than birth names. She'd changed to Fordham at marriage, then slowly back to Silverstream over the years since divorce. Would she take another name if an unthinkable second marriage were to materialize? Kellaway, Mrs Kellaway? As soon as she thought it she remembered his knighthood and mentally corrected herself, Lady Kellaway, is that who she'd be? Oh how her colleagues in the office would laugh at that one. But the thread of name changes, or even name giving, was interesting.

Whoever Freddie's Linda Thompson might have been, she was important to him now and yet her name was far from certain. He'd never known for sure what she'd been registered as, and wouldn't have any idea of what she'd grown up as or taken on for herself in later life.

Predictably, Saturday evening meant eating out, and there'd be no skipping it this weekend. In Oxford Lydia hardly ever had occasion to dine out, and would never consider doing so on her own. With few friends and even fewer who would invite her to join them, opportunities were limited. When her trips to Grantchester had become more frequent she'd found it necessary to upgrade her wardrobe, but even those modest improvements left her feeling drab next to Jacqueline's elegant chic. Whether by upbringing, taste or instinct, she had a mastery of wearing clothes that Lydia could never hope to match.

As they entered the contented buzz of Le Chat Noir, new to Lydia but clearly not to Stephen or Jacqueline, many heads turned. Was it her imagination, or was there also a pause in conversations as men and women alike registered the younger woman's face and figure? She noticed too that both Stephen and Jacqueline nodded their hellos towards several groups as they were shown to their table. Along with two others, it was perched by open windows above the dawdling Cam, a step or two up from the main dining area. Across the river, private lawns, brushed gold by evening sunlight, stretched from college houses to the water's edge. Within the restaurant they were overlooked by no-one, yet could survey each table if they chose. It would surely have been the position of choice for any of the diners that evening, but it was reserved for their little party.

A year ago, even less, Lydia would have been daunted by the place. Hadn't she been in a blind panic about even meeting Stephen that night in Oxford, hadn't she tied herself in knots over his title, his distinction, his rarefied life of science and university professorship? The fear and self-doubt had lessened, but she was still anything but comfortable in his world. Mute acceptance best described the way she dealt with her insecurities. Jacqueline, in her understated finery, was a different test, not least because she behaved with such assurance, behaved with all the comfort and ease that Lydia could only aspire to. Little wonder she was the apple of her father's eye.

Across the Cam on the golden lawn a young man stood smoking, uneasily shifting his weight from one foot to the other. After a moment or two, a young woman hesitantly stepped out from around the house, then seeing the man, stepped further and lit a cigarette of her own. Even at a distance it was clear they didn't know each other, all they shared was the lawn and the craving. They stood awkwardly apart, each in their own refugee spaces. Lydia wondered how many lives had been changed by smokers being chased outside from their homes and offices to share draughty corners or corrugated shelters. Lives changed by losing the friendships of the canteen and the tea room, lives changed by the new camaraderie of the car park and the bike shed. Her friend Gloria had said as much, enough to make you stop she'd said, but she hadn't. The two young people on the lawn moved closer together. She could see they were exchanging small talk, puffing nervously at their smokes. It's the little things, Lydia thought, at least as much as the really big things, that change lives.

'Did you get anywhere with our bursar's problem?' Stephen was asking.

Her idle musings evaporated instantly, replaced by guilt and her cheeks burned. For a millisecond she considered lying, a vague untruth but still lying. She hadn't even opened the envelope.

'No, I didn't. Sorry, I will though, tomorrow, definitely,' she said apologetically.

'Freddie's still bugging you.'

Lydia nodded, regretfully. 'I was wrapped up in him, kept going over the same ground, kept thinking about the things he said, trying to see if there was some clue to what he's hiding. I ended up going in circles, literally.'

'Walking.'

Stephen was not a pacer. He would sit calmly at his desk, his references close at hand, and work through a puzzle until it was solved or until he accepted that he couldn't solve it. For him it was a process. Having applied the process, the answer would be apparent. Finding no answer was a result in itself. Lydia had her processes too, but at heart she was a worrier. She'd nag away at a problem, turning it over to look at it from all angles until a solution, or at least a possibility, presented itself. When the opportunity arose to accompany deep thought with a circular walk, she would take it. He'd seen her do so several times, and was fascinated by the intensity she brought to her craft.

'Yes, walking round the garden. You know how I am,' she added a little sheepishly.

'Bursar? Are you talking about the bursar at college, somebody Durham?' Jacqueline asked.

'Yes, I mentioned we'd seen him for lunch.'

'But you didn't say he had a problem, tell me more.' Jacqueline's eyes widened in anticipation.

'Ah, well, it's not that simple, darling,' Stephen said a little awkwardly.

'That's your hush-hush voice, Daddy. Is he a war criminal or something?'

'No, no, nothing like that, it's…' he hesitated, caught between a promise to Laurence and trust in his daughter.

'His problem is a brick wall,' Lydia intervened. 'There's a part of his family history he can't get past, so he wondered if I could help,' she said, as casually as she could, hoping to relieve Stephen of his little dilemma. For a brief moment she also relished their shared knowledge, however slight it might be.

'How far back?' Jacqueline snapped back. Her voice said one thing but her looks said another. Wide-eyes were gone as she fixed Lydia with a stare while the smile froze to her face.

The question was one Lydia had heard a thousand times, although usually in different circumstances. It was as if there were some status in having more generations identified than the next person. Identified or not, everybody's lineage goes back beyond counting and Lydia had never really understood the fascination.

'How far?' she said, keeping the casual note, 'I don't know. I should know, but I haven't looked at his papers yet. His problem might be simple or beyond my help. I'll look tomorrow.' Turning to Stephen she added, 'I promise.'

Stephen beamed, oblivious to the undercurrents of competition between the two women. To him they seemed to be getting along well together. He'd never doubted they would, but he was still pleased to see it. Grasping a hand of each of them on the white linen tablecloth he gave both a gentle squeeze, emphasising his delight at their company.

The meal meandered through the courses, and the conversation meandered with it. Little of substance, nothing of opinion or feeling. Whenever the talk drifted towards something Lydia might share, might have some experience to contribute, Jacqueline guided it back towards her own territory. When reference was made to the pleasures of Oxford and the Thames, Jacqueline brought it back to Cambridge, the Cam and Midsummer Common. When Lydia showed interest or knowledge, Jacqueline introduced a different slant, all the while seeming to be inclusive, asking if she had been to places, enjoyed sights, tasted exotic flavours when it was a safe bet she had not. Out of charity as much as an unwillingness to compete, Lydia chose to believe this was Jacqueline's natural behaviour, not something designed for her. For Stephen's benefit, she smiled and nodded or became thoughtful and serious according to the topic.

As they sipped the spicy richness of cognac, Lydia cast her eye once more round the restaurant. One or two tables had already emptied but for the most part diners lingered over the last of their meal or, as she did, over their end-of-evening drinks. At the furthest point from them a man with his back to her rose from his table to pull back the chair from the lady sitting opposite him. Even across the room, Lydia could see she was striking despite her advanced years. Long grey hair was pulled tight to her head, while jewels at her ears and throat flashed hidden subtleties of the light. Beneath a high forehead and fine nose, her mouth was a crimson slash, all the more severe for its brevity. Lydia felt sure that in younger days she would surely have been amongst the most beautiful of women.

With a start Lydia realised that the man now assisting the lady from the chair was staring at her, much as she was staring at his companion. Embarrassed, she looked away for a fraction of a second before recognition dawned. It was Laurence Durham. With her mouth half open in a distant hello she looked back. He was still looking at her, quite expressionless with no hint of recognition in his face or token gesture of friendship. The silent greeting died on her lips, her half-raised hand diverted to her cognac. She and Laurence Durham continued to hold each other's eyes. As he followed his companion towards the door, he kept his head turned to Lydia. She knew, exactly as Laurence intended she should, that the lady was his mother, she could be no one else.

'Are you all right?' Stephen asked. 'You look as if you've seen the proverbial ghost.' He turned, following her gaze across the room, but Florence Tweddle or Durham, or maybe even Harvey, and her son had left.

'I thought I saw Laurence Durham, but I must have been mistaken, I'm sure he'd have said hello.'

Lydia was certainly one person in Cambridge who Laurence would not acknowledge while in the company of his mother. She wondered if there might be others.

∞

Lydia's night passed miserably in a fitful mix of lucid dreams of Laurence in drag and waking worries of Freddie and his Linda. The Old Rectory, usually so silent and still, seemed full of unfamiliar noises as the wind rose steadily. At six the threatening storm broke in a torrential downpour, hammering on every surface, bending every branch and flattening the summer flowers. Bleary-eyed and yawning, she sat in bed watching and listening as the weather raged around the house. Most likely it would pass soon enough despite the crashing and banging of the moment. She'd always found pleasure in watching the rain from the security of her bed, now the luxury of the bed and the drama of the thunderstorm heightened the enjoyment.

Across the room, on the writing desk by the window, Laurence's envelope lay untouched. A nightcap, and then another had put paid to any thoughts she'd had of opening it last night before bed. Now it lay mutely demanding her attention. Stupidly overconfident that she needn't take any notes of their private lunch, the detail of what he'd said and how he'd said it had already become hazy. Sitting alone with the thunder rolling round the skies, she struggled to recreate their conversation, to recall the expressions, the nuances of his story. All she found were the bare bones. Worse, Freddie Bell's face, Freddie Bell's hollow voice crept into the memory where they had no right to be.

As soon as she pulled out the papers Lydia realised they were not simply secret copies of Laurence's life fragments, they could've been prepared with Lydia in mind. The top sheet was both an index to the contents and a summary of his early life. A few dates were scattered down the list, starting a little sadly Lydia thought, with the entry *'1954 Sep 29: Born in Dover, Kent.'* For the most part the dates were approximate, guesses based on indistinct memories of childhood. Where they were specific it seemed they could only be known because of a document in the slim bundle. In 1967, aged 13, as his life stabilised around a permanent address and regular schooling, the penultimate entry showed his home and school in Cambridge. The final line, for 1976, recorded the move to the house in Trumpington Road, the house he still shared with his mother.

The time to make her own index, record her own notes and observations, would come later, sitting at her desk at home. For now she contented herself with leafing through the remains of Laurence's childhood. The copies were not quite the same as touching the real thing. A photocopy of the front of a football programme from 1964 meant little beyond the date, whereas to hold the original slightly dog-eared *Southend vs Colchester League Division 3 Nov 7 1964* could mean so much more. Was the match significant, was it a father and son excursion, did they know the teams or a player in them, who did they support? Then, in a flight of fancy, she thought how some trace of his father, his fingerprints or a smudge of DNA, might yet remain from that Saturday half a century ago. Such a thing would be beyond her reach, but just possibly not beyond Laurence's. He'd made no extra comment about the programme, it was there on his list as a date, nothing more.

A few pages of postcards caught her attention. They'd been carefully copied, front and back in colour on the same side of the paper. Two from his mother, who signed herself as that but without any hint of love or affection in the briefest of messages.

65

One postmark was blurred beyond recognition, the other was dated May, possibly 1962. Both had pictures of steam engines which to Lydia meant little beyond suggesting they could have been bought and sent from a railway station, at a break in a journey perhaps. The address for both was in Little Shelford near Cambridge.

Of four more postcard pages, two were signed 'love Grannie' and were equally brief; a third with a picture of an ocean liner was blank. Only one was addressed, suggesting that the other two might have been included with a letter, no doubt to his mother. The single address was in Margate, Kent and dated in April 1961. The fourth card was a little more interesting. A Canadian airmail stamp beneath a well preserved postmark declared it had been posted in Halifax, Nova Scotia in February 1963. The card bore a picture of a town by the sea with the wording *Dartmouth as seen from the Angus L. Macdonald Bridge*. The sender thought young Laurence would like to see 'another Dartmouth' and signed herself 'Auntie Em'. Laurence's address at the time was in Devon. Here at least was a suggestion of a relative, although Lydia knew well that an 'Auntie' might be nothing of the kind.

The photocopied images were too hard to sink into, to feel anything about them. She leafed through them with little enthusiasm: a few photos of Laurence with his mother or his grandmother; a school report for two terms when he was eight; a day excursion train ticket from Victoria to Brighton overprinted with 'child' in red; a little poster for Bertram Mill's circus at Olympia; a programme for the Royal Tournament at Earls Courts for July 1960. The pages went on with another dozen or so copies of memorabilia before Lydia found the envelopes Laurence had spoken of. Hadn't one been rescued secretly from a bonfire? On their own they amounted to very little, four envelopes addressed to Mrs F Durham at three different addresses and all postmarked in England at various dates between 1960 and 1964. The fourth, the Broadstairs envelope, was the only one not handwritten, and the only one followed by a copy of the letter it had contained. Reading it for the first time, Lydia remembered the bleakness of Laurence's story as he'd made his plea for her help, how he'd saved this letter, scared to open it, scared of discovery, only to eventually find these handwritten words:

> *Dear Florence*
> *As you'll see, the arrangements previously discussed are now confirmed. I hope they will work out as you wished. Things here remain much as always, there is little prospect of change in this sleepy corner, whatever else may be happening. Do let me know about Harry, I trust he has fully recovered by now.*
> *Sincerely*
> *Paul*

To Lydia, a handwritten letter in a typed envelope, plus the 'as you'll see', meant there was originally another, typed letter, the one detailing the arrangements, whatever they might have been. For Paul to have added his own more personal note suggested that he also wrote that other letter. It followed that Paul held some professional or semi-official role, but was acquainted with Laurence's mother on a more personal level, too. The envelope was dated November 1963.

She would, of course, do her best with the scant information available. At the very least she might be able to construct a few generations of a bare-bones family tree for Laurence, something which might give him avenues of his own to explore. But finding his father appeared to be quite beyond her resources without the active co-operation of his mother, which she supposed was highly unlikely. Lydia wondered what might motivate Florence to behave as she had done over so many years, surely the secret of Laurence's father was only part of the picture. The need to destroy letters and cards, to deny the past, to keep moving from town to town all spoke of many secrets of which the identity of Laurence's father might be only a small part. If Laurence was to be believed then it was all done with the knowledge and support of his grandmother too. The questions also arose of what the family had lived on, of how they'd been able to stop moving and buy the grand villa behind the high hedges of the Trumpington Road.

The torrent had slowed to a steady drizzle, the crash and wallop of earlier had given way to an even dullness laying like a grey blanket across the land. The pleasure of watching the rain hurl itself at the window while she was safe and snug behind it had gone with the thunderstorm. A general dissatisfaction had taken its place, part impotence to resolve any of her puzzles, part grey skies, and part the prospect of the journey back to Oxford, and work in the morning. She should really stop and see Freddie on her way too, although she had little to say to him. Even though she pushed the thoughts away, she wondered about Stephen, wondered where their friendship was taking them. She wondered if it had already arrived at its destination.

∞

'I've sent off for some certificates, birth, marriages, they'll take a few days.'

'Is that it? Is that all you done?'

'Friday, it was only Friday I was here, Freddie. Two days ago. I paid extra for express service too,' she said, sounding slightly more irritated than she really felt.

'Two days?' Freddie Bell looked beyond her, both in time and space. 'Two days?' he repeated, then with more regret than anger, 'You sound like that other cow, did yer know that?'

'Sorry, Freddie, I know two days is a long time, longer for you than me.'

'Yeah. Now you get it.'

She looked at him propped on his pillows, drip and monitor leads trailing off to the machines beside him, the red call button lying by his hand. He's been very low, they'd said at the desk, waiting for you, they said. Always picks up for you, you see the best of him, they said. She wished she'd told them they looked for the worst, that the best of him was there to be seen if only they'd look. But she hadn't, she hadn't said anything. She'd only thought of the reply when she'd sat with him while he woke, smiling when he saw her. She hadn't said anything at all at the desk, she wasn't his daughter and the less she said the less chance there was of that awkward conversation ever happening.

'Freddie, I might be able to find things and I might not, I don't know yet. But if you told me something about this Linda, something more to go on, I might get there faster. It would stay a secret between you and me, nobody else would know, I promise.' It might not be one hundred percent true, but it was true enough.

He studied her face, and for a moment she thought he would give her some insight, some fact that would help her in her search.

'Nah, you got enough. I'll wait, see what there is. If I ain't waitin' here, I'll wait in the next place, eh?'

'The next place? Where's that?' Lydia was thinking of hospitals, an intensive-care bed.

The gurgling that passed for a laugh deep in Freddie's tubes told her what he meant. She forced a feeble smile and nodded. 'Yes, waiting for me there.'

The prospect of death hung close about them, his before hers almost certainly, but he'd drawn her in to the process by suggesting he'd be waiting for her, however lightly he'd meant it. The lightness had fallen away, leaving only the sombre truth that it was waiting for them both one day.

'Since we're on the subject,' Lydia said gently, 'what should I do with your medals, your grampy's medals?'

His hand tightened on hers and he grimaced as another wave of pain swept across him. After a few moments his grip relaxed a little and he opened his eyes. 'Find someone who should have 'em. There'll be someone, somewhere, you'll see. When I'm gone, you'll see.'

Lydia nodded, hoping she understood his meaning, sure at least that she should keep them for now.

'Tell me about the old times, any times you like, any place you like. Tell me about the best of times,' she paused, 'or the other kind.'

'Plenty of the other kind, plenty of that stuff.'

'Like what?'

'Bad things, bad people. Not stuff you'd wanna know, all right?'

'I might.'

He held her hand tighter. 'No, funny girl, you wouldn't.'

She didn't press him, it had got her nowhere previously. He was protecting her from the knowledge, not protecting his own secrets. She'd come across it before, talking about families and their histories, the events that had shaped them, and finding great reluctance to share certain episodes. It was as much to shield the living as to keep the privacy of the dead. The half-formed idea that Florence Durham might be doing the same for her son briefly intruded. Might Laurence's father have done something terrible?

'What about when you were just a boy, what about school, the tricks and games you played, or was that all bad stuff too?'

'Nah, plenty of bad stuff but not the same. We was all right, even if we did spend half the time bunkin' off whenever we could.' The tension left his face, memories of adult evils chased away by the misdemeanours of childhood. 'That's all a long time ago now. Wouldn't know the place now, wouldn't know it was the same planet.'

'Has it all gone?'

'Bombed out, mostly. And what didn't get bombed got ripped down after.'

'And those friends you bunked off school with, were they all bombed out too?'

He looked away from her, searching for a distant memory that escaped him. 'Dunno,' he said absently. 'Some were, the Watsons, they were, caught a whole stick they did.' He paused again, back in 1940, hearing the sirens, tasting the dust, trembling as the walls shuddered around him. 'Yeah, the Watsons went and a good few others. You'd have thought there'd be more but next day we was all there, all there except Mickey Watson.' He spoke with a tenderness, a nostalgia for those far-away days, despite the death and destruction of the time.

'The school was all right, was it, that never got hit?'

'Nah, that was all right.'

'Do you remember where it was, what street it was in?'

'Down Cable Street it was,' the reply was instant, no fumbling for lost words.

'What did you do the day that Mickey Watson wasn't there any more, just carry on as usual?'

'Yeah, someone said they'd copped it and that was that, nothin' else said. Then it was just normal. One of the girls was cryin', who was she, eh? Janice something.' A moment later he had it, 'Janice Beckett,' he announced triumphantly. 'And her mate, little Betty Singer, always cryin' they was.'

The afternoon ticked on, but in Freddie Bell's room nobody noticed. Lydia had at last released memories from Freddie's childhood and was happy to hear them tumbling out. She made no notes, she was not going to spoil his pleasure or her own, but some names would stick. The school down Cable Street, that would probably be enough to find the town, and the Watsons' deaths would pinpoint the date. All that could come later, for now she listened as Freddie talked about his childhood, about playground games and collecting shrapnel, about nights in the shelters and hiding under the stairs, about his best friend Alfie Wilson.

With one hand tied behind her back she'd never find Freddie's Linda. If he thought she was conning him, he'd never forgive her but she felt no guilt on that account. She really did like listening, at least as much as he liked telling. After an hour or so he grew tired and began to doze off between stories. Gently she roused him once more to thank him and say goodbye, assuring him that as soon as she had news she would return.

'Clever girl, eh,' he smiled at her and nodded. He hadn't missed anything.

'See you soon.' She leant over, kissed his forehead and left him to his dreams.

Before setting off for home, she sat in her car and made a few notes, writing the names and events she remembered. When she'd written a dozen items she put a big ring around 'Sarah - sister'. So far as she knew, Freddie Bellinger, born 8 May 1930 in Hampshire had only one sister, Maud, who died in an air raid in Bristol in January 1941.

5

After a week's holiday, the process was depressingly familiar: a few steps in grey drizzle across the footbridge to the stop in Ferry Hinksey Road, a bus into the centre, another out past the mishmash of trades and cultures along the Cowley Road, off at the business park, scuttle through the rain to the side entrance by the smokers' hutch, a swipe of her ID then up the single flight of concrete steps to her own small part of Human Resources.

It was Lydia's habit to be early to work, even though there was no such thing as being late. Flexible hours were part of her contract, she could start when she liked so long as time was made up at the end of a day or a week or a month. But old habits are hard to break, and being first to her post had been her way for many years. None of her colleagues in the section shared her preference, they drifted in as the day and the fancy took them, but all expected to see Lydia behind her desk when they arrived.

Familiarity ended when she opened the door from the stairwell. Her office simply did not exist any more. Where once there'd been a glass partition wall with a door leading into her own space with its desk and computer and filing trays, now there was bare carpet. In place of her two chairs and steel drawers topped by the ever-struggling yucca was a chilled-water dispenser. In the numb moments of disbelief the irrelevant question of whether it was a cooler, in the American way, or the more English dispenser, floated through her mind. The office next to hers had gone too, along with her workmates' desks. In their places were chairs clustered round two hexagonal workstations, cramped little spaces with shelves over computer screens. From above each position a single flexible light protruded on a chrome stalk, reminding Lydia of a water bottle in a hamster's cage.

She turned, wondering if perhaps she had come into the wrong area, climbed two flights without realising. Yet no, when she opened the door and looked down the stairwell she could see the glass door to the car park, see the ID swipe that would open it to let her out again. Could she be in the wrong building? Even in her confused state it seemed unlikely. She turned back into the room, scanning for some familiar feature or object. On a windowsill she spotted the sad brown and green of her pot plant. A pink cardigan hung limply across the back of a chair at the workstation. Certainly Chloe's. For years it had hung either on her chair or round her shoulders when she went for a smoke.

Behind her the door opened and Gloria Fitzgerald, flushed and breathless, fell into the room, her face twisted in anxiety and wailing, 'Oh no, I so wanted to be here before you got in today, I really did.' She came to Lydia with her arms open in a huge embrace before Lydia had a chance to speak. 'I tried, I really tried,' she breathed in her friend's ear.

'Oooh, thanks, Gloria,' Lydia eased herself from the hug. 'What's going on? What's happened?'

'There was some mix-up, it was meant to happen in a month or two, they couldn't do the place they were supposed to, so they came here. There were only the two of us in so...I would have called, but I didn't want, you know, to spoil your...' the breathlessness subsided as her explanation trailed off.

Dimly, Lydia recalled a circular about a program of refurbishment. Dimly, she recalled words like improvement, convenience and consultation.

'So, where do I...?'

'We share. They call it hot desks,' she said glumly.

'Oh.'

Lydia was not strong on status or privilege and she had no real authority over the section. Her seniority was more by years of service and experience than management design. But she was strong on her privacy, and one bonus of those extra years had been her own space with a door which could be closed any time the cackle of gossip rose above a low murmur. And if a colleague, Gloria more often than not, wanted a private word, that closed door came in handy again. When others had tears over husbands or boyfriends, Lydia's little box was far more comfortable than the cold tiles of the ladies' toilets.

'I knew you'd hate it, just hate it, I'm so sorry,' Gloria implored, and her regrets were heart-felt. Her friendship with Lydia, an unlikely alliance, had grown in the last year or so. It was Gloria who'd encouraged Lydia to grab the opportunity of Stephen's interest and friendship, and it was Gloria who remained mystified at their failure to consummate. For her part, Lydia had discovered new insights and refreshing realism in Gloria's uncomplicated views on life.

'Thank you, I suppose we'll get used to it,' Lydia said with little conviction. Her mind was already wandering far from payroll analysis and hot desks.

'Yeah, at least it's not for long,' Gloria added a little gloomily.

'No, we'll see.'

Lydia was all too aware of her own shortcomings, both real and imagined. She could list them almost by rote: boring, staid, frumpy, humourless - the exact description varied as often as she repeated it, but the theme never changed. It had been reinforced at regular intervals since her teenage years by friends and boyfriends, by colleagues and by her husband. Sometimes openly, sometimes whispered, the common thread was a lack of desirable qualities: she lacked grace, lacked humour, lacked ambition, lacked adventure, lacked vision. But of all those missing virtues nobody had ever doubted she was conscientious. On occasions it had even been thrown up as a criticism. She'd been a conscientious daughter and granddaughter, a conscientious niece and sister; she'd been a conscientious girlfriend and wife. At work she'd been a conscientious employee since the day she delivered her first newspaper. She'd given her best, dutifully, to each and every employer, never cheated them of an hour or stolen a pencil, despite far greater provocation than a re-arranged office.

Now, caught unprepared after an unsettling week littered with more perceived failure, she saw all her loyalty, all her conscientious efforts, betrayed in a single trivial decision about the size and placement of her desk. Her instinct was to turn on her heel and leave, perhaps to call in later to claim one of her unused sick days. Instead, she wandered uncertainly round the new space, gave the workstation a cursory inspection and considered the future of the yucca. It did not like being over-watered, neither did it thrive on parched neglect. These, alternately, were the only attention it ever received. The plastic tag outlining the simple instructions for healthy survival lay face down in the desiccated clump of dirt in which the plant unhappily sat. Its last attempt to produce a side shoot of leaves had been broken off.

'It fell over when we moved it. Sorry.'

Gloria was at her elbow, apologising again. When Lydia didn't answer she tried a different tack, one which held far more interest for her. 'How was your week on the country estate? Any news I should be the first to know?'

Her idea of Stephen's house in Grantchester was a little grander than the reality, but not by much. She liked to tease Lydia about it, sometimes calling her the Lady of The Manor. More often she would remind Lydia of her chaste relationship with Stephen, and it would be Sister St. Lydia.

'No, nothing to report,' Lydia said distractedly, continuing to prod the grey dust around the yucca. Nothing to report at all, she thought. No progress anywhere, no achievement, no conclusions, a standstill week. Not even that, hadn't she gone backwards with Freddie? Maybe even backwards with Stephen too. Clouds gathered around her, but she couldn't summon the energy to care. Let it have her or leave her, let the black wave roll in, she wouldn't struggle.

'And how about the blessed Jacqueline, that's her name, yeah? Did you finally meet her, did she welcome her new mummy?'

'New mummy? Gloria, it's not...' she began to protest until Gloria's wide eyes told her she been teased again. 'OK, yes, new mummy, that's a good one. I did meet her. I don't think we'll ever be what you'd call close, even if...' She turned back to Gloria, frowning. 'What did you say?'

'About mummy?'

'No. Not for long, didn't you say not for long?'

'Did I?'

'About hot desks, you said it was not for long. What did you mean?'

75

'Well, we'll all be...' Gloria hesitated, trying to find some alternative to what she took to be obvious. 'You don't know, do you? Didn't you get a letter? With your payslip?'

The little pile of unopened post, unopened because Lydia thought she could tell the contents of each item without opening it. A gas bill, the credit-card statement, the once-in-a-lifetime insurance offer, her payslip in its usual brown envelope with her name and address not quite fitting properly in the little cellophane window. She hadn't given any of them a second thought. Once again solid ground was shifting beneath her feet, order and security replaced with confusion.

'I didn't see it, what did it say?'

'Christ, Lydia, wake up girl,' she said despairingly. 'We're out. Redeployed, re-organised, redundant, take your pick. I've been offered a shot at a job in Banbury, so's Chloe and Vics. Probably the same job. Bastards. I shouldn't be surprised if you have too, which'll leave us out. I don't know what I'm doing yet. But if you don't go for it you don't get the redundancy, do you? Anyway, I might look for something else, I don't fancy Banbury every day.'

Lydia reeled from the flood of information, trying to grasp some sense from it all. None of it seemed real, yet Gloria was not one to make up such an elaborate joke, nor act it out so well. Hadn't it only been a few weeks since the last reassurance that all jobs were safe, even in an age of austerity and shrinking budgets. And why all the new carpet and desks if they were closing it all down?

'Um, not long, you said not long, when is all this supposed to happen, I mean...I don't really know what I mean, it's all a bit sudden.'

'A couple of months they say, but it might be sooner someone said, who knows. The letter didn't say much, most of it's on internal mail. The usual crap but it's just sugar on the shit.'

Lydia looked about her at the once-familiar office, at the space where her desk had been for nearly ten years. She drew the toe of her shoe across the plushness of the blue carpet tiles, still new enough that she left a dark mark in the pile.

'Why the new carpet, new desks, why all the change for just a couple of months?'

'A new call centre. No jobs though, all subbed out.'

Change at every turn, thought Lydia, there were no certainties and few loyalties. She looked at her watch. It was eight fifty-two. To her friend's great surprise, Lydia said, 'Too early for a drink I suppose?'

∞

It was true, all true. Not that Lydia seriously doubted a word Gloria had said. Her section was no longer required in its present form and each member of staff would be offered alternative employment, even if they did have to compete for the available jobs. And even if those jobs were a long way from home or in dismal locations or quite unsuitable for the experience that the applicants had. The twist for Lydia was she could take a part-time job in Henley or volunteer for redundancy, a choice calculated to ensure the latter. The whole object of the exercise was to cut cost while simultaneously demonstrating the humanity and generosity of personnel policies.

Lydia was home before mid-afternoon, having done no work at all, but thinking that she'd save a sick day for the Tuesday. Sick on Tuesdays always attracts less attention than sick on the first day back after a holiday. She'd read everything she'd been sent but taken little of it in. The detail seemed irrelevant when set beside the enormity of the basic facts: no job in Oxford, half a job an hour's commute away. She'd need to play the game to pick up the scraps on offer, or look for a new job. Maybe both. The idea of a new job held no attraction, but then neither did manning a reception desk. Until today she'd been secure and comfortable, modestly paid it was true, but it suited her and mostly she enjoyed the work. The prospect of presenting herself for interview, for inspection alongside the inevitably younger competition, filled her with dread. Perhaps it was the moment for a bigger change, a moment to cash in her assets and go on a world tour, returning only when the sun and the money ran out. Even as she thought such a thing she smirked, knowing all too well that it would never happen that way. More surprising was the realization that she did not really care whether she had a job or not, most certainly not with her current employer.

By five she had a second glass in her hand and was considering an invitation to join Gloria for a meal at a fashionably new restaurant on the High Street. She declined, but to have considered doing so, and on such a day as it had been, spoke volumes of her mood. She was almost light-headed, intoxicated by the novelty of events before she'd even opened the bottle. A small voice was cautious, wary of the sensation, waiting for the crash, alert for the shifting ground to open and swallow her completely. Until it did, responsible Lydia gave frivolous Lydia free rein.

Briefly she thought of telling Stephen of her day, but changed her mind before it was made up. He would be sympathetic, asking how she felt and what she intended to do. She didn't need sympathy and beyond her present surreal euphoria, she had no idea how she felt and even less idea of her intentions. Instead, her thoughts were drawn almost inevitably to Freddie Bellinger and his Linda.

For nearly twenty-four hours she'd savoured the prospect of unravelling Freddie's secret life, congratulating herself on her patience and the subtlety of her approach. Success beckoned, raising her spirits to dizzy heights, fuelled further by the *pinot gris* and the recollection of her little inheritance. Finally she settled at her desk to investigate the names and places she'd scrawled on the back of the envelope. One simple name would be all she needed, and she had it right there - Cable Street, a London street famous for a battle, although exactly when and between who, she was not quite sure. But there was only one Cable Street. In a few moments she had it - 1936 and the violent confrontation of the fascist Blackshirts by the combined ranks of the Left. Yes, it was a very well-known street, but not only that and to her delight, it had a school. Another entry in the list of search results caught her eye - Eastleigh in Hampshire. It too had a Cable Street. In alarm Lydia looked further down the list: Manchester, Lancaster and Formby all had Cable Streets. So did Wolverhampton, Southport and Salford. She cursed herself for taking such a simplistic approach.

What had happened to her careful assembling of the information, her elimination of the impossible, her sifting of the probabilities?

She hesitated over the next step, not as to what it should be, but whether this evening was the right moment to take it. Easy success had been snatched away and the mood and the wine suggested investigation might best be left to another day. It could be a long and inconclusive hunt for the right street in the right town and her other clues amounted to little: an unnamed school plus a few pupils in the 1940s; the area being bombed in the war; close to some docks - but how close? And couldn't it all fit right in with what she already knew, fit in with Bristol? As she stared at her list of Cable Streets she realised that the name of Bristol was missing. Quickly she searched again, this time specifically in that city, and then for Capel and Caple and Kaybull and others which grew more unlikely as she invented them. No results for Bristol. Nothing fitted in with Bristol. She'd clung to her previous diligent research that had produced Freddie so neatly and tidily, albeit with a little luck. She'd hung on to it as being right and now suddenly she must accept the accumulated evidence that it was wrong. The balance of probability swung against it all and, like a steel door closing, it swung with a mighty clang. How could it all be wrong when he was the man she'd sought, and with the certificate to prove it?

Guiltily she thought of the man himself, sitting or sleeping, propped in a bed, drip fed drugs and wired to the machine. The little yellow warning light flickering on then holding steady as some threshold is crossed, too much of this, not enough of that. Somewhere else a buzzer sounds, a minute or so later the unannounced entrance, the waft of sanitizer, a smiley-faced enquiry, *Not ready to die yet, Freddie? Soon though, eh?'* And what then, a hand into his drawer and a note slipped from his wallet? She hadn't really paid much attention to all that. Where was truth, where were lies, and all the shades between? Not for the first time, Lydia recognised how little she knew of the people whose lives she tracked and traced. And of Freddie Bellinger or Bell or Bright or Meadows or whoever, she really knew next to nothing.

The next glass drained the bottle and took her exhilaration with it. She should have taken up Gloria's offer of an evening together. Maybe it wasn't too late to change her mind. No, it wasn't even seven, but it would mean finding some decent clothes. And collecting her scattered wits into some sort of order. She dismissed the notion and settled back into her favourite chair to survey the wreckage of her life.

∞

At five, the first glimpses of Tuesday were too early and too bright. In the last minutes before she'd fallen onto her bed, a tiny grain of sense had demanded she drink a glass of water. Now she was far from chirpy, but the water had saved her from the worst consequences of the night's excesses. With an effort she sat in bed and contemplated her options. It took no more than a moment's thought to decide on a long-overdue sick day. Then some breakfast and a walk to clear her head of yesterday's turmoil. And when she thought more about it, she wondered if perhaps it would take a very long walk indeed to clear all her confusion. Perhaps, like her previously methodical approach to research, she should take one thing at a time. Easier said than done with real life, which had a habit of changing from day to day.

By six she was walking up Hythe Bridge Street to the stub end of the canal from where it runs north, side by side with the Castle Mill Stream, one of many branches of the Thames which permeate Oxford. Some glitter proudly in tourist view while others slide silently between hidden banks, scarcely calling themselves Thames. The city was already awake and starting its day, for the most part with the less glamorous sides of life, the office cleaners and street sweepers, the bin men and the papers dumped by the newsagents' doors. The other Oxford, the one that stayed behind college walls or offered only a glimpse of manicured lawn through a grudging gate, that Oxford was barely yawning into its comfortable summer-school day.

The canal always offered a good walk. Apart from the mud of winter, it generally provided easy going and the interest of all the life along it, whether on the water in boats or wildfowl ducking and diving. The idea of living on a narrowboat held the same romantic attraction for Lydia as for many others. Here, hidden from most of Oxford along the cool watery highway, were the homes of those who lived it for real every day. Despite the season, several that she passed had smoke curling from their little tin chimneys, coal or wood being the only means of heating water or cooking. A few more than she remembered sported satellite dishes while solar panels crowded many rooftops. It all looked like a simple way of life, out of the mainstream, below the radar and off-grid. She guessed the truth to be different, but under the gentle shades of summer beside the brightly painted houseboat homes with their private-joke names, Lydia chose to let romance be her guide. *Dawn Treader,* moored nose to tail with *Narnia,* brought a smile, while further along *Second Chance* and *Belly Dancer* caught her eye, as did *Tardis.* A friendly greeting from another early-riser poking their head into the morning air rounded out the idyllic scene.

A little beyond the lock where the canal links to the river, an acrid smell hung about the towpath. Walking on another hundred yards she came to the sad cause of the stench. Festooned with yellow warning tape lay the listing and charred remains of a narrowboat. The stern half had burned to the waterline while the blackened front remained attached to the mooring by a single scorched rope, pulled tight but still with the strength to hold the hulk. With a jolt she saw the name *Silver Stream* still legible in white paint along the black bow. It brought her up sharp, not just by the name's silent witness to tragedy. The romance of the river fell away as she recognised harsh reality lurking beneath the sparkling surface.

She hurried on, pushing this new disturbance from her mind. It was healing she'd been seeking, not further discord. At the first opportunity she turned away from the canal, heading west across Port Meadow towards the real Thames. The Meadow glistened in the morning light. Save for a few horses quietly chomping, the whole expanse of it seemed quite empty, she alone taking its pleasures. To the south and west the sun glinted off snatches of creeping traffic, the morning grind to desk and factory already well under way. She could easily join them, attend her own place of work or follow her mood and cash in a sick day. One decisive moment later she'd called and left her message. The day was too good to waste. The tiny, silent movements of the distant commuters might as well have been from another planet. A trace of yesterday's exhilaration rippled across her shoulders and down her spine, a physical pleasure she was quite unaccustomed to. It rolled again and such was the intensity, it brought a smile to her lips.

Little wonder, she thought, that a day like today would bring great pleasure to the mind and body. From having more cares than she could count, she suddenly had none. When she reached the crossing at Medley she stopped and found a bench to sit by the water. Where else could she possibly do this? Not in Cambridge, or at least, nowhere that she knew of. From Grantchester her kind of walk was always a bus or car ride away, which immediately created an obstacle. That city might still have a place for her but she had yet to find it. There would be no prising Stephen from The Old Rectory, and why should she try, where else would she ever see him so content? But his wife's ghost still inhabited the place, never more so than when his daughter came to stay. Lydia reminded herself that she too, had, until recently, been as content in her space as Stephen was in his. What held her here, was it familiarity, the convenient groove, or something deeper? The uncomfortable answer that came to mind first was inertia.

Less than forty-eight hours ago her world, her life, had been full of certainties and she'd baulked at the prospects of change. Now the old adage about the certainty of death and taxes came back to her, and of the two it was death that meant most. More specifically, it was Freddie Bellinger's death. It would come soon and her chances of finding his Linda were slim. She would work on Freddie's story today, maybe even visit him later in the afternoon and confront his secrecy. Wasn't the first rule of enquiry to extract every piece of knowledge from the living before asking questions of the dead? And hadn't she stepped too gingerly round his feelings, hobbling herself before she started? No, she'd tease out what she could from Cable Street, a sister named Sarah, Mickey

Watson, and Janice Beckett then she'd get some straight answers from Freddie.

By nine her fresh resolve had brought her back to the house and the debris of her desk. Last night's wine had got in the way of everything, including her tidy methodical habits. The Cable Street search remained on her screen, while the envelope with the scribbled notes had fallen to the floor and might as easily have dropped into the waste-paper bin, never to be seen again. She tidied and cleared then set to work with a new vigour, exhilarated by her early start.

Old schools and streets and playmates were one thing, but a death was quite another. Freddie had claimed that his friend Mickey Watson, presumably aged around ten or eleven years, had failed to come to school one morning circa 1940 after his house was destroyed in an air raid. Records of Mickey and his family would exist and should be easy to find. In finding him the area would be pinpointed and with it the particular Cable Street of Freddie's memory. From there a school could be identified and with the school, its pupils, although that might take a lot longer than she probably had.

It proved to be remarkably simple to find Mickey. The UK World War II civilian deaths register had all the victims conveniently laid out by location and the power of the search engine indexed every entry for her. They were all there on the last-but-one page of the London Borough of Stepney. *Audrey Hilda Watson, age 35, widow of George Andrew Watson, Merchant Navy seaman, on 17th September 1940 at Dock Street Shelter E1,* together with her daughter *Anne Mary Watson age 8* and son *Michael George Watson age 10.* Mickey's house hadn't copped it, they'd been in a shelter and copped it there. It had been in the same register that Lydia had found the deaths in 1941 of Freddie's mother Lillian Edith and his sister Maud. Curiosity took her back to those pages, just to be sure. Mickey Watson killed in Stepney, meant Cable Street in Stepney. It was not impossible for Freddie to have been at school with Mickey and have lost his mother and sister in Bristol four months later, but it wouldn't make much sense.

A check for similar casualties amongst the other families of Freddie's youth, the Andrews, Meadows, Becketts and Brights, brought only one entry in Stepney and that seemed of little value. Nonetheless, in Lydia's more methodical way, she made a note of Elizabeth Andrews' death alongside her daughter in 1944. As an afterthought she looked for Thompson but found nothing. Looking back at her notes, Lydia struggled to make sense of a scrawled name until she remembered the words Freddie had used a week ago, 'Little Caesar,' he'd said. She wasn't surprised when her genealogy searches brought nothing for Caesar Andrews.

By eleven she'd exhausted the potential of the names and places he'd mentioned. A sister Sarah was of very little value without a surname to go with it, which after all, had been the main difficulty all along. Sarah Bellinger brought a few entries which might've been more interesting had Lydia not become convinced that Bellinger was not the name she was seeking.

On a sudden impulse she picked up her phone to call Stephen, and surprise him with a work-day call. To say what? She'd lost her job but didn't care and it's a great day? She let it slide from her fingers back onto her desk. As it did so the silent vibration of the call alert began. He was calling her. The little screen flashed 'Stephen K calling' as if she knew a dozen other Stephens who might at any time call her. She knew only one Stephen, the K was quite superfluous. She let it purr to itself until it stopped. They hardly ever called each other, only a week ago they'd joked that they'd sent more postcards than made calls in all the time they'd known each other. Here she was not answering his call and without any good reason she could think of.

Now she had a reason to call him. She picked it up, feeling its glassy black smoothness on the tips of her fingers.

'Hello, did I disturb you? I just called without really thinking, can you talk or are you hard at it?' He sounded full of enthusiasm, bubbling with something to tell her, not at all sorry to have interrupted her at work.

'It's all right, I can talk.'

'Good. How are you?'

'Surprisingly well.' Lydia looked out to her little patch of garden, leaning towards the window to get a glimpse of blue sky through the greenery. 'Maybe not so surprising, it's a beautiful day. I was up early, walking by the river.'

'Ah, solving puzzles?'

'Maybe.'

'Not Laurence's by any chance? I saw him earlier. He didn't say anything, but he looked as if he wanted to.'

'No, not Laurence's. Soon though.' Her pleasure in the morning, pleasure in her own existence, was having miraculous effects. No surge of unworthiness, no guilty apology for her failure to unravel Laurence Durham's miserable history. Instead, an echo of that earlier ripple sent a shiver of goose bumps across her back and a smile flickering on the corners of her mouth. Sensible Lydia's caution was dismissed: this was altogether too good to spoil with thoughts of the crash or the height of the drop when it came.

'Still Freddie then.'

'Yes, still Freddie. I saw him on Sunday on the way back here. Maybe a little closer. He's playing games with me. The closer he is to dying, the more he's ready to tell.'

'Perhaps he doesn't want to be around for the consequences,' he suggested.

'Whatever they might be. It's an idea. He wants me to know, but doesn't want to tell me. In a peculiar way he thinks he's protecting me from something.'

A pause from Stephen reminded Lydia that it was he who'd called her. He had something he needed to call about even though she was supposed to be hard at work at her office.

'What are you up to this morning?'

'Oh, yes. I've been doing a little bit of research of my own,' for a moment he let the statement hang, teasing her with ambiguity. 'I've been trying to see where and when might fit that formula we spoke of for a holiday. Guaranteed sun plus food, drink and something interesting to do, wasn't it?'

The holiday. Unmentioned in Jacqueline's presence, un-mentioned for over a week, one of those things that seem like a good idea at the time and are then allowed to be quietly forgotten by all involved. He hadn't forgotten at all, far from it, he was actually doing something about it. Her smile widened as the ripple replayed itself across her neck and shoulders.

'Oh, going away. Together. Yes. I don't know what we said.' Then with more courage than she thought she had, she added, 'We said something about being ready to risk what we have.'

'Still ready to gamble?'

∞

With Laurence's index as a guide and so few facts to work with, cataloguing his copied papers and adding her own sparse notes took little of Lydia's afternoon. No pattern of events, no theme or repetition suggested itself when she surveyed the list. Apart from the occasional visit to a circus or the like, the whole of his known childhood was encompassed by a few addresses, half-a-dozen picture postcards, a handful of dates, a solitary birthday card and a birth certificate. His mother, and just possibly his grandmother Alice, were the only ways into his past. Florence wasn't the first mother to have hidden a father's identity, but Laurence's account suggested something spiteful in her refusal.

A search for Florence's birth brought a few Tweddles, along with Tweddels and Tweedles, mainly from the north-east of England in Northumberland and Yorkshire. Amongst them were two potential Florences, although neither would be eighty-two in the next couple of months. Women often age more slowly than men, especially in official records, so it was quite possible for Florence to have shed a few years as the decades passed. Even so, there was nothing to inspire a more detailed sifting of the results.

Florence had been a Tweddle, or so she claimed, and then become a Durham: who was to say she hadn't been a Durham first? Again the search threw up a few vague possibles together with a long list of the extremely unlikely. Setting birth aside, Lydia tried a new tack: a list of marriages of a female Tweddle to a Durham in 1965 - give or take a few years - brought a smile of satisfaction. The single exact match showed Florence A. Tweddle had married a Durham sometime in the last three months of 1959. Coincidently, they'd married in Bedford. One click later she had

Florence's groom as William G. Durham. She'd married Laurence's father? Surely it couldn't be that easy, but she'd changed his name to that of her new husband, so why not? Lydia was wary of such simplicity, recent experience had re-taught her old lessons. The marriage would explain the name change, but it was a long way from proof of paternity. Social acceptance, financial benefit, avoiding awkward questions - all were good reasons to take William's name for her son.

Laurence would have been just five when his mother married. Quite possibly he would have been kept out of sight during the event, perhaps for a while both before and after. The Swinging Sixties might have been just round the corner, but there were plenty of old prejudices still on display. If the marriage had been short-lived he could easily have no memory at all of William G. Durham.

A little more information about William might prove useful. Unlike Florence's birth record, his was easy to narrow down. On the assumption that he was at least twenty-one when he married, a couple of records showed promise. Both referred to births registered in 1930, which would have made him a year or two older than Florence. Speculation on that would take a back seat until she had the details from the marriage certificate. But speculation on the marriage and what happened to William G. were very much in her mind. A quick search of the divorce index found no likely entries, but the death register happily gave up three William Durhams, two who might be those born in 1930 and a third who'd managed ninety-nine years when he died in 1977. Time would tell, but first impressions were that Florence's husband would be far less elusive than the lady herself.

Lydia turned her attention to Laurence's grandmother, Alice. According to Laurence there had never been a grandfather in his life and he'd never dared question his grandmother on the subject. Whether she'd been married or not he couldn't say, but according to their declared ages, Alice would have been just sixteen when she gave birth to Florence. She might have been married but her age and status suggested otherwise. The only fragment Laurence could provide was a recollection of the young Alice having been 'in service'. At the time he'd had no idea what the phrase meant, which is why it stuck with him. Alice used the name Tweddle but Laurence couldn't say whether or not she was born with it. Having recently celebrated her ninety-eighth birthday, his grandmother should've been easy to find. But like her daughter, the search results gave no Alice Tweddles. The closest were Philipa A Tweddel and Mary A Tweddle, registered in Northumberland and Suffolk respectively at the end of 1916. If she was going to learn more about Alice it would have to wait until she'd got closer to Florence. Or Laurence managed to dredge up something better.

Beyond her window the summer sun continued to beam down, while gentle airs brushed through the branches shading her garden. To lounge outside with an afternoon glass, letting the day wrap her and bathe her in its soft warmth was so tempting. Later, she told herself, she would succumb to temptation later, but until then she could enjoy the prospect of it. If ever there was a day to call in sick, this was it. Was that, she wondered, why she'd let Stephen continue to think she was at work when he'd called? To let him keep his good impressions of her? Thoughts of Stephen inevitably brought thoughts of their proposed holiday, discussed and enthused over, but as yet undecided.

She didn't much like the connection, but it was a short jump from that to a honeymoon. Where might Florence have spent her honeymoon? One of Laurence's precious postcards came to mind, not the steam engines but a steamship. In a few seconds she had the photocopy in her hand, the *SS Davina-G* depicted not in a photograph but from a painting. The reverse was blank apart from the printed details of the shipping company and the artist. A search for both gave immediate results. The card was one of a series of paintings commissioned by the line, one that operated cruise ships in the 1950s and 60s. After only a few minutes reading in the specialist world of maritime postcard collectors, Lydia learned that only a few thousand sets had been printed. All had been sold within a few months of their issue in November 1959. Although they were now occasionally available at auctions, at the time they had only been sold on board the cruise ships. Here was a little nugget of information after all, something Florence had sent

Laurence, presumably included with a letter to his grandmother, and being a passenger on the *Davina-G* was the most likely way she would have obtained it.

A few minutes more and there before her was a complete history of the G-Line, along with the ships and the cruise routes they followed, all courtesy of another enthusiast. It was even possible to see where most of the vessels were on a given day. In late 1959 and early 1960 the *Davina-G* cruised the North African coast with visits to Madeira and the Canary Islands from her pick-up point in Pireus. If William G Durham and the new Mrs Durham had chosen the *Davina-G* for their honeymoon, not only would the card be explained but one important, perhaps critical, part of Florence's past would have been uncovered. The G-Line site even had some crew and passenger lists but nothing for the *Davina-G*. It was all speculation, she hadn't even seen the marriage details and it would be a few days before the certificate arrived. She was in danger of getting ahead of herself, but it felt right and the card had come from his mother, Laurence had been certain of that.

Collecting a bottle from the fridge, Lydia made herself comfortable under the willow and considered holidays and honeymoons. It had been many years since she'd shared a holiday, and the few hours she'd spent with Stephen in the Lakes hardly counted. Her only honeymoon had been nearly twenty-five years ago when she and Michael spent an anxious week in Cornwall awkwardly adjusting to the daily intimacy of married life. They'd previously shared a bed many times but not shared the living, not shared whole days and nights one after another. Exactly what she'd expected she couldn't remember now, she could barely remember anything of marriage. He'd expected more, he'd expected some unspecified transformation of their lives. She'd failed him on all counts, remaining the girl he'd married, unaware for years that he'd wanted something she wasn't, something she couldn't pretend to be even if she'd been given the script.

A holiday with Stephen might almost be the reverse of all that. They'd already shared plenty of days, lived together in his house for two, three, even four days at a time and never found cause to complain of each other's company or habits. But they hadn't shared a bed. They might easily have done so over the weekend, but having apparently reached that point, the perfect daughter came between them. It was all in the timing and she didn't want this holiday to be the first time, for it to loom unspoken over their plans. She poured another glass and toasted her new resolve. If they would wake together under some foreign sky then they should do so in Grantchester first. It would not be here in her house in West Street, of that she was certain, he would never visit Osney. No, if it was anywhere it would be The Old Rectory. His wife's ghost would simply have to look the other way.

6

Wednesday dawned as perfect as Tuesday. Lydia stirred at six and drifted sleepily through a replay of her stolen day, hardly daring to check if all that confidence, all that resolve, had evaporated in the night. As she sank back, satisfied, into her pillow, a little gooseflesh brushed her shoulders again. Yes, it was all still with her.

The immediate thought was to take another day, look at what the postman might bring, then perhaps go to Bedford and see Freddie with any discoveries she would make. With luck those certificates, expensively ordered with express service, might land on her doormat today. On days such as these, she thought, skipping work could become a habit. With a slight shock she remembered that it would not be very long before there would be no work to skip, every day would be like this, but without the sunshine or the convenience of a regular salary. How could she have forgotten so easily? All that upheaval was the very reason she'd skipped Tuesday. Bunked off, Freddie would have said. Did he ever wake on such mornings and for a few blissful moments forget his foreshortened future? He was one very good reason to bunk off another day, to do some work on his Linda.

As the idea began to solidify, Lydia remembered Gloria with a pang of guilt. She'd deserted her friend without a second thought. Gloria had been genuinely upset for Lydia, yet it was only a year ago, perhaps less, that they'd abandoned a decade of sniping and become the nearest thing they each had to best friends. Gloria still sniped, especially about Stephen, but also about Lydia's obsession and her special slant on it. Genealogy was, Gloria had declared more than once, the most boring thing in the world, even worse than fishing. But since they'd found unexpected common ground and shared confidences, the snarky comments had lost their barbs and were usually accompanied by a roll of the eyes and a tongue in cheek. When it was all over, when the office had closed and they'd gone their separate ways, she would miss Gloria Fitzgerald more than she would ever have imagined. No, today would be a work day after all, even if it were a short one and no work was actually completed.

Being first into the office gave her the feeling of restoring some normality to an abnormal week, even if it was as unappealing as it had been on Monday. The newness hadn't rubbed off any part of it, it still smelled new, still smelled of plastic. Until her colleagues trickled in around nine-thirty it had looked like a showroom. Apart from the ailing yucca.

No sooner had Gloria parked herself next to Lydia than she needed a smoke. 'Coming?' she asked.

'No, have I been away so long you've forgotten…ah, right. Yes, why not.'

Lydia had never joined the smokers in their exile, never had a reason to. Now she had no reason to do anything else. The day was already warm, relieved by a soft breeze rustling the trees. Standing upwind of Gloria she turned to let the morning sun warm her face.

'How was it yesterday?' Gloria asked tentatively.

'Lovely, thank you.'

'Lovely? Here?'

'Oh no, I thought you meant at home. I had the day off. I was sick.'

'Sick! You're never sick,' she snorted.

'Well I was yesterday, and nearly today too. You weren't in either?'

'No.' Gloria was about to add something but paused and looked away, taking a deep lungful of smoke. A muscle twitched in her cheek. She turned back suddenly, 'Were you sick, really sick, you know, throwing up and all that?'

'No, like I said, I had a lovely day, walking by the river, working a few things out, you know me.'

'Yeah, we know you Lydia. Seen any good gravestones lately?' She laughed, endlessly amused by her own humour. She turned away again still smiling, head back, smoke trailing from her nose then lingering in her hair. 'I got some news,' she said to the sky.

It wasn't like Gloria to be coy, she was straight talking if nothing else. Lydia wondered what might follow the pause. Oh, no please don't be pregnant, maybe just a new job. But it was something Gloria was wary of telling. Still she was smiling at the sky.

'All right, I give up, what's the news?'

'Getting married!' she shouted into the blue, arms wide. Then she turned to Lydia's embrace, beaming with joy and pride.

Lydia was astonished. Boyfriends regularly came and went in Gloria's life and for all she'd declared her intention of hooking one permanently, they had both doubted it would ever happen.

'That's wonderful Gloria, I'm so pleased for you. Come on who, when, where's the ring?' Then the question crept across her face.

'No, I'm not!' said Gloria, then added, 'I thought maybe I was, but false alarm, thank god. Anyway, the lucky man is Eddie. Haven't even told my mum yet. You're the first.'

'Eddie? The Eddie you ditched a few weeks back? Eddie who was too, what was it, too slow to catch a cold? Surely not that Eddie?' Gently teasing Gloria was a rare reversal of roles.

'OK, yeah, that one. We kinda got back together on Monday night.'

'Gloria, really, I'm so happy for you.' Lydia reached out and gave her friend another big hug.

'Listen, we haven't fixed anything yet but will you be my, like, bridesmaid?'

Lydia laughed. 'Bridesmaid? I'm a bit past that I think, and matron-of-honour sounds ghastly, but yes, of course I will. I think they're called supporters these days. I'll be your supporter. I've never been asked before, it's lovely.'

'Don't you start, you'll set me off.'

The unlikely bride-to-be and her delighted and surprised supporter shared another hug and a kiss and a few tears.

∞

They were there on the doormat waiting for her, two envelopes with the 'express service' stickers. The colours of the paperwork gave away their contents. The thicker one with two bluey-grey birth certificates, the thinner one, a single green marriage certificate. Never one to tear open anything in a hurry, Lydia put them to one side until she'd emptied her shopping bags and settled herself with a glass at her desk. Even then she clicked open her notes and spreadsheets for Francis 'Freddie' Bellinger before carefully slitting the envelopes. She smoothed each certificate and laid it out for inspection.

First to view was Belinda Andrews, born to Catherine and Peter Andrews on December 18th 1956 at an address in Mile End, London, registered in Stepney. Catherine's maiden name was Bright. That had certainly piqued Freddie's interest when he'd heard the name, what had he said about Andrews, a sick joke? And it was London's East End again, not a stone's throw from Cable Street.

Linda Thompson's details were just as clear. Born on September 29th 1956 to Sylvia Bright, father George Frederick Thompson, in a nursing home in Ramsgate, Kent. The usual residence was given as an address in Dover. Unlike the first certificate, the informant on Linda's was her mother. Sylvia had registered Linda not in Kent but in London nearly twelve weeks after the birth. So, Freddie Bellinger, if this is your Linda, are you really George Frederick Thompson? Even before the thought had fully formed, Lydia was stopped by the father's occupation shown on the certificate: *Deceased*. Deceased? She'd never seen it written there, it was always in brackets after the dead person's name, for the father of a bride or the widower's long-departed wife. True, it was only a copy of the original entry, a mistake could have been made at either point. It might not even have been *deceased* at all, but a proper occupation, although she could think only of *decorator,* which would surely be difficult to confuse with *deceased.* This was the birth that had caused Freddie the most agitation, perhaps the deceased element was the reason why. If she was ever to find his Linda before he died, it really needed to be this girl.

The third document gave details of Sylvia Bright's marriage to Norman Ernest Brooks at Leyton in 1968. She had the same birth year as the Sylvia who'd born Linda and was very likely the same person, a few more searches and certificates might verify that. Sylvia was recorded as a spinster, her father was George W Bright, a market porter. No mention of deceased, Lydia was pleased to note.

The temptation to take her wine to the garden was strong. Her chair was waiting and the day had several good hours left in it. But how many good hours had Freddie got left? The question came to her with such clarity she wondered for a moment if she'd really heard it or unconsciously said it aloud. She turned guiltily back to her desk and keyboard. There was plenty to look for, plenty of names to check, lives to fill in and those good hours to do it in.

At a little after midnight, surrounded by the dry remains of a sandwich and scribbled notes and printed pages with more scribbled notes upon them, Lydia came to a halt. The credit card had racked up charges for another dozen or so certificates, all express service, plus new subscriptions to newspaper and magazine archives.

Searches and re-searches, cross reference and tabulation were all a familiar part of what Lydia did, even if it was not often done in the small hours. But in looking for Linda and trying to discern how Freddie might be her father, the results of all those searches had taken her further and wider than usual. It had taken her to dozens of pages of the ubiquitous *wikipedia* and specialist web-sites run by enthusiasts of every kind. All anoraks of one sort or another, just as she was, and all dedicated to recording some niche of trivia. She blessed them for their diligence.

She'd found the traces of Linda Thompson, some of it yet to be confirmed by copies from the registers, but she'd found traces of the girl and of the woman, she may even have found the mother she became. More than one marriage seemed possible, but as for most people, there was only one death at the end of it all. That would take a little more work, involving as it did, a death abroad. Until she was sure, really sure, of what she had, Lydia would tell Freddie nothing concrete.

Of Freddie himself, the core of his mystery remained. If he was the deceased George Frederick Thompson whose certificates were among those Lydia had ordered, she would have to reconcile herself to having been chatting with a ghost. Either that or the official record was once again no more than convenient lies. Whether convenient for the mother or the father remained to be seen. A deceased father gains sympathy for the unmarried mother where there might otherwise have been censure. Aside from parenthood, there might've been many reasons Linda's father had found it convenient to be dead, although how he came to be resurrected as Freddie Bell was more difficult to imagine. And if he had become Freddie then what had happened to the real Francis Bellinger?

∞

'To Oxford? Tomorrow?'

'Yes, a last minute thing, a meeting. At a place to the west, Eynsham I think.'

Stephen's Thursday-night call changed the unspoken plan for the weekend. The loose invitation to come down to Grantchester, as had become her habit, was so loose that it may never have been issued at all. But it was understood. And she'd planned to call in to see Freddie in Bedford on the way. Now here was Stephen coming to Oxford instead.

'Are you still there?'

'Yes. Eynsham's not far.'

'No, that's what I thought. Meeting in the afternoon around three. Probably finish by six at the latest.'

'Hmm.'

'I was wondering about staying over.'

Oh. The penny suddenly dropped. It dropped so loudly Stephen probably heard it in Cambridge.

'Ah. Staying over. Yes.' There was simply no alternative, she had to invite him to her house, he was practically asking her to. He'd listened when she'd spoken about always being on his home ground, and now he was doing something about it. She swallowed hard and said, 'Would you like to stay here?' Her voice sounded flat and peculiar, even to her own ears.

'We could,' he said. There was that *we* creeping in again, *we could.* But he didn't sound any more convincing than she had.

'Were you thinking of staying in Eynsham?'

'Not really, it's not a hotel, but I thought we might go somewhere else, somewhere new, for a couple of nights maybe.

You could bring your Laurence and Freddie things, do some work, some walking. It's just an idea. I'll probably have reading to do.'

'Oh yes.'

It was such a relief that he wasn't going to have to squeeze into her little house, agreeing to the weekend in a hotel came without a second thought. Which was lucky, because no sooner had she and Stephen made the arrangements than all the old doubts began to circle in the shadows, threatening her new confidence. Don't look down, that's what Gloria had said. So she looked straight ahead and thought about walking on gentle Cotswold slopes.

∞

He arrived a little before six. After the niceties of welcoming him to West Street and giving him the whistle-stop tour they were out of the house and on their way in no time. For all her fears, it was such a simple way for him to see where she lived. No need to find him space, to fret about beds, make sure there was food in the fridge: it was done in a few minutes and if there was a next time it would not be a surprise, she wouldn't have to apologise. The release from this anxiety left her feeling euphoric once again, dizzy with the pleasure of it all.

They sat in comfortable silence as he negotiated the Friday night crawl along the Woodstock Road. Although they'd travelled little together, Lydia very much enjoyed being driven in his car. For all its Teutonic functionality, it was extremely comfortable. She could sink into the soft leather, adjust every aspect of her position and minutely control the temperature and flow of the air around her. She could choose her music too, although she'd never done so despite Stephen's frequent invitations. Looking sideways at him concentrating on the stop-start traffic reminded her just how fortunate she was to find herself beside him. It wasn't her usual unworthy-to-breath-the-same-air sense of inadequacy. It was more realistic than that. She thought he was a good man, a generous and thoughtful man, good company, a man easy in his own skin. And yes, he was still attractive, he wore his years well, as the lean and long-limbed often do. More, he found something in Lydia to attract him. The slightest tingle ran down her back.

'What did you meet about in Eynsham?'

'Not Eynsham as it turned out. Eynsham Hall, which is a hotel after all, but confusingly not in Eynsham.'

She waited to see if he would tell her, while he waited to see if she would press him.

'I met some people there, Home Office, Foreign Office. Civil servants.'

Lydia recognised the slightly evasive voice she'd heard once or twice before. What had Jacqueline called it, his hush-hush voice? It was a moment not to question further. 'Ah, sounds boring.'

'Well, no, unfortunately, far from. I'll tell you about it one day.'

They drove on, faster once the traffic eased beyond Peartree and out past Woodstock.

'Did you see Freddie today?'

Sometimes he seemed to entirely forget she didn't have the same comfortable semi-retired lifestyle as he did. The occasional lapses were endearing but might easily become irritating. With slight surprise she remembered her looming redundancy, which amounted to much the same thing, only without the comfort.

'No, I was going to see him tonight if we'd been in Cambridge. I left a message. I hope he gets it.'

'Progress?'

'Maybe. I might've found his Linda, we'll see. If it's her there'll be no happy reunion, at least, not this side of the grave. There might be a granddaughter.'

'And Laurence, anything for him?'

'Another maybe. I have some certificates that came today, one might be his mother's marriage, they're in the bag. I'm saving them for later. So far it looks like Florence married a William Durham at the end of 1959.'

'His father? That would be marvellous. I think he'd be very happy about that,' Stephen enthused.

'Hmm, not that easy.'

'No, of course not, but I'm sure he'd be pleased. What's next?'

'I'd like to see him soon, talk over a few things. I'll try and fix something for next week.'

She watched the countryside slide smoothly by as they journeyed to Stow in their air-conditioned cocoon. They could, she thought, be any of ten-thousand tourists criss-crossing the landscape, hurrying to an airport or an evening meal and tonight's bed. The green and rolling hills lulled them in their comfort, manicured hedges and tidy lawns nestling by streams spoke of order and peace, all was picture-postcard perfect in the gentle July evening.

She could see herself swishing past from the windows of the cottages, from a church spire a mile away she could see the glint of sun on the windscreen, in the traffic-camera control-room she watched as the car flashed through the fish-eye image on the screen. The icy embrace of detachment had slipped in like a cold draft in winter. It came stealthily upon her, often at the best of times, always an ambush, always unwelcome. Its ugly sister, self-loathing, was never far behind. Lydia could be laughing, talking, drinking, then click, she was watching herself, hating the watching and hating what she saw. It paralysed her, barely allowing breath into her body, even the tiniest movements becoming impossible without intense concentration. As the shallow breathing dipped the oxygen level in her blood, the edges of her vision faded to black. She blinked fiercely and tried to swallow as the car came to a stop.

'Lydia, Lydia,' he was saying urgently, 'what is it, what's wrong?'

They'd stopped under some trees at the side of the road. Beyond the trees and a low fence, the land slipped away to a sparkling valley to the west. She saw the beauty of it, caught the sight of horses a field away pausing to raise their heads, felt the gentle sway of the car as others sped by.

'I'm fine,' she heard somebody say.

He was at her side, the car door open, almost kneeling to be close to her. 'You didn't speak, I thought you might faint, you were white.'

He took a bottled water from the drinks cooler, removed the top and held it in her hand. 'Drink. Sip it,' he said.

His touch warmed her. She fancied she could feel the warmth flowing back into her hand, up her arm, into her whole body until it reached her face and she smiled. 'Thank you. I'll be fine in a minute, I was a little faint for a minute or two.'

She recovered quickly while he paced back and forth beside the car, looking very serious. After a minute or two she got out and took a few steps with him to demonstrate her return to health. She knew the shadows lingered at the edges of her mind but his intervention had saved her from a longer episode.

'Shall we go back?' he asked when they were settled in the car and the engine was running, 'Or shall we go on? There'll be other weekends.'

'We've come this far,' she said, in something closer to her normal voice.

The Gawcombe Woods Hotel was exactly what they had hoped: a big old country-house hotel in private acres with superb views and modern plumbing. It even had a library with easy chairs and an old-fashioned hushed feel about it.

They settled into their room, a little self-consciously but without great embarrassment, then walked in the gardens before dining, giggling more than might be expected of a mature couple.

When the wine had been brought with their meal, Stephen grew more serious and said, 'Lydia, you've not seemed quite yourself this week. When we phoned there was something, and earlier, before we left the house, there was something then too. I wondered if it was just, hmm, uncertainty, nerves, the prospect of...' hesitation was unlike him, 'of being here. Then nearly fainting in the car. Or am I imagining it and adding two and two to make five?'

'There is something I haven't told you,' she began, then seeing the look on his face added, 'No, nothing that serious. My job's going, I'm redundant. Or strictly speaking I'm being offered re-deployment on a part time basis to a place I don't want to be and a job I don't want.' She let this sink in for a moment. 'I found out on Monday. I didn't tell you before because I didn't know how I felt about it myself.'

He nodded. 'Yes, I can understand that,' he said slowly. 'And now, how do you feel now?'

'I'm still not sure. Half the time I keep forgetting about it, and sometimes it just feels, well, liberating is all I can think of.'

After a few more moment's thought, Stephen lifted his wine in a toast. 'Then here's to liberty,' he said and they clinked glasses. 'I'm very glad, you worried me in the car.'

She thought, 'I worried me in the car,' but she said, 'Thank you.'

Lydia woke from a contented and satisfying sleep as if surfacing from a beautiful deep-sea dive. Reluctantly she left the soft sea-bed, ascending slowly through the blue towards a sparkling surface, past colours and currents that could've detained her longer, reaching out to floating strands as she rose above them. Her eyes opened to an unfamiliar darkness, with flickers of half-light through curtains that gently billowed at the open window. Stephen was somewhere close by. Even in such a huge bed she was sure that she need only reach out a little to find his body close to hers. She held her breath to catch the sound of his but could only feel its silent rhythm.

She let her fingers find his skin. He didn't stir as she let them settle like a butterfly on his back or his thigh, she couldn't say which for sure. She'd forgotten, or had dared not remember, the simple pleasure of the touch of another's skin. When they'd first been naked together and held each other, the surging intensity of contact had almost overwhelmed her. For a moment it had seemed they clung to each other as drowning swimmers might cling to rescue. Then she'd recalled how his touch at the roadside had been the antidote to her demons, had suffused her whole body, and she'd relaxed her frantic grip and his relaxed in response. They were both unpractised in love-making, both tentative in their touches, hardly daring more than feather-light strokes across back and breasts until their confidence in each other grew.

Since their talk of risking friendship they'd explored each other a little further in their brief embraces but those small rehearsals had not prepared her for his solid reality. If she'd imagined anything at all it would have been that his leanness, his muscularity might have been an illusion of movement, or an impression created by clothes and style. Her own far-from-lean puffiness only served to emphasise his sinewy strength. Thankfully, near-darkness hid her inadequacies from them both and they'd rolled and curled and

101

cuddled with each other with no thoughts for the past and few for the future. Now she lay beside him while he slept, her nerve-endings still touching his, he and she still an entity for all their separation. It was unfamiliar territory, but she was happy to explore unguided, let the memory of pleasure mingle with anticipation for the new day.

The swaying curtains hinted at dawn light beyond the window and the urge to stand in it grew impossible to resist. She slid from the sheets and felt the delicious shiver of silk across her skin as she gathered her robe - his unexpected gift - around her. At the window she paused to see if Stephen stirred. He did not. The door to the balcony opened silently and she stepped out into the cool morning air. Across the valley towards Bourton the hard details of the land were hidden in a soft purple haze, lightening and shading to pink. Even as she watched, the trees along the crest of the distant hills caught the first golden tint from the rising sun. All was still and silent save for the stirrings of unseen animals. She thought she had never seen anything quite so perfect.

On another day she would pull on her jeans, push her head into a sweater and be off walking to Stow, or more likely down in the valley finding the river and a path to take her close beside it. Maybe there would be such a day in another week or a month or a year, but today was a day to resist the solitary impulse, the singular pleasure. Today was a day to relish the perfection of the moment, to find a different start. A cool breath of air moved across the balcony reminding her of nakedness beneath the silk. The purple haze had all but gone, hard edges were taking their usual places in the scene. On the hillside above, the yellow light of morning was creeping down the fields.

She stole in silently beside him, warming herself on his body heat. After a few moments he rolled towards her. 'How's the day look?' he murmured.

Their grandly appointed room was lacking only in one respect: it contained a single writing desk. They'd meandered through breakfast, strolled round the grounds and debated a longer walk to Bourton or The Slaughters. But by mid-morning they were both itching to look at yesterday's unopened paperwork. And since his was tinged with confidentiality if not actual secrecy, and hers was open for anyone to see for the price of a paperback, well, the desk in their room was clearly the place for Stephen. Not that Lydia minded, the quiet library looked ideal for her. On a summer Saturday morning she was sure she'd find few others using it.

She had three envelopes to look forward to. If she had it right, then along with Florence Durham's marriage she'd also have her husband's birth and death certificates, which would be a huge step forward from Laurence's anaemic list of life events. She opened the marriage details first, the key to success elsewhere, and spread it out beside her keyboard. It was all she hoped and expected apart from one thing: the William Gordon Durham who'd married Florence Tweddle on Dec 12th 1959 at Bedford Register Office was aged seventy-two years at the time. Seventy-two? She'd guessed at something much less than that, had ordered certificates based on those guesses. Seventy-two? She did the maths quickly. He would have been born in 1887! Florence was twenty-seven and William was seventy-two. The symmetry of the numbers was not lost on her, but it still seemed bizarre. And it meant those birth certificates were wrong before she'd opened them, they were for Williams born in the 1930s, not this old boy marrying the young Florence.

Lydia sagged back in her chair. Hardly the progress she wanted. Only one answer, one that raised even more questions. What was Florence thinking off, marrying a man more than forty years older? Laurence's mother was certainly full of surprises. With little enthusiasm, Lydia copied all the vital facts - and lies and half-truths for all she knew - into her spreadsheet records. He was a retired solicitor, declaring himself as a widower with an address in Bedford and whose father, also William, was deceased. Florence was a spinster, whose father's name was Jack Buchanan. Now that was truly a new piece of information, maybe a new piece of misinformation. Whichever it was, it had been witnessed by her mother, for there at the bottom of the form was her name *in the presence of M Alice Tweddle.'* Possibly an aunt or sister, just conceivably a cousin, but for Lydia it would only be one person, Laurence's grandmother. He'd called her bloody-minded and signing yourself in that way somehow seemed to confirm a perverse outlook on life.

Having had time to recover from the marriage surprise, Lydia realised that the birth and death certificates might yet be valuable. And so it proved. She'd hoped for William G senior's birth when she ordered them, but she had, by luck it seemed, received details of a son. William Henry Durham, 2nd Feb 1930, born to William G and Gwendoline Durham formerly Forester. One of the death certificates appeared to be the perfect fit for William Henry: in 1968 at a hospital in Sussex after what Lydia recognised as a heart attack. It took no more than a few minutes to be satisfied that William G had married Gwendoline Forester in the second quarter of 1928 in Wellingborough. She hesitated over ordering the certificate, there was no doubt the expenses were mounting up. Would it be of interest to Laurence? She made a note of the details and let ordering wait for future developments.

With new information came the urge to make fresh enquiries, especially regarding William G's death, for by now he must certainly have died or be the oldest man alive in England. Someone, somewhere would have recorded that event and someone else would have added it to a database. Her logic was flawless but it still did not produce a record or a reference she could find in her searches. Even so, despite an uncertain start, the morning had already fulfilled its promise.

She'd hardly been at the desk for half an hour, yet already her concentration was wandering. The day beyond the windows remained seductive and the impulse to look in on Stephen was becoming almost irresistible. She was loath to disturb him, she didn't need to ask anything or fetch anything from the room, but she did want to see him, wanted to see him sitting at the desk reading and making notes just as he would at home, just as she had seen him do many times in the last few months. She wanted to see him look up and smile as she entered, unquestioning but always open to receive news of her discoveries.

He'd chosen this place, chosen neutral ground for their weekend, yet his choice had brought them to somewhere so like The Old Rectory it might as well have been in Grantchester. Perhaps he just had an instinct for a place that would suit them both. She was not unhappy, like his home, she found it an easy place to be. And he remained an easy person to be with. Now that they had slept together, now that it was a thing in the past, it seemed they had risked nothing of their friendship by sharing a bed. The idea that it could have risked anything at all seemed incredible, too ridiculous to have even considered it. On the contrary, they had added to it and subtracted nothing.

When her thoughts drifted towards the future, albeit an unknown and obscure one, their ages inevitably surfaced in those thoughts. Or rather, it was inevitable that the difference in their ages should feature, for they had more than twenty years between them. At what age did it stop mattering, at what age did it start again? Today it mattered nothing at all, but in another five, ten, what then? Of course it would depend on health and fitness and hormones. Which took her back to Florence and William. The attraction must have been great to bridge a gap of forty-plus years, regardless of health or hormones. It's never difficult to see the attraction a younger woman holds for an older man, but is the reverse always as cynical and obvious? William would likely have been comfortably placed as a retired lawyer, but was unlikely to have been in the millionaire class. Money, sex, position or what? Love? She wouldn't discount it altogether.

Lydia circled the room, absentmindedly looking for distraction as much as something to concentrate her thoughts. The walls were lined with hundreds, probably thousands of volumes, nearly all behind locked glass doors. She could read the titles of only those on the lowest four or five shelves and many of those were too faded to decipher past her own reflection. Immediately above the writing desk hung a full-length portrait of a man and a woman. Squinting, she could just make out the inscription on a small plate on the bottom edge of the frame. *Sir Nathaniel Wykham and Lady Elizabeth Wykham.* Lydia guessed it might have dated to around 1910. Even allowing for men appearing older than they were and ladies being made to look far younger, the couple appeared to have many years between them. Again the question: money, sex or position? Perhaps an arrangement to suit both parties and to suit

105

both families? Perhaps an urgent need to produce an heir? With William G certainly deceased, along with his only known son, had Laurence come into the reckoning for inheritance, as surely his mother must have done?

Rather than look for the record of death, look for the results of death, look for a will. A retired solicitor would surely have had a will signed and sealed long before his nuptials with the young Florence. There might be no official record, it might have all been handled privately but it cost nothing to find out. The main index available to Lydia had nothing later than 1966 so it was not a great surprise when her search for a will for William Durham gave no results. The nearest was a Walter G Durham in 1963. Out of simple curiosity Lydia clicked through to see the entry. It was not what she was looking for, but it did give her an idea. The entry read *'Durham Walter Granville otherwise Wallace otherwise Wally...'* Like many people, Walter had been known by different names by different people and probably at different times. His closest friends might never have known him as anything but Wally, while Wallace had been reserved for the taxman.

Ignoring a first name, Lydia established the list of all the recorded Durham wills up to 1966, then she set about inspecting each of the entries. She was prepared for a longer search than it took. In the first volume for 1960 she had her answer. *Durham Bill otherwise Billy otherwise William Gordon of Roseland Rothsay Road Bedford died 7th January 1960 at Clinica Santa Sophia, Funchal, Portuguese Madeira. Probate 21st June Bedford to Robert Ballard solicitor and notary public. Effects £173,291 11s 8d.* Lydia couldn't quite believe it, a treasure chest of information in four typed lines. She was so excited she hardly knew what to look at first. A double check of the address with that given on his marriage certificate less than a month earlier confirmed it was the same man. Less than a month - William G was surely still on his honeymoon when he died in Funchal. And he left a handy sum for his beneficiaries, it would be a fine amount today, but back in 1960 it would have been called a fortune. Out of curiosity she found a calculator which would tell her exactly what it was worth in today's money and was shocked to find it was close to £3m. Lucky

Florence, assuming that she was the main beneficiary. A copy of the will would reveal that and maybe a few other things, it might even throw light on the identity of Laurence's father.

She could wait no longer. Scooping up her things she ran up the stairs to their room.

'You look very pleased with yourself,' he said with a huge smile of his own.

'I am. A discovery in Laurence's saga. I'll show you.'

In the afternoon they walked down into the little valley below the hotel, across the water-meadows by the Windrush into Bourton and its summer busyness of tea-rooms and made-in-China trinkets. They loitered over jars of local honey with Jacqueline vaguely in mind, and hesitated over boxes of fudge with local postcards stuck to the lid for Gloria's sweet tooth. At a bookshop they were politely refused entry until they'd finished their ice-creams, then spent half-an-hour browsing the packed shelves without finding anything compelling. At four they took coffee and scones with strawberry jam and clotted cream beside the sparkling river and ignored the endless traffic creeping through the town. By five-thirty they were back at the hotel, Lydia noticeably more breathless than Stephen after the climb back up through the woods.

To their mutual surprise and no little pleasure they fell onto the bed and made love before they had a chance to notice it was still daylight or remember they were no longer teenagers. Spontaneity gave them the wings that tired limbs would have denied them and they drifted in a contented embrace for almost an hour before bathing.

As they sat to their meal on the terrace, surrounded by the quiet chatter of expensive dining, Stephen said, 'Lydia, I was wondering...'

She cut him off immediately. 'Please don't, don't wonder about anything today. It may all be a dream for all I know, we may wake tomorrow and it'll all be gone, it'll be raining and cold and I'll be in Oxford and it will all have been a terrible mistake. If it is then it is, but today is today. Sorry, I just don't want to wonder about anything, or hope for anything or regret anything. Now is lovely.'

It all tumbled out with far more force and certainty than she expected or intended. The very next moment it felt selfish and ungrateful. 'Thank you, I should say thank you,' she added quietly.

She didn't see Stephen frown at her outburst, she had her eyes closed and was trying not to gulp down her wine. She knew without hesitation that it was she who had burst the bubble in her anxiety to preserve the idyllic moment. Whatever it was he was wondering about wouldn't have changed a single jot of the moment, the loveliness of now would have been quite unsullied by a gentle speculation of this or that or what path they might walk on in tomorrow's sunshine. She felt sick at her ability to spoil perfection with a childish desire to make it last for ever.

Whether Stephen understood quite why or how, after a few moments to consider, he found the perfect healing response. 'You're right. If ever there was a time to live for the present, live for the very minute, it's now. Tomorrow will take care of itself.'

7

The little entrance area at Willoughby House was noisier than usual. It normally had the hushed tones of a funeral parlour, as if those present were practising their regrets and condolences while their relatives boxed in their little rooms along the corridors were still living. But as Lydia pushed through the swing door late on Tuesday afternoon she became aware of angry words being exchanged at the reception desk.

A woman in a print dress with a large floral pattern stood hands on hips with her back to Lydia. It was, she thought, singularly ill-chosen, both in design and fit. It was not a particularly hot day but a faint V of sweat darkened the dress from shoulder blades to waistline. The woman spoke with that hissed whisper which ensures all can hear. The member of staff was hidden behind her, but Lydia immediately recognised smiley-face's nauseating sympathy and chose to stay out of sight to hear what complaint was in progress.

'And after all you've done too. So unfortunate, he can be very difficult.'

'And the language! You wouldn't believe it!'

'Oh I know, he can be,' she leant forward as if to be discreet, 'so, explicit, if you know what I mean.'

'Explicit! Disgusting, more like. Thinks he can get away with anything he likes, the dirty old man. Well if he thinks I'm doing anything else...' her voice trailed off as smiley-face peered round her and recognised Lydia waiting patiently in the woman's shadow.

'Hello there,' she said in a voice uncomfortably placed between sympathy and smiles.

Lydia nodded a greeting and the woman turned to see who had interrupted her flow of invective. Small black eyes in a pasty face swept Lydia from tip to toe, then rested back on her face, defiant, suspicious, unashamed of anything Lydia might have overheard. She half turned as if to confront Lydia, confirming her place at the desk and her right to be attended to before anyone else.

'I'll just go down, shall I?' Lydia suggested, avoiding naming names.

'Yes, do,' said smiley, then added mischievously in her brightest nursery-nurse voice, 'Do you know Monica Sanders, Freddie's neighbour? I wasn't sure if you two had met.' It was as Lydia had feared and half suspected, there would not be many residents of the hospice who'd readily give foul-mouthed abuse to a visitor, not many Freddies cursing their well-wishers. 'This is Freddie's daughter, Linda Silverstream.'

'You? Silverstream? You're the medal woman aren't you?' Monica Sanders pulled herself up to her full height and crossed her arms over her chest. 'You never said anything about being his daughter,' she added indignantly.

'No, I don't think I did,' Lydia said, surprised at the ease of her own deception.

'Well, you're flavour of the month now. He never said a word about you all these years he's lived next-door to me.' She stretched her head forward, closer to Lydia's face, 'You're welcome to him. He owes me money for his papers, you goin' to pay me?'

'Have you asked Freddie?'

'He knows.'

'I'll ask him. He'll pay what's owed.'

Lydia turned away down the corridor to Freddie's room, ignoring smiley-face's belated reminder to sign the visitors' book. It was far easier to behave as Freddie's daughter than she would have believed, although she did think afterwards how a real daughter might have slapped Monica Sanders very hard and brought a little colour to those pale cheeks.

She paused at his door and knocked, but there was no answer. Tentatively she opened it a little, gently calling out his name. His bed was empty, but she could see he was slumped in his chair by the window, his back to the door. Beside him stood the IV and the monitor. Involuntarily, her eye was drawn to the glowing numbers, and the slow rhythm of the wave across the screen. She wondered if she'd have the courage to approach him if there'd been no pulsing wave, if the numbers were zero. She called out again and saw his hand raised, vaguely beckoning her into the room.

'Hello, Freddie,' she said softly, fearing to disturb him, even though she knew he wasn't asleep.

'You, is it.' That deep hollow voice was slower than before, each word an effort. He opened his eyes and it seemed to Lydia that the colour had almost gone. Dilated pupils under white lids.

'Yes, it's me, Lydia. Come to see you and talk about old times, maybe talk about some people you might know.'

'Took yer time.' A week ago this gentle prod would have been a curse, now he said it as if out of habit, all venom gone. Lydia thought that he'd shrunk a little more too. The once great bear of a man nothing but a shell.

'I met your neighbour, Monica. You've upset her.'

He half snorted, half gurgled what might have been a laugh. 'Good.' He drew another breath. 'Worth the effort then.'

It occurred to her that Freddie must have put a lot into abusing Monica Sanders. What she saw now was the result, all his energy spent on cursing and calling her bitch and whore and no doubt more besides.

'Yes,' she smiled a disapproving smile, 'certainly worth the effort.' Quite why she had taken such an instant dislike to the person who'd put her and Freddie together, she would've been unable to explain.

He lifted his head a little and looked her in the eye. He seemed expressionless until his right eye closed in a slow wink. 'Clever girl, eh.'

'Maybe. Do you remember why I first came to see you, why I keep coming back?'

'Yeah. Medals. Still got 'em?'

Lydia nodded.

'Linda.'

She nodded again.

'Well, what yer got?'

'Something. Maybe nothing.' She leant closer to him. 'Only you'll know if it's something or nothing. You don't want to tell me anything, answer any questions, I don't know why. All right, I won't ask any questions then you won't have to answer. I'll say things and if you know they're wrong you tell me. If you don't know or if you do know and they're right, you say nothing. What do you say, can we do that, will that save you from telling me things you don't want to tell?'

'You,' he struggled to find the breath for the question, 'you ever been a copper?'

'No.'

'You shoulda been.'

'I don't think so. Are you sitting comfortably? Then I'll begin,' Lydia said, hoping the old catch-phrase might stir a memory for him.

A hint of a smile crossed his face. 'Get on, girl,' he said.

'Let me tell you a story,' she began, 'although exactly when it began is hard to say. It's about a girl, but it starts with a man, we'll call him Freddie although his proper name was something different, something like George Frederick Thompson. Freddie grew up in the East End where he went to school as a child in the 30s. He was still a child when the war came. He saw and heard a lot of bad things, people killed, his friend Mickey was one of them.' His eyes were closed. Again the involuntary glance at the monitor where the wave continued its flow across the screen.

'Freddie had a lot of adventures in the war years and afterwards too, most likely. One of them was with a girl he knew, a girl called Bright, Bright as a Button he used to say.' She saw his lips move slightly to repeat the familiar words. 'One day in September 1956, the twenty-ninth to be exact, the girl called Bright, Sylvia Bright she was, this girl had a baby, another girl. She had the baby down in Kent, away from her family in the East End. She called the baby Linda. Which was funny in a way, because a little while later Sylvia's sister Catherine also had a baby girl and she called her baby Belinda. So there were these two baby girl cousins called Linda and Belinda. Another funny thing happened a little while later when Sylvia came to register her baby. She put down that the baby's father was the man we started with, she put down that George Frederick Thompson was the father.'

Lydia paused to check her notes. He opened his eyes. 'Is that it?'

'No, far from. Tell me if you're too tired and want to rest.'

'Get on.'

'The really funny thing was that poor Freddie was dead when she put his name down on baby Linda's birth certificate. Of course he might not have been dead, but she said he was. Why would she have done that? Maybe he was dead, poor man, and poor baby Linda had no daddy. But maybe Freddie's name was just a handy one to put down, because if he was dead, he wouldn't complain would he? And Sylvia couldn't be blamed for not having a husband, could she?

'Whatever the reasons, little Linda probably grew up without a daddy, although she probably spent a lot of time with her cousin Belinda and Belinda's parents Catherine and Peter Andrews. It seems that Linda and Belinda went to school together and when a few years later Linda's mum Sylvia decided to get married...'

'No,' he interrupted her, disbelieving.

'No? Something you're sure of? Or maybe she did.' Lydia reached out and touched his hand. His skin was translucent, paper-thin, criss-crossed with dark blood vessels, blotched with brown spots.

'Never thought.'

'We never do. Nobody ever thinks. Shall I go on?'

He nodded and shrank back, turtle-like, into his collar.

'So it seems that in 1965, when Linda would have been nine, Sylvia married Norman Brooks. They lived in Leyton and had a listing in the phone book from 1966 onwards for a few years. But it seems Linda didn't change her school, the one she went to with her cousin Belinda. It was just a couple of streets away from where Belinda lived, which was still in Stepney.

'We have to skip forward here, because I can't find any mention of Linda again for a few years, and certainly no official record for quite a while. Then, when she was almost sixteen, it seems she tried out for a little part in a film. The story goes that she was turned down and told to change her name because there was already an actress called Linda Thompson.'

Lydia looked to see if this fresh mention of the Thompson name would bring another reaction from Freddie. His lips again moved silently, but he made no sign of approval or otherwise.

'Before I go on, the idea that she changed her name from Linda Thompson to something else does at least tell us that she used the Thompson name, and it's likely she knew the name of the father on her birth certificate. And those two things seem to me to suggest that he was her real father, but we might never know for sure.'

She was fishing, hoping for an answer to a question she wasn't asking, but Freddie remained silent, shut away in his own world of memories, fed by his narrator.

She continued. 'Now suddenly it's easier to find traces of Linda, they're littered all over the place. Her acting career never hit the heights, but she had the looks and was in a whole list of little films, B films they used to call them, and even one or two more well known. She used the name Lynn Brighton. Did you ever hear of her?'

Freddie shook his head. The movement was so small that it might have been no more than a tremor.

'Here's something. I hope it isn't too difficult for you, maybe you don't want to look. I've printed it as big as I could. It's a picture of Lynn Brighton, one of those black-and-white studio portraits, a publicity photo. She would've been about eighteen.'

He opened his eyes and his mouth fell open, a mix of suspicion and amazement on his face. After a few moments he fumbled with his grimy glasses and extended a shaky hand to receive the photo. It trembled in his hand so much he couldn't see it properly.

'Let me clean your glasses.'

He passed them to her and she went to the sink and washed and dried them. They looked as if nobody had done that small thing for him in a long time. He was peering at the picture through a little magnifying glass when she returned to sit beside him. The trembling had lessened and he rested the paper on a cushion on his lap, looking long and hard at the young woman in the photo. It showed a typical wannabe-actress pose, leaning forward with a low neckline, a faraway look in big eyes, an elegant hand resting on her cheek. Everything a casting director could want: a dramatic gaze, slim and elegant, curves well hinted at. *Always Lynn Brighton* was handwritten across the bottom of the picture, whether in the starlet's own writing or her agent's would never be known.

'What d'yer think?' he slurred through suddenly thick lips.

'What do I think, Freddie? I think she's Lynn Brighton. I think her parents were Sylvia Bright and George Thompson. I think she might be the Linda you wanted me to find. What do you think?'

'She's Sylvie's girl, yes.' He let trembling fingers trace across the face in the picture. 'Just like her mother, pretty as a picture, bright as a button.'

'And I think you're her father.'

He was silent.

'Freddie, there's more to this story. Not about her father, not about that, but about Linda and her life as Lynn Brighton. Would you like to hear it? I should say it's not all a happy story, there's not much happiness in it.'

He considered for a moment before he said, 'She's gone?' and when Lydia didn't answer immediately he knew she had. 'She's gone before me, eh? I reckon it was her that day on Oxford Street, swinging along like she hadn't a care in the world.'

'Yes, probably. If she looked like her mother, then yes, probably.' What did it matter, she thought, whether it was his girl or any other, far better he should think it was.

Lydia couldn't quite understand why she was nervous of presenting her next discovery, but she hesitated over telling him, trying to gauge his fitness for another surprise. One way and another he'd had a taxing couple of hours.

'How are you? Is this all right for you, going on the way we are? Or do you need to rest?'

'I'll rest a long time soon. Get on, girl, I asked yer and yer done it. Lot of work, eh?'

'Not really. Other people have written all about her being an actress, other people have recorded all the dates and so on. I find what other people have done and sew it all together.'

He nodded and spoke silently to himself, then looked up and smiled at her, motioning with his head that she should continue.

'Did you ever have a computer, Freddie? Or use one at the library or a friend's?'

He shook his head. 'Nah, never did.'

She fished her laptop out of her bag and set it up. 'I think you'd be amazed at all the things you can see and read. I found something I thought you'd like. It's one of those films from the 70s, one that Linda was in. She only has a little part, I think she was referred to as 'third beach girl' in the credits. I watched it all but her piece is only a minute or two. I have a copy to show you. It was called *Confessions of a Lifeguard.* Are you all right?'

He'd sunk down deeper into his seat, and the little waves followed each other more quickly across the tell-tale monitor. *Always Lynn Brighton* was scrunched in his hand as he gripped the arm of his chair. The air rasped in his throat as he tried to control his disobedient body.

'There's time,' she said, 'Take your time.' She rested her hand on his holding the photo and regretted her hesitation at that first meeting. Human touch. She could imagine all too well the need for human touch at the end.

In a few minutes the spasm of pain subsided and his breath came a little easier. 'Good girl,' he said and smoothed out the crumpled picture of his Linda. 'A film? Long?'

'No, I have it ready for just the scene with her in it. When you're ready I'll show you.'

He nodded and she clicked on the snippet of *Confessions of a Lifeguard.* A young man in swimming trunks and a bathing hat with the word 'lifeguard' written round it, emerges from a gentle sea with a young woman in his arms. After a couple of staggering steps he lays her on the sand. Two other girls in skimpy bikinis stand close by, anxiously watching. The lifeguard looks earnestly at the prone and apparently lifeless swimmer, then rolls her on her side. As he does so she coughs and allows some water to trickle from her mouth. She briefly opens her eyes and winks at her two friends. The lifeguard does not see this, and clearly embarrassed, says he must perform mouth-to-mouth resuscitation and prepares to do so, rolling the girl onto her back again. He has no idea where to touch the girl, who has large breasts, exaggerated by the low camera angle. Once the lifeguard has his mouth over the girl's, her recovery is immediate and she wraps him in a tight embrace. The

116

second girl says, 'Oh look, that's done the trick, lucky thing.' Then in a head-and-shoulders shot all to herself, third beach girl says, 'I think I might need some of that.' The lifeguard, looking dazed, extricates himself from the first girl's clutches, whereupon third beach girl falls on him. The small crowd that has gathered round applaud. The scene ends with the lifeguard being chased along the beach into the distance by the three giggling girls.

Lydia had the exact place on the recording noted and quickly moved it back to show a single frame of Lynn Brighton just before she spoke. Freddie had a thin smile and was nodding. 'Must be,' he said, 'Couldn't be anyone but Sylvie's girl. Her mother all over. Cheeky, too. That was Sylvie.'

'It's short, like to see it again?'

He nodded, and they watched the action together. When it finished neither of them spoke. If he wanted to know more, Lydia knew the story was not a happy one. She was in no rush to taint his pleasure. Freddie let sight and sound of his daughter soak into him, become part of him after an absence of nearly sixty years. The slivers of knowledge expanded infinitely to fill the void where memory should have been. They told him nothing real of the person, nothing of her life or her troubles. But they told him she'd been lovely, cheeky like her mother had been, full of energy and life and he savoured every second.

At length, when he had her securely inside him, or as much of her as he ever would, he said, 'She's gone then?'

'Yes,' Lydia said softly, 'she died quite young, she died before her mother too. I don't have the details,' she lied straight faced. 'No certificate or anything, but according to a couple of writers she died in Munich when she was just forty-two.' No need to tell him anything of a desperate, lonely end in a grubby hotel room, no need to speak of poverty or addiction. What he had was true and he'd never know what was missing.

He nodded, as if she were confirming what he'd suspected all along.

Having given him news of his daughter's death, Lydia felt safe to speak of Sylvia's fate. 'Freddie, your Sylvie's gone too, did I say that? More than ten years ago now, she died in a place called

Wanstead, not that far from where she'd lived most of her life in Leyton.'

'Wanstead? The Flats we called it. Lived out there did she? All gone, and me too, nearly.'

'Well, maybe not quite all gone. Do you remember Sylvie's sister Catherine?'

He looked puzzled, shook his head slightly, shaping the name on his lips. 'One little sister she had, she weren't what you said. Can't think of it now.'

'It doesn't matter. But maybe she's still alive, she may know more, she might know more about Linda. I could try to find her? She was Belinda's mother, your Linda's cousin. She married Peter Andrews.'

He raised his hand, waving urgently. 'Nah, nah,' he gurgled, 'you promised, just you and me. You can't talk to 'em. Nobody.' The anxiety gave him strength, pushed the blood round a little faster, made the yellow tell-tale twinkle on his monitor.

She had much more she could tell him, records of unhappy marriages for his Linda, traces of her life on the fringes of show business, places she'd called home, courts she'd appeared in. She knew the address in Leyton where his sweetheart Sylvie had lived for thirty years with her husband Norman and the phone number they were listed under. She could tell him another dozen facts but one more thing might be really important, more important than the random events that trace someone's existence in the world: it seems his Linda may have had a child, a daughter. To find her, to even be sure she existed, might take more time than she had without some outside help. Of the survivors, Catherine would certainly be best placed to provide that help.

'It's all right Freddie, I won't.'

She was greatly tempted to hint at a granddaughter, he might excuse her from her promise, perhaps even give him reason to keep his grip on life a little longer.

'Yer can't, it's the deal,' he pleaded. The man from a week or so ago who'd gripped her tightly by the wrist and made plain his demands had already left the room, only his shadow remained.

'Yeah, it's a deal,' she said patting his hand, soothing away his fears.

∞

Stephen and Lydia had not spoken since their fond goodbyes of Sunday evening. Their weekend had changed everything and changed nothing. For the future everything and anything was possible, although they'd avoided talk of such things. For the present they had familiar spaces in which to continue their familiar lives, even though Lydia knew she must prepare for change in hers. Their routines did not include daily communication but she was pleased to find a postcard from him on her doormat on Wednesday. An aerial view of Cambridge was backed by her address and the wonderfully clichéd phrase '*Wish you were here.*' Without fuss or extravagance it stated what she hoped she knew already: the weekend had been as good for him as it had for her. The memory made her smile and a frisson of pleasure ran down her spine. She would call him later.

She recognised a second envelope too, from the solicitors dealing with her ex father-in-law's estate. She put it to one side for a few minutes, preparing herself for the news of the promised inheritance. Like dreaming of a lottery win, she played with ideas of just how much would make a real difference to her life. With the prospect of being jobless getting closer every day, she decided that quite a small sum would make a big difference. True, she indulged herself with her investigations and spent far more than she ought in that respect, but otherwise she was careful with her money. The last cheque had been banked, finally, into her modest savings and remained untouched. By the feel of the envelope another cheque was stapled to the letter.

The third piece of mail came from her employer, reminding her of the appointment on Friday morning to discuss her options in the forthcoming re-organisation. It was formal notice of something previously arranged, but the mealy-mouthed wording of it all emphasised her sense of betrayal. The ill-concealed intention to be rid of her and her colleagues with the minimum cost and maximum speed was insulting. Idly she wondered if it was all

119

calculated to annoy, calculated to encourage angry resignations and unauthorised absences. Both were certainly tempting.

The opening of the solicitor's letter would be a little ceremony for one. She took the envelope and a glass of wine to the garden, then in case a second might be called for, took the bottle in a bucket of cold water. Anticipating the unknown was delicious. Even a lottery winner would know how much was involved, but this was a mystery. She tasted the wine, savoured it a moment as if about to pronounce on its quality, then carefully slit open the envelope and withdrew the contents. Heavy, bonded paper with the name of the firm embossed upon it. Two sheets of paper stapled together, not one sheet and a cheque. No matter, the details would be there, a bank transfer would be arranged. But the details weren't there. The letter indicated only that a 'substantial amount' was involved, that there were still some 'outstanding issues' and what they called 'groundless challenges' to the final distribution. She was invited to attend the lawyer's office at her convenience with a provisional appointment having been set for Friday at three.

The ceremony was over before it even got going, nothing to celebrate beyond the vague promise of 'substantial'. She took a gulp more wine and slumped back into the chair. Friday would certainly be interesting: two appointments to decide her future, then a journey to one of those futures via Freddie's past in Bedford. The cleverness of her thoughts briefly amused her. Freddie's past reminded her that a book she'd ordered had not arrived. Nor had the additional certificates in Freddie's story or those for Laurence Durham's somehow sadder quest. There was plenty more she could look at and theorise about, but she'd been deflated by anticlimax and the energy had drained from her. The warmth of the evening sun, the soft fuzz of the wine, the pleasures of not-quite-identifiable memory, all conspired to keep her in her chair. She even had a wrap should it become chilly later in the evening. And besides, she could research her puzzles as easily here as anywhere else. She found solutions in her head as much as her computer, turning her problems this way and that, considering possibilities, divining probabilities. Finding information and then making some sense of it didn't usually happen by chance, it happened because Lydia asked the right questions, tried the unlikely and imagined the what-if.

By seven the bottle had gone, and the evening was cooler than she would have liked, even with the fleece wrapped round her. She'd drifted on the edge of sleep for an hour, her dreams a jumble of half-truths, imagined scenes and ancient history. The lawyer's letter had done more than disappoint, it had opened a window on the lost world of her marriage. There would be only one person offering a 'groundless challenge' to John Fordham's will, and that was his son Michael. He'd never been close with either of his parents and Lydia had sometimes wondered if she'd filled that gap as much as the daughter-they-never-had role. Now most likely it was Michael challenging that place she'd held in his father's heart as much as challenging the will. The Fordhams had lived well, never wanted for anything, so far as she knew. There would be plenty to share out when everything was sold off, Michael should have no cause for complaint.

Absentmindedly she wondered about the other will, the one she'd found at the weekend and been so excited to tell Stephen about. Had she ordered a copy? She couldn't remember doing so, but she certainly remembered intending to. She remembered running up the stairs and seeing Stephen in their room. She remembered clearly how good it felt, sharing her discovery with him a few minutes after making it. Perhaps that had been it, the thrill of discovery more important than the discovery itself. She reached for the wine, and found the empty bottle bobbing in the bucket.

On the way to the fridge she found Stephen's postcard face down on the floor. *Wish you were here* stared up to rebuke her for the wasted evening. She could at least have called him. Do it right now, she thought, do it now or you'll hate yourself. Five rings then his answering service clicked in. Wednesday, supper in college. She should tell him about Gloria's wedding plans, ask him to fix up a meeting with Laurence, check if Jacqueline would be there at the weekend, let him know about Freddie, the solicitor's letter, her Friday interview.

'Hello, it's me. I got your card. Thanks. See you Friday.'

The offices of Ffynne & Co were tucked away in one of those medieval alleyways behind Oriel. Star Yard is half thoroughfare, half courtyard, still cobbled and unlikely to be otherwise so long as the college owns it, which will probably be another few centuries at least. Lydia wondered how John Fordham had chosen this firm to be his executors. Perhaps it was tradition, the Fordhams had been an Oxford family for many generations. Family lawyers tend to remain in post unless they do something very wrong.

Geoffrey Spencer was a small man, shorter than Lydia. His premature baldness gave him an older look than his thirty-odd years, a look he cultivated rather than contested. His hairless dome rose from a semi-circle of wavy brown hair above large horn-rimmed glasses, exaggerating the size of his head in relation to his body. Immaculate collar and tie, with perfect cuffs under expensive pinstripes were similarly at odds with his cluttered office. Lydia couldn't see that it was dusty, but it seemed like the sort of office which might easily be so.

He was polite but straight to the point, as befits a lawyer with his last client on a Friday and a weekend stay with friends near La Rochelle uppermost in his mind.

'John Fordham's will has proved to be somewhat difficult to execute, although these difficulties are now resolved. The will is clear enough, but the results are probably not what he intended. I'm sure you're concerned about your own position, but you need not be, yours, and one other's, are fixed bequests and are easily covered by the value of the estate.'

'I have no idea of what he left me, or really why I'm here at all. I assume the difficulty has come from his son Michael, my ex.' It seemed slightly indelicate, a little money-grubbing, to ask the size of the inheritance, although Lydia could hardly contain herself.

He peered at her over his glasses, dark brown eyes over dark brown frames. 'Certainly. I'll try to be brief,' he said, glancing at his watch. 'John Fordham was most careful in making his will. You and a charity are the only two beneficiaries with fixed bequests. The remainder goes to his son Michael. That is perfectly straightforward. But he also stipulated that the whole of his estate should be for the use of his wife, Cicely, during her lifetime if she survived him. Which as you know, she did. The bulk was made up of the family home, some investments and savings accounts.

'In the intervening period the total value has shrunk considerably. There are many reasons for this, not least the economic downturn, the crash of 2008, but also some poor advice. Of course advice is only poor or good after the event. At the time it is simply advice.

'The result of all this is that the charity is now the largest beneficiary, your bequest is the second largest and the residual amount is small in comparison.' He peered at her again. 'I expect you can see the difficulty this leads to.'

'I think so. I end up with more than Michael.'

'Exactly, Miss Silverstream, in a nutshell.'

'And he's challenging that, er, process?'

'Again you are precisely right. He is challenging the process. He is quite understandably looking for someone to blame for the loss of the inheritance he believes his father intended.'

'But not challenging the will?'

'Not directly. This morning I heard he has been independently advised a challenge to the will would be unlikely to succeed.'

'My bequest, Mr Spencer. Exactly how much is involved?'

'Oh. Yes, I'm sorry. It is £350,000.'

Lydia stared at the little bald lawyer in his crisp blue-and-white-striped shirt with his perfectly knotted blue silk tie. It was a great deal of money. It was more money than she would ever accumulate herself, no matter how careful she was. She swallowed and fought down a rising tide of panic with what she hoped was a sensible question asked in a sensible voice. 'And Michael currently stands to receive how much?'

'A little less than £48,000.'

'Which at one time might've been a great deal more.'

'Difficult to say exactly, but probably nearer ten times that amount.' He glanced at his watch again. 'I wanted to meet you to see if there was anything we could do to help. We can simply issue a cheque, probably next week, or make some other transfer.'

He continued with some banking details and the need for Lydia to sign her approval of accounts but she wasn't really listening any more. Her head was a kaleidoscope of questions all competing for her attention. She could understand Michael's position, a far from happy one, and wondered if she should offer to help remedy it. The morning interview with her employer had been far less rewarding than this one with the solicitor. When, a little mischievously, she'd added a throwaway comment about seeing a lawyer, a sudden frost had descended on the conversation, which was terminated soon afterwards. And then again, what would she do with so much money? How much to give away - and to whom? Who would she leave it all to, and should she now have a will of her own? Through this confusion she was dimly aware of him offering to introduce advisers, offering to act in property matters, or any personal affairs if needed. When she focused her attention once more on the moment, she saw that he was straightening his papers, and closing the buff covers of the file. *Fordham, John Arthur* was written across it in a meticulous black script more appropriate to a previous century.

'Miss Silverstream?' He looked expectantly at her. 'You'll let me know about the transfer?'

'Yes,' she said dumbly.

'Was there something else?'

'Have you made a will, Mr Spencer?'

He peered over his glasses, frowning. 'For myself? Well, no, not yet.' He smiled awkwardly. 'I'll tell you that you really should, especially now, but I'm no better than most people. I'll wait until I'm sure of what I want.'

'And when you do, let's say it was next week, would you ask one of your colleagues here to be the executor?'

'Why do you ask?'

'I wondered if it would be the usual thing for a solicitor to ask someone in his own firm, or not.'

'There might be a conflict of interest, although right now I can't think of one.' He glanced discretely at his watch again.

'How many partners do you have here?'

'Three others, we're a small practice.'

'Do you know who you'd choose?'

'If I did I'm not sure…'

'No, quite right. It's some research I'm doing. For a friend. A solicitor died and left a will and I wondered if he would have asked a colleague. It was a long time ago.'

'Ah, right,' he nodded. 'It will say in the will, it will say who's appointed as executor. Or it should. A solicitor should have got that part right.' He smiled and rose from his chair to indicate the meeting was over. 'You'll let me know?'

'Yes, thank you,' she said heading for the door which he opened for her. On the point of leaving she turned to him again. 'The other beneficiary, the charity, what did John leave to them?'

'Ah, an easy sum to remember, half a million.'

'God,' she said without thinking, 'I hope it wasn't a cat's home.'

He smiled at this. 'Many people do,' he said, 'but not John Fordham. It will go to a very small organisation here in Oxford, a mental health charity.'

8

'Have you slept in here before?'

Lydia was lying on her side, her head resting in the scoop between his shoulder and chest, her hand on the flat of his stomach. She was wide awake, more stunned than drowsy from lovemaking. Stephen lay stretched on his back, in total relaxation and thinking of little, yet with a mind far from empty. A happy collection of past scenes replayed themselves for his exclusive pleasure behind closed eyes. Among them were fond memories of when they'd first met, the walk they'd shared by chance, the pub lunch with each paying for their own.

'I don't think so.'

He had slept there before, he knew he had, he remembered very well. He and Elspeth had slept there while their room was redecorated, he'd slept there after she'd died and the house was so empty when Jacqueline was away. But he knew the answer Lydia hoped for, what would please her, and pleasing her was more important than the precision of memory.

'Good.'

She'd mentioned it almost as soon as she'd arrived. There would be a time when they might sleep together in the main bedroom, his bedroom, the marital bedroom, but for tonight, their first together at The Old Rectory, she wanted him to stay in her room. It was, and always would be, Jacqueline's room, but Lydia had grown comfortable in it, despite his daughter's apparent ambivalence towards her. And besides, hadn't she insisted that Lydia sleep in her bed? Lydia didn't suppose she'd intended it to be with her father, then scolded herself for such cattiness.

'Did you talk to Jacqueline this week?'

'Yes, briefly. She's in Boston for a few days. Went on Wednesday I think.'

'Everything all right?'

'Sounded like it. Yes, I'm sure it is.' He turned his face to her and kissed her forehead squeezing her a little as he did so. 'And about you and I, yes, everything is all right about that, too.'

She tilted her head to return his kiss. 'Thank you.'

Talk at six on a summer evening of where they would sleep together had encouraged them into bed before seven. Now at eight they were unsure of the evening, whether it was too late to be restarted or too early to end. It was certainly too light for sleep beyond Stephen's post-coital doze. These were unaccustomed pleasures for each of them, neither quite remembering what should come next.

'I called on Wednesday, then I realised you'd be at college.'

'Yes, I got your message. You sounded different. I'm not sure how exactly. I'd wondered if you'd had second thoughts, wondered if the risk had been worth it, or whether we'd lost the gamble.'

'No, I think we won,' she said, but the excitement of victory was missing. 'Wednesday was a funny day. Actually, every day has been a funny day this week. Things have been going to happen for ages, like you and I were something that was going to happen one day. Now suddenly it's happened, is happening. Nothing is the same.'

'Something else? I know there's your job, any news on that?'

'Not really.'

What should she tell him? Details of an unsatisfactory meeting to have the exact terms of her redundancy spelt out? Or how disorienting it was to have that safest of anchors removed while simultaneously gaining a fortune? And all the while she had the guilt of her puzzles remaining unsolved and neglected while the time for action dribbled away to nothing. She'd lunched with the once unmarriageable Gloria and listened while she planned her wedding. Now here she was making love with him in Jacqueline's bedroom. She couldn't tell him how there was a part of her wishing none of it had changed, how the newness had already worn thin and she wished it could all be as it was. In the old world she knew pretty well how to behave, knew her limitations, knew the couple of things she was good at. Nothing in this new world was familiar.

As her thoughts carried her away from him, she saw them both lying there, posed in the classic position for lovers who've made their love. They even had the sheets drawn loosely but discreetly around them lest some inquisitive sparrow should observe them through the open window. Beyond this fanciful out-of-body drift lay the paralysis of disconnection, so appealing to slide quietly into. He'd pulled her out of the quicksand just a week ago and the memory made her grip his flesh to stay afloat again. He flinched a little as her nails bit.

'Bad dreams?'

'Yes. Sorry. Gone now.'

Stephen waited until the moment had become history before he said, 'Do you have anything for poor old Laurence? I mean anything you're ready to tell him?'

'Only what you already know, but yes, I meant to ask you about seeing him.'

'You might be in luck then. If we go to the Botanic Garden tomorrow he may be there. He may even be there with his mother. He tells me they sometimes go for lunch on Saturdays. I know you've wanted to go so I said we might bump into him there.'

'With his mother! Oh, yes can we go?' Lydia begged, half sitting up, suddenly animated, like a child promised ice-cream.

'Only if you swear not to say anything. Laurence was insistent you should say nothing in front of his mother. You mustn't know him, all right?'

'Of course! I wouldn't say anything in front of her!'

'I said we'd probably go, see if we meet and take it from there.'

∞

Lydia hadn't been prepared for the extent of the gardens. Her previous views from the top deck of a bus had given little clue to their size and she'd imagined them to be similar to those in Oxford, something akin to the gardens of a large country house. But in Cambridge she found a huge area more like an estate than a garden. After they'd walked for twenty minutes or so she wondered how they might know they were even in the same area as the Durhams, never mind bump into them.

A little after noon, Stephen steered them towards the café. 'We'll circle round for a while and see what happens.'

Sure enough, within a few minutes they spotted the round figure of Laurence Durham strolling towards the café with his mother on his arm. Age blurs the difference between the generations but even at a distance there was no mistaking them for husband and wife. With a little acceleration in their step, Stephen and Lydia contrived to arrive at the entrance at precisely the same moment as their quarry.

'Hello Laurence,' Stephen greeted his colleague with a good show of surprise.

'Good heavens! Stephen, what are you doing here? We've never seen you in the gardens before,' said the equally surprised Laurence. He turned immediately to his mother who was staring stony faced at Lydia and Stephen. 'Mother, this is Professor Sir Stephen Kellaway from college. Stephen, my mother, Florence.'

Stephen held out his hand and Florence extended hers, limply, so that he might touch it briefly. At the sound of his titles she'd looked up at him with a softer face and forced a pinched smile to the corners of her mouth. She continued to study him for a moment before looking back at Lydia. No question that this was the same woman as Lydia had seen in the restaurant. Same long grey hair pulled back from her face, same short slash of red lipstick. The same traces of a former glory.

'And you, who are you?' she said directly to Lydia, looking her up and down, assessing her worth, her value, from the clothes she wore and her hairdresser's skill. In a second sweep of her figure, she removed the clothes and assessed the body, in the manner of a horse dealer considering the merits or otherwise of a new mare. By the expression on her face, Florence Durham was unimpressed.

It occurred to Lydia that she knew a great deal about the woman in front of her while the woman knew nothing of Lydia. It gave her strength to introduce herself and even manage a smile. 'Lydia Silverstream,' she said, offering a hand.

Florence appeared sceptical at the name, and ignoring the hand, looked back at her son. 'Do you know her?'

The colour drained from Laurence's face and Lydia saw the struggle taking place. Hadn't he said something about being weary of all the lies?

'I think we met at college once,' he said hesitantly, looking at Stephen as if he might confirm such a possibility.

'Yes, possibly, I think so, yes,' Stephen said uncertainly. Then, as if dismissing such irrelevant questions, 'Shall we share lunch together?' Without waiting for an answer he continued, 'Good, come on,' and pushed open the door to usher Laurence's mother into the Garden Café. 'After you Florence. May I call you Florence?' Old-world charm can sometimes soften the hardest of hearts.

Lydia settled for a watching role at first, there was nothing to be gained by engaging in polite conversation and talk of any kind might suddenly trip her up. Florence seemed to adopt a similar policy and for the most part the eating was interrupted only by Laurence and Stephen engaging in college talk. It didn't require great effort, nor great acting, both were in their natural habitat, dining with a colleague with whom one had little in common. The question of holidays and where to take them arose between Laurence and Stephen and Lydia spied an opportunity approaching, and on a subject which wouldn't embarrass Laurence. With enough encouragement Stephen might be nudged into introducing the subject of cruises.

'We've been thinking of getting away in September, haven't we?' she asked him almost absentmindedly, but without daring to look him in the eye for fear that Florence would detect the conspiracy.

He took a moment to respond as she wished, but eventually mentioned the possibility of a cruise. It was difficult to maintain the innocent onlooker pose, but Lydia managed, 'I'm not sure about it. Have you ever tried a cruise, Florence?'

The older woman looked straight at her. 'No,' she said, after briefly considering her answer.

A lie right up front was economical. It removed the need for more lies as the inevitable questions and conversation followed. No need for half-truths or even whole truths, which so often sit uncomfortably with a host of little lies. And a lie to shut off those enquiries of when and where and who, told Lydia it would all be denied, the marriage, the honeymoon, her new groom's death, everything. For Florence that history was fiction, they were events that did not happen. Florence had lied, or at best withheld the truth, for many years, she was good at it, it was second nature to her. Consistency demanded that she lie again now, a lie retold doesn't have the weight of a new lie, it rests comfortably on the old.

Stephen took up the baton, asking Laurence, 'What about you? Ever taken a cruise?'

'No, we're not great ones for taking holidays,' he said, looking a little anxiously for approval from his mother.

Lydia wondered what he would do with the insights she could already give him, insignificant as they were. How would he carry that knowledge without it further distorting his peculiar relationship with his mother? What if Lydia did find something that indicated his father's identity, what then? Surely Laurence wouldn't confront Florence with it, he could never have actual proof, she could always deny anything he said. Perhaps he'd inherited her ability to deceive, to withhold knowledge. Wasn't that how she came to be here in the first place?

'It was so easy when you were a child, wasn't it?' Lydia said wistfully, keeping the thread but changing the subject. 'Bucket and spade, a beach and rock pools to catch crabs in. We used to go to Dorset, Lyme Regis and Swanage I remember. I think we went to Lulworth Cove one year. Maybe we just spent a day there. I got sunburn, I remember that.' Turning to Florence again she said, 'Funny the little details we remember from so long ago.'

'No, we...' Florence began, shaking her head. For an instant a softer shadow brushed her face, then the mouth tightened again. 'We didn't have holidays.'

Lydia took this as a small victory in an undeclared contest. Florence did lower her guard, albeit for only a second or two. And at least she was speaking, and speaking with strength in her voice, a little lower than in her youth but far from the croak of an old woman.

131

'Did you travel far today?' Lydia asked. It was so easy to be ignorant. Across the table she was aware of Laurence staring grimly at her, as one who watches a trapeze artist perform without a safety net.

'Travel?'

'To come to the gardens.'

'No,' she said with ill-concealed irritation, 'we walked.'

'You're so lucky to have this right on your doorstep,' Lydia persisted brightly.

'Lucky? If you say so.' And with that she dismissed further conversation with her empty-headed inquisitor.

Lydia's phone lay on the table and in a pretence of checking it for a message, she set the camera ready. In one simple movement she held it out as if about to pass it to Stephen but instead said brightly, 'Ready!'

Before the surprised mother and son could complain she'd snapped their picture.

'Will you do us now, please?' she asked the ashen-faced Laurence.

He had no opportunity to answer before Florence rose abruptly from the table.

'Laurence, I'm going into town. I don't need you with me, stay here with…' she indicated Stephen and Lydia with a vague gesture, 'Don't be late.'

'Right.'

When Stephen rose to say goodbye she honoured him with a token smile and a nod of the head.

Florence Tweddle left the building without a backward glance and they sat in mesmerised silence watching her go. Fit as a flea, Laurence had said, and so she was, walking briskly away and with more assurance than some people half her age. Only when she disappeared from view did anyone speak.

'She's remarkable. I was going to say for her age, but she's just remarkable,' Lydia said.

'She is,' Laurence said flatly. He appeared shell-shocked, pale and colourless on a warm summer day, beads of sweat following their curving tracks down his round cheeks.

'Shall we get some air?' Having convened the lunch party, Stephen continued to play host.

For a while they wandered with little apparent purpose, finding flowers and shrubs to feign interest in, stooping to read labels that Laurence knew by heart. They were none of them willing to broach the subject that had brought them together on a Saturday afternoon. It was as if they needed a certain amount of time to elapse between Florence's departure and the purpose of their contrived meeting.

At length, near the rose garden they found a shaded bench set a little back from the path. Stephen sat then immediately got up. 'I meant to get some ice cream. Laurence?'

'No, thank you. I appreciate it but there's no need to leave. If Lydia has something to tell me, I'm sure you've heard it already.' The longer they'd walked with no mention of her investigations the more he'd recovered his composure. Now he began to gulp the air again, swallowing on a dry mouth.

'I'll bring some water anyway.'

Lydia leaned forward, studying the grass beneath their feet. She still hadn't quite decided what to share.

'Laurence, I haven't brought any certificates with me. I can give them to you any time, but I didn't trust myself to have them with me today. I have one small piece of paper with a few notes on it.'

'Thank you, if I'd known you might bring some documents I'd have found a way not to come at all. Please tell me what you've found.'

'First, and most important I haven't found who your father was. I may never. At the very best I may find someone who might have been your father. Possibly I've found such a person already. You won't be surprised to hear that his name was Durham, William Gordon Durham, also known as Billy. He was a solicitor and...' again she hesitated on the brink of revelation.

'And? Is he dead? Yes, I expect he is.'

'Yes, he's dead, but that's not it. Trying to find your father is one thing, it's all about you which is fine. But I can't even get close without discovering something of your mother's life, discovering things that she's chosen not to tell you.'

'I'm confused. I thought that was what you were doing, finding the things she refuses to tell.'

'I want to be sure that you want to know. It will change things, knowing something that she thinks is a secret. You might end up throwing it back at her in a moment of anger. You might be different for knowing and she may see that difference in you.'

'Yes, I understand, and thank you. But just talking to you, asking you to see what you could find, that too changed things a little. It's another secret to keep, along with my stamp album and my little envelope of photocopies. I assure you I'm perfectly used to keeping secrets. I may not lie very well, I don't like out-and-out lies, but I can keep my mouth shut. I'll be no worse off with whatever else you have for me.'

'Yes, of course. Sorry.'

With no more than a few dates, a marriage and a death, even with so little she was reluctant to give it up and was a little ashamed. Concern for Laurence seemed no more than an excuse.

'I have copies of your mother's and your grandmother's birth certificates. No big surprises. Your mother's father is given as Buchanan, is it a name you've heard before?'

'Never as my grandfather, he's never had a name, he's a non-person. From somewhere else maybe, I'm not sure. Another name for the collection,' he added thoughtfully.

'I can't say for sure, but I think your mother probably changed her name, and yours, to Durham when she married William in 1959 at Bedford Registry Office.' Lydia let this new information sink in before she continued. 'William died less than a month later. He was quite a lot older than Florence.'

'Not my father though?'

'A candidate. Certainly a candidate, but why wait five or six years, and why the secrecy? Yes, you were born before they were married, but really, is that reason enough to keep it secret today?'

In that moment of asking, Lydia wondered if perhaps she might answer it herself. Just like denying the cruise, maybe everything rested on a lie, undo one and something would slip, undo the next and the next and the whole edifice might fracture and collapse.

Maybe Florence couldn't tell Laurence anything without risking it all tumbling down.

'I can let you have all the copies, I'll give them to Stephen and he can pass them on to you at college, if that's all right.'

He nodded.

'William Durham left a will. I'll be getting a copy of it. It may throw some more light on events. Did you ever hear anything of an inheritance? It could've been for you or your mother.'

'No, never.'

'I think William already had at least one son, so it won't be a surprise if he inherited everything. I'll be in touch if there's anything worth knowing.'

'Anything else?'

'Quite a lot, but only little details. Addresses, telephone numbers, the trivial little records we leave as we move through our lives. Sometimes they point to something substantial. Most often they don't. I've written it all down.'

They fell silent, Laurence finding the right place to file these snippets of fresh knowledge, Lydia unsure whether to tell him more of his mother's honeymoon and William Durham's death. If she told him now he'd recognise her deceit at lunch, better to leave the details buried in the paperwork for him to make his own discoveries long after the conversation would have faded.

'Can I ask about money? I wonder how your mother bought the house, and even now how she pays the bills?'

'I contribute a fair amount. She calls it rent, but it's nothing as formal as that. Cash every month. My mother likes cash. I don't think she has a credit card. Cheques and cash are what she works with. And no, I don't know where her money came from or maybe still comes from today. She'll have a pension of course, but I assume that won't amount to much. I think she has at least two different banks. So does my grandmother.'

'Thanks. It was just an idea. You said so far as you knew she'd never worked, but it must have come from somewhere.'

Through the rose garden Stephen could be seen bearing ice cream and bottled water. Too late, he held the ice creams away from his body to avoid the drips speckling his clothes. As he came to them Lydia saw the white stain on one new blue shoe and two trails down his right trouser-leg. For once he looked anything but the revered professor with a knighthood for services to forensics, more like the harassed father of young children.

'Had to queue, then they'd run out of carriers.'

Lydia decided not to mention the shoe or the trousers.

They ate their ice creams while Laurence sipped from the water bottle, their conversations exhausted but no one quite ready to leave. A steady stream of visitors passed by, some at a distance, others close enough for them to catch a word or a snatch of conversation. All dawdled, many arm-in-arm, a few with awkward space between them, the rare singleton. First-timers had their noses in guide books, regulars and locals strolled untroubled by the details.

Lydia noticed a second and then a third young couple stop by a massive tree a little distance away. Having examined the information sign half-hidden in the long grass, each couple took a picture of one or other of them standing by it. One girl went so far as to hug the tree, even though her arms didn't reach halfway round the huge trunk. Curious, Lydia made her way across. The little sign declared it to be *Ailanthus Altissima - Tree of Heaven.* What better memento for young lovers to take from the gardens? Even as she stood looking, another couple came to read the inscription and then to find its meaning in a tourist phrase book. Wide smiles spread across their oriental features as they handed Lydia a camera and signed for her to snap them posing by the tree.

∞

'Two weeks.'

She'd asked, in a roundabout way, for the prognosis, and he'd told her, forcing the words through his unwilling tubes to her unwilling ears. Just because she'd asked didn't mean she wanted an answer, not one as precise as that. The simple maths struck her: she'd sat there six days ago when he had twenty left and now she'd frittered away nearly a third of his time.

'Oh. They can be that sure.'

'More,' he gasped for air to complete the sentence, 'or less. Nearly done.'

'Freddie, is there anything you'd like? I wondered about going somewhere, seeing something, but I could bring you something if you wanted it.'

'Nah.'

She really wanted to know what he wanted after his death, what he wanted of her, whether she should continue her search, find a grandchild if one existed. And if so, to tell them what? That someone they didn't know and was supposedly unrelated had died alone and unloved in an anonymous room at the end of an anonymous corridor?

'I know we have our unfinished business, but is there anything else that should be settled, decided before…?'

He closed his eyes, his lips moving slightly in consideration of the idea. What he rehearsed, what possibilities he entertained and dismissed, she didn't know. At length he shook his head.

'Do you want me to go on, looking for Linda and her life?'

'Ain't yer done?'

Tell him now or tell him never.

'What else?' It was written across her face and he saw it there. 'A kid? She got a kid?' He stretched himself up at the prospect.

'Maybe. I don't know for sure, but someone wrote that she did, wrote about a child, a daughter. Yes, you might have a granddaughter.'

His breath came faster, mimicked by the waves chasing each other a little quicker across the machine. Irresistibly drawn to the numbers, Lydia noticed for the first time that it was called Vitalyf. He and the machine were as one, she thought. Ridiculously, it occurred to her that it kept him alive, if it were unplugged, detached from him, then he would die.

She spoke to him softly but clearly, as serious as she felt, as blunt as the moment. 'Freddie, if you want me to go on, if you want to know more, if there is more to know, tell me some of your secrets without me having to guess. If I find something, find somebody, it can be a week to get the details, get if confirmed or proved wrong. If it's wrong it can take another week.' He kept his eyes closed

137

while she talked, leaning in to him to be certain there was no mistaking her words or her meaning. 'Let me see if I can find Belinda or maybe Sylvie's sister.'

'Nah!' He held up his hand and shook it as vigorously as he could, 'Nobody, not Kate, not nobody. We said.'

He held her wrist as best he could but it was no more than the grip of an infant. He put all his strength into holding her, insisting she didn't find these people from his past, people who might open the way to knowledge of his Linda, a name for his grandchild. She closed her other hand gently around his fingers.

'Kate? Your Sylvie's sister? I think that was Catherine. Why not, Freddie? After all these years, why not? You can trust me, you know that.'

'The deal was no talking, no saying nothin', it's what kept me goin' till now. I got a deal and I kept it. I'm gonna keep it till the end.'

His determination had briefly energised him, at what cost Lydia could only guess, two weeks might have become one in the space of their conversation.

'All right Freddie. I promised, just you and me.'

She would continue looking, she would bring him any news she thought he would like, she wouldn't speak of him or his search to anyone. They sat together as his day drifted to a close with the sun still high in the sky, Lydia giving him glimpses of her weekend in Cambridge, her return to Oxford when she left him.

'Got that computer wiv yer?'

'Yes, want another look before I go?'

He nodded.

She set it up for him again and together they watched his Linda perform at one of the high points of her young life. It was easy to imagine her having no need to act the part, imagine her being that bright, cheeky girl chasing the boys along the beach.

'Do you remember those films, Freddie? Did you ever see any of them?'

'Yeah, maybe, I dunno. Lovely girls, eh? Full of fun.'

Lovely girls indeed. His Linda was no longer lovely, but the others, what had happened to them? And there was a whole host of such girls, a chorus line of such girls who populated all those saucy *Carry Ons* and *Confessions*. All with little walk-on parts and one-line roles and most with figures to match expectations. Who had told their stories, Lydia wondered, and wouldn't such an idea be a wonderful excuse to track them down, track down their mothers and sisters and cousins and boyfriends. And no better place to start than with the knowledge she already had. The project came alive the instant she conceived it.

'Freddie,' she leaned close to him, held his hand before he held hers. 'Listen, what if I didn't know you, knew nothing of you, and had another reason to contact Kate or Belinda, what then? No mention of you, I promise.'

He considered this for a moment, then gripped her fingers and looked straight into her. He nodded and a lopsided smile curved his mouth. From deep inside came, 'Couldn't stop yer, could I?'

∞

'Crete and Ephesus. Two weeks gentle cruising. What do you think?'

'How gentle?'

'Very. More like a private yacht really, thirty or so passengers, all mod cons, optional lectures, library on board, plenty of stopping and looking.'

'Sounds good.'

'I'll book it then? At the end of September?'

'Yes, why not?'

'Marvellous, consider it done.'

'My treat. I'll pay.'

'Oh, Lydia, it's not…I don't know…'

'I do. My treat. I can afford it.' In her hand she held the latest letter from Ffynne & Co. It confirmed all that Geoffrey Spencer had told her. The money would be in her bank on Thursday, just two days away. She still had no idea what to do with it all, so two weeks in the Aegean on a private yacht sounded as good as anything.

'Maybe, but I'll pay my share.'

'All right, if it'll make you feel better.'

'It will. Is your redundancy finalised? None of my business, but, I wondered.'

'Not yet. It's something else, I'll tell you about it another time. And whatever happens, I've decided not to take that job in Henley.'

'Good to have that settled at least. You sound really bright. Good week?'

'So far. I've actually done some work on Freddie and finally ordered a copy of that will for Laurence.'

She almost added that it had been two days since she'd opened a bottle of wine, a fact of which she was unduly proud. It was true, but only because she'd managed to make the one she'd opened on Sunday evening stretch till now. The last mouthful was in the glass in front of her while the bottle waited to join its fellows in the blue recycling box.

'I've ordered a few more things for Freddie, or George Thompson as I think he really is, or was. With luck they'll be here tomorrow. Might be interesting, especially the death certificate. And, here's something you probably weren't expecting, I've written to the three people I think could be Linda's aunt Catherine, and two others who might be her cousin Belinda. Of course, they could've all moved or died by now, my little lookup-file is getting a bit out of date. I've even resorted to a website for old school friends. And by the way, I am now officially researching a new documentary on the bit-part starlets of yesteryear. I've called it *The Carry On Girls*, do you like that?'

She was very pleased with her own invention and hoped Stephen would like it too, but he didn't seem to appreciate the humour or originality.

'Yes. Good. I know you don't much like using me or anyone I might know, but if I can help, you know what I mean, with Freddie being short of time.'

Once before he'd been the vital information finder and it had felt like cheating then and still did. But he might provide a shortcut through the bureaucracy, although Lydia wasn't quite ready to make that enquiry. She had enough to be doing with wills and her make-believe TV program. Every now and again she remembered that she also had those medals in their velvet-lined case, medals that certainly weren't going to find a home with Freddie.

'Yes, thank you, maybe, I haven't quite got the question yet. I phoned tonight to ask about Freddie. They said he'd had a good day but I never know what to believe when they say that. I suppose it means he's still alive. His doctor's going to see him tomorrow.'

'A sad business.' Stephen waited long enough to mean it before brightening with, 'I'll get on and do this booking, send you all the bumf.'

'Lovely, see you at the weekend.'

'Er, I'm in London this weekend,' after a slight hesitation he added, 'You could come with me, meet me there.'

'Oh, I forgot that, sorry, yes. No, I have a lot to do anyway.'

She cursed herself for forgetting, for making him tell her again, for dragging an invitation out of him, one he hadn't offered when he'd first mentioned his weekend meetings with unnameable Whitehall mandarins. She liked seeing him every weekend, she liked the way their gamble of sleeping together had been good for them, hadn't damaged their friendship but deepened it. And she liked sleeping with him, not only for his touch and their pleasure but for the ease of it, the pure companionship of it. Her list of lovers was short, as was her list of suitors, and such companionship had never previously been a feature. When she thought about it more, it seemed quite natural for their pleasure in each other's company to continue into the bedroom. But it hadn't been obvious before they'd been lovers.

When they'd said their goodbyes, Lydia went to the fridge and retrieved a cool bottle, replacing it with the last one from her store cupboard. Looking round she saw it was not only the wine supply that had dwindled, practically everything else had too. There was nothing that attracted her, either to cook or to eat. At only eight in the evening she still had countless ways to feed herself and to feed herself very well. Within a mile there must be a hundred pubs and restaurants and all those pizzerias anxious to deliver right to her door. But they all seemed extravagant indulgences, despite the fact that she'd cheerily committed thousands on a holiday. She hadn't asked him the cost, it hadn't mattered, but splashing out a tiny fraction of that on a table for one was out of the question. Tomorrow, she'd get some groceries tomorrow. For now there was always the jar of dry pasta waiting to be boiled.

∞

'No, me neither. That makes two of us going quietly. Eddie's not keen on me working in Banbury, in fact he's not keen on me working at all, but we'll see about that, we need the money and I can't sit around all day. Well I could, I could sit around and listen to people saying Mrs Culley this and Mrs Culley that.' Gloria laughed at herself and her fanciful expectations of married life. Her excitement at the prospect was undiminished.

'Mrs Culley.' Lydia tried out the full version to satisfy Gloria's urging, 'Mrs Gloria Culley. Not bad. You won't keep Fitzgerald then?'

'No way, horrible name, can't wait to get rid of it. Everyone thinks you're Irish. Culley has a much better ring don't you think?'

'Maybe. Names are such funny things aren't they? I think we grow into the sound of what we're called.'

'And how's your name-change project getting on?'

'Oh, Gloria, you'd hardly believe it, there's more than one, I've got the poor man Freddie in Bedford who's really George and who has some awful secret and asked me to find his daughter, or at least what became of her. Then there's Laurence in Cambridge who doesn't know why he has the name he uses and whose mother won't tell him anything. I met her last weekend and she is truly amazing.'

Gloria had adopted a hands-on-hips pose and her most bored expression to which she added further disapproval by rolling her eyes.

'No, you silly cow, not all that graveyard stuff, I mean are you any nearer being Lady Whatsit of bloody Camchester? It took me long enough to get you into bed with someone, anyone, then you pull off the catch of the bloody century with Lord Fit 'n' Rich. So yes, I would like to know about that project and less about old Freddie. Is His Lordship looking after you as a girl should be looked after?'

'But it's not a project…'

'Jesus, Lydia! I know! But you always rise to the bait!' Gloria practically bounced up and down in frustration.

'Yes. It's very good. I think so, very good. Not sure that there'll ever be wedding bells.'

'But he's coming to mine? You asked him?'

'Yes, of course he'll be coming.'

She hadn't asked him at all, it hadn't crossed her mind once while she'd been with him. She couldn't even recall whether she'd mentioned the wedding. With no date set, no venue, it still seemed slightly vague, something that might as easily be cancelled as not. Stephen would want to come, for Lydia if not for Gloria, but he'd want the time and the place and an entry in his diary. He had an unseen life of appointments and deadlines, commitments and understandings. Juggling them for something as vague as a possible wedding didn't compute. She could easily excuse herself with such reasoning and never mention that she'd forgotten.

'He probably won't remember me anyway, and you've kept him well out of the way.'

'What about you and Eddie, do you know where you're going to live? You've not long been back with your mum, she'll miss you, leaving her again.'

'He shares with his brother. It's all right, he's away half the time, but it's tricky. There's a place near Kennington we like, but I think it's too much for us even if we could get a deposit together. We'll rent somewhere for a while and see how it goes. I'll get something then we'll see how the money is.'

The temptation was too great, the impulse too strong. Even though she heard herself starting to speak, there was nothing she could do to stop the words leaving her mouth. 'I'll give you the deposit. A wedding present.'

9

With time running out, Lydia had trusted to instinct and experience to gather as much information as she could about Freddie's new identity and the family she was building for him. To her there was no doubt he was Linda's father, there could be none other than a father who would have spoken as he did, or looked as he did, or had the tears well in his eyes. Where it would all lead she had no idea, except that knowing the real family might be useful if she were ever to find a grandchild. Such details would certainly not be among the certificates on her desk. Her search for a child of Linda Thompson or even Lynn Brighton had thrown up nothing worthy of further enquiry. Evidence for the child's existence was a single passing comment on a wiki website.

From the first of her envelopes came a new birth date and confirmation of a name: *George Frederick Thompson born in Mile End, July 1930 to George and Esther Thompson.* The *Esther* pleased her greatly, hadn't Freddie called his mother Tess when he'd been reminiscing? And with a father called George there was nothing easier than to use the son's second name to avoid any confusion. Who, she wondered, had first called him Freddie? Perhaps he couldn't wait to change from George at the first opportunity he had. And it had stayed with him, even when he became Francis Bellinger. A sister's details followed, Sarah, born two years later, then brothers Charles and Andrew in 1934 and 1936, all born in Mile End. George and Esther had been married there too, in 1928, she going to the altar as Esther Sarah Glynn, daughter of William Glynn. Glynn was a name Lydia had come across before, although in what context she couldn't recall. It was a name she liked, so perhaps it was the only reason it stood out for her.

With the family details came their address, just one covering all the events in front of her. She didn't need to look at her A to Z to know it would be close to Cable Street. It had survived the war too, because there it was again on sister Sarah Elizabeth's marriage in 1952. She'd married Peter Wilson, he a couple of years older than she and from Canning Town.

The Thompsons could be any one of thousands of families, unremarkable, straightforward records of marriages and the babies that followed, the cycle repeating itself down the generations. But for the Thompsons, Lydia was sure there'd be at least one exception to the norm in her last envelope, a death certificate for George. It might yet be the wrong George, it might be a completely false trail but she enjoyed the moment as she slipped the knife under the flap and carefully sliced the official brown paper.

August 9th 1956 HMP Wormwood Scrubs, Middlesex, George Frederick Thompson also known as Freddie Thompson or Tommy Quick, male, born 14th July 1930 Stepney, casual labourer. What a bounty, more than enough to satisfy her, this was the same George Thompson whose birth certificate also lay on her table, although *Tommy Quick* was new to her. As if to confirm it, the usual address shown was in Chapman Street E1, not more than a few hundred yards from the original family home in Sutton Street. Lydia noted that the informant was no ordinary copper, but *Ernest R Bowker, sergeant* whose address was given as *Met. Pol. Svc. New Scotland Yard.*

The cause of death was even more unusual. *Cardiac failure as a result of knife wounds severing a) the pulmonary vein, b) the inferior vena cava, c) rupturing the right atrium, d) loss of blood from other non-fatal injuries. After post-mortem without inquest. A C Morrison, Coroner.* George had been stabbed to death and here was the cold anatomical catalogue of the injuries that killed him.

As she stared at the paper it took on the weight of a great burden. She even fancied that the single sheet grew heavier in her hand, too heavy to hold and it slipped to the table, obscuring the details on the birth certificate. She'd seen dozens of death certificates, browsed through lists of countless more, but never before had she been so close to such violence. One read of such things, a hundred films have shown a man stabbed, more than one in a prison fight, yet to hold a copy of the matter-of-fact record brought a new perspective: it was close, it was personal, it was real life, real death, one man killing another. It was a jolt to catch herself drawn into the drama, feeling the blade slide up under the ribs, silently, shockingly, painlessly. The horrified surprise on the victim's face, close enough to the killer to taste his breath, close enough to realise the cheapness of life.

Lydia shook her head as if to loosen the images conjured there, opened a new bottle of *pinot* and poured a large glass. No lingering over this one, she took a big swig and returned to her desk. She reminded herself of how she'd got to this point. The death certificate she held was pure fiction, George was still alive, just, in a hospice in Bedford. There'd been no gruesome death in prison, there'd been a life in a dozen places round the globe. This was the big lie that he'd been living since 1956, the big lie that had cost him sight of his daughter, the love and laughter of his family, a life with his sweetheart. Somehow he'd become Francis Bellinger, and Francis Bellinger he'd doggedly stayed for the rest of his life, even though he'd never parted with being Freddie. Having lived as such, he would die as such, there'd be no changing that.

With a pang it occurred to her that the whole certificate might not be a lie, it might only be the identity of the victim. It was one thing to give a corpse a false name, but another to invent the corpse itself. It would have involved so many more lies if there'd been no stabbed and bloodied body to lie about. Which meant that although it wasn't Freddie, it was still someone, still someone's son or husband, someone's father or grandfather who'd bled to death on a grubby floor.

Lydia wondered if the victim, whoever he was, might not have been a prisoner, but a visitor or someone else with good reason to be at Wormwood Scrubs. How that would lead to the killing or Freddie being named as the victim, she couldn't quite imagine. And who was Tommy Quick? There was a nickname with a meaning if ever she saw one.

A story might fade from the headlines, might even be lost to living memory, but it seems it can never be forgotten by the web. *Tommy Quick 1956* brought up a dozen likely references with the first enquiry. Only one proved to be enlightening, the page which listed the name among a number of small-time violent criminals murdered in gang warfare during the struggle for control of the East End in the mid-fifties. The tit-for-tat killings had reportedly spilled over into the prison system and dock labour unions. It was short on specifics but did have a link to a newspaper archive and referred to a book, *Clean Sweep: Forty Years on the Force*. A quick search found no book with that title currently available. The newspaper archive had only been digitised as far back as 1959 so it would mean a visit to turn real pages. But their index of names and events was comprehensive and contained several entries for Tommy Quick, the first in March 1956, the last in February 1958. For Freddie Thompson, a single entry which referred to the same 1958 issue. The archive was housed on an industrial estate somewhere near Gravesend. Maybe one day, if the need was urgent.

Lydia tried the same searches with the other names listed in the original article but without making further headway. Each took her to the same or similar sketchy information, each was linked to the criminal gangs of the East End in the 1940s and 1950s. She also came across two more references to *Clean Sweep*. The city library had been very helpful in the past. Another visit was called for.

No wonder Freddie had stuck to his name. At one time or another he'd been George, Tommy, Francis and maybe more besides. She wondered when he'd settled for Freddie and stayed that way, when he'd stopped being on the run perhaps?

Her collection of certificates had been rewarding, a family confirmed, hints of his life till he was just twenty-six, till just before Linda was born, till George died in a prison fight and Freddie left the country. All fascinating and one day no doubt useful, but Lydia wasn't sure that it added up to anything vital now. She took another glass into her garden and paced around it a few times. It was a small square, not quite big enough to really get her brain going. Unlike The Old Rectory garden with its choice of paths and flora, her West Street patch offered only clockwise or anti-clockwise. She would miss seeing Stephen, the weekends had become a happy habit.

∞

The librarian had been more than helpful, he'd located a copy of *Clean Sweep* in neighbouring Berkshire's reserve holding of old books. And in doing so he'd identified the ex-police inspector whose memoir it was, a William Kingsley. A small fee was paid and the book would be available in a few days. In the end it might be nothing more than a curiosity, but it might be an interesting diversion.

While she was in the library Lydia browsed the shelves for anything related to the British film business of the 1970s, Lynn Brighton's heyday, if that was not too grand a term for her brief career. There was a small selection, but nothing she thought would be worth wading through on the chance of finding a snippet of information. But seeing what was available made Lydia wonder if there wasn't a real documentary to be made or even a book to be researched and written. She felt quite confident of the first element but less so of the second, although as things stood she would soon have the time for both. For the present, she vaguely thought if Catherine or Belinda were to contact her, it would be prudent to have some knowledge of the subject she was supposedly researching.

Once home, she set about finding the names of actresses who'd played those bit parts and one-liners. With so many enthusiasts providing information, and the industry itself so keen on detail lists of credits, Lydia's difficulty was not finding information, but the volume of it. Method and patience served her well, as they so often did in her researches. Starting with *Confessions of a Lifeguard* she made a list of the actresses with the roles similar to Lynn Brighton. She collected eight names quickly and from there was able to find the whole career of any one of them.

On reflection, she decided to widen the list to include the young men who'd played the little roles, wouldn't they have different memories of the girls on the roster? In a couple of hours she assembled information on more than thirty starlets and a dozen assorted actors. What surprised her most was that so many had such long careers, some were even still active. Most had continued to be in the chorus line rather than the lead, but a handful had become well known character actors in later life.

Lynn Brighton's acting began in 1971 with an uncredited appearance in *Grave Mistake*, a low-budget horror film. Two more quickly followed until a break in 1973, then from 1974 it meandered through a dozen other titles via *Confessions of a Lifeguard* and a couple of *Carry Ons* to end in 1980 with *Naked Garden*, soft porn posing as art. Another part of her life Freddie needn't hear about. The two-line biography suggested she left the film world to become a singer.

To round-out her credentials as a researcher, Lydia tracked down details of the agent representing two of those actresses still active, and sent a note asking about possible interviews to reminisce about the old days. The more she played her new role, the more she enjoyed it. *The Carry On Girls* was still no more than a convenient invention, but it began to feel like a real project.

Settling into her garden chair, brushed by the soft evening air, she began dreaming of a TV show and the book to go with it. Not that she had any connection to anybody in film or publishing, but the dream was nice. And there was always Stephen, he had connections to everything, he'd get her an interview with anyone she wanted. And no sooner did she have the thought than she remembered she did know someone in television, she knew Jacqueline. It should have been a happy realisation, but instead it drove all thoughts of a documentary from her mind. If it were to be anything it would be a book, TV would take care of itself when the book had caused enough interest.

The evening lapped round her with deepening shadows. She lit two big candles, then, enchanted by the light, lit two more. With another bottle she brought out her newly purchased brie and the rare luxury of fresh bread. Why, when it was so close and so good, did she so often ignore shopping in the Covered Market? As the warmth of the day slipped away, she drew a blanket around her and counted her blessings. When had she ever had so few cares or worries? When had her future held better prospects?

Hovering round the glow of well-being was the question of her new wealth, both the agent of freedom and cause of nagging anxiety. She'd checked her bank account as soon as she'd got home. True to their word, Ffynne & Co had transferred the money from John Fordham's estate. She immediately moved nearly all of it into her savings account, leaving only enough to cover her recent extravagances and perhaps one or two more to come. Tucked away out of sight, she might be able to ignore it for a while, let the novelty wear off before thinking what to do with it all. Perhaps that was the key, do nothing with it, she'd be paid for a couple of months yet and there'd be the redundancy money to live on for a while after that.

She still hadn't told Stephen, nor anybody else. Gloria had flatly refused her offer of help with a deposit, saying she would simply tear up the cheque. Lydia had no significant debts to pay off, neither did she have a pet charity or good cause to endow with thousands. With no children to pamper, the next best thing should be her nieces, who she hadn't seen or heard of for several months. They'd never been attentive to their aunt and had received little encouragement from their parents. Lydia's brother lived only a forty-minute drive away, but they'd hardly spoken to each other in months. Most likely he would be pleased to have a share of her good fortune, and she might yet give him something, but the idea did not immediately appeal. Brian had done little to deserve such generosity, but no sooner had she thought such a thing than she felt the guilt of doing so.

As her only close relative, her brother would almost certainly receive all her money if she were to die. Not just her money, but her house too. She resolved at once to make a will, to avoid such an outcome. Brian would get something, so would his daughters, but they wouldn't get it all. Why it mattered now, when it hadn't a week ago, she wasn't sure, but it suddenly mattered very much. She would do her best not to die until she'd seen Ffynne & Co to have the papers drawn up. Who would have what, she wasn't sure, but Gloria could hardly tear up a cheque from a lawyer. Her friend Dorothy down on the South Coast might benefit from a mention too. And what of Michael, her ex, he'd be none too pleased at seeing his father's money - he would certainly see it as such - distributed without a mention of himself. Like John Fordham, she might also include something for a charity, but it would not be Michael.

The warmth of the night, the slow dance of the candles along with the wine and good food inside her, helped her drift into sleep. She didn't fight it, didn't think how she shouldn't or how she'd feel in the morning. She embraced it, welcoming the prospect, settling her head more comfortably on the cushion. And as she floated away, she dreamed she was sleeping on the deck of a private yacht as it bobbed beneath an Aegean sky.

∞

Not so good, they'd said, then asked if she was going over to see him. They'd never said that before when she'd called. What they'd meant was, if you don't come over soon, you might never see him again. So straight from her office, straight from an early end to a late-starting day, she drove to Willoughby House. Smiley face was at reception, but selected her deeply sympathetic expression once she saw Lydia.

'Sandra's with him now,' she said, somehow suggesting that the presence of Sandra indicated a defining moment in his decline. It occurred to Lydia that perhaps Sandra was the local priest and was hearing a confession or administering the last rites, although she doubted that Freddie would tolerate such nonsense if he still had the power of speech.

At his door Lydia hesitated, listening for raised voices or the lowered ones of a private conversation, but she heard nothing. She knocked and paused a fraction of a second before entering. Freddie was propped up in his bed, apparently asleep. His face shocked her, more skeletal in a week than she'd have believed possible. In a chair beside him sat the sad-eyed member of staff Lydia had encountered before.

'Freddie,' she said softly, 'Your daughter's here to see you, Lydia's here.'

He made no sound or movement, neither did the numbers on his monitor change.

The 'how is he' question almost formed itself before Lydia choked it back. It didn't need asking and it certainly didn't need answering. Lydia pulled another chair across and sat opposite Sandra.

'Hello, have you been sitting with him long?' she said quietly.

'Just ten minutes or so. He was asking for you, and rambling too, but he was upset you weren't here. I said I'd stay for a while.' She was holding his hand, gently stroking it as she spoke.

'I'm not his daughter, you know. People think I am, but I'm not. I never said I was. Freddie knows that too. He said it once to…'

'I know. He told me. But he wishes you were. He told me that too.'

'But if you know, why did you still…'

'He forgets he told me.'

Lydia said, 'Thank you,' because she was truly grateful and because she couldn't think of anything else to say.

'I'll leave you with him. The buzzer's there if you need it.'

'Is he asleep?'

'In and out, I think.'

Sandra patted his hand and slipped from the room. The only sound she left behind was Freddie's breathing, alternately coarse and laboured then briefly and alarmingly smooth and silent. In his wrist where her fingers lay across it, Lydia could feel the tiny trace of a pulse keeping time with the green peaks running across the monitor.

She studied his face for a few moments, wondering if he would ever see her again, ever manage another curse through his sagging lips or force a laugh from failing lungs. He was a stranger to her, she had no duty or loyalty to him, and yet she sat with him. He concealed his own, perhaps wicked, life from her but sought her help in revealing it. Was it misguided compassion that had kept her coming back or something to satisfy her own conceit and prove her cleverness? And when he was gone, as he soon would be, what then? If she continued his search it would surely only be to reward herself, even though she might dress it up with fine words. If she gave him a granddaughter today, would it be for him or for him to think well of her?

He stirred slightly and she said his name but he gave no answer.

She hadn't sat with her grandmother through the night of her last hours, even though it had been suggested. They'd said it was a chance to say anything that needed to be said, to let the old lady go with no unfinished business. Lydia had said and heard all she needed to say and hear a long time previously, so she stayed away. Whatever she said to Freddie today or tomorrow or next week, there would be unfinished business for him. She couldn't collect his lifetime of missed memories and replay them all in the time they had left.

Like a TV screen in a bar, sucking attention from friends or conversation, the numbers on the monitor were irresistible. Her finger on his artery, her eyes on the screen, slow but steady bump, bump, bump, bump. Did he miss one? Urgently she scanned the disappearing trace to find a break in the pattern, but it was gone before she could be sure. The little yellow tell-tales stayed unlit. She'd half reached for the buzzer, now she froze in mid-stretch. Imagination, just imagination.

'Freddie,' she said, 'it's Lydia, come to see you and talk about the old days. I was looking at all sorts this week, when your mum and dad were married, when your brothers and sister were born, all sorts. When you spoke of your grampy, I wonder if you were talking about your mum's father or your dad's. Your dad's father was Frederick, maybe people called him Freddie too, and your mum's was William. Maybe he was Bill or Will, I haven't looked up details for either of them. Were they Londoners, East Enders like you and your family were?

'I saw your mother's name before she was married, it was Glynn. That's a name I've always liked for some reason. It's quite unusual, like Silverstream. You've had a few names in your time, eh Freddie. Did you like one any better than the others? You've ended up as Freddie Bell, I wonder if you like that best. All sorts of games people play with names, especially as kids. You'd have had a few games played with yours at school if you'd been a Bell in those days.'

She fell silent and would have gone to the window had her hand not still rested on his. She feared that moving away from him might break the spell, disturb his peace.

'Who was that other Lydia, Freddie? The one you spoke about, the girl on the beach. Was that here or somewhere halfway round the world? I wonder how you knew her, what you knew of her. You know nothing of me do you? I have a friend, Stephen, who lives near Cambridge.'

She was surprised to hear herself talking of him so easily. Of all the things she might have said about herself, it was Stephen who came to mind first.

'I often see him on a Friday evening, but not this week. He's away for the weekend in London, some important meeting. I'd drive from here to his house and stay until Sunday, then call back here on my way home to Oxford. Did you even know I live in Oxford? A little house, a very little house by the Thames. A little place called Osney, Osney Island. I wonder if you've ever heard of it, most people haven't.'

What else should she add, and what would he care anyway? She had decades of trivia she could recite but it all amounted to very little. He had no need of talk for talk's sake.

'I haven't heard from anyone about your Linda. I sent out some letters to a few people. I was hoping one might be Belinda or her mother, Kate you called her. They might've gone away or been the wrong people. If I don't hear tomorrow, I'll see about calling or maybe I'll drive over to the addresses I have, and find out.'

Lydia had no need to say this, she had no plan to do any such thing. Freddie's fingers contracted a little, enough for her to feel the pressure on her hand. Pure coincidence of course, an involuntary spasm as vivid dreams flittered across the brain cells. One of the numbers on the machine rose a couple of points then fell back.

She took the opportunity to stand and cross to the window. The early evening scene was no different to any other time of day: the tended lawn, the path around it and four deserted benches. It seemed such a waste of time and effort when nobody seemed to use it. Perhaps they took pleasure from it being there, a reminder of different days. A sound, a little groan or a slurred word, made her turn.

'Over here by the window, Freddie. It's Lydia, I got up to stretch my legs.'

Did all the rooms in Willoughby House have the same utilitarian furniture? Were they all devoid of anything personal, any photo or trinket to remind their occupants of their previous lives? It reminded her of a waiting room lacking even the small luxury of an out-of-date magazine. A prison waiting room, or worse, the room for conjugal visits. Bland magnolia walls over two-tone beige carpet tiles. Maybe the blank canvas encouraged relatives and friends to fill the void with snaps of smiling grandchildren, flowers from the garden, a television, a few books. Lydia was that friend and she'd never brought him anything apart from the velvet-lined box of medals which she'd immediately taken back home.

'I'll bring you some flowers next time I come in. Any preference?'

∞

Lydia's letters had given the maybe-Catherines and Belindas every opportunity to respond by whatever means they chose. By Saturday morning none had opted for the self-addressed envelope she'd included. It didn't surprise her, who wrote letters any more? She looked again at the addresses for the five people she'd written to: four in suburban Essex, one in leafy Bushey, close to Watford. She could do nothing but wait, and hope her out-of-date people-finder would serve her well just this once more.

The postman had not been completely empty handed. Aside from the junk, there were two letters. She recognised Stephen's careful handwriting on a large brown envelope from Cambridge and guessed it would be the details of their holiday, a pleasure to keep for later reading. The second, from the Wills and Probate Office, would certainly be a copy of William G Durham's last will and testament. It was already a week since she'd seen Laurence and his mother in Cambridge, a week with nothing new to tell him. Here was another summer's day, would they be in the gardens again this morning, taking a light lunch in the café? That was one engineered encounter that could not be repeated, Lydia would need to see Laurence by appointment in Cambridge when they next met.

She took her cereal and coffee and the will to the garden. It didn't take much reading, it was as short and to the point as should be expected of a solicitor, even a retired one. It was dated a few days before his marriage to Florence and very precisely named three beneficiaries. The precision was a pleasure to Lydia's eyes, if only every will were written as William G's, how much easier her work would be. After a single specific bequest his son would receive half the estate. The precision was in the naming: '*my son William Henry Durham, born to my deceased wife Gwendoline Marie Durham formerly Gwendoline Marie Forester on February 2nd 1930.*' It was so exactly what she needed to read, Lydia wondered if William G could have been a family historian himself. His equally well identified wife-to-be, *Florence Ada Tweddle*, would also receive half. These two halves were after the special bequest of '*Ten Thousand Pounds to Laurence Harvey Durham, son of Florence Ada Tweddle, born September 29th 1954, to be held by her in safe keeping until he reaches the age of twenty-one years.*'

Lydia put the paper down and considered her breakfast. Laurence had been quite definite, he'd never heard of an inheritance for himself or for his mother. Which was not to say that Florence hadn't put the money in a bank account for him, or been dishonest in any way, but she didn't have a record of openness. Or honesty. Despite the concealment and lies, the idea persisted of a well-intentioned Florence acting in her son's perceived best interests. Whatever the reason, she'd hidden his father's identity all these years, so why not a few thousand pounds? Although forty or fifty years ago it represented a lot more than a few thousand today. At first glance the bequest seemed quite natural, provision for his new step-son was a generous act, but hardly remarkable. Yet as Lydia considered it more, she wondered if it was so normal. Surely at the age of five it would have been sufficient to leave Florence half the estate and rely on her to provide for Laurence. Why the specific bequest to a child who wouldn't see it for sixteen years? The more she thought about it the more it seemed wrong.

The will certainly explained how Florence had been able to afford the houses they'd lived in and the succession of private schools for Laurence. A mother would not deny her son his inheritance, she would find a way of giving him the benefit without him knowing the source.

It occurred to her that concealing the source would be entirely consistent with hiding his father's identity. Florence wouldn't speak of having been married, wouldn't mention the inheritance and wouldn't tell Laurence anything of his father. She couldn't say anything about any one of them without the rest unravelling. She'd never been on a cruise, she'd never done anything at all. Once denial becomes a way of life, once 'no' becomes the default answer, it must be easier than the complexities involved in telling the truth. But did all this confirm the idea of William G being Laurence's father? Or was that the biggest lie of all, the one from which everything else flowed? Still Lydia could not see a motive for the concealment, although a little wickedly, she could see a huge motive for marrying and then being rid of an ageing husband.

If Florence had profited so well from one will, might she not also have done so from another? It was a subversive thought and Lydia lacked the tools to explore it, but it would help explain a comfortable life unsupported by work. Finding if someone had left a will was one thing, but without a clue as to the name of the deceased, finding a beneficiary was quite another. The idea would have to wait, be tackled by a different route, perhaps after a short list of potential benefactors could be established. Today's new information was another small step. She still had Robert Ballard, the solicitor who'd been granted probate to follow up and more of William G's legal career might be found from checking The Law Society's records.

It seemed there was nothing that couldn't be tracked or traced. Keeping secrets was all the harder when anyone's marriage, or birth certificate could be found in seconds and ordered up in a few more. Whole lives and as many deaths were available for dissection with only a few keystrokes. Yet lying had never been so easy either, no sooner had it been said than it was repeated a hundred times and then a hundred times more. Even if some correction came limping along behind, the lie could never be quite undone. Like the old church complaint of the devil having the best tunes, the lies were always more seductive than plain old truth. When Florence had started out with her big lie, whatever it was, she could never have imagined how easy it would be to uncover so much of what she'd concealed. Having worried away at Freddie's big lie with perversely little help from him and yet still found his Linda, Lydia told herself she could surely do at least as well for Laurence.

∞

Late in the day, Lydia made the decision to visit Freddie. She was almost there, about to turn into his street when she remembered the flowers. It took her another twenty minutes to find a service station and purchase an expensive bunch of sad carnations - the last-minute token of a hundred hospital visits. Their mean little buds already fringed with brown made her wish she hadn't bothered the moment she put them in a vase in his room. Freddie was just as they'd said he was, unchanged. He lay where she'd last seen him in a peaceful, drug-assisted sleep. She took her laptop to play the clip from Lynn Brighton's starring role with the lifeguard a couple of times, in case he could hear it, on the chance that it might bring him some kind of comfort, but nothing disturbed the rhythm of the numbers. She stayed half an hour longer, talking to him about wills and certificates and a holiday cruise to ancient places.

She was home again by eight-thirty and mellow with half a bottle of wine an hour later when her phone rang. An unknown number. She studied it for a few more rings as if the numbers would by magic identify themselves. She didn't answer unknown numbers, and would have let it ring out had she not suddenly realised it would be Stephen calling from his hotel.

'Hello, how's it going?'

'Yeah, all right,' said a slurry female voice.

'Oh, sorry, wrong person.'

'Yeah? Who's this? Are you the one what wrote me that letter?'

'Oh, sorry, yes, yes. I'm Lydia, I wrote about...' she stumbled over who she'd written to, what she'd written about. 'The project, the TV show. The Carry On Girls!' she said triumphantly when it finally clicked into place.

'You still looking for her, looking for that Linda Thompson? Lynn Brighton she was, know that?'

'Yes, I knew that. Did you know her?'

'Oh yeah, I knew her. I wasn't gonna call, all a long time ago that was.'

'Yes, I know. You didn't say who you are.' Having gathered her wits, Lydia was keen to keep this lady talking, whoever she was.

'I'm Bella Wentworth.'

'Bella Wentworth?' Lydia struggled to get the names disentangled. 'I need my notes and some paper. You knew Linda Thompson?' Then, to avoid focusing solely on one name added, 'You knew some of the girls back then, in those old films?'

'Yeah,' the woman laughed, 'oh, yeah, I knew 'em all right.'

Having got her notes open, Lydia looked down the list of the five she'd written to. 'Oh, you're Belinda Wentworth, in Bushey, is that right?' Lydia was overjoyed, 'You used to be Belinda Andrews!' She practically danced round the room hugging herself.

'Yeah, I did. Used to be Bella DuBois too, and Bella Michelle. Somebody else too, I think.'

Michelle meant nothing but DuBois was a name on Lydia's list of starlets.

'DuBois? You were Bella DuBois? That's wonderful, I had no idea.'

'Yeah, well anyway, what's it about?'

The Carry On Girls project was up and running. Lydia dropped a couple of other names to underline her knowledge and sincerity, then spoke of high hopes she had of the whole idea, how she'd spoken to a few people and how much they'd liked it. She was at pains to say it was in its early stages, that nothing was fixed, that she had to come up with an interesting slant to get the big players interested. As she said it she wondered if 'players' was a good word, if it might be too clichéd for a real insider to use, but Bella didn't seem to notice.

'Just digging up dirt, are yer?' Bella said, and for a fleeting moment Lydia heard her uncle Freddie speak.

'No, not just the dirt. Maybe a few laughs, a few tears too I expect.'

'Plenty of them.'

'I expect you have so many stories to tell. How did you get started in it all?'

'Usual stuff, someone yer know's got a friend who's got a friend.'

Lydia knew she wouldn't get much of substance from this conversation, but it might be the gateway to another. There was nobody better placed to tell her Linda's secrets than her cousin who'd not only grown up with her but shared her almost-famous career.

'Can we have a talk? Can I come over to see you? I'm in Oxford, you're in Bushey, right? I could come over tomorrow.'

'Nah, we got family over. Maybe in the week.'

Family over? Oh to be at that lunch table. But Lydia felt Bella slipping away into a vague arrangement she'd think better of when she woke sober on Sunday.

'Monday then, I'll come to you, we'll go out for a drink, maybe some food. Is there a nice place near you?'

10

The idea of Florence Durham being a beneficiary of other wills or generous gifts would not go away. It seemed unlikely that such good fortune would occur twice but, try as she might, Lydia could think of no other way in which Laurence's mother could have supported such a comfortable lifestyle for so long. Half of poor William's estate would have bought a lot in 1960 and with careful investment might have been stretched out for a good few years, but it wasn't enough for a lifetime. There was certainly no inheritance from her mother, Alice, who remained alive and reportedly well in her late nineties. If she was anything like her daughter she might go on for a long time yet. And Alice's own position appeared to be similar, a life with invisible means of support. She was someone who could certainly throw more light on the family's affairs if she chose to, yet according to Laurence the chances of her doing so were nil. Even so, she and Florence's father, Jack, might be worth further investigation, although as far as Lydia could tell, Florence's birth and marriage were the only instances of him and Alice appearing together in any record.

Perhaps both mother and daughter were professional gamblers, or had hidden careers as successful performers or writers, although keeping such things hidden from a son would be difficult and surely unnecessary. Lydia considered the idea of an essential lie, something that might justify the deception and Florence's refusal to reveal what any son had a right to know. Simple theft might be at one extreme while at the other might be an affair with a prince or prime minister. And if there were no limit to the might-have-beens then why not spies, retired from active service and living on pensions from a grateful nation. There seemed no middle ground between the mundane and the incredible.

For a couple of hours on Sunday morning Lydia fiddled at research and found nothing of importance down all the blind alleys that Google offered her. She hadn't realised just how many family history sites held lists of the beneficiaries of wills. They were nearly all for specific areas, counties mainly, and nearly all concerned themselves with mid-19th century fortunes left by local worthies. And none had an index of those mentioned by name. But with little direction in her searches, the details were seductive, soaking up her morning satisfying idle curiosity. Apart from one she found for a local celebrity in Blackpool, none had any commentary with them, leaving her only to wonder at the circumstances which led to special bequests to maids and gardeners, vicars, shopkeepers and doctors. No doubt they all performed their duties admirably, but surely other stories lay concealed by the dust of decades.

From vaguely looking for Tweddles and the source of their affluence, Freddie's predicament played on her mind. She should probably see him again, yet she had nothing to offer, nothing until she'd met Belinda and charmed or bribed some secrets from her. Apart from having to get herself dressed it would take little effort to drive over to Bedford, and he'd surely be pleased to see her if he was awake. She caught herself playing lady bountiful again, the dispenser of charity and visits to the needy and dying, gathering their gratitude to confirm her own importance. She would phone and leave a message, that would be enough.

Instead of driving for a couple of hours, her time would be better spent preparing for supper with Belinda Wentworth, or Bella as she was now. If she tried hard enough, Lydia could convince herself that the picture she'd painted of her research was not really that far from the truth. Bella had been curious enough to respond, even if it had taken a little Saturday night drink to turn curiosity into action. Flattered by the attention and the prospect of more, most likely. Perhaps finding some specific details of Bella's life and times would be rewarded with an easier interview over a pub meal. And besides, it dawned on Lydia that she had little else to do. The avenues of enquiry open to her for both Freddie and Laurence had narrowed almost without her noticing. If Bella couldn't, or wouldn't, tell her anything of Lynn Brighton she had no plan B for Freddie's saga. She didn't even have a plan A for Laurence. What she had for him raised more questions than it answered. He might be William's son: that was it, that was really all she'd found in answer to his plea for help.

Bella Wentworth, née Belinda Andrews, had enjoyed a long but undistinguished career as Bella DuBois. Lydia had the bare bones of it from her previous searches, now as she looked closer, it seemed there was little more of substance to be discovered. As Bella Michelle she'd fared little better, confined mainly to roles needing little acting and few clothes, the bikini being her usual costume. She ranked just above background and had regular speaking parts. When her bikini days had passed, her credits became less frequent. Even so, she'd appeared in more than twenty films and had several years in seaside summer shows - always the support, never the star. By the time she'd finished making a comprehensive file, Lydia thought she probably knew more of the details than Bella would remember. But it wasn't these details she was really interested in, it was personal memory.

Just as she thought she had enough for her *Carry on Girls* project to be credible, she followed one last link and found clips from hundreds of British films from the 1950s through to the late 80s. The site specialised in naming the extras and background actors, especially those who subsequently progressed to bigger parts, even to leading parts. The link presented Lydia with a familiar scene, the beach with the hapless lifeguard a few seconds before Lynn Brighton delivers her line. A still shot had two faces circled in the crowd that gathered round, one was labelled Bella Michelle, the other a name Lydia didn't recognise. If it hadn't been placed in front of her she would never have noticed the girl, the shot was too quick to allow recognition, and if she had she would have said it was Lynn Brighton playing both parts. In a moment she had the original clip she'd made for Freddie and paused it to compare the two faces. They could have been twins.

Lydia sat back and considered the frozen faces side by side on her screen. Linda and Belinda, childhood playmates, schoolmates, then paired as cheesecake in the same second-rate films. And cousins, yes, that was easy to see, the likeness was striking. Was this a glimpse of another dark slice of Freddie's old life, had he seduced not only his bright-as-a-button Sylvie but her little sister Kate as well? Or did imagination and suspicion run away with her, were their looks no more than a family likeness? Maybe both girls were the spitting image of their grandmother and Freddie had nothing to do with either of them.

The date with Bella took on an added interest: her looks would have been Linda's looks if she'd lived that long, it would be like dining with a ghost, a vision of a different destiny. Photos! Lydia suddenly thought of photos, she should have asked Bella to bring photos. She would certainly have some, albums full of them no doubt. Twenty-something films rubbing shoulders with some of the once and future stars of the industry would have produced a lot of photos. Lydia grabbed her phone and dialled without further thought. As it rang twice she remembered the family visit to Bella's house, the reason they couldn't meet today. Much as she would have wished to be there, to meet all and every one of them, she didn't want to pester Bella. Something told her that Bella would need to be treated with great care if she were to give up her secrets willingly. After a third ring it was too late to hang up, after a fourth she could only hope for an answering machine. Her prayers were answered when a man's voice told her that Trevor and Bella would call back if she left her number. In as matter-of-fact way as she could muster, Lydia asked Bella to call when she could spare a moment.

∞

The place was crowded, people milling about looking for a table when there were none to be had, all driven in from the terrace by the drizzle blowing in from the west. A few determined souls kept their places under umbrellas, shielded from the worst of it by the willows bending down to the Thames. Gloria had called, rousing Lydia from her Sunday lethargy and insisting she meet for late lunch with her and Eddie at The Rose Revived, out by Newbridge, well away from Lydia's usual riverside haunts. She hadn't had the energy to refuse and was feeling a little guilty that she'd shown so little enthusiasm or interest in Gloria's big day. She couldn't even remember if she'd ever met Eddie.

164

As she scanned the bar she felt a hand on her shoulder and a familiar voice breathed beer into her ear, 'Over here, you dozy cow!'

She turned into Gloria's beaming face and outsize hug, then followed her to a corner table being defended by a man with a weathered face and a shock of steel-grey hair curling round his shoulders. She'd expected someone younger, fatter, louder, someone different in every respect. No, she hadn't met Eddie before, she would have remembered intense blue eyes and an easy smile.

'Lydia, meet Eddie, the soon-to-be Mr Fitzgerald,' she said with a theatrical wink and laughed at her own joke. 'Eddie, this is Lydia,' then, adopting a cut-glass accent, added, 'of whom I have told you so much,' and gave an equally large wink.

'Hello,' he said quietly, offering his hand, 'nice to meet you, Gloria's always talking about you,' which in its own modest way gave Lydia quite a surprise. She was prepared for dull ignorance, or overwhelming exuberance, not for soft-spoken and polite.

'Quiet you,' Gloria commanded, 'Go and get the lady a drink.'

Eddie did as she asked but not obediently, more as if it was his own idea. Lydia turned to her friend and tried by facial expression alone to indicate her surprise and approval. It was as if her own new status of being in a relationship qualified her to judge, where not long ago she'd have had no opinion at all.

'He's all right, eh? You reckon?'

'Very much so, yes. He seems, well, very nice.'

'Too nice for a tart like me?' Gloria laughed again, 'Yeah, well don't tell him that, OK.'

Eddie returned with drinks and they raised their glasses together and toasted each other and their futures. Gloria was naturally full of her plans for the wedding and Lydia couldn't help noticing how they seemed to be very much her plans and not their plans. But Eddie smiled and nodded where he should and otherwise paid attention to Gloria without competing with her or attempting to deflect the flood. Lydia was irresistibly drawn back to his face, those eyes in particular, and since he was speaking so little he noticed each glance she gave him. A full head of hair disguises a man's age, but she put him at late forties, a good ten to fifteen years older than Gloria. He was certainly a cut above anyone she'd previously been involved with, despite being 'too slow to catch a cold.' Lydia chose not to remind Gloria of that dismissive comment, maybe slow old Eddie was just the tortoise that Gloria's hare needed.

'I know you're not going to remember all this, so I've written out all the important bits, times, dates and places. We'll do the proper invitations next week.' She fished an envelope from her bag and passed it to Lydia. 'We'll have a little night out the week before, when you'll have to make sure I get home safely, and you'll,' she looked at Eddie, 'have to make sure you're nowhere to be seen.'

Eddie nodded, 'I can do that, I'm quite good at that.'

Lydia opened the envelope and looked at the details Gloria had neatly written out, and how she'd added cryptic little notes and smileys beside the bare facts of times and places. Lydia recognised the venue as being one of Gloria's preferences, but there'd been some question of availability.

'You sorted it all out then?'

'Yep, everything fell neatly into place, including him!' she poked him playfully and he nodded and smiled at his good fortune. Yes, he really liked her and that thought pleased Lydia immensely.

When Gloria's recounting of all the wedding details and plans had run its course, Lydia took advantage of a lull to ask Eddie what he did, hoping that Gloria had never told her.

'Work on the estate at Blenheim. I say Blenheim, but could be anywhere, it's a big estate.'

'Anything in particular?'

'No, whatever's needed, depends on the season. Often involves driving a tractor, though.'

'Wasted, he is,' Gloria suggested, 'could be anything he wanted to be.'

'I am what I want to be.'

'I know, lover, I know. But you could be a hundred other things.'

'Not many can say that,' Lydia said with some feeling. 'I still don't know what I want to be. Have you made any decisions yet?' she asked Gloria.

'Oh yeah, Mrs Culley of course,' was the wide-eyed reply. 'But no, I'll have to work, we can't do on Eddie's money, but I'll get something. I've been behind a bar before, I can do it again if I have to.'

'What about the house at Kennington? Anything happened on that?' Lydia asked, avoiding direct reference to their previous conversation.

'No. And don't get any more ideas, thank you. Eddie's put in for an estate house, we might be lucky, there's one coming up at Hanborough soon.'

'Gloria told me about your detective work,' Eddie said. 'Could you earn a living at that? She's said how much it means to you, how good you are.'

'No, nobody would pay for that,' Lydia said quickly, amazed and embarrassed that Gloria would have spoken of her in such terms.

'You might be surprised, people pay for a lot of things these days.'

He was right, people did. One of her current preoccupations would probably pay handsomely for all the work she was putting in to find his father. And in different circumstance the other would've happily given money for news of his daughter.

'It's a thought. I'll need to do something. Eventually.'

∞

She'd half expected a call from Stephen by the time she was back in Osney, but none came. At eight, after she'd fiddled with a few long-overdue domestic jobs and made herself spaghetti topped with butter and pesto and pretended it was real cooking, she called and left a message. Even then she worried he would think her too needy, after all, they'd often gone a lot longer than a few days without speaking. But the change in their friendship, adding the physical, had drawn her closer, she did want to see him more often, stay closer when they were apart. If not, then what was it for, just the pleasure of the moment? Having denied herself the possibility of such things for years, even with Stephen, the desire to hold him, to be held again, was unfamiliar yet insistent.

A few hours with Gloria and Eddie had served to remind her how much she missed him. Once the showers had passed, they'd walked a mile or two by the river, Eddie at one with the sounds and smells and the light of the earth and the water, while Gloria felt her way in alien territory, happy to be guided by his quiet words. Playing gooseberry is never easy, the more so when one of the pair is so attractive and their coupledom underlines what the gooseberry lacks. Lydia found herself forming the question of how Gloria of all people could have landed such a catch and rebuked herself for her lack of charity. Hadn't Gloria as much right to find a good man as anybody? Didn't she have a good heart beneath her abrasive shell, wouldn't she love a man better than most men deserved? Might others not say the same about her and Stephen, indeed, Gloria had called her a lucky cow more than once. As she dragged herself to bed at ten, still adjusting to the shapes and shadows of her changing world, Lydia reflected that now there were two lucky cows.

Sleep wouldn't come, no matter how many times she rearranged her body and fattened her pillow. Drowsy visions of Eddie, of Stephen and even Michael, swirled round with Laurence and his mother. Geoffrey Spencer sat waiting behind his desk at Ffynne & Co while Freddie languished in Willoughby House, at the mercy of the moon-faced girl and her nursery-nurse ways as his numbers ticked down. She owed all of them something, whether it was time or attention or apologies for unspoken thoughts.

Around eleven she heard her phone ring downstairs and cursed her thoughtlessness. She wouldn't reach it before the voice-mail clicked in, so for a minute or two she contented herself with the knowledge that it would be Stephen, that he had called and it would be enough to settle her. But not answering, not returning the call when he'd made the effort only added to her burden. She stumbled down, collected her phone and fell back on her pillow before dialling.

'Hello, were you asleep? You said to call any time.'

'Did I? Yes, good. In bed but not asleep. Are you home?'

'No, on the way. At King's Cross, leaving in about ten minutes.'

'Oh. Long weekend then.'

'Yes, spent most of it in Paris, but not a lot of fun.'

'Paris? Let me guess, not something you can talk about.'

'One day, but not now. Anyway, it might take me away for a month or so later on. We'll talk about it. How was your day?'

'It wasn't Paris. Lunch with Gloria and her new man. He's nice.'

'Good. We should have them over, if you like.'

We. Yes, we should, shouldn't we. All her anxieties, the thin edges of doubt that creep in during the restless night were banished in a single word. She'd been super-sensitive to it from the first time he'd said it and it had lost nothing of its potency. We. It warmed and embraced her, it said we are still we and happy to be so.

'Hmm, yes, maybe,' she said sleepily, but had already forgotten what she was agreeing to.

'Anything else before I let you get to sleep?'

'Freddie's saga continues, I'm going to meet someone tomorrow who I think may be his niece.'

'Interesting. The *Carry On Girls* project. Good luck. Anything for Laurence? I'll see him tomorrow. He won't ask, but he'll want to.'

∞

Lydia was up early and into work by seven. It took no more than a couple of hours to clear her inbox and extract and prepare the figures for the more urgent queries. She didn't send all the results of her work immediately. Instead she kept them ready to send at intervals through the day. It was work she did well, as she had done for many years, but now anything less than urgent she put aside until another day. In the absence of any interest or guidance from above she'd also become the sole arbiter of what was urgent and what was not. She would deal with any new requests through the day with the same even-handed policy.

Satisfied, she turned to the first of her own tasks, spending a few minutes writing out a list of names, then putting a number against each. After considering the list carefully and changing two numbers, she called Ffynne & Co and begged a late morning appointment with Geoffrey Spencer. He, reminded of her inheritance, invited her to lunch, which suited her well. It enabled her to put 'solicitor's re employment law' on her personal availability diary for the day without lying, even though it stretched the truth very thinly.

The news from Bedford was little changed. Freddie had a comfortable night, in and out of sleep and asking for her. She sent him her love - why, she was not sure, it just seemed natural. And also to say she was getting closer and she'd see him soon. They promised to tell him.

Before she settled to her laptop and the prospect of an enjoyable morning looking for clues to Florence Tweddle's life and times, she called the library and discovered that *Clean Sweep* had arrived and awaited her collection.

∞

Bushey turned out to be a shorter journey than she'd imagined. Even taking the back roads by Thame and Wendover along the Chiltern Hills it took little more than an hour, which left time to find the pub and still have plenty to spare. She could sit and drink, which was tempting, but Lydia knew she'd need her wits about her if her first performance as a writer was not to be her last. This was as close as she could ever have hoped to get to Freddie's Linda, for his sake alone she mustn't fluff her lines. So rather than drink, she chose to find Belinda's house and snoop a little. Wasn't that what all good researchers did? It would give her an idea of how Belinda had fared in life, at least financially, and the size and age of the car or cars in the drive would amplify that.

When she realised where the house was, Lydia understood why the pub had been chosen: it was no more than a two-minute walk away. Driving slowly up School Lane told her something but not a lot. A straggling row of terraced houses, all extended till they looked like bursting with loft conversions and porches and glimpses of conservatories. A few, like Bella's, had front gardens tarmacked over to squeeze a car off the crowded road. It was a neat and tidy road, with neat and tidy houses, convenient for the school but not for parking. It told her a little of what Bella might be, a little of what she was not. She was not wealthy, she drove a modestly-sized car, and had probably extended her mortgage a few years ago when she and Trevor had extended the house. The need to extend suggested children. She circled past again, then stopped at the pub, there was nothing to be gained and she had no wish to be discovered in her snooping.

She ordered an orange juice when she really wanted white wine, selected a table in a quiet corner and arranged her notes and laptop ready for Bella. To pass the time she took out *Clean Sweep* and read the blurb, then turned a few pages before putting it down. It was too distracting to be sucked into that 1950s gangland world of cops and robbers when she was here to think about Bella DuBois and Lynn Brighton and their world of *Confessions* and *Carry On*.

'Are you Lydia, Lydia Silverstein?' asked a tentative voice. A middle-aged woman with dark hair cut short stood in front of her, frowning, looking intently at Lydia.

'Yes, it's Silverstream, Lydia Silverstream. You must be Bella, thank you for coming. Let me get you a drink, we'll order some food later if you like.'

'OK,' she nodded, 'dry white wine.'

Lydia studied Bella's face for a moment, searching for the girl in the picture, the girl on the beach, searching for her cousin Linda. She may have caught an echo, the way the elfin haircut framed her features, the shape of her mouth, but the distance was too great for anything more.

'I'll get a bottle.'

They sat a little awkwardly together, exchanging strangers' small talk, Lydia uncertain how to proceed, how a real researcher would proceed, Bella wondering why she was there.

'Is that part of it?' Bella said, motioning to *Clean Sweep*.

Lydia was caught off guard, forgetting that if the book touched on Freddie's life then it might also touch on Bella's. 'Oh, no, no,' she said hastily, 'that's something else, from the library today, I haven't even started it, it was in case you didn't…you know…'

'So, what's all this about then?'

'Well, a project, an idea for a book, maybe a TV thing too, about the girls who were in the films, the *Carry Ons* and *Doctors* and *Confessions*.' Lydia became aware of how garbled it all sounded, how disorganised she appeared, and steadied herself. 'Look, there might be some real stories, sad and happy about those days and how your lives have turned out. I thought it would be better to concentrate on maybe a handful of the more interesting stories, but include as many as possible.'

Bella nodded and took another sip.

'You're a bonus really,' Lydia continued, 'I wrote to you about Lynn Brighton, or Linda Thompson as she was, let me check, I've got so many names running round my head.' In her deceit Lydia couldn't remember exactly what she should instantly know and what she should be unsure of.

'No need, she was Linda Thompson,' Bella said.

'Well, I didn't know you were Bella DuBois or Bella anybody when I wrote. So for you to say, well, that's wonderful. Anyway, how did you get those names, DuBois and Michelle?'

'My boyfriend, he fancied himself as a manager. He liked the French sound, thought it was sexy I suppose. He was brought up on Brigitte Bardot. Never did much for me though,' and she laughed, relaxing into comfortable memory.

'When you told me, I looked up all I could find about the films you did. I found this with you and Linda, I wonder if you remember it?' She clicked play just as she'd done for Freddie and the lifeguard staggered from the sea once more, but this time she was looking for a different reaction, and this time she was sitting with someone on the screen.

Bella studied the clip intently, half smiling, a little regretfully Lydia thought.

'Blink and you'd miss me, eh? Funny thing is, I never saw that on the screen before. When it went out I think I was cut from what got shown. It was only a second or two but they cut it.'

'Do you remember it being made?'

'Oh, god yes. They used to do all those sunny seaside bits in bloody winter when no one was about. Freeze our arses off down at Littlehampton or wherever they took us.'

'Did you and Linda work together often? I know about this one, I thought there might be others.'

'A couple. She always got the lines, I never got them if she was around.'

'You looked so alike, you could've played twins.'

'Yeah, that's what I said, but Lynn wouldn't have none of it. You know we was cousins, right?'

'Yes, that's how I wrote to you,' then, in case that took her to questioning how, Lydia added, 'Sounds like you and she had different ideas. Were you ever close?'

Bella laughed. 'Close? Bloody right we were close. Sisters, more like.'

'In London, the East End wasn't it? You were born, what, mid-fifties? Tell me how it was, how you came to be sisters and *Carry On* girls together.'

'Her mum and mine was sisters. She lived with us for a while when her mum got married again and moved out. I dunno why she didn't go with her, but she lived with us. Went to school together we did, everything.'

'Her mum was Sylvia and yours Catherine, right?'

'Aunty Sylvia and Kate really, nobody calls her Catherine.'

'Still going strong?'

'Sylvia died a few years back, ten or so, but Mum's still going, I don't know about strong, but yeah, she's all right. Her and Dad still putting up with each other.'

'So Linda lived with you for a while?'

'Yeah, she was all right, we got on. Usual stuff about boys when we discovered 'em, but we was all right really.'

She took the bottle and topped up her glass. Lydia reluctantly declined.

'So how did you get into films?'

'Linda was mad keen on it, always wanted to be the star. She got in with someone who knew someone, the usual kind of thing. We must've been about fifteen or so and Mum says no, she couldn't go anywhere meeting some bloke to get her pictures done without I went too. So I did, we went to a studio up West, off Regent Street it was, and had some photos done. Mum would've had a fit if she'd seen us, but we were all right. Next thing we know, I get a call to go for a part and Mum says the same, not without Linda goes too. We never got the part, neither of us, but it set Linda off. She had the taste for it, she wanted it. I was just along for the ride really.'

'Was it always like that?'

173

'Pretty much. Poor Lynn, she had a rough time.'

'Yes, I think she must have. I've read all I can find about her, it doesn't add up to much, but I thought it sounded like a tragic life she had. It was really her that set off the whole idea of telling the story. Listening to you, I wonder if maybe it would be your story as much as hers or anybody else's.'

Lydia calculated that Bella was now sufficiently relaxed and engaged to be interrupted by food and more wine so they ordered and chatted on like old friends. Every now and again she remembered why she was there and the truths she stretched each time she spoke, drawing Bella into her false sincerity. Not that it felt false, it seemed real enough as she talked with her new friend. As the meal arrived and Bella began asking Lydia about her life and Lydia honestly told her the bare bones, she wondered why she was keeping a promise to an old man a few days from death and who would never know anyway. But unless they were flattered or deceived as Bella had been, who would have met a stranger in a pub to talk intimately of family secrets? The food was good and a second glass of wine eased Lydia's conscience.

'And you, Bella, do you have children?'

'Two. Grown and gone, thank goodness. No, that's not fair, they're pretty good, but it was good to get the house back to ourselves. They're not far away and we see them often enough.'

'Did Linda have any children? I read she was married, one place said married twice. And I read about her death. Was that true about children?'

Bella paused for the first time in their conversation, and contemplated her forkful of Welsh lamb. 'Are you writing all this, you know, for the book or is this private?'

'One day I hope so, but not without your approval. If you told me anything that's already public that would be different. The important thing is for tonight it's just between you and me, if we take this thing further we'll do it properly and I'll make notes and record things. Tonight is great because I can get a real flavour for how it might be done, what interest there might be. Nostalgia is a big seller.'

174

She was suddenly aware of the dangers of overplaying her hand, getting carried away with her new persona. *Nostalgia is a big seller?* Had she really said that? She needn't have worried, Bella had only needed reassurance, not a signed contract.

'Yeah, poor Lynn had a crappy deal all along. She loved the life, the parties, the promises, but she listened to the wrong people, made bad choices.' Lydia nodded sympathetically. 'She had a kid, Claire, and I know because Mum brought her up. She lived with us. I was there until I was twenty-one or two, Claire was maybe four or five by then. Mum and Dad kind of adopted her, she was theirs, Lynn was never any good with her. Lynn wanted it all hushed up anyway. She went to one of Mum's cousins in Scotland somewhere, she was going to leave the kid there but she came back later with little Claire Sylvia. She was such a sweetie.'

Lydia could scarcely believe what she was hearing, the very thing she'd hoped to uncover was there in front of her, and delivered by eye-witness testimony. Freddie had a granddaughter. She struggled to stay focused on what she should be interested in, her head suddenly filled with the thought of telling him, of finding a photo. The photos! She hadn't mentioned photos.

'Did Lynn see much of Claire as she grew up?'

'Not really, she came over now and again, but she was never close, she was never really a mum. Mum did all that.'

'What about later, did they get together when she was older?'

'They saw each other a few times. I lost touch with Lynn. She was all over the place, then she ended up in hospital a few times. You know she was living in a hostel when she died, poor sod. Wanted the moon and ended up with absolutely sweet FA.'

'That must have been so awful, how did Claire take that, was it a very bad time?'

'She was in Canada, she's never come back so far as I know. She stays in touch with Mum, she's got married, got a couple of kids of her own now. Funny thing is she married someone in films out there, not an actor, but like my Trev, an electrician I think.'

'Is that how you met him?'

'Yeah, we'd kind of known each other for a few years, on the set and that, and he kept asking. In the end I gave in, you know how it is.' She laughed at the memory, enjoyed sharing it.

'So he's probably got some memories, some stories of those days too? I never thought about all the people making the films. Do you think he'd be interested?'

'Probably not, knowing him. He'd have to stop watching the football. But you could ask him.'

'Oh, and I meant to ask before, did you keep any photos from those days? Not just you and Linda, but family photos, parties, off-duty snaps of some of the girls, I'm sure you know the kind of thing.'

'We got boxes of 'em. You should come and have a look, it's only two steps up the road. Come back and have another drink. You can meet Trev.'

Lydia would have loved another drink, and an opportunity to see the photos could not be missed. But with each embellishment, each step on the ladder of deceit she grew dizzier. It already seemed an awfully long way down. Another drink might easily see her fall.

'Yes, that would be fantastic,' she enthused, 'but I mustn't stay long.'

They stayed a few more minutes in the pub, Bella making sure that the bottle was drained before they climbed the slope of School Lane to Bella's house. As she had predicted, Trev was firmly settled in front of the TV, barely acknowledging their entry. The night was warm, with light lingering in the summer sky, so they sat at the back of the house with the French doors open, a new bottle from the fridge and three shoe boxes of Bella's photos from the cupboard under the stairs.

'There's all sorts here,' she said, attempting some kind of order in the handful she first picked up. 'You always wish you'd written on the back don't you? You think you'll never forget who that was, or when it was taken, but you do.'

'Maybe we could find some of you and Linda,' she said, then casually risked, 'or you two with Claire.'

'Don't really know what's in here.'

She rummaged further, selecting photos then dropping them back without passing them to Lydia. In an instant the box slipped from her lap and scattered its contents across the floor. Bella followed it, scrabbling around on her knees trying to gather the photos back into the box.

'Let me help,' said Lydia, joining Bella on the floor. The second photo she picked up was of Bella and Linda, arms round each other in big jackets that hung open enough to show their bikinis underneath. 'Is this what you meant about freezing your arse off?'

They both laughed like friends laugh together and Lydia felt a surge of desire to tell the truth about why she was there, sitting on the floor of her lounge holding a photograph of Bella and her cousin Linda Thompson. She desperately wanted to tell her about Freddie and the medals in a velvet-lined box that still had no home. Instead she fought down the urge and took up a handful of photos and began leafing through them. They were mainly of the young Bella, sometimes smiling, sometimes pulling a face, sometimes serious, always the actress looking for a role. In a few she was pictured with vaguely familiar faces, stars of their era, off-duty but ever conscious of the camera's presence. Several were signed with hearts and kisses added to the dedication 'for my lovely Bella' or a little more subtly 'ma belle Bella.'

'You know, I wonder if a few of these might be worth something, did you ever try and sell any?'

'Nah, they're all just personal. Trev's got masses of 'em too. He always used to get autographs or something small off the films he was on.'

'You'd be surprised, I think some of these would fetch good money, they're real photos, not the usual mass produced things. You must have had some of those done yourself.'

'Yeah, by the bucket load, but they never did any good.'

'Who's this?' Lydia held a square Polaroid of a young Linda and Bella, on a swing-seat by a pool with an older man, dark haired and lean faced, squeezed between them, an arm round each. In one hand he held a glass, in the other a cigarette. He appeared to be blowing a kiss to the photographer. A note was scrawled under the image: '*Spoilt for choice! L xx.*'

Bella thought for a moment. 'Larry, I remember he didn't like that, he was really snotty about it. He was Laurence something, an actor. We were fooling about at a pool party, somewhere down south, like Chichester I think. He was famous back then, really well known, Hollywood and all that, not just Borehamwood.' She laughed at her own often-repeated joke. 'Like I said, Mum would've had a fit if she'd known half the stuff we got up to.' She rolled her eyes and shook her head. 'Makes me go cold to think about it now. God knows why she thought we'd be all right if we was together. There's loads of stuff like that, I used to keep it all in a box under the bed. Look here's another one.'

She passed over another Polaroid. Again she and Linda were bikini clad, this time they were posed kissing the cheeks of the older man between them. He, playing to the camera, was wide-eyed as if surprised by their attention.

'He looks familiar, but I don't know his name.'

She took it back and held it for a few seconds. 'God, nor do I. I should do, we shared a cab once, all the way to a party in Maidenhead or somewhere out that way. Bit of an ordeal that was, I can tell you. Can't even think of his name now. Peter was it? Dickie something?' She let it drop on the pile. 'They're all gone now.'

Together they sat passing photos backwards and forwards between them for another half an hour. Some were unmarked and the faces no longer instantly recognisable, others featured the best-known names of British film in the 1970s and needed no reminder scribbled on the back and sealed with a kiss. There were a few studio shots but mainly they were private, off-duty snaps. Bella recited half-remembered stories while emptying another bottle and Lydia forgot why she was in Bushey.

When it came time to leave, the two embraced with genuine affection. Bella was never more sincere than telling Lydia whatever happened it had been brilliant to talk about the old days with someone who was really interested. At the door Lydia paused, collecting her thoughts as someone might check their pockets for all their belongings before leaving a train. There were names she must be sure of, dates to be cross-checked, faces to memorise. She had no notes, no recordings, no copies of photos.

'That photo of you and Linda on the seat with that actor, the first one we talked about when we sat on the floor. Do you think I could borrow it? I know the box it's in, it's on the top.'

'Yeah, 'course.'

She went directly to it and brought it to Lydia.

'Bella, something else. I wonder, do you think it would be OK to get in touch with Claire?'

'Yeah, can't see why not.'

11

'Freddie, how wonderful.'

The surprise was on her face and in her voice. Freddie was not only awake, but dressed and sitting in one of the chairs by the window. Lydia bent to give him a squeeze and a kiss on his forehead.

'What d'yer reckon then, come to see if I was dead, did yer?'

'I'm very glad you're not. I'd have had a wasted journey, wouldn't I?' She smiled to remind him of their pact, their understanding of give and take and shared secrets, but her lightness found no response in him.

'Yeah, all right. What yer got?'

'Well, it's what you've got that's interesting. I was in a pub last night with Belinda Wentworth. She's your Sylvia's niece, Kate's daughter. You know who I mean?'

'Yeah.' He sounded tired of the whole affair, willing it to be finished, yet now there was something else to contend with. 'Found her, eh? Clever girl in't yer? What else?'

'Here's the essence of it then, Freddie. Your Linda did have a baby, you have a granddaughter. Her name is Claire Sylvia McCreadie, I think she's in Canada, out west in Vancouver probably. She's married and has children of her own. You have great-grandchildren.'

'Bugger me,' he said with feeling and closed his eyes, his face briefly relaxing as if asleep. 'You sure?' he growled at her suddenly.

'I've ordered the certificates but yes, as sure as I can be. I wouldn't tell you otherwise.'

'And all quiet like, nothing said? You know what I mean.'

'No, nothing said.'

He seemed satisfied and shut his eyes again, apparently oblivious to Lydia's presence. It was gone seven on a wet Tuesday evening, she'd left work later than intended and hurried, as best as traffic would allow, to see him. She'd had nothing but a service-station sandwich to eat, but had still arrived happy and breathless, anxious to share her discoveries and share his pleasure in hearing of them. Now, in less than five minutes, it was over and done with. Perhaps such news needed time to digest, time to find the reaction, the emotion that goes with the knowledge. Perhaps it was a matter of wonder and not of joy. It could never happen to her, she could never discover a grandchild, no one would ever come to her in thirty years and say 'I think you're my granny.'

She turned her attention to the garden, lush and green in the warm August rain. It struck her as a good size, a manageable size, soulless certainly, but well proportioned. For the first time since the inheritance had provided the means and looming redundancy had provided the opportunity, Lydia knew for sure there was one thing she wanted: a decent garden to tend and to walk round when there was thinking to be done. And in the same moment she knew that she wanted the puzzles to think through, whether anyone paid her to do so or not.

'Freddie, you awake?'

'Yeah,' he gurgled.

'You know that film clip I showed you with your Linda on the beach?'

'Yeah.'

'I found out that her cousin Belinda, the one who told me about Claire yesterday, she was in the same clip. Want to see it again?'

He nodded, eyes still closed.

She set it up on the table beside him, let it run through from start to finish while he peered at the screen, leaning forward in his chair.

'Never saw it.'

'No, blink and you miss it, that's what Belinda said. Look again.' She paused the playback at the vital moment and pointed to the face, then to Linda's.

Freddie squinted at the image. 'Like bloody twins.'

'Your Linda wasn't so good with kids. Claire was brought up by Sylvie's sister Kate, kind of adopted. Belinda must've helped a lot too.'

'What yer tellin' me that for?' he suddenly struggled for air to give the words the force he intended.

Lydia put a hand on his. 'I get the idea your Sylvie must have missed out on being a mum, too, and on being a grandmother, like you missed out.'

He made as if to snap something else at her, but nothing came and he turned his head away. A little yellow tell-tale blinked by the numbers on his machine.

They sat in silence for a minute or two until the sad-eyed Sandra crept into the room. She and Lydia exchanged smiles and nods while Freddie seemed unaware of her presence. She looked at the machine but her expression gave no clue as to the meaning of the digits. Freddie looked up and saw her over him.

'What yer want?'

'Came to see how you are.' She stooped to his level and gently held his hand. 'Any pain right now? I can up the dose a bit if you have.'

'Nah. Piss off.'

'Yes, Freddie, on my way.' She turned to Lydia. 'Will you be here long?'

'Not sure, for a bit, unless you want me to go.'

'No, stay as long as you like, but Freddie will need some help getting to bed in a while.'

'He seems so much better today, I was so pleased to see him up and dressed.'

The carer nodded, but paused before replying. 'Yes. Seems is the right word. When he knew you were coming he insisted on getting dressed, didn't you Freddie?'

He turned his head and closed his eyes again, unable to argue, unable to determine who should be in his room or when, who should hold his hand or speak of him as if he were elsewhere. A turned head, closed eyes, were among the few independent actions still allowed to him. And cursing, that was one pleasure they couldn't deny him.

Sandra slipped from the room as quietly as she'd entered.

'Why are you so hard on them?' Lydia said softly, almost to herself, not expecting an answer.

'Thieving bitches,' he replied with something of the old force.

'Sandra? I can't see it.'

182

'Huh,' he grunted, as close to conceding the point as he was likely to get. 'Some of 'em. I caught 'em.'

'Freddie, are you going to help me with what to do with those medals?'

'Do what yer like.'

'What I'd like is to hear it from you. But I'm going to read a book about you instead. A policeman's memoirs. Apparently, you're mentioned. I'm hoping it'll explain why I'm still talking to you and yet have your death certificate.'

'Yer got a lawyer? Solicitor?'

'Yes,' she said hesitantly, 'only just.'

'Any good?'

'He's OK.'

'Get 'im 'ere.'

'Just like that? I could ask him, but he's in Oxford.'

Freddie considered this for a moment. 'I can pay.'

'What shall I tell him it's about?'

'Changing my will. And something else.'

'All right, I'll ask tomorrow, but he might not. Shall I get someone local to come in? They must know someone in town here.'

'Nah.' He reached to her hand and held it as tight as he could, pulling her slightly to him. 'Clever girl ain't yer? But time's nearly up.'

∞

She opted for a late start in the office, never her preference, but a convenience for the tasks in hand. There was today's begging call to Ffynne & Co, a detective's recollections of saving London from East End gangs, plus the worry of her car, which had noisily struggled to complete last night's journey home. On a purely domestic front there was a shortage of clean underwear. Somewhere in her day there should also be a place for Stephen, neglected since Sunday's call. Paris? Why would he have gone to Paris? If only she were not so preoccupied with Freddie and will-making she might give Stephen more thought. It took physical determination to remind herself to just stop for a minute or two and remember how they were together, how they would be again if she gave it half a chance, how it would make decisions about priorities really quite straightforward.

He answered immediately, bright and welcoming, 'You're an early bird.'

'Thought I'd catch you before I get started.'

'How was Bushey?'

'Really good if you count getting Freddie's granddaughter identified.'

'Good, but?'

'And fantastic if you were researching the starlets of the seventies.'

'So far so good.'

'And even better if you like deceiving people and conning them into telling their family secrets.'

'Ah, yes, there is that. You could fix it though.'

'How? It's done now. Bella's nice too, we had a good laugh, it was a nice evening.'

'You could actually do it, really tell those girls' stories.'

'I can't do that.'

'Maybe not. Anyway it's a thought and it would mean you weren't telling all those lies and it would let you enjoy yourself. For what it's worth, I think you'd be very good at it. I think you are good at it.'

'Well,' she conceded doubtfully, 'something we could talk about.'

'You'll be here at the weekend?' It was unlike him to ask, he sounded as if he needed reassurance, as if some doubt had crossed his mind, a doubt that needed to be quickly dismissed.

'Yes, if that's all right.'

'Very much so.'

No sooner had she said goodbye than she remembered her car. It was so long since she'd had anyone look at it she had no idea who to call. It would have to wait, she had yet to persuade Geoffrey Spencer to drive over to Bedford to see Freddie.

His secretary was polite but unyielding. Mr Spencer was in court all week, there was no chance of him even sparing five minutes in Oxford and certainly he would not be able to travel to any new clients. She could not even guarantee he would see or hear any messages until at least Friday afternoon. The vague idea of going to the courts and waylaying him crossed Lydia's mind, as did the thought of a small paragraph in the Oxford Mail, headed *Woman Arrested For Stalking Lawyer*. And no, the secretary continued, unfortunately Ffynne & Co had no legal partners in Bedford that she could recommend, the Law Society web pages would give her a comprehensive list.

Which was all very true and professionally correct, but not what Lydia wanted to hear. Nevertheless, she took the advice and in a few moments was confronted by the details of two hundred solicitors within twenty-five miles of the centre of Bedford. One near the top of the list caught her eye immediately. With it came the nauseous sense of having failed to follow up on something important. Ballard, Edwards & Joyce were less than half a mile from the centre and had all the badges and accreditations she could wish for, but it was not their location or their qualifications that attracted her. It was the first-named partner, Ballard, that jumped off the page.

It took only a few seconds to retrieve her notes and William Durham's will. They confirmed her first thought: June 21st 1960, Robert Ballard, solicitor and notary public of Bedford had been granted probate of William's estate, valued at precisely £173,291 11s 8d. She looked to the screen, to the notes and back again, hoping some excuse might manifest itself. How long ago had she planned to check on Robert Ballard? For how long had she thought it would be useful to know if he was a partner at the same firm as William had been? And there was Stephen thinking she might be able to research the stories of ten or twenty people at the same time, yet she couldn't even manage two. Laurence's faith had been misplaced. Stephen's too.

She could so easily walk away from it all, tear up her notes, shred the photos and burn the certificates, declare herself no longer interested, retire from the business of puzzles. The temptation was great but somewhere in the gloom, weakly, a yellow tell-tale light briefly blinked on. A miserable, cursing old man who would not thank her for her efforts, wanted a solicitor. Today. Mechanically she clicked on the entry, checking on the names of the solicitors in the practice. There was still a Ballard partner, a Derek Gregory Ballard. A link took her to the firm's web pages where a brief history informed her that since its founding in 1903 there had always been a Ballard partner, with the exception of 1943-46. The modern firm, enlarged and merged with two others, had been fashioned in the 1980s by the then senior partner Robert Ballard, great grandson of the founder Charles Ballard. It was all there, all laid out for her. It had taken only a minute or two to discover so much and yet she'd neglected to do so. This was not the stuff of the inspired investigator, only of a diligent one. She felt certain that a simple enquiry to Ballard, Edwards & Joyce would easily determine whether or not William Durham had ever been a member of the firm.

It was with great difficulty that she got past the receptionist, who, like many of her kind, saw her prime function as defending her masters from the rest of the world. The senior partner's secretary was no less easy, but susceptible to the extra pressure of a dying man's needs. Any solicitor, even a legal assistant would do for Freddie, but Lydia had her sights set on Derek Ballard. As the secretary wavered, Lydia casually threw in a mention of the old days and Robert Ballard and the scales were tipped.

'Did you know my uncle?' asked the latest in the Ballard line when she finally made contact.

'No, not personally, but I knew of him. He acted for someone I know, it's how I came to be calling you.' Not an outright lie, room for interpretation, but the truth content was minimal.

'I understand there's some urgency, tell me what I can do.'

So she did, she told him exactly what he could do and where he could do it and gave him an idea of how to prepare and the kind of person he would be dealing with. And he, to his credit, grasped the situation quickly and agreed to call at Willoughby House on his way home after his golf. She would have preferred sooner, but in the circumstances thought she'd done well enough.

'I might be there or I might not, it's not important. But if you need a witness for anything, ask for Sandra. There'll be others, but he doesn't trust them. He doesn't really trust anybody.'

'He trusts you, though.'

'More than he should.' She hesitated over her next request, unsure how to switch the subject without treading further on the thin ice of her supposed connection to Derek's uncle.

'Whatever happens with Freddie, could you spare me a little time too?'

∞

Inconveniently, frighteningly, embarrassingly, Lydia's car died before she'd even left Oxford. Most inconveniently it meant she would not see Freddie that evening, not find out how the interview had gone, not have a chance to talk about *Clean Sweep*. Frighteningly her car came to a smoking, shuddering halt in the wet and greasy middle lane of the Ring Road by the works at Cowley, a little before the evening shift change. Many who passed had the time to open their windows and curse or make obscene gestures, but none had the time to stop and assist. To her great embarrassment she was rescued by a police patrol who set out cones in the road and under blue lights directed traffic round her stranded vehicle while generally behaving as if she, as a woman, could not be expected to know anything about cars. But they did call a breakdown service to come and tow hers away.

When the drama had subsided and she was seated in the back of the police car like a criminal, feeling stupid and vulnerable, she realised how pathetically ill-prepared she was for a simple mechanical malfunction. Or any other malfunction, be it emotional or physical. Despite herself and her surroundings she felt her lips grow fat and the tears welling in her eyes. As she scrabbled for a tissue one of the officers consoled her that it was only a car, that it could have been a lot worse stuck out there in the rush-hour madness. She nodded and managed to concentrate on the car but it didn't help. Yes, it was only a car and she'd had no particular attachment to it until this moment, yet here was this shaven-headed policeman speaking of it casually in the past tense. It still had her belongings in it, it still existed, it was still her car even if it was broken.

187

A little less than gracefully, the patrol took her home, an exception they said, as she was in shock, normally they were under instruction to go to the nearest bus stop and no further. Nonetheless, she was grateful for their help and had recovered herself a little by the time she bolted the door behind her. Luckily there was still wine in the fridge. With only a moment's hesitation she ignored the remains of last night's and opened a fresh bottle. A thin drizzle put her garden out of reach, although she let herself play with the idea of walking in it anyway, what difference would it make to walk in the sun or the rain, what harm would come to her for being wet from a summer shower? But the ingrained wisdom of staying dry, the instilled folklore-fear of catching a chill, sent her reluctantly to her chair.

She sat for a long time, her car only one of a myriad failures to contend with. Yet it seemed whatever she did, whatever action or resolution she attempted would produce no more than cosmetic change, it would fix the way something was for now or for a few weeks or months, but it wouldn't truly change anything. There would be plenty more failures lining up to take its place. That was how it had always been, always would be, that was the truth she must deal with, a succession of disappointments, chief amongst which was Lydia herself. She could easily buy a new car, a new house with a garden to walk round, new clothes to replace her everyday threadbare, new hair, a remodelled face, brighter teeth, perfect nails; she could cruise the bluest, sunniest sea, dine out on lobster under the stars; she could brush Laurence's lost father aside, she could pay for Freddie's funeral, she could even become pretend friends with Bella. All things were possible, but why bother with any of them?

If only she didn't think so much. If only she could turn off the thinking, stop trying to solve puzzles, stop trying to second guess the right answer before the question was even posed. If only she couldn't see herself the whole day long, see how she walked and talked, see what she ate, see what she thought and see no future in any of it. She reached to fill her empty glass, conscious that she drank more than she used to, conscious that it was becoming a habit. It didn't help her to stop thinking, she never thought it would, but was it a subconscious desire, to make thought impossible through the haze of alcohol? It never worked, or she never drank enough to make it work. It made her feel marginally better for a few hours before making her feel marginally worse in the cold light of day. A zero sum at best. Which could not be said for her hips.

With the thought of weight, of fitness and health, came thoughts of Stephen, or more exactly, the feel of his body. He ate and drank as she did, appeared to take less exercise, though she took little enough, yet he was pleasingly lean and firm and walked like a man half his age when needed. He too was a puzzle-solver, a man with an active mind, commitments and loyalties that often pulled in different directions, yet he seemed at ease with it all, the very opposite of her struggles. Did he have his own black fog descend upon him in the silent solitary times, did he question his purpose at every turn, yet keep those greedy doubts pressed further down than she could?

Her hand moved to the bottle again and found it empty. On the floor beside it her bag hung open, its contents escaping onto the carpet, amongst them *Clean Sweep* with Gloria and the girls' shared lottery ticket slipped in as a bookmark. That was one thing she'd be happy to be finished with, the collecting of money, the monthly purchase and the occasional distribution. She should finish the book too, even though it was hard going and was yet to provide any insight into Freddie's old life or death.

Beyond her window the rain had almost stopped, although the clouds still hung low and heavy. It would stay light for another hour or so at least, and the urge to be outside, to be in the air, to be walking by the river was as sudden as it was strong. With it came the realisation that wherever she might live, wherever that manageable garden with its path for thinking might be, she wanted it close to other walking places, preferably the Thames, but failing that, another good-sized river.

There were no new paths from West Street for Lydia, she'd trodden each a hundred times, but some offered the prospect of change, others guaranteed the familiar. The towpath beyond the lock, winding round to Folly Bridge promised both. Munsey's boatyard at the old mill, the bridges, the monuments, all provided familiar landmarks, the summer busyness of the river ensured a changing scene. In the soft grey light nothing was hidden by shadow, although wisps of mist had begun to appear across the path, sodden from the day of rain. From the ground and hedgerow rose the simple smells of the plants and the earth, from the water itself came the complex odours that make one stretch of the river a fraction different to the next. Underlying it all was the thick, fat smell of lazy flowing water. Taken together it all reminded Lydia that she was alive, and should be glad to be so.

A little past the railway bridges her eye was taken by an approaching boat. She'd seen hundreds of boats on the Thames: barges, narrowboats, cruisers, gin-palaces of every kind, but never noticed one quite so elegant as the white-hulled delight gliding serenely towards her. It was under a gentle and quiet power, white masts fore and aft lowered to pass under the bridges. The running lights were lit, as were those in the cabin, glowing warm and welcoming. It was a boat for living on, if not for ever then certainly for a good stretch. She stopped to see it better as it passed on its way upstream and saw a woman at the helm. Beside her in the cosy cockpit sat a white cat, staring through blue eyes at Lydia as the boat, *Mijn Zwerver*, slid past. The woman glanced across, half smiled and raised a hand in greeting. Something in her smile told Lydia she was quite accustomed to admiring looks from the river bank.

The old romance of the river came straight back to her, impractical yes, cramped certainly, but suddenly hugely desirable. That was a boat she could be in, sleep in, live in. And thanks to her new wealth it was a boat she could probably afford. It had no garden, no walking space, but she'd have the whole of the river and all its walks at her front door. Such was the wave of enthusiasm, had the boat been for sale, had the money been in her pocket, she would have bought it right there and then, no questions asked.

She turned and walked on, no more than another twenty steps before she realised the light was failing more quickly than she'd realised. The cabin lights had been so welcoming because they shone out in gathering gloom. Her euphoria died as quickly as it had arisen. She turned and headed for home, surprised to see the stretch of river quite empty save for the fingers of mist reaching across it. The white boat with the white cat had disappeared. For a confused moment Lydia fancied it might've been an apparition, a vision conjured in her own head and nowhere else. It might even have been herself she saw at the helm. She fought down the first hint of panic with studied reason: no, the boat would be snugly moored with all the others in the marina by the mill, the entrance was not far along, time and speed and distance were all deceptive in the half-light before darkness.

As she walked resolutely back towards the lock and the safety of her house, she couldn't resist looking across several times to see just where *Mijn Zwerver* was moored, to see a cat silhouetted in the cabin window. Unusually, there was no sound or light from any boat in the marina that night.

As she sat in her bed, slowly warming after the damp had crept into her, she wondered if moving away from her cramped little house, away from her beloved river, might really be for the best. They held her there, she was their prisoner. Now she had the means to leave, the key to the lock. But her other jailer, inertia, still had her shackled.

∞

Thursday brought mixed news.

Word had passed round that the section was closing, which resulted in a surge of requests for information and analysis, mostly marked as urgent. Some were no more than five minutes work, easy enough for anybody, but others required time-consuming collection of figures and then establishing the right formulas and graphs to demonstrate meaning from the data. In a week or so, those asking for the information would be expected to retrieve and manipulate it for themselves. For the moment it was her job, it was what she did, but now, at the fag end of her time, Lydia had planned other ways to spend her day.

Around mid-morning a sympathetic garage man called to say her car was beyond economic repair. As a favour they would waive the towing fee and the disposal fee and ensure it was dealt with properly. Could she come and collect her belongings and sign the paperwork? Soon? She thanked him half-heartedly, wondering what she should do next. Did she really care what car she drove, so long as it was comfortable and reliable? Surely she could find such a vehicle without assistance, yet she had a sneaking feeling she'd be eaten alive if she walked into a car showroom without any knowledge or prior research. But the prospect of analysing her requirements and possible solutions was unappealing, it really did come down to comfort and reliability. For now, she'd simply hire a car for as long as she felt like it.

Slightly better news awaited her at home. A letter from her employers offered improved terms of redundancy, terms which they claimed protected the value of her pension and made allowance for her long and valuable service. Too little, too late for appreciation, she thought. Lydia had her own spreadsheet with all the vital figures plugged in, so checking the claims was a matter of moments. It was true, the offer was slightly improved, but it was at a price - clean break, no early pension claim, no offer of redeployment anywhere in the county, and she would need to clear her desk within a matter of days. All of which suited her well, not least because it removed the lingered doubt of alternative posts and dates and holidays. When remaining leave days were taken into account, she'd have to work just two more days, Friday and Monday. She had only to sign and return the form and it would be done. She did so immediately, and felt better for it. Then, doubting her own resolve, walked to the post box.

A call to Willoughby House brought nothing new. Yes, he did have a visitor as she'd told them, and the same man had called again today and seen Freddie. Sandra had been with them, too. As for Freddie himself, he was hanging on. Friday evening? They'd tell him, it would keep him going, something to look forward to. It struck Lydia that although their purpose as a hospice for the terminally ill was quite obvious, their principal therapy appeared to be giving patients something to live for, to hang on for, as if there were a prize on offer for the one that exceeded expectations by the greatest time. What about the people concerned, what about their wishes and desires in their blank, bland rooms? Perhaps keeping the dying alive as long as possible was for the benefit of their nearest and dearest. When Lydia's turn came, what then, would the culture have switched to the opposite extreme, would her end be hastened by the latest sweet-dreams chemical?

∞

'It's all right, I was going along to look in on him anyway. We can walk down together.'

'How is he?'

Sandra stopped a little way short of Freddie's room and put her hand on Lydia's arm. 'He hasn't eaten since yesterday morning, he had some porridge for breakfast, since then nothing.'

Lydia frowned, uncertain of what to make of this fact. 'He saw the solicitor yesterday morning?'

'Yes, I was there. Did you ask for me to be a witness to his signature?'

'Yes, I think Freddie trusts you. As much as he trusts anybody.'

'Thanks. The not eating, it's often how it takes people.' She paused looking directly, intently, at Lydia. 'Near the end. He's been waiting to do something or say something, you probably know more than I do, but whatever it was, I think it's done. Now he's said enough is enough.'

Lydia nodded and mumbled, 'I see,' but the truth was this entirely expected event caught her by surprise. In some illogical way she'd begun to think that as long as she was on the case, his daughter, granddaughter, the medals, the puzzle of him being twice dead already, as long as she was still working on all this, then he would stay alive to hear the results. Now it seemed he had all the results he wanted and was calling time. It felt unfair, there were so many more things she wanted to hear from him, all the stories he'd filled his lives with.

'I don't know if he's awake or not. In and out, I expect. Let's go and see him.'

It was Lydia's turn to delay the visit. 'How long? I mean usually, from here?'

'It takes different people different ways. Some say that's it, I'm done and they're gone in hours. Others it can be longer.' She spoke with kindness, but with complete frankness, choosing her words carefully. She was familiar with the dying and the manner of their deaths. Those she usually spoke to in this corridor were not.

If it hadn't been for the machine, she would have thought Freddie was already dead. The numbers blinked resolutely on, the peaks on the trace may have been a little further apart but appeared steady. The man himself was little more than a shadow on a white pillow, his long arms stretched out over the covers of his unruffled bed. His mouth was a half open, drawing constricted, shallow breaths to struggling lungs.

They sat one either side of him, each with a hand on his, not holding, simply touching. After he'd sworn at her, holding his hand had been the first thing he'd asked her to do. Remembering the moment, Lydia felt a little ashamed of her reluctance.

'Freddie,' she said gently, 'it's Lydia, come for a while, a chat if you like.'

He made no sound or movement in response.

'Well, I'll talk to you anyway, or just sit for a while. Sandra's here too, she says you saw the solicitor, sorted out what you needed. I'm going to see him about something else next week, he seemed nice on the phone.'

Sandra nodded her agreement.

'He might help me with a little puzzle, not your puzzle, not the medals, someone else. Someone who's looking for their father, or at least would love to know who their father was. We never really talked much about your father did we? George wasn't it, George and your mum was Esther. Tess, you said she was called. Do you think George ever bounced your Linda on his knee?'

He might have moved his fingers, or it might have been a spasm. He might have said, 'Yeah,' or it might have been an extra rasp in his breathing.

'Sandra, is Freddie in pain, do you think?'

'Hard to tell for sure, but probably not. Thankfully, that sense sometimes shuts down, but he's still on the drip.' She motioned to the IV bag and the little see-through valve. Like the digits on the machine, it had a rhythm of its own, blink and you missed the next colourless drip of fluid.

'Can you increase it?'

'No, not any more, that's it.'

The sat across from each other, Freddie prone and all but lifeless between them. Each saw a fraction of what the other was thinking, about hastening a death, helping the slide down the dark slope, easing the painful way. Each also saw there was no need to speak of these things, the slope grew steeper by the moment and the way seemed smooth enough.

'Do you think I should go and see Bella again, Freddie? She was nice, I did mislead her though.' Lydia and Sandra glanced at each other, Sandra with a faint surprise in raised eyebrows. 'Stephen says I could put it all right by doing the book we were talking about, the book about your Linda and Bella and all the others in their kiss-me-quick tops. Think I could manage it?

'And what about Claire? I'm not sure what I'd say to her, even if I got in touch, she might not want to know. Have you thought of that, she might not want anything to do with you and your past. I'm still reading about that. You never told me, never told anybody, I'll give you that, but my guess is you had good reason to keep quiet. There were a lot of bad things back then in your old world, not just bad things, terrible things. I don't know how much you did, I haven't come to your part in any of it yet, but I can guess how much you knew.'

'Lydia.'

'Yes, sorry, I'm rattling on a bit. God knows what I'll be like when I'm his age.'

'He's gone.'

'Ooooh,' she said, the single sound catching in her throat. She looked up urgently at the machine, willing it to resume its counting. Three unblinking yellow lights under three sets of zeroes remained obstinately unchanging, the peaks and troughs had merged to a single line, running to infinity.

They sat in silence for a few moments before the door opened and another carer, one new to Lydia, put her head round the door. 'I thought you were here, Sandra. Do you need anything?'

'No, I'll be out in a minute or two.'

The door closed behind her.

'I'll need to go and attend to a few things, in a minute. Will you be all right if I leave you here, what do you want to do? When you leave we'll need to sort a few things out and then we'll lock the door.'

Lydia nodded dumbly, tears silently flowing down her face.

'I know you're not family, but you're next best thing most likely. Do you know if he has family, anyone we should contact?'

'Not family he knows, or is in touch with. There's a granddaughter but she's never heard of him. Locked up? Is that what happens?'

'Yes, then nobody comes in by mistake,' she paused before adding, 'and nothing walks out.'

Lydia immediately looked to the cupboard where she'd last seen his old brief-case. She went to it and opened the door but there was no case.

'The solicitor took it, I saw him. He left a receipt for it, just a note he wrote out. It's in the drawer by the bed.'

Lydia opened it and took the slip of paper. 'All right if I take this do you think?'

'Yes. Will you be in touch about his other things? He doesn't have much.'

Lydia nodded. Having left Freddie's side to look for his case it seemed artificial to sit beside him again. Instead she stood, hovering between staying and leaving. He hadn't quite left the room, or so it seemed to her, and to leave before him was somehow unkind, deserting him in his last few minutes, despite what the numbers said. She knew for sure that if she left, even for a minute, she would find it empty of him when she returned. While she hovered so did Freddie.

'I must go,' Sandra said softly and in doing so broke the spell. The room emptied in an instant, as if a window had been thrown open and all the stale air had rushed out.

'Yes, yes, I should too.' She turned back to Freddie, relaxed in the final sleep. 'Should we...?'

'Yes, if you like.'

One each side of him they put his arms under the covers and lifted the sheet over his face.

12

'When will you tell Jacqueline about the, er, change in our arrangements?' Lydia nestled a little closer under Stephen's arm, wrapping herself in the warmth of his body, the smell of his skin. They'd kissed, although he'd barely woken, but the question had pressed on her from the moment she'd opened her eyes and found herself once more in Jacqueline's room, in Jacqueline's bed with Jacqueline's father, watching Jacqueline's curtains float lazily across the open window.

'I mentioned it last weekend, when we had supper together on the Friday, in London,' he said thickly, 'I thought I said something.'

Perhaps he had, but Lydia had no memory of it. She felt sure that it would've been something she'd remember, it was important.

'Was she, well, was she all right about it?'

'Yes, she was. Did you think she wouldn't be? We're old enough to make our own decisions, and she's not a child.'

'No, no, of course not, but,' she struggled for the words to continue, he seemed a little prickly, a little defensive, as if perhaps the conversation with Jacqueline hadn't been quite as simple and straightforward as he was suggesting. 'She does have a special place here, and with you, I wouldn't want her to feel I was, well, taking anything for granted.'

He rolled round to look at her, his face close to hers. 'No, she doesn't think you are. I don't think you are. She's very, very pleased for me. You do not come between us. She does not come between you and I.' As if to demonstrate the point he pulled her closer to him, wrapping his arms around her body, his legs around hers. If she hadn't wept so much the night before she would surely have started the day with tears.

She'd arrived late, pleased to be there, pleased to be with him again and secretly relieved to discover Jacqueline wouldn't be there until Saturday and then only stay until the evening. They ate and drank and spoke of work and cars until Stephen said, 'so, how was Freddie today?' and she didn't know how to simply say he was dead. Her face told him immediately, and he comforted her with warmth and words. He'd brushed a tear from her eye once before, but he hadn't seen her weep like this, not shudder and cry out with a running nose and thick wet lips and dribble down her chin and be unable to speak, like a child who's fallen and seen their own blood scraped red across their skin for the first time.

He'd mistaken her misery for a closeness he hadn't appreciated, for a loss greater than he'd realised. But even as the tears flowed, Lydia knew them to be tears for herself, for a broken car, a lost job and false friendships as much as the shock of covering an old man's face. Poor Freddie was indeed a loss, a loss which had crept up unexpectedly, but he was the trigger for all the emotions to rise as one, bubbling, writhing, disabling.

At length she'd recovered, cleansed by the outpouring. Afterwards they'd gone early to bed with no discussion of which bed, which room, and slipped so easily into each other's arms they would've been the envy of many lifelong partners. Lydia had slept soundly and deeply, Stephen less so, with old torments of his own stirred up by the evening's events.

When he'd properly woken and brought them coffee, they sat close and comfortable and reflected on their lives. It seemed as good a moment as any, and better than most, to finally share the facts of her inheritance with him. He saw immediately why she hadn't mentioned it, saw too that it introduced its own uncertainty, asked its own questions of her.

'Your job is settled, that's something,' he said almost absently. 'We go away in a few weeks, why not come and stay here until then, you can do all you want to get done from here as easily as anywhere.' When she didn't answer immediately, he added, 'Just a thought.'

'I'll need to think about it,' she said cautiously. 'I mean, thank you, it's a lovely idea, but I'll need to think about it.' After a few moments she said, 'Do you mean as a kind of try-out for something longer-term?'

'I suppose I do. I hadn't planned to ask, it just seems like a good idea, something we'd both like.'

'Right.'

Because it was a morning for saying things, a morning when anything could be said, she told him about weeping in the back seat of the patrol car and the police taking her home and later how she'd seen the white boat and the woman with the white cat. She told him how, taken all together, she'd begun to wonder about her sanity, what was true and what was not. She didn't tell him about the bottle of wine because it had already become mere trivia in the background blur.

Stephen, hearing the events of her week, understood a great deal more of what lay behind last night's outpouring and caught something of the scene at the river. 'Was it a beautiful boat? It sounds quite wonderful.'

'Yes, I thought for a moment I saw myself waving back at me.'

'The police car was real enough.'

'Yes.'

'Then it doesn't matter if the boat was a dream or not.'

He could have said anything, but he chose dream, not imagined, not hallucination, not nonsense, but dream. Yes, she might have dreamt it.

'I'll go home tomorrow, then I have the farewell day. Tuesday I'll see Freddie's solicitor. We'll talk about it again before I go back, how's that?'

When they'd had their pyjama'd breakfasts Stephen reminded Lydia that he had a little work to complete, mails to attend to, before Jacqueline arrived for lunch. When she simply said 'Paris?' he'd nodded. He dressed and took himself to the seclusion of his study. It was never off limits, but so long as he was in there, it usually meant he had work to do. Lydia lazed in the robe he'd given her, torn between idleness and showering.

Clean Sweep lay where she'd left it, the lottery ticket three-quarters through it. It was not one of the world's great reads. The ghostwriter had clearly done his best with some uninspiring memoirs and turgid prose 'as told by' Inspector Kingsley. Most of it was fairly run-of-the-mill cops and robbers but some of the war-time stories had been more interesting and a lot nastier. Much of it described police activity which probably broke the law, but in earlier times they'd frequently taken it upon themselves to dole out a rough justice, especially for lesser offences. The urgency had gone with Freddie, but curiosity remained and his altered identity might yet hold the key to finding a home for the Brenton medals.

She settled on a sofa in the sitting room, remembering the first time she'd sat there, her first visit to The Old Rectory, how like a comfortable country hotel it had seemed. It still did, but visit by visit it was feeling more like a home. If she wished, she could make it her home, for a few weeks at least, although she knew the hope was for a permanent arrangement.

She opened the book and began half reading, half enjoying the wonderful relaxation of the moment, the sheer luxury of lounging her way through a Saturday morning, all cares forgotten for the moment. But after a few more pages *Clean Sweep* took her attention more fully as Inspector Kingsley told the story of Tommy Quick.

> *Then in the early summer of '56, we had a bit of luck. And we were able, by one means or another, to turn that bit of luck to advantage. Good luck for us was bad luck for all the 'partners' in that set up, with just a couple of exceptions, the infamous Tommy Quick being one.*
>
> *Tommy was a junior partner, but he had family connections that gave him more clout than he should've had. Not that he needed any more, he was a tall man, and strong. People used to wonder why he was called Tommy Quick, but they never asked him and they never called him that to his face. He was Tommy because he was one of the Thompson boys, George Thompson was his real name. And he was Quick on account of two things: one, he had a fuse about two seconds long and he'd hit you before you'd finished speaking and two, he was fast. There was nobody ever got away from Tommy Quick, not in the playground as kids, nor later when it was dished out for real.*
>
> *Some of the old bombed-out buildings were being torn down ready for new flats to be built. Dozens had already gone and we'd been told that with them had gone a lot of secrets. They were, apparently, handy places to hide things*

away and you can understand why. A lot of rubble, some still dangerous to be in and many getting overgrown with weeds and covered in rubbish of all kinds. One of the informants we had then said we should look very carefully at a block that was coming down the next week as we might find something interesting, but we'd need to be quick because the contractors didn't stop for anything unless it was a bomb, and even then they'd sometimes take a chance it was a dud.

We got it all set up, then let them start work clearing the site getting the old walls down. Once it was flattened and the top layer of bricks and rubble was scraped off, we moved in on a Tuesday night with the bomb squad. By morning it was all roped off and we cleared a few people out of their houses in the next street so it all seemed right. We got the squaddies, sweating in their bomb kit, to dig in the cellar we'd been told about. Sure enough a couple of hours in they found a body. Back then, there were still bits of bodies, bones and so on, being found from the war, so it was nothing special to get an ambulance up and have it taken away. We knew what was going on, the squaddies had an idea and most of the people round there knew something was up, but we kept the game going so nobody was really sure and we didn't scare off the big fish.

It didn't take long to find out the body wasn't from the war, it was fairly recent and was that of James Andrews, a nasty piece of work who was probably responsible for two murders himself. He'd started off small time, then worked a black market scam through the docks in the war. They called him Little Caesar on account of his middle name, Julius, and he fancied himself to be more than he was and set up in competition to some of the rackets already covered in the East. He upset a few people who were nastier than he was and disappeared around May that year, just after he'd been to a wedding. The word was that he'd gone on a long holiday. In his pocket there was an unused train ticket, a *single to Skegness. Whether it had any other significance we never knew.*

James Andrews had been shot in the head with a bullet from a Roth M07, an old World War I pistol, not very common. Hundreds, maybe thousands of handguns of all sorts were in circulation around that time, mainly souvenirs brought back from the war. It was known that a lot of these were in the East End and one of the Thompsons had been caught carrying a Roth, although no charge had ever been brought. It supposedly belonged to an uncle who got it in Italy in '44. Wherever he got it, it was unusual and so were the bullets it fired.

A second piece of intelligence came our way. It implicated the Thompsons but wasn't specific about which one, or who had ordered Little Caesar's killing. At that time, things were getting out of hand with armed robberies and little crooks getting too big for their boots. Word came down that we were to arrest as many of the possible culprits as we could find as well as all the little hangers-on, and charge them with anything that might stick or at least stick long enough to keep them out of circulation. The idea was that if they were all inside and kept apart then we'd find at least one who'd crack.

How it never got out I don't know, but we filled the nicks all over north London that night, spread them about so nobody knew who was where. And because all the little errand-boys were in the net too there was no communications left for those who gave us the slip and nobody to do the running for the ones who pulled the strings. Of course we couldn't keep them all but we kept a lot and had a few successes too. Enough to make holding the rest that little bit easier.

Weeks later, just as it was beginning to dawn on a few of them that we didn't have much in the way of evidence, we had another stroke of luck. That gun, the Roth M07, turned up in a shoe box left in a bag on the Underground. Handed in at Whitechapel of all places and no record of who did the handing in. The bullet from Little Caesar's head was badly misshapen and wasn't a perfect match to the gun, but it was close. We didn't much care about that, but we did care that the Roth had some lovely clear prints from one of the Thompson boys: George Thompson, Tommy Quick as we called him, though his family all called him Freddie. Bingo, we could nail him, although a good lawyer might have had some fun because his prints weren't on the vital points you'd like them to be. Usually the whole lot of them would hold the gun, which would tie them all in to it, then they'd draw lots for who pulled the trigger. This looked a bit different, but no matter, it was a pressure point at the very least. He'd know he'd held the gun, and he wouldn't remember whether he'd touched the trigger, chances were that he had.

We thought we'd have some fun at Tommy's expense, run a few ideas past him, see how he reacted, just to test the waters, see what we might really have. He was in Wormwood Scrubs, on remand, already charged with being an accessory to Little Caesar's murder. Because it was the summer and the courts weren't sitting for the big cases there was a lot of them on remand. Some of them were held where they wouldn't normally be, and some of them were rubbing shoulders with those we knew were sworn enemies. They were in all the prisons in London and a few further out too. The idea was sooner or later there'd be trouble and then that'd be something else we could keep them on, and more than likely get a conviction too. And if they killed each other in the process, well who was going to worry about that?

The day we went to see Tommy Quick, he had an accident. He fell down some stairs, pushed more likely but we never found out the truth of it. He was bruised and a bit battered and first of all nobody noticed he'd been stabbed too. It was a bit of a mystery until they found the knife in his pocket. It looked like he'd stabbed himself as he went down the stairs. We ended up seeing him in the hospital wing as he was being stitched up. He looked a mess but mostly it was superficial stuff, although it had properly shaken him up, which suited us very well. All he said about the knife was that he'd never carried a knife, which was as close as he'd come to saying he'd been stabbed and set up.

He was lucky, another inch and he'd have been dead, and we told him that, but it gave us an idea too. Supposing he was dead, he'd be free to give us the inside story on the whole crew, if he had a mind to and if he had a little inducement. We had to act fast and keep it within a very small circle. We didn't have the whole thing worked out, it was just done to give us a breathing space, but we got the nod from someone at the top.

We told Tommy about the gun and his prints and that if he wanted out this was his chance, probably the only one he'd ever get. Play dead and he could have a new life, give it away and he'd be dead in a month anyway. He said he'd play dead. We knew once he'd started there'd be no going back, he'd have burnt his bridges. Then we played a little game of charades and got the doctor in quick and made out he was dying. We made sure that a couple of the orderlies, trustees who worked on the wing, got involved, fetching and carrying, everyone in a tizzy trying to save poor Tommy. Then while they were both outside Tommy died. Just as they came back in we were covering his face and shushed them outside again. Then we had a really good argument over how there'd be hell to pay for letting this happen, not getting him to a proper hospital and so on. We did it well and Tommy played his part, he was so still we thought he'd really gone. Then we would've looked fools.

Next we had to get him out, so it was all done as it would be if he was really dead. The room was sealed up to protect any evidence, and a coroner's van was borrowed and brought in. Tommy went out in a coffin. Under escort of course. We took him to the mortuary and booked him in, all properly done. We gave him a uniform and he walked out and got in the van. The drawer he was supposed to be *in was left locked. Considering we'd cooked it up in a few minutes and here he was a few hours later, dead for all the world knew, we were pretty pleased. He slept in a flat out by Hammersmith that night, handcuffed to the bed post.*

Compared to what we'd done on the spur of the moment, all the rest seemed to take for ever. It was easy enough to find a corpse to take his place, we just used the next one floating in the Thames. Took it in the same way as Tommy had gone and popped him in the drawer. He was the right size too, Tommy was a big man. I still don't know who was cremated out at Manor Park a fortnight later, but he got scattered as George Thompson, aka Tommy Quick.

We had him at a place out in the country for a few days, he wanted to see his girlfriend who was in the family way and we said no, never. That's when he got the hang of it, realised there was no going back. That was the only moment I ever felt sorry for him, seeing it dawn on him that he'd lost everything. He knew we could throw him to the lions any moment we chose. We got the deal we wanted and he gave us everyone, everyone except his brother Andrew, but that was no great loss. It was all done up properly, we had a lawyer there making sure it was all covered. It was just the date that was adjusted, to a week before he was killed. And of course, him being knifed in prison, that confession and all the names he gave us would have been the reason for it. What he got out of it was a few quid in his pocket, about a hundred I think, a new name with all the trimmings and a chance to have a life. I remember it all came down in a brown envelope, a little man with a little moustache brought it in person from the Home Office, made sure it went straight into Tommy's hands and no other. Even made him sign for it. He paid the price though, no contact and a secret to be kept for ever, that was the deal. There are probably still people who'd like to kill him again, and if not him then someone close they could get their hands on more easily. Whether he made any good I don't know, there were rumours about him a few years later, but we've never heard from him again.

With his statement signed and sealed, we put a bit of pressure on a few others, and that led to one or two more deals being done. Nothing as elaborate as Tommy's, but that was all done on the spur of the moment, most likely wouldn't have worked if it had been planned. We never knew for sure who killed Little Caesar, but we did put a few nasties away for a good many years, one of them probably did it. Maybe it was Tommy all along. He always said he never knew, maybe he didn't, maybe it was his brother.

Lydia read on for a few more pages, learning how these events had changed the criminal landscape in the East End, how other names came to dominate and how the police themselves were sucked into the gangs as the stakes got higher. In the end, Inspector Kingsley lamented, the conviction and sentencing of less than a dozen of the smaller fry had little effect on the criminal culture of the East End, a culture which he concluded was 'inbred'.

She turned back to the passage on Tommy Quick and read it again. It should have been difficult to reconcile the text with the man she'd sat beside as he died in a lonely, bare room in Bedford, but it wasn't. Involuntarily she rubbed her wrist when she recalled how tightly he'd grabbed her as she'd gone through the list of possible Lindas. She'd check later, but wasn't there an Andrews in there? Of course there was! It was Belinda, she'd been born Belinda Andrews. Little Caesar, was he her father? Had Freddie killed Belinda's father?

She rushed upstairs and dragged her laptop from its case. It took its usual time about starting, long enough that Lydia added a new computer to her list of desirables she could now afford. Yes, there he was, James Julius Andrews, not Belinda's father, her grandfather. Died before she was born. And there was another curiosity: if Kate, Belinda's mum had married an Andrews and Sylvia had a child with Freddie, a Thompson, then the two sisters got together with boys from two warring gangs. Lydia wondered if they were ever together for Sunday lunch at the Brights. Now that would have been a question to ask Freddie. 'Bleedin' sick joke,' he'd probably have said.

Thinking of him again, it suddenly occurred to her that all that secrecy, living his life as Freddie Bellinger, never going back, never telling what happened to anyone, not even in his last days, it was all wasted. His secret was out in 1976, and what she'd just read might not have been news even then. He kept his part of the deal but Inspector Kingsley didn't keep his. He'd probably have given away his name too, if he'd have known it. There'd be a file somewhere, the Home Office most likely, with his name on it, or rather, both his names on it. She imagined it in a cardboard box with other such files, stored in a warehouse with mile upon mile of racking stacked ten shelves deep. Unindexed, unfindable, a very safe secret.

∞

'Wow, that looks fantastic. I'm very jealous,' Jacqueline said, with sufficient feeling that it sounded quite genuine.

They were passing round the brochures for the cruise which Stephen and Lydia would be taking in a few weeks. Although he'd sent most of the same information to her, Lydia hadn't spent any time looking at it, in fact she'd half forgotten exactly what he'd arranged. What she did remember was how much she was looking forward to it and the longer she put off knowing the details the longer it would be something to look forward to. But once Stephen had brought the subject up over a lazy supper, Jacqueline's enthusiasm and questions could only be satisfied by seeing everything. When the glossy paper details were exhausted, the online sources, previous passengers' opinions and photographs, the insider tips, the cafés with the best menus, the ideal beach to swim from, all these things and more were examined in depth. After half an hour Lydia was beginning to feel as if she'd already been on the cruise, walked the streets of Ephesus and lounged on the beach at Kusadasi - the most favoured part, of course.

She took it all with as good a grace as she could find. Stephen was in high spirits, clearly enjoying his daughter's company and very pleased with himself that he'd identified and booked such a trip, one which had met with her approval.

'I never asked about your passport, I presume...' he left the question unasked but it sent a tremor through Lydia. Hers was where, exactly? And how old and out-of-date might it be?

'Er, yes, I never gave it a thought. I might need a new one, how long does it take?'

'Only a couple of days if you go and wait in the office for them to issue it,' Jacqueline said.

'Don't worry, there's plenty of time to get one,' Stephen soothed her concern, 'I'm glad I mentioned it.'

'And I must get off and leave you two to your own devices.' Jacqueline made big eyes at her father and rose to leave, 'I have an early start tomorrow.'

Lydia stood and they embraced lightly while Stephen beamed at his two favourite women getting along so well. While he went to kiss his daughter goodbye and see her to her car, Lydia sank back into the sofa. She was cross that she hadn't been quick enough to say her passport was fine, bang up to date, no problem. Instead she felt foolish and inadequate. Again. No harm done, she supposed, it made no difference to anything.

Beside her on the cushion were all the papers for the holiday. Despite having missed the chance to discover it all for herself, she still relished the prospect of the trip. It was exactly the kind of thing she'd often dreamed of, now Stephen's company would make it better than any dream. Idly she opened the white envelope marked 'Your Travel Documents' and leafed through the half-dozen papers. One was the detailed itinerary with flights and expected sailing times. She studied it for a few moments before fixing her eyes on the departure date. Their outward flight was from Gatwick, two days before Gloria's wedding. She'd been mistaken before about the date and there remained a faint glimmer of desperate hope she might be wrong again. In her heart and in the empty pit of her stomach she knew it was false hope.

She heard the car on the gravel and shoved all the papers back in the envelope and picked up the brochure as Stephen returned.

'Are you all right?' he asked, 'You look very pale.' He had a clear memory of how she'd looked that day on the journey to Gawcombe Woods.

'Yes, yes, I'm fine,' she said, which was a very long way from the truth. She wanted to hide in a dark place and not come out until she'd found a solution and if that meant never coming out then that would be fine, that would be for the best.

'Are you sure? You don't look it.' He brushed the holiday papers aside and sat beside her, an arm ready to close round her, to coax colour back to her drained cheeks.

She couldn't speak to him, couldn't trust herself with a single word or sound. She couldn't trust herself to even look at him, he would see straight away what was in her head, see her for what she was and brochure dreams would be just that. Her breath came in little gasps, as it had when she'd wept in his arms last night and he held her again, thinking that the shadow of Freddie's death touched her once more. But last night she'd turned into him, buried herself in his shoulder, now she turned away, stiffness and tension in her body.

After a while she said, 'I need some air, I'll be OK,' and went into the garden.

Stephen didn't follow her. He wasn't sure what was wrong, but he knew enough to know it was not air she needed but space. His desk work from the morning was incomplete, cut short by Jacqueline's arrival, now he went back to finish it. Lydia would come round in her own time. 'I'll be in the study,' he called after her, 'Come and see me.'

By the time they were in bed, Lydia, having spun it out to delay the moment of contact, had recovered herself enough to speak. But the conflict remained locked inside her, a solution beyond her grasp. The nearest she could come to an answer was to delay her flight and join the cruise later. It was a lame idea, to do such a thing would change all the time between now and then and might fatally cripple the whole event.

When he put his arms round her she made to snuggle into him as she'd done before, but traces of the tension remained, there was no comfortable spot for her head, nowhere her arms were not awkwardly placed. Stephen eased away from her as she rearranged herself for the third time. He lay on his back with his eyes open to the almost-darkness of the August night. He wasn't waiting for an explanation, but he wasn't completely surprised when she spoke.

'Stephen, I've, um, messed up. Big time.'

She felt like a child, but couldn't help herself. It was easier to speak in the dark, she didn't have to suffer his expression, his disappointment. To be doubly sure she closed her eyes. But one way or another she had to share her distress. When he didn't speak, she went on, 'It's about the holiday, our cruise.'

He remained silent, but she felt him turn to look at her and she stole a look at him, a grey outline with a spark of light reflected in one eye. Please god, she thought, don't say something trite, like do you get seasick.

'I don't know how, but the dates, they overlap with Gloria's wedding. She's getting married on the Saturday after we fly out on the Thursday. I should've checked. Before now, I mean. I should've checked before now.'

Still he waited, as if he wanted to be sure she'd finished with the whole of her confession.

'Sorry,' and when he said nothing she squeezed his arm and said, 'Please say something.'

'I'm not sure what to say. Or do,' he said, as much to the darkness as to Lydia.

'We could book something else,' she said tentatively.

'Yes, we could. Not the same, though, they're all different tours, different places. They're not like buses, miss one and another one'll be along in a minute. I think ours is the last of the season.'

Unsettlingly, he didn't sound angry, barely disappointed even, just thoughts running through his head. Lydia suddenly wanted him to at least be cross, even if he couldn't manage angry, if he was nothing then what had she been so worried about?

'And I don't suppose there's any possibility of Gloria's wedding changing. Or missing it, either,' he said absently.

'I'd rather not, but...'

'Tricky, then. You realised after we'd looked at it all with Jacqueline.'

'Yes.'

'We'd better see what's possible.' He stretched his head towards hers and kissed her, more in the old way than the new, Lydia thought.

In the morning he was early to rise, trying to slide from the bed unnoticed, but she stirred and held a hand out to him.

'I'm going to get to the study,' he said softly, 'no point lying awake thinking about it. I'll bring some coffee up in a while.'

But the spell of sleep was broken, the escape from her dilemma over, and a numbness settled on her. Was this his way of being angry with her, did he handle all disappointment with the same cool calmness? Was there real work in the study or could he not bear to be in bed with her? Or had nothing changed but her own guilt, her own pit of disappointment? She got out of bed and wrapped the silk robe around her, reminded of how much she liked it, how carefully he must have selected it. Oh no, no, don't let Jacqueline have helped him choose it. She pushed the idea away, filling her thoughts with Laurence, with Ballard, with poor Freddie, with anything she could conjure that was not about Stephen or his daughter.

She put her head into the study. Stephen was at his desk, papers spread out, a pen in hand. He looked up smiling.

'I've put coffee on,' she said. 'If you're up I thought I might as well be.'

'Right.'

She turned to leave as he called after her, 'We'll sort things out, leave it a day or two.'

'I thought I'd probably tell Gloria I couldn't, I mean we couldn't, go.'

'No, leave it, let's see what can be done.'

So, it was just an inconvenience to him, something would happen, something would turn up and a solution would present itself. He did seem supremely unconcerned, but she didn't have his faith.

The early morning sun was already warming the conservatory as she curled in a chair under its greenery. As it warmed her, it soothed her anxieties, let her mind wander to other, quite different, problems. The Brenton medals had begun to nag at her again. They'd acquired sentimental value, which was not part of the plan, although they did look extremely good tucked in their leather and velvet. How often she developed an attachment for her lost things in need of re-homing. Not unlike a stray dog service, she imagined. The medals were never going to be Freddie's, she should've seen that in the first minutes and walked away instead of involving herself the way she had. There was still the puzzle of how he came to be Francis Bellinger, by what mechanism had that happened? Is that who'd arrived in an envelope brought from Whitehall, or had he become a pioneer of stealing identities? Changing names, re-inventing yourself, was once common enough, especially amongst those who crossed the oceans to start new lives in a corner of the Empire. Many a family tree had lost a branch or two that way.

With coffee poured and delivered to the engrossed Stephen, she brought her laptop back to the chair, with no particular purpose other than to browse for answers to unformed questions. The first ping of the day was from her email, the regular newsletter from one of her genealogy subscriptions. She did little enough real family history these days, but there were sometimes interesting curiosities that she tucked away for future reference. She looked quickly at the list of topics: more newspaper articles available, a photo competition, War Graves action, a pilot beneficiaries index, Scottish burial records. In all, very much the usual thing. Until she flicked back and looked again: a pilot national beneficiaries and executors index. There were already several county databases, mainly for centuries past, but a national index was something quite new and might be her longed-for key to Laurence Durham's mystery.

It took only a moment to click the link and find a disappointingly clunky web page which was not encouraging. It required a modest payment to become a member for a few weeks. Membership would entitle her to search the currently 'very

212

limited data available, only 11,000 names in the first batch, mainly from Suffolk wills of the 19th and 20th centuries. Copies of the listed wills may be ordered directly from the site.' And there she might have stopped, thinking it was little more than another county index of old wills, had it not been for the example given to illustrate the method of enquiry. The sample search was for *Tweddle M,* giving the result *Tweddle MA (B)* in the will of *Cunningham GK,* probate given *3rd June 1938 at Ipswich.* A glance at the key told her the B was for beneficiary, as opposed to executor, probate or witness. Lydia almost let her computer slide off her knees, such was the shock. Of course it might not be Laurence's grandmother, but probability and instinct told her it was.

When she'd signed up with shaking fingers and twice-typed credit card, she tried a search exactly as the example had shown, to be sure it hadn't been a random coincidence. No coincidence. The same result. Then she reversed the process, entering Cunningham as the deceased to find other beneficiaries, even the executor. She hovered over the search button. Sometimes this delving into other people's past seemed more like spying, even when the information was as public as the telephone book, just a click away.

GK Cunningham's will had three beneficiaries, The National Canine Defence League, MA Tweddle and FA Tweddle and one executor, WG Durham. It was witnessed by WG Durham and N Bateson and probate was given at Ipswich, Suffolk on 3rd June 1938 to WG Durham, solicitor. Facts as bare and plain as they could be, facts that most certainly were no more than hints of a deeper story lurking behind them. Presented as they were, to a casual observer they would be as dry and uninteresting as the next dozen entries or the previous thousand, but to Lydia's eyes they meant a great deal. Mother and daughter both beneficiaries in a will, the executor also a solicitor who would thirty-one years later marry the daughter, who would then inherit half his wealth within months. It was, at the very least, an unusual chain of events. Probability, Lydia's favourite marker, suggested more than coincidence.

She was still staring openmouthed when Stephen sat beside her.

'More Freddie surprises?'

'No, no, not Freddie. Laurence this time. I don't know the story behind it yet, I only just found this,' she said, showing him the screen.

'WG Durham, is that the Durham who might be Laurence's father?'

Lydia nodded.

'And Cunningham? Is that a name I should know?'

'It's new to me, it means nothing.'

'There was something you were going to ask me, something about Freddie I think, just before Jacqueline arrived yesterday.'

'Yes, there was, I forgot. It was a favour really.' Yesterday it would've been easy, today she didn't feel like asking a favour of him, she felt as though she might already have asked too much.

'Anything.'

His eager response coaxed it from her.

'Could you ask your man at the Home Office about something. It's not personal, although Freddie is the example. Could you ask him if there's any record of how a person was given a new identity, like Freddie was. What I mean is, how the new identity was selected, what were the mechanics of it back in the 1950s.'

13

'What? Today? You're finishing today?'

'Yes, today. The rest of the week is holiday, then that's it.'

Gloria turned away, blew smoke into the wind. 'It's all just fizzled out, hasn't it? All these years we've been here,' she turned back to Lydia, more serious than often she was, 'and not always like we are now. Next week we'll all be gone.' The reflective moment passed and her more usual spirit returned, wide-eyed she asked, 'What about a drink? Monday night doesn't seem right somehow. Never mind, we've got my hen-night for all that, we'll roll it all into one and drink double.'

'Double, yes.'

Lydia hadn't decided how or when or even if she would tell Gloria about her problem. Not until it was beyond recovery, not until Stephen's let's-see-what-can-be-done had been seen and failed. But standing here in the car park sharing a smoke break with Gloria, talking of hen-nights, thinking of wedding days, it felt mean and deceitful to say nothing. In a day or two or next week when she had to tell her, when she had to confess, Gloria would remember standing here and Lydia saying nothing, and how she'd let her continue believing her chosen supporter, her only bridesmaid, would be at her side for her great day.

'There's something else, too,' she said tentatively.

'Sounds ominous.'

'About the holiday that Stephen booked.' Oh how wonderful if there was someone else to blame, but confession couldn't rely on a second lie. 'I mean, we booked.' She willed Gloria to see what was coming, to have her ask, so all Lydia had to say was yes and not spell it out.

'What about it? You two haven't fallen out of bed have you? Only just got in!'

Lydia gave her a few more milliseconds to guess, then took the icy plunge. 'The dates we booked clash with your wedding.'

'What?' Gloria's expression froze before the humour drained from it. Her face crumpled towards tears and she cried, 'Oh Lydia, no, don't say that, please don't say that, don't joke with me.'

'No, I wouldn't do that.'

'Jesus Christ, one day, one fucking day, Lydia, that's all there was to remember,' and tears fell down her cheeks.

'Gloria, I'm so sorry. I feel so bad about it,' and she too wept and snivelled into a tissue.

'What am I going to do now?'

'Stephen said I shouldn't say anything, not for a couple of days. But it's the end of the season, and it would be, well, you know, quite special.'

'So would my wedding, that would be quite special,' she wailed between heaving breaths.

'I know, I know, I didn't mean that. Something might happen, I don't know what, it might work out, but I couldn't talk about it without telling you, I just couldn't.'

'So what, you might not go? I don't get it.'

'By the end of the week, I don't know, I don't know what I'm doing, I don't know what he's doing.'

'Bloody hell, Lydia, I always said you were a silly cow and you bloody are.'

Of all her days working in the section with Gloria and Chloe and the others, her last day was one of the worst.

For years Lydia had seen it as more than a humdrum job to be endured without satisfaction. She'd performed her tasks conscientiously, enjoyed the challenges, the steady progression, the security too, yet for much of the time the social aspects had been less attractive. She'd been the odd one out, the older one, the one a little apart from the group, the one who didn't get drunk, didn't have sex and certainly didn't compare notes on the subject. Gloria had been her chief antagonist, sometimes with a hint of malice but more often from the habit of making Lydia the butt of the joke. A chance meeting with Stephen had been the catalyst for change and in the space of a few weeks they'd become accepting of each other, then confiding and finding common ground. Some of the teasing remained, but lately it had been given as well as taken.

But the last day was meaningless. The rest of the section, including Gloria, were either serving out their time to the end of the month or on holiday. It was only Lydia's last day, no one else's. From the morning agony with Gloria it stuttered uncomfortably to the earliest moment at which she could leave, then a couple of see-you-soons and stay-in-touches and it was done. After the morning distress Gloria had been quiet, and when Lydia gathered up her few possessions, the tears flowed again.

'I'll call you. I won't leave it,' Lydia assured her, 'A week at the most. I promise.'

'You'd better,' was her parting shot, fired from her usual spot by the car park.

The house was never more welcoming than when she slipped the key in the door that afternoon. It could be mean and damp, tight and awkward, the more so when she'd spent time at The Old Rectory, but it was at its best, as if to compensate for the unhappy day. The fridge was well stocked and Lydia took a bottle and a glass into her patch of garden. There was no better time than a sunny, late afternoon in August. The willow gave shade and light in just the right amounts and the sleepy arm of the Thames running, more dawdling, a few yards away lent coolness on a hot day, an earthy smell when the city stink threatened to invade.

How easily it was ended. She had left work only a couple of hours and already it was passing into history. The space between then and now was expanding even as she thought of it. And how wasted it now seemed, all that diligence, all that loyalty and honesty, all those extra miles she'd gone, all for what? For a slightly better pension deal, a slightly bigger severance payment? Surely there must be something more, something she'd forgotten, she'd given more than many women give their husbands, was there no more to it than a few thousand pounds? It was another divorce, another divorce not on her terms.

Tomorrow all this would be a day away. Tomorrow, when she sat in the offices of Ballard, Edwards & Joyce in her new full-time role of family investigator - she liked the idea of that title and poured another glass - tomorrow, she might learn something more of Freddie and, when she'd deftly switched the conversation, of

Laurence, too. In a few days, when she'd had sight of the Cunningham will, another conversation with the solicitors might be called for. The exact wording might provide fresh insight or confirm a suspicion, although it was unlikely to be as precise as William G Durham's had been with its birth dates and spelled-out relationships. Which made her think again about that special bequest made to Laurence. He'd been specifically named as Florence's son, whereas William's acknowledged son was identified unequivocally as 'my son.' If William was Laurence's father then he must have had a very good reason to avoid saying so, for maintaining a deception, even after his death.

Letting the questions drift, to settle where they would, was a fanciful method of enquiry, but an enjoyable one, especially sitting in the sun with her glass bright and shiny with wine. Drifting allowed the impossible and the unlikely to dance with the highly probable and consort with the certain. More than once it had jolted a conviction or provoked new questions. Laurence and his mother, his grandmother and the solicitor, were all bound together by Cunningham at least, possibly a great deal more. She let them swirl round her dance floor, looping and gliding while she sipped her wine and completely forgot everything she'd ever known about payroll and budgeting and data selection, extraction and analysis.

When the music stopped, two stray dancers left the floor hand-in-hand. Laurence's birth certificate and the conversation she'd had with Bella Wentworth while they looked at the photos in her shoe box. She had the photo, she'd borrowed it on a last-minute impulse. Both items were on her desk, one in Laurence's file, the other in Freddie's. She reminded herself of the birth certificate first: Laurence Harvey Tweddle, father Laurence Harvey, 29th September 1954, born to Florence Ada Tweddle. The photo by the pool of Linda and Bella, one each side of the actor, he with his arms round them, blowing a kiss to the camera. The girls in bikinis, the actor in a loose shirt and swimming trunks, and underneath, the unambiguous note: *Spoilt for choice! L xx.* And according to Bella that *L* wasn't Larry but Laurence, a big name, she'd said, a Hollywood name. Lydia could only think of one famous Laurence and it didn't look like him, but if he was a

Hollywood name then there would be pictures of him, there would be an entire career with every part he'd ever played and every girlfriend he'd ever had.

And so there was. It took no more than a few clicks to find a 1972 photo which identified *L*, absolutely confirming Bella's memory. The actor's name was Laurence Harvey. It seemed as though the glass and the cigarette were something of a signature. Lydia read more about his life and early death, his wives and mistresses and doubts about his sexuality. The more she read the more the pose with Bella and Linda appeared contrived. He may have enjoyed the company of young girls, but his known partners were mainly older women. In all she read, Lydia found no possible connection to Florence Tweddle. Which, as she well knew, didn't mean there wasn't one.

Many of the hundreds of images were taken from studio publicity shots, signed like Lynn Brighton's had been, with an 'Always Yours' message and a mechanical signature. None that she could find had simply *L* or anything personal. The *L* was quite distinctive on Bella's Polaroid, the long tail underlining the two kisses, just as it underlined his whole name on the standard photos. As she'd first thought, Bella was probably holding a valuable collection of snapshots in her shoe boxes. Another name changer, she thought, from his unpronounceable native Lithuanian to the very British, Laurence Harvey. How long did it take to get that signature so consistent and perfect? And how many times was it signed, even allowing for the studio secretaries doing half of them? And how many programmes, how many scraps of paper thrust out by anxious fans, how many autograph books held that practised *Laurence*?

A sudden thrill rippled down Lydia's back, a physical anticipation of a pleasure that was hardly even formed in her mind. Laurence Durham had an old autograph book, one he thought he'd been given by either his mother or his grandmother in his childhood. He hadn't seemed to take any interest in it, although the exact reference escaped her. Might it hold long-forgotten secrets, clues to other lives? Might Laurence Harvey have had it pushed in front of him at some appearance, some function and signed it with that long-tailed L under his name? She wanted to see that book now, she wanted to reach out and pull it from her shelf and turn the pages slowly until she found the signature.

Tomorrow she'd be in Bedford in the afternoon, but she could be in Cambridge by four. Could she risk a visit to Laurence's office in college without an appointment? Too late to call him now, but she could call Stephen, ask him to set it up. Yes, she could call Stephen, and while she was doing so she could give him the answer as to whether or not she was going to live with him for a few weeks before their cruise, an answer she'd promised him before she left and yet had avoided giving. He hadn't mentioned it again, hadn't prompted her. Even now she didn't know if it was what she wanted. More, she struggled with the thought that it was not what she deserved. She who forgot important dates, she who let down her best, her only, friend, she who seemed better at playing parts than running her own life. She felt the ground shifting, opening beneath her feet, the numbing fear of falling into the abyss from a great height rendered her motionless. As the corners of her vision began to darken, breathing became a conscious effort. She could barely manage the smallest gasp and the darkness was so inviting, so comfortable, promised such relief.

It would be like this at the end, this is how it was for Freddie, soft velvet blackness then effortlessly floating up, seeing her body slumped over her desk, a breeze from the garden ruffling her hair as she slept the long sleep. Who wouldn't want to do this, who wouldn't want the pleasure of hovering, swooping, swimming in the air? Who'd want to go back to the misery and the guilt, who'd want to endure constant failure when there was such freedom?

Despite the euphoria, Lydia felt a thirst and tested her tongue on dry lips. Slowly the vision dissolved to a sideways view of her garden through open French doors twitching in the evening airs. Her head was resting on one arm and she'd drooled over her keyboard. Just another day in the life.

∞

'Miss Silverstream,' Derek Ballard welcomed Lydia to his office, a comfortable room that seemed more social than business-like as they were seated in easy chairs either side of a coffee table. His desk, a huge affair justifying that old label of a partner's desk, was on the opposite side of the room, which fell somewhere between old-fashioned courtesy and new-fashioned informality. This particular partner was a balding, bespectacled man, slightly stooping as tall men often are in later life. His still-dark hair was combed in wisps across the top of his head. Lydia guessed him to be mid-sixties, close to retirement, close enough to take afternoons off playing golf. It occurred to her that he would be a contemporary of Stephen, yet for all his golf and Stephen's lack of it, Stephen seemed ten years younger.

'I was so sorry to hear that Freddie Bellinger had passed away on Friday. I gather you were close.'

'Yes, in a way, but I've only known him a few weeks.'

'Oh, I had a different impression. He didn't say much, I don't think he was able, but he spoke well of you. How did you know him?'

As the secretary brought tea and coffee, Lydia gave an account of her time with Freddie and how she'd first come to visit him. The solicitor seemed fascinated by the story, and pressed her for more detail at several points.

'Thank you,' he said, as she drew to a close, 'what a fantastic thing to do. I should love to be part of such a project.'

Which was music to her ears, since in a small way he was already, and in another, bigger way she hoped he soon would be.

'Is there anything I can do regarding Freddie's affairs?' Lydia asked, wondering vaguely about his personal effects at Willoughby House.

'He didn't say anything to you, about his will?'

'No, nothing. Is this a new will, made last week?'

'Yes, was there another one?'

'I've no idea. I wondered if you were quite happy about his mental state, sometimes he could be only half there and wander off.'

'It's a delicate thing, but yes, I was satisfied he knew what he wanted even though he was in pain. I drew it up and he just managed to sign it. The carer, Sandra, was a witness. I privately asked her opinion about his mental state too, if it worries you.'

'No, it doesn't. I suppose as a solicitor your opinion would be significant if there were any questions raised.'

'Do you expect there to be?'

'No, just something I was concerned about. But I interrupted you. No, he said nothing to me about his will.'

'You're mentioned twice and he assured me that you would be happy with the arrangements. First you are a beneficiary, not a vast amount. It's not written down as such, but Freddie suggested it would be something to cover expenses. It's £2000.'

'I never imagined he had much to leave. There are no expenses, it's just what I do. I was passing his door anyway.' She hadn't expected tears again today, but she found herself blinking them back. 'I'll have to find a home for that.'

'The other formal reference to you is as an executor, I should say jointly with me, or at least, with the firm.'

'Oh, yes of course, but I know almost nothing of his friends or his affairs. I only know about his history.'

'He was very keen that you were involved, he said you were the person for the job. I suggested that making you an executor would help. There are only two other beneficiaries, both needing to be identified. He said you had the key, the knowledge to do this, you knew the people. One is a lady Freddie referred to as Bella Andrews, is she known to you?'

'Yes, I've met her, she's a cousin of Freddie's daughter Linda. His daughter died many years ago. Bella Wentworth as she is now, born Belinda Andrews. Her mother was Kate Bright.'

'Well, it's not in his will, but he hoped Bella could receive her money without any knowledge of the source. I told him it was unlikely. For your ears only, he said it was for her grandfather. Does that make sense?'

Bella had one grandfather who'd lived to a good age, but she'd never known the other one. He went on a long holiday with a bullet in his head and a ticket to Skegness in his pocket.

'It might,' she said a little unsteadily. 'Who else is there?'

'A lady who's name is Claire and who might be in Canada. His granddaughter he said. Do you know that lady?'

'She's Claire McCreadie I believe. Yes, I know how to get in touch with her. Through Bella's mother if I need to.'

'Good. Is she his granddaughter?'

'Yes, as sure as anyone can be anybody's anything. She probably doesn't know who Freddie was. If she knows anything it'll be that he died before she was born. We could do DNA tests I suppose.'

'No, Freddie trusted you, I trust you. Show me your evidence of who's who and how and so on and I fully expect that to be good enough.'

'Is there much money involved? Any property, will it all take a long time to sort out?'

'No, it won't take long, there's no property, few possessions, ah, yes something for you in a minute, but the estate is only money, after expenses and your bequest I expect the remainder to amount to around £25,000. I have his bank books and have written to them this morning. Divided equally. So no, not a lot to be done once you've done your bit.'

'Something for me, you said, what did he have?'

'He had an old briefcase, insisted I take it away and give it to you, insisted I didn't look inside.'

She gave him a sideways look and asked with a smile, 'And did you?'

'It was a great temptation. I was slightly concerned it might be full of money or drugs.' His expression suggested his concerns were not serious.

Straight faced, Lydia said, 'Oh it might be yet.'

'It's not in his will, it's nothing formal, he just asked me to give it to you, I'll ask Angela to get it from the safe.'

While they waited, Derek Ballard tidied up the formalities, had Lydia sign the required papers and described what evidence he'd like her to provide regarding Bella's and Claire's relationship to Freddie. She already had all that he wanted, she had only to assemble it.

'Shall I open it now?' Lydia asked when the briefcase was delivered.

'Up to you, I've done my bit,' he said, but the disappointment was plain.

She slipped the latch and opened the jaws of the case. A musty aroma, the scent of age, of rarely opened pages greeted her. There on the top was his birth certificate, back where she'd found it. Beneath it she saw notebooks and loose papers, lots of them, and when she took a few from the top there were more below. She picked one at random and carefully opened it. Small, neat handwriting covered the pages, a commentary on a journey through a fertile valley beneath snow-capped mountains. She opened another, notes of a town called Freemantle, dated January 1968. A third described a woman, her curves, her skin, the way she lay on a bed, on the next page a pencil sketch of a nubile figure. The same woman? The Lydia he'd known, the girl dead on the beach with sand in her nose? She took out a few more until her eye caught a different bundle near the bottom. Carefully she lifted it out, holding it in the palms of both hands as if presenting it to the solicitor.

'Not quite what you feared, but still money.'

She held a bundle of US $10 notes, still in their yellow bank wrapper denoting a value of $1000. To judge by the perfect alignment of their edges, they had never been removed.

'What should I do, I mean, we do about this, add it to the estate?'

Derek Ballard thought for a moment. 'I think not. Apart from the questions I would have to ask, for which there will be no answers, it was a gift during his lifetime. It's yours. And the books and papers, anything interesting?'

'Not sure, stories of one kind or another, might be fact, might be fiction. It looks as if there's a lot of them. When I've nothing else to do they'll keep me busy through the winter evenings. No, if there's something important, I'll let you know.' She paused and considered her next question carefully. 'What would you have to ask?'

'Money laundering, proceeds of crime, that kind of thing. Things I have no interest in asking unless you have suspicions yourself.' He spelled out the words slowly, holding her gaze as he spoke, making quite clear the answer he needed.

'No, none at all.'

'Good. Now, all this is very fine, excellent that you're here. An unusual day in the life of a country lawyer. Now it's your turn, what can I do for you?'

'Something different again. A man in Cambridge, not unlike yourself in age, also a professional person, this man has asked me to help try and identify his father. He has very little to go on and the more obvious sources of information haven't been much help. I suppose I should add that all this is completely confidential.'

Lydia hadn't rehearsed any of this, and she hoped she could say enough to engage his interest before getting to the nub of it. Her surroundings gave her courage, endorsing her right to be discussing such things. The country lawyer nodded and put his fingers together as if in prayer, pursing his lips in thoughtful anticipation of the help he might give her.

'I wonder if you've ever heard the name William Durham? He was William Gordon Durham, but also known as Will, maybe something else too. I think he died in early 1960. The thing is, I think he might've worked here at some time, possibly as a solicitor.'

Derek Ballard continued nodding, his lips pushed tighter together, his hands still in prayer. But before he spoke Lydia knew the answer was yes.

'Well, Miss Silverstream, you are full of surprises.'

'Lydia, please.'

'Yes,' he nodded again. 'The name William Durham is not one I expected to ever hear uttered in this office again. I'm not sure it's a welcome sound.'

It was Lydia's turn to nod sagely and wait for him to continue.

'I probably don't know enough to really help you, he was long before my time here. You're right, he was a partner in the firm at some time, he retired in the late 1950s I think. Might he be the missing father?'

'A possibility, that's all I can really say, and the truth may never be known. But I like probabilities. The man I spoke of, the man who I'm helping, he'll be pleased enough to know possibles and probables.'

'I could give you a few snippets of things I half remember, but you should speak to my uncle Robert, if he'll speak to you. I think he will, I'll talk to him.'

'He knew William Durham?'

'Yes.'

'You said his name was unwelcome here.'

'Did I? Yes, my uncle will not be pleased to hear it again. I'm sure he'll tell you himself, I think William Durham nearly broke this firm. My uncle and his father, my grandfather, rescued it, kept the good name of Ballard out of the headlines, and probably the courts too.'

∞

At The Old Rectory Stephen was warm and affectionate, showing no sign of irritation with her late decision to stay. It was for a while, she said, not for a given period and she may come and go a little, she hadn't shut up the house in Osney. It wasn't a trial for something permanent, it was a comfortable escape for a few days, maybe a week or two.

They talked of their days and the days to come, how Laurence would expect her at ten in his office, how he'd been keen to see her, to have news of her enquiry. Stephen's contact at the Home Office had been unable to answer the question about new identities and had passed it on with an 'urgent' sticker attached but any response might still take a while. Of their cruise he seemed disinterested, unwilling to consider alternatives or give any thought to poor Gloria's unhappy situation, instead repeating the same vague 'let's see what can be done.'

They examined the $1000 together and over supper speculated wildly on reasons Freddie might've had the money in such an unusual form. On an impulse Stephen suggested looking at the design of the notes to see if they could be dated, which they could - to a first issue in 1963. Their true value might lie in the low serial numbers and the fact they were uncirculated. As collectible notes they might be worth three times their face value. As a pristine bundle the value might double again. But she knew that for the foreseeable future they'd remain a curiosity in a bag of notebooks.

Those notebooks would need a longer look to even begin to understand the chronology or connections.

The wine, the comfortable ease of the house, his company and their conversation all combined in a mellow cocktail. In a few moments of silence between them, her skin tingled in anticipation of touching his, of being touched, not as a fingertip might pet or stroke, but as his whole body might wrap hers. As her thoughts turned to an early night, he excused himself to attend to work and retreated to his study. It left her a little nonplussed and without a purpose for the rest of the evening, although her wine glass was again full. For a while she sat and wondered how it was she'd gone from her fixed and predictable existence of two, perhaps three years previously, to this wholly altered universe where nothing, not even her innermost thought, could be trusted to remain consistent. On the edge of frustration she picked at the bookshelves, sampling the how-tos-for-dummies - how could there ever have been a dummy in The Old Rectory? - the worthy but dull, the popular and the predictable. Nothing held her attention and after an hour or so she wandered to the study, pausing at the doorway.

'Sorry to interrupt, I'm going to bed, I might take something to read,' she said lightly, hoping she sounded neutral about him staying or coming too.

He started as she spoke, he'd been so engrossed in his work he hadn't heard her footstep. As he turned to look at her she noticed he clicked to a different tab on his screen.

'I'll be a few minutes, no more,' he smiled, 'Sorry, it needs to be done tonight.'

'Paris?'

He pulled a face and shrugged. 'Yes, Paris, if you like.' he said, happy to have found a code word for whatever he was doing.

He was as good as his word. No more than five minutes after she'd settled into the bed he was sliding in beside her, snuggling close with his arms around her, satisfying her half-formed desires in an immediate rush of pleasure.

'I'm glad you're here,' he said, speaking softly into her neck. 'I know it's difficult. These are the between times, between what was and what will be and we don't ever know what will be. Stay as long as you want, go as often as you want. I mean it.'

'Yes,' was all she could manage. She could scarcely breathe, such was the intensity of being wrapped by his limbs. She could stay in this sensual overload for ever, basking in his body heat, arching herself against him. One hand moved slowly over her until with a little cry she seized it, holding it still, overwhelmed by the surge unleashed by the gentle friction. 'Too much,' she gasped, as if he needed any explanation.

After a while his muscles relaxed, his hand submitting to her vice-like grip as the currents and colours flowed through her, little groans and twitches marking their progress. At length they slowed, a natural rhythm of breathing returned. She drifted across a lilly-strewn lake, propelled by silent oars, dimly aware that Stephen was the pillow she lay on. 'Sorry,' she said, when her mouth was again able to form words.

'Beautiful,' was his drowsy reply, whispered into the nape of her neck.

She woke again at two, the soft night enfolding them, both lying exactly as they'd fallen asleep. She would sleep again in a minute or ten or an hour but there was a pleasure to being awake while another slept beside her. The freedom of being alone blended sweetly with companionship to make a secret thrill. Sometimes, as now with perfectly remixed hormones tipping the balance, she could allow a few minutes of watching herself without the fearful paralysis threatening her. But who was she watching? Was this the same Lydia who earlier in the day had been both the bereaved friend and the subtle detective? Or were they her Bedford faces, surpassed in quality only by her *Carry On Girls* researcher, played to the unsuspecting Bella? Now she lay naked, covered only by a sheet and Stephen's arm, weighing heavier now, resting where she'd released it. She felt perfectly content, yet such contentment was unfamiliar, untrustworthy. Was this contented lover another part she played, a role she'd taken on and wore like a costume for the Grantchester scenes?

She felt changes in them both, even if there were no easy words to describe them. He, breathing steadily beside her in uncomplicated sleep, would deny it, would say there was no change between them that wasn't a better, deeper, warmer version of their former selves. She saw other shifts. Having gained this one exquisite privilege of intimacy, she was aware of other, lesser, favours not granted, confidences not shared. Privacy, and respect for it, was one thing, yet there was a fine line between the private and the secret. Once they'd chosen physical disclosure she'd imagined privacy in all things would erode and fall away, instead it was hardening into evasion and secrecy. And as she sensed him holding back knowledge, even opinions, so she felt herself concealing her own doubts and fears. Her independence was a precious thing, hard won through the solitary years, and to be protected now, for who knew when she might need it again. For tonight and tomorrow, the days ahead, perhaps to the cruise and beyond, the trade-off would work. The pleasure of sharing themselves, sharing excursions and experiences, smiling together over wine, paddling in warm seas, all that and more, would outweigh the small deceptions, the unspoken exclusions, the hidden priorities. But as she felt them breathing together, lying together, she saw these things might eat away at the heart of it.

∞

Laurence Durham grinned foolishly as he showed Lydia into his office. The roundness of his face grew rounder still as his cheeks puffed up in the pleasure of anticipation.

'I have it here! And I think I know exactly what you want to see!' He could hardly contain himself, such was his excitement. Lydia hadn't seen this side to him, an almost schoolboy delight in the unmasking of the little snitch from 3b. Was this the Laurence who'd never left his mother's orbit, was this the child still in the man?

'You might be right!' Lydia said, trying to match the glee on the other side of the desk. A little desk, she thought, surely too little for a college bursar, certainly a long way from the partner's desk of yesterday.

'Here it is,' he announced triumphantly, taking the book from a drawer. The cover was padded under a pink and purple cotton fabric. 'Can I show you what I think you're looking for?'

Lydia nodded, 'Yes, do,' she enthused.

He'd placed a little paper marker in the page and flipped the book open, turning it for Lydia to inspect. He was right, it was the autograph she'd hoped was there, The flamboyant L that drew a line beneath the *Laurence*, the tail of the Y drawn back under *Harvey*. No personal message, nothing to say the book's owner meant anything to him, just *Best Wishes* and beneath the signature *London '53*. On the same page in the same ball-point ink she read *To Fleur Best Wishes Stanley Baker*. Might he be another actor? The name seemed familiar from somewhere. But Stanley Baker was insignificant compared to the dedication, *To Fleur*. Not a giant leap from Florence, same meaning, same root no doubt, just a touch more exotic, a name someone might use if they wanted to be someone they were not.

'What do you think?' he said excitedly.

'Oh, yes, sorry, I was looking at the other name too. What do I think? I think it may be the answer to one little riddle, to why your mother said it was just a joke. I think it's possible that she put Laurence Harvey down as your father and gave you the name because she'd met him briefly when she was twenty-one or so and had his name in her book. And to be honest Laurence, I don't think it gets us any closer to your father.'

'No, I know that, but it has to be the joke, what else could it be? And I've had the answer all along, sitting in this old book. This is quite a day.'

'Didn't you ever look through it, notice the name, think it might be how you got yours?'

'No. I've had it since I was a child, but the names meant nothing to me then, and really they mean nothing to me now. I don't think I've looked at it for forty or fifty years. It must have been my grandmother's before my mother's, the first page is dated 1924.'

Lydia turned the pages. The first was taken up by a ditty, written in an adult hand but tailored to a young girl's amusement, *For Mary, By hook or by crook I'll be first in your book. Marjory*

230

Richardson 10th July 1924. It had an answering rhyme on the last page, *Your friend to the end. Hellena Forbes.*

'Do you remember when your grandmother's birthday is?'

'July, I'd have to check the date.'

'I think it's the tenth. It looks like this was a birthday present.'

Laurence was still beaming, loving every moment of the discovery. He couldn't have been happier if she'd brought him incontrovertible evidence of his actual father. Perhaps this understanding was as important as finding his father. His name, the joke of the birth certificate, both might have worn thin beyond endurance in the years since he was first taunted with it. Now, rightly or wrongly, he had a satisfying answer. More, he had an answer he'd found for himself in the pages of his own book. True, Lydia had been the catalyst, but it was Laurence who'd listed the book amongst his possessions of childhood and Laurence who'd opened it and recognised the significance of a celebrity's autograph. She wondered if finally getting the joke wasn't more important than identifying his father. Maybe Laurence really knew all along that her task was impossible, only his mother could ever know that truth. Maybe too there would be unwanted implications with such knowledge, the more so if it were obtained without Florence's involvement or consent.

'Do you mind if I borrow it for a while? I'd like to go through it carefully, it looks full and there are a lot of names in here.'

'I did wonder about copying it all for you,' he said with enough hesitation to show he'd rather keep it.

'A copy would be fine, yes.'

'I'll do it now.' He set about the job, standing by the copier in the corner of his office.

'I'm seeing someone, Friday I hope, someone who knew William Durham,' she ventured, testing his feelings about finding his father.

'Good, good,' he said without pausing. 'Do you think anything will come of it?'

She'd been right, his matter-of-fact tone, almost polite disinterest, was a change from their first meeting with its sad confessions and desperate plea for help.

'Another clue, maybe more, I'll let you know. One thing I've already heard is that William left behind some kind of difficulty when he retired. Just thought I'd warn you.'

'Why am I not surprised?' he said with resignation.

In a few more minutes he finished the copies and handed her the sheaf of paper. They would be an interesting evening read.

'One thing, I forgot to ask, does the name Cunningham mean anything to you? '

He thought for a moment before answering. 'No, although I feel as though it should. Why?'

'It seems your grandmother and your mother were beneficiaries in a GK Cunningham's will. I haven't seen the details yet, hopefully I'll get a copy in a few days.'

'Really? When was this?'

'Mid 1930s I think, yes I think your mother was only a child.'

Only as she said the words did it occur to her that it was another oddity, a small child and the parent being beneficiaries in a will. Laurence and his mother Florence had gained the same benefit from William Durham's will. Once was unusual enough, but for successive generations to have the same good luck was surely more than coincidence.

∞

After early lunch by the river at Midsummer House, Lydia and Stephen walked across the common by the Cam, then along Riverside on their way to the Newmarket Road.

'We don't do this enough,' he said. 'There are plenty of walks in Cambridge, plenty to take the eye and the ear. And all better for sharing.'

'Yes,' she said, while thinking the Cam was not the Thames, although it might grow on her with time.

'We've never walked into town from home, there's a path all along by the river,' he said as if to read her thoughts.

'By the Cam? I thought it was called something else, I forget which.'

'So do I, it's the Cam or the Rhee or the Granta, there are several branches and as many names.'

She found this slim connection to the Thames with its different names according to whether you were local, tourist, map-maker or historian, somehow comforting. It provided scope for discovery and exploration, where previously she'd seen little. Different names meant different histories, intertwining and diverging over the centuries. Like her puzzles, maybe even like Fleur and Florence, certainly like Freddie Bell and George Thompson, different names for different uses.

By the Museum of Technology they cut up from the river to the superstores where Lydia deposited her faithful laptop with its drool-damaged keyboard. She'd ordered a new machine and arranged for everything to be copied from the crippled one to the shiny new one. Only a couple of hours, they'd promised.

An hour each way would take them comfortably out along the river to Fen Ditton for a prowl round the parish church. They took Garlic Row down to Stourbridge Common, walking easily together in the August sunshine.

'You'll be in college for supper tonight?' she asked, pleased that she'd remembered his Wednesday evening ritual.

'Ah, no. I forgot to mention, I have a call to make at seven, maybe another after that. A conference call, at least it's better than travelling, but it may take a while, I'm not sure.'

'Important? Silly question, you wouldn't miss college if it weren't.'

'Yes.'

As they approached the corner of the common with the railway bridge in sight, a chill breeze swept round them, ruffling the water. Within a few more steps the first sprinkles of rain were wetting their backs and they hurried forward, glancing over their shoulders at the shower clouds streaming in from the west. By the time they reached the shelter of the bridge they were wet and breathless and laughing at their foolishness.

Stephen said, 'We'll make a break for it when this has passed. We can get an umbrella at the supermarket, then pick up your computer and get a taxi. I just don't like the idea of being wet through and on a bus with a lot of other wet people.' They laughed again and kissed like awkward teenagers on a first date.

14

The copied pages of Laurence Durham's autograph book should have been more interesting. They had great potential but little which Lydia could sink her teeth into. She knew part of the problem was the copying. That little soft-padded book with its different pressures and inks and pencils and smudges was one thing, a special thing, a thing held by a hundred hands if not more. Her plain white copies were accurate for sure, but quite soulless. The book kept everything in the original order whereas her copies needed numbering before she'd turned more than half a dozen pages. One thing she noticed as soon as she'd done it was the absence of a true sequence. Like a passport stamped with a new visa on any blank page, so the autographs of the unknown friends and acquaintances were scrawled or carefully signed wherever the book had fallen open.

Each name probably held a story of friendship, local notoriety or passing fame. Lydia thought there might be relatives too, hidden behind the little verses and drawings of cats and dogs, but as she looked at each she saw no uncle or auntie before the names. She supposed cousins might remain a possibility, although she'd uncovered none in her researches. Most were friends, or perhaps friends of parents and nearly all wrote clearly, probably because they were in no hurry and they wanted their messages and witticisms to be read and admired. These were curiosities from another age, whereas the few scrawls which might have started with *Best wishes* and then degenerated into a squiggly line were more interesting, if only for the puzzle they presented.

It was one of these scrawls that caught her eye towards the end of the book. It certainly started with *Mary*. As was common with names unfamiliar to the writer, a little more care had been taken in forming the letters. It was probably followed by *All good wishes*, but the signature line was not recognisable. It was the last few letters which made Lydia pause, they looked like *clanan*, perhaps *Suclanan*. The more she looked the less apparent the letters became. She tried squinting, she tried looking away then glancing at the page. The S changed to P and back again. The first letter became D which could give *David Suclanan* although there was no gap to mark the end of one name and the beginning of the next. It was a signature collected in 1931, presumably by Laurence's grandmother. The words in the book would be exactly the same as on the paper she held, but how Lydia wished she had that original page in her hand. That signature meant something she was sure, yet the significance eluded her, hovering on the edge of her consciousness. To hold the actual book, feel the fabric of the cover, see the precise colour of the ink, these might draw out the meaning.

She tried a different tack, thinking of a name she might find in the book and seeing if it might fit. It wasn't a Tweddle or a Durham, certainly not a Harvey and oh how she tried to make Cunningham fit, but it wouldn't, no matter how much she twisted it. But that made her think of whether there might be a Cunningham in there somewhere, especially a GK Cunningham. Carefully she turned the remaining pages until, close to the end, she saw it. A brief *Good luck* was signed by *Ghislaine K Cunningham* in an educated script, unsteady with age. A woman. It had never occurred to her that it would be a woman, she'd never checked. A lady with an unusual name too, someone whose birth and death records, perhaps more, should be easy enough to find.

Her new computer was still in its box, but what better moment to try it out and see if the techies had been as good as their word setting it up for her. Stored passwords might be a problem, they'd said, and some old software should be replaced with newer versions, otherwise it should all be fine. All was not fine. It looked and felt different, it had almost no charge in its battery, no memory of being connected to the web at The Old Rectory and ridiculously required an 'overdue' update to the next level of operating system. Cursing the need to change for change's sake, Lydia made the necessary connections and started the process, only to be informed that it could take an hour and should not be interrupted.

Her old laptop would be good enough for one more day, especially as Stephen had suggested plugging in a spare keyboard.

It worked as required, with no mention of overdue updates. Ghislaine Cunningham had died in Suffolk during the second quarter of 1938. A few clicks later showed her birth registered in 1855 in Lincoln, where she appeared on every census until 1901 when she popped up in Bury St Edmunds. After a quick search the evidence of the censuses suggested she had not married.

Lydia ordered the certificates and hesitated over the address to have them sent to. She was more likely to be in Grantchester than Osney, yet it felt like another step. She tried it out to see what her name looked like above Stephen's address. If Gloria wrote to her she would probably put Lady of The Manor now that the taunt of Sister St. Lydia had lost its edge. The thought made her smile until she remembered she owed Gloria a call or at least a message. Tomorrow, she'd do it tomorrow. She clicked confirm and the deed was done, another small step.

Stephen was still at his desk, shaking his head in frustration when she looked in on him.

'How's it going?' she asked, knowing that he could answer without any hint of confidential subject matter.

'Not ready to talk in London yet, someone else has been called away, all very annoying.'

'Yes, it must be.' For Stephen it certainly would be, when he made an arrangement that was it, no question but that he'd be there on time. 'I'm about done for today, I'm going up, I'll read for a while.'

'Ah, before you go, a message from my contact at the Home Office about your identities question. I think you'll like this. Apparently after the war and up until 1962 they invented them for military people, but for civilians after 1949 they used a missing person's identity taken from a special wartime list. It was called the Register of Presumed Civilian Deaths from Enemy Action. They kept this register for anyone they thought was dead but couldn't find, or couldn't find enough of to confirm it. If a body was discovered and identified they'd cross it off the list and issue a death certificate. They changed in 1962 to something more contrived. The register was destroyed in a fire in a storage unit in Uxbridge in 1964. How's that for service?'

'Fantastic, thank you. I knew they couldn't have made up Freddie Bell. He was from the register. The real Francis Bellinger probably died with his mother and sister in Bristol in the raid. Dead twice already, Freddie said, and he had been. Once in the war, once in prison, now he's really gone. Well that's another piece of that jigsaw. And thank your man, too.

'All I have to do now is find someone else who should inherit the Brenton medals.'

∞

Lydia woke urgently, alone, in the dark, and struggled against it, the dream had been so much better, she could just drift back into it. But it had dissolved already, there was nothing of it to go back to, beyond a sense of it being pleasant. What was so important to take her from it? Her arm was caught in the sheet and in the confusion of the dream and the waking she couldn't remember where the light was, or even if there was one. Buchanan! That was what had woken her. The name Buchanan, the signature in the autograph book, it was Buchanan. And, if her memory was right then so was the entry on Florence's birth certificate in the space headed Father's Name. She needed to get up and find it then write down the name, and work out the first name, and where was Stephen? Not still talking to London, surely? She freed herself and fumbling, found the light switch. Two-thirty. First things first, with a pen from the drawer she wrote *Buchanan* in blotchy green ink on a tissue. As she watched, the blotches ran together and the name was lost again. No matter, she wouldn't forget it now.

She opened the door quietly and listened for sound in the silent house. Nothing, no distant voice speaking softly to London, nothing at all and only darkness to hold it. Had he gone out, been called away suddenly and left without a word? She slipped back to the room and collected her phone with its torch light to show her the way. The darkness downstairs confirmed he was either out or sleeping elsewhere. In the drawing room she flipped through her papers to Florence's birth certificate. Father's name given as Buchanan. What it meant could wait until a sensible time, for now finding the connection was enough. Perhaps that pleasant dream could be rediscovered after all.

In the kitchen she found the note he'd left her. *If you'd like company you'll find me in my room. Didn't want to disturb you, S.* She wasn't sure if she was pleased or not, and for a moment wasn't sure if she wanted company. Somehow they seemed to be going back to a previous existence, tiptoeing round each other's sensibilities. Perhaps her own uncertainties were showing, colouring his behaviour. He'd always travelled at her speed before, he was only doing the same again.

At the top of the stairs a crack of light showed round his door. He must've heard her go down. She hesitated, unsure of anything. Last night his touch alone had given her such pleasure and now she was back second-guessing intentions and desires. She turned left, to his door, whispering 'Are you awake?' as she opened it.

'Just about,' he mumbled, holding out a hand. 'Coming in?'

As she slid in beside him he turned out the light.

'You wouldn't have disturbed me,' she said.

'No, I wouldn't. You went down, everything all right?'

'Yes. Buchanan. That name in the book is Buchanan, I'm sure.'

He turned so he could wrap an arm round her, pulling her close. 'Working in your sleep. Like me. We'll talk about it tomorrow.'

∞

Again she woke alone, slowly stretching, squinting one-eyed at the unfamiliar room. A glance at the clock by the bed showed it was still early, early enough to turn over and doze guilt-free. Was this what Elspeth would have done? She'd pushed Stephen's wife far away last night as she'd joined him in bed but her spectre couldn't be resisted forever. Was it even the same bed? It was definitely the same room. She held her breath and listened for an echo of those times but heard none. She'd slept an untroubled sleep in Stephen's arms, slept through him leaving the bed, and now she felt nothing of Elspeth around her. If there were a photo of her on the dressing table or the chest of drawers then she'd be ready for it.

Eyes open she found no more ghosts than eyes closed. She'd looked into the room before, out of curiosity, but from her position in the bed it seemed bigger than ever. It occupied a corner of the house, looking across the meadows towards the river on one side and the church on the other. Could it ever be her room, hers and Stephen's? She would give it time, it was too new, she was too much the visitor in it to know that answer. But she could sleep here with Stephen, she'd done that. Another step.

He came in with a tray and coffee, put it down and stooped to kiss her. 'Good morning,' he said, with obvious affection, and climbed in beside her. They sipped their coffee in contented silence.

'Up early, working already,' she said, catching his habit of statement instead of question.

'Briefly. Most things were sorted out last night, eventually.'

After a moment staring into the distance, he turned to Lydia, the lightness of his mood replaced with seriousness.

'Sorted out enough. It affects us, the work, the Paris work. We can't go on our lovely cruise. I have to be elsewhere, in Havana. There'll be an announcement today, it's a United Nations thing.'

He paused, letting the effect on their own lives sink in before getting to the cause.

'You know what I do, or did,' he said to answer her questioning look.

Lydia nodded, although she hadn't quite seen the connection between Cuba and being a professor of forensic archaeology.

'A multiple burial site has been discovered. We don't call it a mass grave, too many bad vibes with that. It's in the south-east of the island, not far from the American base. You can imagine how political that could become, even though it's probably very old. It already has. The UN has agreed to oversee the investigation. I'm part of the team. Apparently I'm acceptable to all, even the Americans.'

Lydia nodded again, seeing the connection now, but struggling with how such a thing, such a terrible thing, could come from the other side of the world to directly touch her life. Everything else shrank to nothing by comparison, there was nothing to be said, no protest to be made, no ifs or buts, it was decided.

'I'm really sorry about the cruise, we'll do it another time, I promise. Don't worry about the cost, disruption compensation they call it. All covered.'

She hadn't paid anything yet anyway, the cost meant nothing.

'How long have you known?'

'Last night for certain, it was in the air just after we'd booked it. That's why I went to Paris. I couldn't say anything, it's too sensitive.'

Sitting there with him in his bed, sitting where Elspeth must have sat, she wanted to ask him if he would have told Elspeth, trusted her with his secrets, let her go on fretting over the cruise and Gloria's wedding and it all being her fault when he knew it might be off anyway.

'Stephen, that's not fair. You could have said something without telling me anything secret. I didn't know what was going on, I've been thinking all kinds of things.'

'I thought it was better to wait and be sure, one way or the other. We must trust each other, you should've said something too, if you were thinking things.'

'All right,' she said, not because she agreed but because she was too confused to discuss it sensibly. 'Anyway, how long will you be gone?'

'Probably six months, no more than nine. I'll be back here every fourth week, three weeks away one week back. But that might not be precise, it'll depend on what's happening at the site.'

'More than the cruise postponed, then.' She couldn't resist saying it, and risked the rising bitterness leaking into the words.

'Nothing else, we can go on, you can live here if it's what you want. You can even come to Cuba every couple of months, conjugal visitations they call it. Part of the deal. They wanted me enough, there was no argument. If you wanted to stay there with me you probably could, they'd agree. There's no rush to decide.'

He seemed to have every base covered apart from trusting her sooner, and even there she could have said something herself and the problem would've disappeared. Speak and - poof! problem solved.

'And college?'

'College will be delighted, they love having their people recognised, it reflects well on them. It impresses donors and wealthy families who might otherwise send their favourite sons elsewhere.'

Tick. All wrapped up.

'I suppose Gloria's wedding hasn't been moved to Havana has it?' She wanted it to be light but it came out sour.

If he heard the sourness he chose to ignore it.

'No, sadly not, that is one thing I'll miss.'

He put his arm round her and drew her to him. She felt as though all the soft and pliable had drained out of her, leaving nothing but wooden stiffness. His easy stride seemed to clear any hurdle while she stumbled on the smallest pebble.

'We've had a bit of a false start, but it'll come right if we want it to,' he said softly. 'Maybe we've tried to do too much all at once. We'll have another go at that cruise next year, or one just like it. And I know it's all a bit of a surprise and it'll take time to adjust, but really, come to Havana, at least once.'

'Maybe,' she said, 'I keep forgetting I've got nothing else to do.'

'Well there's always Laurence. You came to bed excited about Buchanan, who's that?'

'I'll show you at breakfast, you can tell me what you think.'

By the time they'd showered and readied themselves for the day, another hour had passed, an hour in which Lydia felt a better humour creeping back into her. She wanted to be indignant about being excluded from the whole Cuba affair, but the prospect of an adventure to Havana was appealing despite her wanting it not to be. The United Nations had at least helped her out of a pit of her own making with Gloria. She sent her what was meant as a light-hearted text, *Cruise cancelled, bridesmaid not*, but received only a curt *OK* in response.

While they ate toast and licked butter and jam from their fingers, Lydia showed Stephen the page from the autograph book.

'I can't see anything but Buchanan, but I'm not sure about the first name.'

Stephen examined it with a magnifying glass and then announced, 'The Silverstream theory would have it as Buchanan because it can't be anything else, and I agree with the theory. Is it a famous Buchanan?'

'I don't know, are there any?'

'Well, I think there was a boxer, a golfer too. When was this, 1930s?'

'Yes, there, 1931.'

'There was an old-time music-hall star, maybe films I'm not sure, he was Jack Buchanan I think.'

'But Jack's the name on Florence's birth certificate, that's her father. Let me see again.' She seized the paper as he passed it back. 'I can't see how you could get Jack out of that. That's hardly a J, more like a D and there's no k in there at all.' She stared at the signature trying desperately to make it Jack, but the doubts about the Buchanan flooded back in, the B was an S again and the h had collapsed into an l.

'Look it up, there's bound to be an autograph somewhere, on some film memorabilia auction.'

'Can I use yours, mine's not talking to me.'

Leaning close over him while he clicked the search, Lydia noticed some of the scribbled notes he'd made on a pad the night before, *back every 3 weeks* and *Lydia to Havana* both with ticks beside them, as did *cruise comp* a little further down.

'Look at that,' he cried, 'couldn't be closer. And across a photo, too.'

He was right, the signatures on the paper and the screen were almost identical. Neither looked like a Jack, but several more examples all certified that this was his signature.

'Does it mean anything?' Stephen asked, unsure of how important identifying an autograph might be.

'Probably not, except that Laurence's birth was registered with an actor's name as the father and so was his mother's, and both had signed the same autograph book. I still can't see that it means anything, but it's a strange coincidence at the very least.'

'According to Laurence, his mother called it a joke, something she got from her mother?'

'Yes, what did he say about them, his mother and grandmother? Two of a kind, that was it.'

'Where now?'

'Nowhere with Jack, nor Laurence Harvey, convenient names to laugh about, names to answer a question with, names to fill in a space. I wonder if Laurence has made that second connection, probably not if he's never seen his mother's birth certificate.'

Stephen was aware a sudden gear shift, an enthusiasm for the chase that had been missing of late. It wasn't quite the passion he'd first been attracted to, but it was still welcome.

'They're blind alleys, there's nothing there for Laurence,' she announced firmly. 'They always looked that way and yet they could never be discarded. But take the two together and the chances are almost nil. They're a distraction, a deception to muddy the water, which I suspect is what they always were. Two more chances. Something in the Cunningham will or the conversation with Robert Ballard. That's tomorrow after Freddie's funeral.'

∞

'No Eddie tonight?'

'No, got a job on, mending something.'

Gloria wasn't happy. And it was more than Eddie working late on a fine summer's evening when he could have been with her on the Cowley Road, picking at a chicken tikka as she was. Lydia had tried a few different topics, steering clear of the wedding plans, but her friend couldn't muster more than a few words on anything. At first she thought Gloria might still be hurt and angry for Lydia having double booked her special day, but it wasn't like Gloria to let something fester, she'd say it straight out.

At length Lydia thought she'd risk the subject most on her mind.

'I'm really, really, sorry for messing you about.'

'Yeah.' Gloria didn't look up or stop prodding her food. 'You always was a silly cow.'

'Well, I'm back on track, is everything else working out?'

'Oh yeah, fantastic. I haven't got a job yet, seems it's a difficult time. The house in Hanborough won't be available after all, we've put in for another one but it's out at Charlbury. What else? Eddie's brother won't be coming, they've fallen out. My mother's got very sniffy about something stupid, I forget what now. Oh yes, and Eddie's having second thoughts, wondering if I really want to get married. No, other than that, everything else is working out just fine. I wish we could bloody smoke in here.'

'Eddie's brother, the one he shares with, the one you might share with too?'

Gloria nodded.

'Are you, you know, wondering if you really want to?'

'I wasn't, till he said. I dunno now. Any ideas?'

'Me? No idea at all about anything. But if you've got a doubt then don't. You don't have to, try it out for a few years, see what happens.'

'Is that what you and Lord Snooty will do?'

'I don't know, we're not sure, and I don't know why. Your Eddie seems a really nice man, like Stephen in some ways I thought. Stephen called it a false start and he might be right. Maybe that's you and Eddie. I can't see us getting married, but never say never, eh?'

There was something else taking shape in Lydia's mind, but unlike the previous occasion with Gloria, she managed to say nothing, biding her time until she had it clear in her own head before blurting it out. Talking with Gloria, really the only person she ever spoke to about such things, putting ideas and half-thoughts into words, helped see how it might all fit together. She was leading a life of snapshots, scenes in a play, where she had roles on the stage and sat in the audience too. Tonight she had Gloria sitting beside her, comparing notes about the real world and passing comment on the performances.

'Eddie's all right, yeah, a nice man. No, he's a lovely man, the best I've had or likely to. It's me I suppose, I want it all, I'm used to doing what I want when I want it, with nobody else to say yes or no. And if I don't know what I want then I don't have to know. Eddie says 'well, what do *you* want?' and mostly I haven't a clue, or

I don't care. I know he's only being Eddie, asking what I want. There's not many who've ever done that.' As she said this, Gloria rolled her eyes and Lydia had a glimpse of usual spirits returning.

'I want what I can't have, I want it all back how it was.'

'Yeah, well, I dunno about that. I'll keep Eddie, thank you very much.'

'Good for you.'

She meant it, Gloria did know what she wanted, and was a lot more certain than Lydia. Did back-to-how-it-was mean Stephen then, or Stephen now? Hadn't she been the one who'd wanted it to be more than just good friends?

'Smoke time. Sorry, I can't finish this. It was nice but, just not in the mood.'

'Wait, before we go. You need a house and I've got two. No, don't say anything, use mine for six months, see how it goes. I'll stay in Grantchester while Stephen's away. I might go on a few trips myself, maybe visit him in Cuba for a while. And I might come back now and again and use the spare bedroom, just to annoy you two. Talk to Eddie. It'll be cheap and it's better than living with a brother you're not speaking to.'

∞

A grisly accident had closed the main road that bypasses Bedford, forcing all the eastbound traffic through the town. Bad enough for Lydia's journey to the crematorium, but compounded by her own late start from Osney. The mail often rattled her door before she was out of bed, but on a day when she really wanted it before she left the house, there was no sign. So she'd sat in the car waiting until she could wait no longer, then as she turned at the end of West Street, she saw her familiar postman standing chatting in the sunshine. After he'd rummaged in his bag she grabbed the two envelopes, gasped a hurried thanks and rushed away.

When she eventually arrived at Norse Road, the place seemed surprisingly busy and she wondered if perhaps Freddie's funeral had coincided with that of a local celebrity. It took her a few more minutes to find somewhere to park and then to find the right entrance. In her sweaty anxiety she was sure the service would be over, so she was a little surprised to find herself only a few steps behind the coffin. It was calm and cool in the chapel. She took a deep breath and walked quietly to the front where the two other mourners were standing.

She slipped into the pew beside Derek Ballard. From the other side of him Sandra from Willoughby House turned and nodded a greeting. The three were outnumbered two-to-one by staff from the undertaker.

'I thought I'd missed it, the traffic's awful,' she said to the solicitor.

'Everything's running late, glad to see you.'

'I wondered if his neighbour, Monica Sanders might be here.'

'I spoke to her in the week. I think she lost interest when she found out she wasn't a beneficiary. She said Freddie owed her money for his newspapers. Told me to be careful of you, too, said you weren't his daughter.'

Before Lydia could find a reply a woman in a grey suit and black gown came in from a side door. As she did so, the funeral muzak ceased. She stood for a few moments in silence beside the coffin, then turned to the three mourners, introduced herself as Carol and welcomed them to a sad occasion. Lydia wondered if she'd said the same thing a hundred times before, perhaps a thousand, usually to only a handful of people. When there was little left to say and nobody to say it, Carol would be the one to step forward. They would, she said, have an opportunity to speak of, here she quickly referred to a note in her hand, to speak of Freddie in a few minutes. She turned again to the coffin, bowed slightly, then read a short speech about why they were there and eternal mysteries which would always be beyond understanding, and something else which Lydia hardly heard. She'd closed her eyes and drifted away, wondering how she came to be there on such slight acquaintance with the deceased, yet knowing more of his life than anyone else in the room, perhaps on earth. Lives, she corrected herself, more of his lives. There may be a little left in his story, another name or face, a grandchild to be spoken to, but his book was all but closed. Freddie's mysteries, his unspent dollars, his bodies on beaches, murders and mistresses, all real and imagined in equal measure perhaps, they'd all remain unsolved unless…unless on a winter evening by the fire in The Old Rectory his notes and journals told a different tale.

'Would anyone like to say anything?' Carol asked in her practised hushed voice, close and directly to Lydia.

'Oh, yes, please.' She paused and swallowed before finding the words. 'Thank you, Freddie,' she said, as much a surprise to herself as anyone else.

'That's lovely,' Carol said, and it seemed she meant it. As she turned away an unseen hand started the coffin on its final journey, accompanied by beautifully calming music which came to a surprising climax as the curtains closed before returning to a more sombre rhythm.

'Stay as long as you wish,' said Carol as she shook their hands before leaving through the side door.

'That was short,' Lydia said.

'I didn't think we needed much else, I hope you're both all right with it,' said the solicitor.

'Oh, yes, it was fine, thank you for arranging it, and you too, Sandra. Nice music at the end.'

'I like it, it seemed all right. I have it marked down for myself when it's my turn in the box. It's Grieg, The Peace of the Woods.'

His words seemed somehow too light for the moment, something a younger person might have said, yet there was a frankness to them that Lydia liked. It gave a glimpse of a man with humour and music in his life, which reminded her again how little she knew of those around her. What music had there been in Freddie's life? Surely there must have been some, he couldn't have lived through the times he had without there being music.

They left the quiet of the chapel to the sudden noise of cars and confusion as the congestion of funerals in the waiting area grew worse.

'Thank you for coming, Sandra, and for everything else.'

'That's all right, someone always comes. Sometimes we're the only ones here. Sometimes the place is packed with family and friends.'

'Are you going back to work straight away?'

'No. I'm going to another in an hour or so, a lady who hadn't been with us long.'

'Would you like to come to lunch with us?' Derek asked.

'No, I brought some, but thank you.'

'Can I walk with you a minute? Do you mind Derek?'

The two women who'd been at Freddie's bedside at his last moment of life wandered off together and found a quieter corner of the grounds.

'I wanted to ask you about something, it's a little awkward, it's about Willoughby House, one of the staff.'

Sandra nodded, but said nothing.

'Freddie thought someone took money from his wallet, did he ever say anything, make a complaint?'

'No, not formally. I know what he thought though.'

'He kind of suggested there was something else,' Lydia hesitated, she wasn't really sure what Freddie had suggested and he might've imagined it all. 'Something inappropriate, if you know what I mean.'

'I think so,' Sandra nodded.

'So long as you know. It might all be nothing.'

'Probably wasn't nothing. You're probably thinking of one person in particular. Sharon. You saw her a few times. Freddie wasn't the only one. People said things and when two people say the same kind of thing, you know it's not dementia or drugs. She wasn't right for the job, she gone.'

'Good, it's been on my mind, thank you.' And having been relieved and grateful, Lydia had a sudden thought. 'Not to another hospice?'

Sandra sighed deeply. 'No, not a hospice. A retirement home, she's a cleaner. It's very hard to get staff, she'll be a carer again somewhere someday.'

'Can't you do something?'

'No. What's to do? It's all just talk, nothing proved, nothing official. I've been called a witch but I'm not.'

They walked back in silence. At the car park they said their goodbyes, embracing each other as even slight acquaintances do at funerals. Derek Ballard and Lydia watched as Sandra made her way back towards the chapel, perhaps to hear Carol speaking about the unknowable mysteries of the universe once again.

Derek had suggested lunch together before they visited Robert, and he took her to a place by Bolnhurst, no more than a few minutes from his uncle's house. After the usual small talk, Lydia could resist the envelopes in her bag no longer. One was Ghislaine K Cunningham's will.

'You might be interested in this. Or maybe it's one for your uncle, it's a will from 1938. The executor was that well known solicitor William G Durham. I haven't seen it myself yet.'

She drew out the two sheets of paper, one the covering note, the other a copy of the typewritten document set out on standard printed stationery. It was extremely short, occupying less than half the page. After the usual preamble the crucial elements were two bequests with the residue of the estate going to The National Canine Defence League. Mary Alice Tweddle 'my devoted maid' received £2000 and Florence Ada Tweddle, Mary Alice Tweddle's daughter 'and my adopted granddaughter' also received £2000, to be held in trust by her mother until she was twenty-one. It named William G Durham, solicitor, as the executor and was witnessed by him and by Norah Bateson whose address was shown as the same as Ghislaine Cunningham's and whose occupation was 'cook'. The will was dated May 2nd 1938.

Lydia passed it into Derek's eager hand while she considered the contents.

'What do you think?' she asked when he'd read it.

'Do you know how much the Canine Defence League received?'

'I think the whole estate was about £44,000, so roughly £40,000.'

'Doesn't sound like much does it, but it was a huge amount in those days. Even £2000 was huge, you could buy a couple of houses with that. But it looks all right, do you think it might not be?'

'Funny the cook didn't get anything, but the devoted maid did. Funnier that the maid's daughter had some in her own name, too.'

'They'd have needed another witness if there'd been a bequest to the cook. She couldn't be a witness and benefit from the will. When did this lady die?'

'I'm not sure yet, second quarter 1938 I think.'

'Looks like May or June. Not long before her death, it's probably all right.'

'Nothing suspicious then?'

'Not really, you make me wonder, but no, not in the words, not in the form, the signatures look all right, they certainly are three different signatures. See what my uncle thinks.'

Lydia looked again at the scrawls at the foot of the typed contents. Bold and dark from the first witness, clearly William and presumably Durham. Careful and stuttering from Norah, the cook. Ghislaine K Cunningham had signed in exactly the same educated script, unsteady with age, that Lydia had seen before.

15

Robert Ballard's cottage was a modest affair with a pretty garden, the last house in the village before the farmland stretches away to Wyboston, five or six miles to the east. The old man himself was shrunk with age, but moved well enough and rose from his garden seat to greet Lydia and Derek as they came in by the side gate. He hugged his nephew, then turned to Lydia, raising his sunhat in an old-fashioned greeting.

'Derek says I should talk to you, he says you're to be trusted. Should I trust you Miss Silverstream? He says you've come to rake up some very old dirt.' Age had thinned his voice and lifted the pitch but he still spoke very correctly, the King's English it would once have been called, required pronunciation in the private schooling of his youth.

'I've told Derek the truth,' she said steadily, 'not all of it, some names remain confidential for the moment. I'll tell you the truth, even though sometimes lately I've found myself telling lies and half-truths. If you tell me something that's not to be repeated then I won't.'

'Very forthright, Miss Silverstream, very confident.'

'Not really, just plain speaking for a change. I'm trying to do more of it.'

'Please sit down. Derek, would you get some drinks. Now, tell me how you come to be here in my garden asking about things I thought were finished with before you were born.'

He settled himself back in his cushions and despite the warmth of the day, pulled a rug over his knees.

'There's a man, similar in age to your nephew Derek, also educated and with a responsible job. He's unmarried and the only family he's aware of are his mother and his grandmother. The grandmother is in her late nineties and the mother is possibly of an age with you. They presumably know many things but haven't told the man anything of his father. They either cannot or will not. The man asked me to see if I could find or identify his father.'

Robert Ballard had his eyes closed with his hands together as if in prayer, his lips pursed as if ready to kiss his fingertips. It was exactly the pose his nephew had adopted when Lydia had told him the same tale. Now Lydia filled in more of the detail, adding in all that she had learned in the last few days, but for the moment kept back the Cunningham will she and Derek had examined over lunch.

'So,' she concluded as he rejoined them, 'I wonder about many things, but it's William Gordon Durham who's brought me here. He might be the man's father, although there's little evidence. It's no more than a suggestion at present. In fact there are a couple of things that might suggest he wasn't. And I hope you can help, if nothing else you could tell me about William Durham.'

'This man who's looking for his father, is he a friend of yours?'

'Not really, he's a work colleague of my…of a very close friend, a man of great discretion himself.'

It wouldn't surprise her if Robert Ballard knew of Stephen, but she was shy of his titles herself and was not about to drop them into the conversation.

'Well, first of all he wasn't ever called William that I know of. He was Bill Durham. I suppose you know he did have a son, also called Bill or William?'

'Yes, the son of his first marriage to Gwendoline Forester. She died around 1954 and the son died quite young, more than twenty years ago now.'

'You've been thorough. Is the man in question the son of the second marriage?'

'He's the son of the wife in the second marriage, the question is who is his father?'

'Then we're talking of Laurence, and we can dispense with the anonymous man.'

The older Ballard sipped his elderflower cordial, weighing what might be said and what should not. Lydia said nothing, she'd told her tale and asked the question. No need for pretence today, no need to be a researcher checking up on old cases, no need to be anything but what she was.

'Your William Gordon Durham was a very bad man, a thief who abused the trust of clients and whose actions killed my father.'

'Allegedly,' added his nephew dryly.

The old man snorted his disapproval.

'He can sue me. My father died in 1964, before his time. His heart problems began soon after Durham's death. Hard work and terrible anxiety finished him off.'

'Were you the executor for the Durham will?'

'No, that was my father, he was also Robert. I was Bobby until I grew too old to be a Bobby and became Robert. You've seen the will?'

'Yes, it's one of the things that might suggest Bill Durham was not Laurence's father. But the special bequest to Laurence could mean he was.'

'You take your work seriously, Miss Silverstream. Anything else?' he asked, as a schoolmaster might encourage a slow-thinking pupil.

'It was a lot of money.'

'Yes, a great deal of money. I've been looking through some papers and my diaries since I knew you were coming, but I didn't need reminding it was a lot of money. My father thought so too, that was what first made him suspicious. A year or so before Durham retired, a relative, a niece I think, of a long-standing client who'd died a year previously came to my father and asked if he knew about the old lady's will and how she came to be missed out. Although she'd lived abroad most of her life, the niece was sure her aunt wouldn't have forgotten her. My father found that the old lady had left most of it to a charity with a couple of smaller bequests. No mention of a niece. And nothing wrong with the will, which Durham had drawn up and had witnessed a week or so before the death. There were a couple of letters in the file too, everything was as it should be.

'There's nothing unusual about a disappointed relative turning up to question who got the money. In this case it was a well known charity, Dr. Barnardo's, who actively encourage such generosity, so there was no possible reason to challenge it. The niece left empty-handed. Move on six months and a similar thing happened, the details don't matter. It was a different charity, but the picture was the same. Another will drawn up and executed by Durham. The other witness was also the same, his secretary. Again, quite normal, who better than the solicitor's secretary, almost as reliable as the solicitor himself.

'My father asked Durham about both wills. Quite vague and unconcerned was how my father put it, unsure of the details, that sort of thing. Fair enough, he thought, everything in order.'

Robert Ballard was warming to his story, becoming more animated with each flourish. Lydia would have liked to have interrupted with a question, but she let the story unfold as the old man wanted it.

'Then Durham retires, apparently quite suddenly, although he was well past the age. More surprisingly he announces that he is to marry, and not only marry, but marry a young woman less than half his age. Imagine the talk! But there was more. An unmarried mother!

'I never spoke to Durham about any of this, but my father did. I don't know what was said, it may have been no more than the two of them talking, as men do, about the ladies, perhaps at the club or somewhere like that, but my father told me afterwards that Durham was very happy to let everyone think Laurence was his child. And if you knew the mother, Fleur, when she was younger, you'd understand why. A very striking woman.'

'Fleur? She still is,' Lydia confirmed.

'I remember her, even though I only met her a couple of times.'

'Yes, me too. She's remarkable. Laurence still lives with her. But please go on.'

'No sooner are they married than Fleur turns up one day telling my father Durham is dead, buried abroad, would he execute the will. My father said he never even knew the firm held the will, but naturally he did as he was asked. And had the same surprise that you did, it involved a lot of money. It actually involved a lot of property which amounted to a lot of money. One day, my father wondered where all this property and money had come from. He told me how worried he was as he checked through the firm's client accounts, praying there was nothing missing. He checked the whole ten years that Durham was with him. All in order. But it nagged at him, and as he worked on the property details he saw that most of it had been purchased in the previous five years.'

He paused and took a drink, looking suddenly tired.

'Are you all right?' Derek enquired.

'If you're too tired I can come back,' Lydia said.

'I'm fine, it's a long story, Derek's heard it all before. Am I missing much?'

'I'd forgotten most of it. You tell it as if it were all yesterday.'

'You'll see, everything seems like yesterday when you get to my age. Where was I?'

'Your father was working on the property details when something happened.' Lydia prompted.

'Ah, yes, the name. Quite unconnected, a client of father's died suddenly. He'd made a will years previously, the usual distribution to family, a couple of friends and a charity. Once again Dr. Barnardo's. It made my father think about the niece who'd come looking for her inheritance, so he dug out all those papers again. He told me the night he did that he thought he might as well shoot himself.

'You know that Fleur as she called herself, was really Florence, a pet name she told my father, but it was probably just more convenient to be someone else. Well, my father had of course seen her name in Durham's will, but hadn't connected it to anything else. Sure enough, one of the beneficiaries in that earlier will was Fleur, under her Florence name. He told me that when he'd stopped shaking he went to the second will that had been questioned and found the same story. He knew before he looked any further that this wasn't a coincidence, the two of them had been doing this together for years. He didn't know and we don't know to this day, whether the wills were forged or properly signed by people who didn't read them and trusted they were what was needed, what they'd asked for.'

'What did he do? Surely he couldn't take back the money, he didn't know what those people really would have wanted.'

'You have a rest for a minute, uncle,' his nephew interrupted. 'What he did was to go through everything that Durham had touched. He started with all the wills, all the wills that Durham had drawn up. Most were fine, no mention of Florence or Fleur or charities. But there were a considerable number that did. All made close to death, all single people or widows who'd either made no previous will or who'd made a will like the new one, a will involving a charity. All of them had bequests to that woman or to another woman who he never traced.'

'And the Durham will itself, did Florence get her share?'

'No,' Robert Ballard answered before Derek could speak. 'His son got his portion, but Laurence didn't get his and Fleur got a quarter of what was stated.'

'How did he manage that?'

'He told me what happened. He called her in without saying why, just a detail point on some property. He told her how lucky she was to inherit money and to do so as often as she had done. She blustered and threatened, but she knew she was discovered. He told her he was keeping most of her share and she could do what she liked. It was still a lot of money.'

'What did he do with what was left?'

'He did something good with it. He set up a charity, a fund to support legal services to the aged and infirm, especially those who have limited funds. He built in as much protection as he could. Derek?'

'The work we did for Freddie, we'll charge a nominal fee to his estate because he can afford it. But if he couldn't or it had been something else he needed, the fund would probably pay.'

'It still exists?'

'It was a lot of money and it's been well managed.'

It was a perfect fit for everything Lydia knew, but it left the question of fatherhood unanswered.

'May I ask again, do you think William Durham was Laurence's father?' she asked Robert.

'He'd known her longer than anyone realised, known her long enough to be the father.'

Lydia looked at Derek, and moved her hand towards her bag, to ask him whether she should show his uncle the Cunningham will from 1938. He nodded slightly.

'Uncle, Lydia has a little more information, I think she'd like to share with you. Are you happy to carry on?'

He nodded.

'Before that, a question,' Lydia said. 'Do you remember the name of William Durham's secretary?'

'I do,' said Robert immediately, 'Her name was Mrs Richardson. She was pleasant enough, although my father wasn't so keen, I remember he said she could sometimes be very coarse. I think she left before Durham retired, I don't know if he had another one.'

'Do you remember her first name?'

He thought for a minute, but shook his head.

'I had it there but it's gone.'

'I wonder if it might've been Marjory?'

'Marjory, that was it, Marjory. Yes. How on earth did you know that?'

'A guess, I'd have said Mary or Alice as a next guess. Let me tell you about a little book of names.'

So she told the two men about Laurence Durham's little autograph book that he'd inherited from his mother and grandmother, how Laurence Harvey and Stanley Baker had signed a page where she first saw Florence had used the name Fleur, how Marjory Richardson was first in the book and Hellena Forbes was last. There were other names, too many to remember, but it seemed when a name was needed for a father, a new identity or a signature, Florence or her mother would take one from the little book. Even the name Fleur, Lydia thought had probably come from the autograph of Fleur Robinson, a few pages from the front.

'I'm confused,' Robert Ballard said. 'Mrs Richardson can't have been Florence.'

'No, I think she was Florence's mother, Mary Tweddle. The little book was hers first and Marjory Richardson was the first name in it in 1924. I imagine her as being a respectable older woman, an image which stuck with Florence's mother, so when she needed to be such a person and not a cleaner or a housemaid, Marjory Richardson was the name that came to mind.'

'But if Mrs Richardson was her mother, then…' his voice trailed of as the implications became apparent.

'Then Mrs Richardson was part of everything,' Derek Ballard concluded unhappily.

'Let me show you this. It's from long before you'd ever heard of William Durham.' Lydia handed the Cunningham will to Robert Ballard. 'The same characters, the same pattern with another charity receiving the bulk. I wonder how often they repeated this over the years? Often enough to live very comfortably, I think. They still do.'

'Marjory Richardson is still alive? Where did she go?' Derek asked.

'She went back to being Mary Alice Tweddle. She lives near Cambridge.'

'That wretched man knew them all those years.' Robert sank down in his seat, his enthusiasm for the tale exhausted. His reward for confiding the awkward truth was to be told worse, another betrayal. 'He knew Florence when she was just a child. I wonder what else they got up to. I hardly dare think.' he added blankly.

As they'd spoken new doubts had formed, at first more feeling than questions, then suddenly taking solid shape and form. Might William G's will have been a forgery as well? Florence and her mother had ample opportunity and many examples to borrow from. And his death at the Clinica Santa Sophia, was that as simple as the record showed? Lydia pushed the ideas away, this was not the time to give an old man new anxiety. She sighed, deeply and with feeling and brought herself back to the moment.

'Meanwhile there's the identity of Laurence's father. Here's a funny question for you. Do you remember if the office had blue lino and what was called austerity furniture in those days we've been talking about, at the end of the fifties?'

'Yes, no doubt about it. That lino was still there when it all came up about twenty years ago. It had been covered by all sorts. I don't think there was anything special about the furniture, it might've been new soon after the war.'

'Thank you, Laurence remembers such an office when he was five or six. Now I wonder if you'd mind looking at a photo, see if it means anything to you.'

She scrolled back on her phone to the day in the Botanic Garden in Cambridge and the picture of the scowling Florence beside Laurence in their ambushed pose. Robert Ballard cupped the little screen in his hat and squinted at the image.

'Is that Mrs Richardson? She's aged well. Better than I have, wretched woman.'

'No,' said Lydia, 'that's Fleur, or Florence as she is now, I've never met her mother. That's Laurence. Do you see a likeness to William Durham?'

Lydia zoomed in on Laurence's head and shoulders and the old man looked again.

'It's hard to tell, a resemblance perhaps. He had his photo in the paper once, he was at some function with my father, he got quite angry about it, so my father said. Durham had a moustache, did you know that? One thing though, he always wore a bow-tie, I'd forgotten that.'

'It's not genetic,' Lydia smiled, 'but I'll tell Laurence when I see him. I don't really think I'm any closer, despite your help, but perhaps I know why his mother won't give him a straight answer. She has a lot of secrets, unravel one and the rest might follow. I think his father was probably connected to all this in some way and the one obvious candidate is William Durham. Perhaps with this knowledge Laurence will be able to confront her.'

∞

It was a very long way to the surface, but the time had come, there could be no putting it off any longer. There were people she must find, people who needed her best wishes and goodbye kisses, a school friend, her brother, Chloe from work, the white cat with blue eyes, and Trevor watching TV. None of them paid her any attention as she left, despite her calling out. They had lives to get on with and their backs were already turned, their eyes focused on other things.

The cold bit into her at such a depth, but far above a few splinters of light penetrated. One deep breath now, then the steady ascent. A moment later and she could hardly make out the smooth sandy floor as it shrank into blackness. Above, the beckoning light drew her on, although it was even further than she'd realised. Stay calm, just don't breath yet, the light was almost within reach and with it the air. The nearer she got the slower she rose. She tried to reach out a hand, to touch the surface, draw down a few bubbles to her mouth, but they slipped through her fingers. She kicked with all her might but her feet wouldn't move beyond the tiniest twitch. She stopped rising, hanging there, suspended a few feet from the sparkling sunlight. There could be no resisting the urge any longer, she would have to inhale, even knowing it meant death. A serene calm surrounded her as the moment approached. The dancing sunlight made jewels of the ripples around her. They would wrap her corpse in light and colour. Breathe in.

She struggled and coughed, gasping, clutching desperately to anything solid, unable in the moment of waking to tell dream from reality. Wailing like a baby, she blinked into the day, panting air into her lungs as she dug her fingers into Stephen's arm.

'Bad one?' he said gently as he brushed her hair back from her face.

She fought him off, pushing his hand away, still seizing her breath, until the nightmare receded and the room and the day and his solid reality gained the upper hand.

'I couldn't breath,' she cried. 'Drowning, dying. I was ready, I'd given up.'

Stephen put an arm round her and held her loosely to him, helping the horrors drain away. Slowly he felt the tension leave her and softness take its place.

'Thank you,' she said after a few minutes, 'You know I'm glad to be here. I don't say that often enough, but I am.'

'Is this our fresh start?'

'Yes. But there might be others, I haven't got everything quite worked out yet. Will that be all right?'

They lazed and cuddled together for an hour, interrupting their dozing with soft words and snatches of thoughts for the weekend and ideas for the rest of their lives. At length the business of the day called them, neither quite comfortable that they should still be in bed when Jacqueline arrived.

'Post,' Stephen said quite casually as if it was an everyday event, passing over the envelopes with G K Cunningham's birth and death certificates. Perhaps he really had no idea they were the first to be addressed to Lydia at The Old Rectory. She paused to look at her name in the little address window and was pleased to see how totally unremarkable it was.

'Anything interesting?'

'Not really.' Lydia passed the documents across their breakfast. 'Confirmation. Ten days between the will and Ghislaine's death. Long enough to be genuine, short enough to be fake. Do you know what *Pn post CVA* means as the cause of death?'

'I think so, but we can check. I think it's something like cerebro vascular accident. It means she had a stroke. I don't think it's used any more, these days the doctors are supposed to be more precise. The Pn is probably a shorthand for pneumonia. Doctors always like to be obscure if they can.'

'So she could've been immobilised after a stroke, caught pneumonia as a result, then died a few days later?'

'Sounds like it. I think it's quite common in the elderly. Maybe less so nowadays, but back then, probably very common. We can check.'

'Lucky she had her will sorted out. It can't have been more than a day or two before her stroke. I think they forged it, used the signature from the autograph book.'

They sat in thoughtful silence over the last of their toast. The simple death certificate seemed to confirm a deeper, darker conspiracy than three generations of Ballards had imagined. Robert Ballard senior, Derek's grandfather who'd first suspected wrongdoing, he'd feared enough for such crime that he'd thought he might as well shoot himself, but he'd found nothing beyond embezzlement and breach of trust and neither of those provable. Not that anything was provable with the Cunningham will, but probability, Lydia's reliable friend, whispered in her ear. She would add it to the report she'd write for Laurence, the one she'd started to compose in her head, ready for their next meeting.

Having owned her new laptop for a week, Lydia finally sat with it after breakfast, determined to get to grips with its newness. Each time she'd needed it, she'd turned in frustration to her grindingly slow old machine, hobbled as it was by a malfunctioning keyboard, but familiar in all that it did and the way it did it. The techies had promised her a seamless transition, but had failed to deliver. Now, while Stephen attended to some problem with his travel to Cuba, she would familiarise herself with its workings.

It was easy enough to see that the reliable and regular features of her spreadsheets and databases were all in place. They were newer versions, of course, with symbols changed for the sake of change and terminology upgraded to create new buzzwords, but they were there. Even while the machine had sat unused overnight another raft of updates had downloaded ready for her approval. Taking her time to get it right first time, she set the new installations to behave close to how the originals had done. Then it was the connections and browsers with their puzzling new expressions and unlikely options. If she'd been asked, she would admit there were some useful improvements in all of this, but the new clothes they came in were nothing but annoying.

Once she'd done the standard fare, the utilities she couldn't do without, she turned her attention to the critical genealogy software. She'd used the same program for years through all its upgrades and novelty additions. It had taken much trial and error to find exactly the one which suited her best and she'd stayed loyal to it ever since. Apart from her own family she had a dozen more which, for one reason or another, she'd researched and documented, sometimes with no reward, more often with great satisfaction. Among the dozen were the three of current interest. First was the Brenton medals family which had taken her to Freddie Bellinger. Second were the Thompsons and Brights she'd identified in finding Freddie's Linda. Least satisfying of all was the bonsai tree of Laurence Durham, his mother and grandmother, with little else for facts but plenty of notes and aliases. It hardly qualified as a family tree at all.

As she opened the file of her own family with its hundreds of entries and meticulous notes, she saw that there were yet again new options, new defaults to be dealt with, but at least it opened correctly. It was always her test after each update, to see if her own family details were readable and correct. So far so good, but then she opened the Brenton medals family to find it had been updated with additional members. The thing was doing its own research, looking for likely records and grafting them onto her own findings. A new and unwanted default setting. In dismay she looked at the Thompsons and Brights and they too had dozens of additions. She could delete them, reject the automatic, reject the connections made to the ill-founded speculation so often mistaken for real research, but that wasn't what made her so angry with the machine. Even if all the suggested links turned out to be right, where was the satisfaction in any of it?

The stunted Tweddle sapling, the one place where she might've welcomed help from any source, remained obstinately free of suggestions.

But worse was to follow. In dealing with more than one family at a time, the wretched default setting had merged the Brentons into the Thompsons, and the Thompsons into the Brentons. Now she had two family trees each suggesting that it belonged to the other. Yes, she could unpick every miserable mistake, nothing was irretrievable, but it was deeply frustrating. And it was not the seamless she'd paid for.

When she'd walked round the garden and taken in the air and the sun, she found a little more perspective on the problem. It was still annoying, but in an hour or less, all would be as it was. She made coffee for them both, checking on Stephen's progress with his own irritations, then calmly returned to the mess. She would unpick the additions one by one, checking as she did so if there might be any validity in the links proposed.

She started with the Brentons, she would need to be doing work with them again soon or else resign herself to keeping the medals. As Freddie had said, they were pretty, and maybe one day she'd find a good home for them.

She hadn't really been interested in James Edward Brenton's forebears, it was his descendants she'd been keen on. Freddie, in his Francis Bellinger persona, had been the perfect result and quickly found. She'd previously noted James as being the only son of Nathaniel Brenton and Marie Loving, now she saw that James' wife Ada had been given parents: Albert Percival Hiscock and Edith Witte or Witt. They looked plausible, but that Witte or Witt was a warning in itself. Spellings varied too often to really bother about and consistency was no guarantee of accuracy, but it increased the possibility of error. Instead of deleting the links, Lydia tested the record. What if she'd been seeking James Brenton's mother- and father-in-law, would Albert and Edith have been her best answer? Without certificates it would rely on transcriptions and probabilities, but good enough for her purposes.

Within twenty minutes, she was reluctantly conceding the suggestion proposed was the same as she would have come up with. There were few choices, the dates were a perfect fit and the Witt or Witte was quite acceptable. In twenty more, Edith also had parents, Nathaniel Witte and Margaret Bailey, born, married and buried in Ellingham, Hampshire. They too matched the suggestions exactly. Now Francis 'Freddie' Bellinger had not only great-grandparents, but great-great-grandparents.

It was difficult to not keep referring to the combined Thompson-Bright-Brenton family that had been constructed by the software, but these two, Nathaniel and Margaret, were the bridge where they joined. If the other links were as potentially reliable as those Lydia had tested, the merging of the records would be valid. A little unwillingly, she worked through the few Witte descendants that affected her own projects, ignoring those of the wider family. Edith Witte had an older sister, Sarah, who'd married George Cutler in 1880, also in Ellingham. Amongst their offspring was their first daughter, another Sarah, born in 1882. In 1904 she married William Glynn in Mile End. Lydia checked twice through the process, but found the same result each time - it was the same William Glynn she had identified as George Frederick Thompson's grandfather. Unless there had been a glaring mistake in the original record or a consistent error in transcription, Lydia's Brentons and Thompsons shared Nathaniel and Margaret Witte as a common ancestor.

For a while the practical implications did not occur to her. She sat in the gentle warmth of the conservatory, gazing at the garden and its timeless delights, her laptop set aside. This default setting challenged all that she did, invalidated her talent, such as it was. There was nothing that could not be found. Where once such automation had little common sense or quality in the results, now it seemed more discerning in the suggestions it made. In a year or two it would be Lydia who made the suggestions to the software, it would choose whether to accept them or not. When she offered a name or date that the program had overlooked and, wonder of wonders she proved to be correct, it would no doubt give her the reward of a little *Good Job!* message.

At the exact moment that she heard Stephen call her name, she realised that George Frederick Thompson, aka Tommy Quick, the Freddie who'd died holding her hand, was a cousin to Francis Bellinger, third or fourth she couldn't quite calculate in the dizziness of realisation. Against the odds he'd been given the identity of a cousin he'd never known or heard of.

Stephen slipped in beside her. For a minute or more she didn't speak or even look at him, just allowed her hand to be covered by his. Still gazing at the garden, apparently studying it intently, she told him about the discoveries her computer had made without being asked, how annoyed she'd been, how she'd been ready to dismiss them all until she'd begun checking through them. In its way it was a small confession, although she didn't include how empty she felt, how pointless her passion for discovery now seemed, how she might never look at a marriage record or passenger list ever again.

'You felt the same over things you asked me to help with,' he said without any hint of reproach, knowing very well what she hadn't said. 'You set it all up, you found the connections that no computer would find, you talked to the people, listened to their stories, lingered over their photo albums, held his hand when there was no one else. This automatic thing is just another tool. You'll still want to verify every suggestion, every proposal, and be delighted when you prove them wrong, as you will, more often than not.'

He was right, of course he was right, but it didn't lift her, didn't make it all better in an instant.

'Am I right in thinking this solves the problem of the medals?' he added.

'The problem of the medals? The only problem with the medals is who…ah, yes, I see.'

∞

With Stephen playing host, they met once again in the Armoury for lunch. The room and everything in it was identical to their previous visit apart from the college servant who waited on them. An older man, slightly built and with grey locks tied back in a ponytail had taken the place of the beautiful youth. His view of the proceedings must have been the same, for he too glided silently in and out precisely on cue. Their small talk was of Cuba and Vancouver, of summer students and the approaching Michaelmas term. As on their first meeting, Laurence seemed reluctant to broach the subject which brought them together. Only when the last dishes were cleared away did he come to the point.

'I'm not sure how to ask what you've found.' He hesitated, clearly struggling with what else he wished to say. 'The truth is, now we've come to it, I'm not sure that I want to know. Sorry, I know you must have done so much work.'

'You said as much when we talked about the autograph book. It's no surprise, Laurence. You're not the first to change their mind. I found a lady's whole family once, verified some stories, proved others false and wrapped it all up with photos and six generations of ancestors and cousins she'd never heard of, but she didn't want to know until after her parents died. She knew there were untold secrets and couldn't bear to know them and have to face them.'

'Thank you, that is so much easier, thank you,' he said with relief.

'But I will tell you some things right now. Everything else I've written out, dates and places, events and the people involved.' She reached down to her bag and pulled out two envelopes and lay them on the white tablecloth. 'Here in this envelope is all that you gave me, and here,' she tapped the slimmer one, 'are the details of what I've found. You can open it whenever you wish, or never.'

Laurence Durham pulled it towards him and rested a hand on it, his fingers moving gently back and forth across the seal as if he were stroking a cat behind the ears.

'First, I cannot tell you who your father was. I can give you all the clues that I've found, I can give you an opinion, but not the fact. In the end there's only one person who can answer the question for certain.'

She let her blunt statement find it's place in Laurence's world of lies and secrets. He nodded and smiled while his fingertips continued their tracing.

'Laurence, it seems to me that your mother and grandmother have many guilty secrets. Whatever they are now, they might once have been...' she trailed off, unsure of the best word to describe their activities.

'Was it criminal?' Laurence asked, blinking hard behind his round spectacles.

'Yes, I think it was.'

He nodded.

'And my father too?'

'If he was the person I suspect he was, then yes, him too. If it's of any use to you, then I think your mother is scared of saying anything at all, in case it all comes out. At this stage, even if it did, I don't think there'd be any proof. There are some people who think the same as I do, people who've been helpful. They might even be guilty of covering the whole thing up, but I believe they did it with the best of motives.

'I've put all the details down on paper, but there were little discoveries along the way. Remember you told me about an office with blue lino? I think I've been in that office, although the blue lino is long gone. And another thing, all this probably started a very long time ago, before your mother was old enough to know. She was brought up to it, although I don't know when she became really aware. It's no excuse, but it might mean something.'

'You're putting the best light on things.'

'Maybe. You can make your own mind up if you want to. And if you really want to do something yourself, then there's at least one more thing you could do, something I haven't done. In the archives of a local newspaper in a town not too far from here, there's probably a photograph of the man who might be your father. I haven't seen it so I don't know if it would suggest one thing or another. I do know that the man we're talking of was in the habit of wearing bow ties.'

'Huh, that would be funny,' Laurence laughed unconvincingly. 'Let me explain. My mother has never much liked me doing so, always telling me how old-fashioned it is. I was given a yellow one with red teddy bears on it when I was a child. I don't know who gave it to me, but I loved it. It disappeared years later, probably in one of my mother's purges. I was in my twenties when quite by chance I found its twin. I bought it immediately. The first time I wore it my mother was in a bad mood for a week. It became a habit, and then part of what I am. A bit of an oddity.'

'Will you open it, Laurence?' asked Stephen, 'or let it lie.'

'One day I will. Probably. I'll get used to the idea that it's there first.' He tapped the envelope. 'I'll enjoy the fact that it exists, that I have a way into my past.'

∞

Lydia had dozed fitfully for the last two or three hours of the flight, flitting between past and future, each as impenetrable as the other, memory as unreliable as hope and wishes. Then, just when a deeper sleep beckoned, the plane shifted and banked as the announcement of final descent into Vancouver cut through the endless videos. Between cotton-wool puffs of cloud she glimpsed the Gulf Islands scattered in a shimmering sea. No, not a sea, she realised, but the Pacific Ocean. Her first sight of a different ocean, a moment to remember for any traveller.

The still-unmarried Gloria and her non-husband Eddie had insisted on seeing her off, to make sure she really went, Gloria said. To make sure they wouldn't be disturbed in her house in West Street, Lydia said. There was a hint of truth in both, Gloria and Eddie had their wedding day without actually getting married and moved into Lydia's house two days later, so were naturally keen to get Lydia off the premises. Lydia had wobbled more than once after Stephen had gone, suddenly an awkward misfit in The Old Rectory, while her travel plan had seemed more ambitious the nearer it came.

The wine that came with a seat near the front had settled and soothed her after the anxiety of the airport. She'd gazed at the expanse of the Atlantic for as long as it took to cross, feeling at once superhuman and utterly insignificant above the blue-green vastness.

Over the wastes of Greenland she'd read *Our Man in Havana*, a parting gift from Stephen as he'd kissed her goodbye two weeks previously, heading to Cuba via New York and Mexico. In a fortnight she would join him there and they'd play tourists during a week of leave from his grim task.

As the barrens of Nunavut had passed endlessly beneath her, she'd dipped into *The A to Z of Carry On*, borrowed from Bella Wentworth. Bella had so liked Lydia's *Carry On Girls* that she'd begun contacting old colleagues and organising a re-union. Lydia still liked the idea too, but had promised nothing beyond her pledge to stay in touch. Bella had been a little cool when she learned the truth of their first meeting, but thawed when she understood the connection to her unexpected inheritance. In their exchanges since, there'd been a warmth that might last into a longer friendship.

More than once in the flight Lydia's hand had gone to her bag, reaching into its depths for the smooth, reassuring shape of the medal case. It had provoked curiosity from the scanners and genuine interest when she'd opened it for inspection. She took the case out one more time, lifting the lid to enjoy them. The three nothing-special medals looked good, Claire Sylvia McCreadie would be delighted to have them, she'd said so already.

Who's who - Linda's Pedigree

Linda Thompson born on Sep 29, 1956 in Ramsgate, Kent, died on Mar 22, 1998 in Munich. Registration: Dec 20 1956 Stepney. Occupation: Actress, singer. Cremated in Munich.

Parents

George Frederick Thompson (Freddie) born 14th July 1930 in Mile End, London.

Sylvia Bright born in 1938 in Mile End, London (Reg, Stepney), died in 2004 in Wanstead, London.

Grandparents

George Edward Thompson born in 1906 in Mile End, died in 1978 in Ilford, Essex.

Esther Sarah Glynn born in 1906 in Whitechapel, Middlesex, died in 1991 in Ilford.

George Walter Bright was born in 1917 in Ramsgate, Kent and died in 1988 in Ilford.

Margaret Wilson was born in 1919 in Whitechapel.

Great-grandparents

Frederick Sinclair Thompson born in 1875 in Whitechapel.

Elizabeth Nicol born in 1880 in Trewarth, Cornwall.

William Glynn born in 1872 in Bermondsey.

Sarah Cutler born in 1882 in Hampshire.

Great-great-grandparents

Frederick James Thompson born in 1847 in Mile End.

Alice Donna Sinclair born in 1850 in Dumfries.

Daniel Nicol born in 1848 in Trewarth.

Jane Bethan Griffin born in 1855 in Trewarth.

William Glyn born in 1847 in Ireland.

Hesther Merchant born in 1852 in Salisbury, Wiltshire.

George Cutler born in 1855 in Ellingham, Hampshire.

Sarah Witt born in 1859 in Ellingham.

Great-great-great-grandparents

Nathaniel Witte was born in 1831 in Ellingham.

Margaret Bailey was born in 1837 in Ellingham.

Nathaniel Witte's descendants

Nathaniel Witte born in 1831 in Ellingham, Hampshire. He married Margaret Bailey in 1858. Margaret was born in 1837 in Ellingham. Their children were **Sarah**, born in 1859 in Ellingham, and **Edith**, born in 1865, also in Ellingham.

2nd Generation (Children):
Sarah Witt married George **Cutler** in 1880 in Ellingham. George was born in 1855 in Ellingham. Their child was **Sarah**, born in 1882 in Hampshire.
Edith Witt married Albert Percival **Hiscock** in 1885 in Ellingham. Albert Percival was born in 1862 in Ellingham. Their child was **Ada May**, born in 1887 in Ellingham, died 1930 in Southampton.

3rd Generation (Grandchildren):
Sarah Cutler married William **Glynn** in 1904 in Mile End, London. William, son of William Glyn and Hesther Merchant, born in 1872 in Bermondsey. Their children were: **Esther Sarah**, born 1906 in Whitechapel, Middlesex, died 1991 in Ilford, Essex; **William David**, born 1908 in Whitechapel, and died 1912 in Mile End, London.
Ada May Hiscock married first **James Edward Brenton** in 1909 in Ellingham. James Edward, son of Nathaniel Joseph Brenton and Marie Constance Loving, was born in 1885 in Southampton and died 1919 in Birmingham. Their child was **Lillian Edith**, born in 1910 in Ellingham, and died 1941 in Bristol. Ada May married second Claud Anthon Matel in 1922 in Southampton. Claud Anthon was born in 1894 in Caen, Normandy, France. Their children were: Claude Ernest, born in 1922 in Southampton and Marie Ada, born in 1926 in Southampton.

4th Generation (Great-grandchildren):
Esther Sarah Glynn married George Edward **Thompson** in 1928 in Mile End. George Edward, son of Frederick Sinclair Thompson and Elizabeth Nicol, was born in 1906 in Mile End, and died in 1978 in Ilford, Essex. Their children were: **George Frederick**, born

14th July 1930 in Mile End; Sarah Elizabeth, born in 1932 in Mile End, died 2010 in Ilford; Charles Graham, born in 1934 in Mile End, died 1962 in Grantham; Andrew Michael, born 1936 in Mile End.

William David Glyn died 1912 in Mile End.

Lillian Edith Brenton married Ernest Alfred **Bellinger** in 1928 in Southampton. Ernest Alfred, son of Dennis Henry Bellinger and Martha Sussana Gulley, was born in 1908 in Southampton and died 1943. Their children were: **Francis**, born on May 8, 1930 in Hampshire; **Maud**, born in 1933 in Hampshire. Lillian and the children died on Jan. 2, 1941 in Bedminster, Bristol.

5th Generation (Great(2)-grandchildren):

George Frederick Thompson, met **Sylvia Bright**, daughter of George Walter Bright and Margaret Wilson, was born in 1938 in Mile End, London and died in 2004 in Wanstead, London E17. Their child was **Linda**, born on Sep. 29, 1956 in Ramsgate, Kent and died on Mar. 22, 1998 in Munich.

Sarah Elizabeth Thompson.

Charles Graham Thompson died in 1962 in Grantham.

Andrew Michael Thompson.

Francis Bellinger died on Jan. 2, 1941 in Bedminster, but his death was not recorded.

Maud Bellinger also died on Jan. 2, 1941 in Bedminster.

6th Generation (Great(3)-grandchildren):

Linda Thompson died on Mar. 22, 1998 in Munich. She had a child, **Claire Sylvia**, born in 1973 in Kilmarnock, Scotland, by an unknown father. Linda married James Terrence Miller in 1975 in Chelsea.

She married Philip George Boscombe in 1981 in Holborn.

7th Generation (Great(4)-grandchildren):

Claire Sylvia Thompson married Simon Alexander **McCreadie** in 1999 in Vancouver, BC. Simon Alexander was born in 1970 in Canada. Their children are: Phillipa, born in 2001 in Vancouver, BC; Lynda, born in 2003 in Vancouver, BC.